Torch

Torch

Cheryl
Strayed

Houghton Mifflin Company

BOSTON   NEW YORK

2005

Library of Congress Cataloging–in–Publication Data

Strayed, Cheryl, date.
   Torch / Cheryl Strayed.
      p. cm.
   ISBN-10: 0-618-47217-7   ISBN-13: 978-0-618-47217-8
1. Women in radio broadcasting—Fiction.   2. Cancer—Patients—
Fiction.   3. Mothers—Death—Fiction.   4. Cancer in women—Fiction.
5. Minnesota—Fiction.
I. Title.
   PS3619.T744T67   2005
   813'.6—DC22   2005010333

Book design by Anne Chalmers
Typefaces: Janson Text, Clarendon

Printed in the United States of America

QUM 10 9 8 7 6 5 4 3 2 1

For Brian Jay Lindstrom

and

In memory of my mother,
Bobbi Anne Lambrecht,

with love

Acknowledgments

I am grateful to Syracuse University, the Julia and David White Artists' Colony, the Constance Saltonstall Foundation for the Arts, the Sacatar Foundation, and the Wurlitzer Foundation for the gift of time and financial support while I wrote this book.

A heartfelt thanks to all the people at Houghton Mifflin, whose hard work and passion helped bring this book into the world. I am especially indebted to my editor, Janet Silver, for her insight, brilliance, and kindness; to Meg Lemke, who guided me expertly along the way; and to Megan Wilson, publicist extraordinaire.

A deep bow to my agent, Laurie Fox, who said she would be my fairy godmother, and was.

I couldn't have written this book without the encouragement and love of my friends and teachers, too many to name here. Special thanks to Paulette Bates Alden, Christopher Boucher, Arielle Greenberg Bywater, Mary Caponegro, Arthur Flowers, Lisa Glatt, Corrine Glesne, Sarah Hart, Aimee Hurt, Tom Kilbane, Gretchen Legler, EJ Levy, Emillia Noordhoek, Dorothy Novick, Salvador Plascencia, Lee and John and Astia Roper-Batker, George Saunders, Anne Vande Creek, Bridgette Walsh, and Devon Wright.

I'm grateful to Karen Patch, Leif Nyland, and Glenn (Benny) Lambrecht for all those years together, and for being modern pioneers with me.

My deepest debt is to Brian Lindstrom, for everything and then some. For love and for life. For keeping the faith and carrying the torch.

PART I

The Woods of Coltrap County

Yet it would be your duty to bear it, if you could not avoid it: it is weak and silly to say you cannot bear what it is your fate to be required to bear.

—Charlotte Brontë, *Jane Eyre*

1

SHE ACHED. As if her spine were a zipper and someone had come up behind her and unzipped it and pushed his hands into her organs and squeezed, as if they were butter or dough, or grapes to be smashed for wine. At other times it was something sharp like diamonds or shards of glass engraving her bones. Teresa explained these sensations to the doctor—the zipper, the grapes, the diamonds, and the glass—while he sat on his little stool with wheels and wrote in a notebook. He continued to write after she'd stopped speaking, his head cocked and still like a dog listening to a sound that was distinct, but far off. It was late afternoon, the end of a long day of tests, and he was the final doctor, the *real* doctor, the one who would tell her at last what was wrong.

Teresa held her earrings in the palm of one hand—dried violets pressed between tiny panes of glass—and put them on, still getting dressed after hours of going from one room to the next in a hospital gown. She examined her shirt for lint and cat hair, errant pieces of thread, and primly picked them off. She looked at Bruce, who looked out the window at a ship in the harbor, which cut elegantly, tranquilly along the surface of the lake, as if it weren't January, as if it weren't Minnesota, as if it weren't ice.

At the moment she wasn't in pain and she told the doctor this while he wrote. "There are long stretches of time that I feel perfectly fine," she said, and laughed the way she did with strangers. She confessed that she wouldn't be surprised if she were going mad or perhaps this was the beginning of menopause or maybe she had walking pneumonia. Walking pneumonia had been her latest theory, the one she liked best. The one that explained the cough, the ache. The one that could have made her spine into a zipper.

"I'd like to have one more glance," the doctor said, looking up at her as if he had risen from a trance. He was young. Younger. *Was he thirty?* she wondered. He instructed her to take her clothes off again and gave her a fresh gown to wear and then left the room.

She undressed slowly, tentatively at first, and then quickly, crouching, as if Bruce had never seen her naked. The sun shone into the room and made everything lilac.

"The light—it's so pretty," she said, and stepped up to sit on the examining table. A rosy slice of her abdomen peeped out from a gap in the gown, and she mended it shut with her hands. She was thirsty but not allowed a drop of water. Hungry, from having not eaten since the night before. "I'm starving."

"That's good," said Bruce. "Appetite means that you're healthy." His face was red and dry and cracked-looking, as if he'd just come in from plowing the driveway, though he'd been with her all day, going from one section of the hospital to the next, reading what he could find in the waiting rooms. Reading *Reader's Digest* and *Newsweek* and *Self* against his will but reading hungrily, avidly, from cover to cover. Throughout the day, in the small spaces of time in which she too had had to wait, he'd told her the stories. About an old woman who'd been bludgeoned to death by a boy she'd hired to build a doghouse. About a movie star who'd been forced by divorce to sell his boat. About a man in Kentucky who'd run a marathon in spite of the fact that he had only one foot, the other made of metal, a complicated, sturdy coil fitted into a shoe.

The doctor knocked, then burst in without waiting for an answer. He washed his hands and brought his little black instrument out, the one with the tiny light, and peered into her eyes, her ears, her mouth. She could smell the cinnamon gum he chewed and also the soap he'd used before he touched her. She kept herself from blinking while staring directly into the bullet of light, and then, when he asked, followed his pen expertly around the room using only her eyes.

"I'm not a sickly woman," she declared.

Nobody agreed. Nobody disagreed. But Bruce came to stand behind her and rub her back.

His hands made a scraping sound against the fabric of the gown, so rough and thick they were, like tree bark. At night he cut the calluses off with a jackknife.

·   ·   ·

The doctor didn't say cancer—at least she didn't hear him say it. She heard him say oranges and peas and radishes and ovaries and lungs and liver. He said tumors were growing like wildfire along her spine.

"What about my brain?" she asked, dry-eyed.

He told her he'd opted not to check her brain because her ovaries and lungs and liver made her brain irrelevant. "Your breasts are fine," he said, leaning against the sink.

She blushed to hear that. *Your breasts are fine.*

"Thank you," she said, and leant forward a bit in her chair. Once, she'd walked six miles through the streets of Duluth in honor of women whose breasts *weren't* fine and in return she'd received a pink T-shirt and a spaghetti dinner.

"What does this *mean* exactly?" Her voice was reasonable beyond reason. She became acutely aware of each muscle in her face. Some were paralyzed, others twitched. She pressed her cold hands against her cheeks.

"I don't want to alarm you," the doctor said, and then, very calmly, he stated that she could not expect to be alive in one year. He talked for a long time in simple terms, but she could not make out what he was saying. When she'd first met Bruce, she'd asked him to explain to her how, precisely, the engine of a car worked. She did this because she loved him and she wanted to demonstrate her love by taking an interest in his knowledge. He'd sketched the parts of an engine on a napkin and told her what fit together and what parts made other parts move and he also took several detours to explain what was likely to be happening when certain things went wrong and the whole while she had smiled and held her face in an expression of simulated intelligence and understanding, though by the end she'd learned absolutely nothing. This was like that.

She didn't look at Bruce, couldn't bring herself to. She heard a hiccup of a cry from his direction and then a long horrible cough.

"Thank you," she said when the doctor was done talking. "I mean, for doing everything you can do." And then she added weakly, "But. There's one thing—are you sure? Because . . . actually . . . I don't feel that sick." She felt she'd know it if she had oranges growing in her; she'd known immediately both times that she'd been pregnant.

"That will come. I would expect extremely soon," said the doctor. He had a dimpled chin, a baby face. "This is a rare situation—to find it so late in the game. Actually, the fact that we found it so late speaks to

5

your overall good health. Other than this, you're in excellent shape."

He hoisted himself up to sit on the counter, his legs dangling and swinging.

"Thank you," she said again, reaching for her coat.

Carefully, wordlessly, they walked to the elevator, pushed its translucent button, and waited for it to arrive. When it did, they staggered onto it and saw, gratefully, that they were alone together at last.

"Teresa," Bruce said, looking into her eyes. He smelled like the small things he'd eaten throughout the day, things she'd packed for him in her famously big straw bag. Tangerines and raisins.

She put the tips of her fingers very delicately on his face and then he grabbed her hard and held her against him. He touched her spine, one vertebra, and then another one, as if he were counting them, keeping track. She laced one hand into his belt loop at the back of his jeans and with the other hand she held a seashell that hung on a leather string around her neck. A gift from her kids. It changed color depending on how she moved, flashing and luminescent like a tropical fish in an aquarium, so thin she could crush it in an instant. She considered crushing it. Once, in a quiet rage, she'd squeezed an entire bottle of coconut-scented lotion onto the tops of her thighs, having been denied something as a teenager: a party, a record, a pair of boots. She thought of that now. She thought, *Of all the things to think of now.* She tried to think of nothing, but then she thought of cancer. *Cancer,* she said to herself. *Cancer, cancer, cancer.* The word chugged inside of her like a train starting to roll. And then she closed her eyes and it became something else, swerving away, a bead of mercury or a girl on roller skates.

They went to a Chinese restaurant. They could still eat. They read the astrology on the placemats and ordered green beans in garlic sauce and cold sesame noodles and then read the placemats again, out loud to each other. They were horses, both of them, thirty-eight years old. They were in perpetual motion, moved with electric fluidity, possessed unconquered spirits. They were impulsive and stubborn and lacked discretion. They were a perfect match.

Goldfish swam in a pond near their table. Ancient goldfish. Unsettlingly large goldfish. "Hello, goldfish," she cooed, tilting toward them in her chair. They swam to the surface, opening their big mouths in perfect circles, making small popping noises.

6

"Are you hungry?" she asked them. "They're hungry," she said to Bruce, then looked searchingly around the restaurant, as if to see where they kept the goldfish food.

At a table nearby there was a birthday party, and Bruce and Teresa were compelled to join in for the birthday song. The woman whose birthday it was received a flaming custard, praised it loudly, then ate it with reserve.

Bruce held her hand across the table. "Now that I'm dying we're dating again," she said for a joke, though they didn't laugh. Sorrow surged erotically through them as if they were breaking up. Her groin was a fist, then a swamp. "I want to make love with you," she said, and he blinked his blue eyes, tearing up so much that he had to take his glasses off. They'd tapered off over the years. Once or twice a month, perhaps.

Their food arrived, great bowls of it, and they ate as if nothing were different. They were so hungry they couldn't speak, so they listened to the conversation of the happy people at the birthday party table. The flaming custard lady insisted that she was a dragon, not a rabbit, despite what the placemat said. After a while they all rose and put their heavy coats on, strolling past Teresa and Bruce, admiring the goldfish in their pond.

"I had a goldfish once," said a man who held the arm of the custard lady. "His name was Charlie." And everyone laughed uproariously.

Later, after Bruce paid the bill, they crossed a footbridge over a pond where you could throw a penny.

They threw pennies.

On the drive home it hit them, and they wept. Driving was good because they didn't have to look at each other. They said the word, but as if it were two words. *Can. Sir.* They had to say it slowly, dissected, or not at all. They vowed they would not tell the kids. How could they tell the kids?

"How could we not?" Teresa asked bitterly, after a while. She thought of how, when the kids were babies, she would take their entire hands into her mouth and pretend that she was going to eat them until they laughed. She remembered this precisely, viscerally, the way their fingers felt pressing onto her tongue, and she fell forward, over her knees, her head wedged under the dash, to sob.

Bruce slowed and then pulled over and stopped the truck. They were out of Duluth now, off the freeway, on the road home. He hunched over her back, hugging her with his weight wherever he could.

She took several deep breaths to calm herself, wiped her face with her gloves, and looked up out the windshield at the snow packed hard on the shoulder of the road. She felt that home was impossibly far.

"Let's go," she said.

They drove in silence under the ice-clear black sky, passing turkey farms and dairy farms every few miles, or houses with lit-up sheds. When they crossed into Coltrap County, Bruce turned the radio on, and they heard Teresa's own voice and it shocked them, although it was a Thursday night. She was interviewing a dowser from Blue River, a woman named Patty Peterson, the descendant of a long line of Petersons who'd witched wells.

Teresa heard herself say, "I've always wondered about the art—I suppose you could call it an art—or perhaps the *skill* of selecting a willow branch." And then she switched the radio off immediately. She held her hands in a clenched knot on her lap. It was ten degrees below zero outside. The truck made a roaring sound, in need of a new muffler.

"Maybe it will go away as mysteriously as it came," she said, turning to Bruce. His haggard face was beautiful to her in the soft light of the dashboard.

"That's what we're going to shoot for," he said, reaching for her knee. She considered sliding over to sit close to him, straddling the clutch, but felt tied to her place near the dark window.

"Or I could die," she said calmly, as if she'd come to peace with everything already. "I could very well die."

"No, you couldn't."

"*Bruce.*"

"We're all going to die," he said softly. "Everyone's going to die, but you're not going to die *now*."

She pressed her bare hand flat onto the window, making an imprint in the frost. "I didn't think I'd die this way."

"You have to stay positive, Ter. Let's get the radiation started and then we'll see. Just like the doctor said."

"He said we'll see about *chemo*. Whether I'll be strong enough for *chemo* after I'm done with radiation, not about me being cured, Bruce. You never pay attention." She felt irritated with him for the first time that day and her irritation was a relief, as if warm water were being gently poured over her feet.

8

"Okay, then," he said.

"Okay what?"

"Okay, we'll see. Right?"

She stared out the window.

"Right?" he asked again, but she didn't answer.

They drove past a farm where several cows stood in the bright light of the open barn, their heads turned toward the dark of the woods beyond, as if they detected something there that no human could. A thrashing.

2

THE SOUND of his mother's voice filled Joshua with shame.

"This is *Modern Pioneers!*" she exclaimed from all four of the speakers in the dining room of the Midden Café and the one speaker back in the kitchen that was splattered with grease and soot and ketchup. Joshua listened to the one in the kitchen as he scrubbed pots with a ball of steel wool, his arms elbow-deep in scorching, soapy water. Hearing his mother's voice made his head hurt, as if a dull yet pointed object were being pressed into his eardrums. Her radio voice was exactly like she was: insistent, resolute, amused, wanting to know. Wanting to know everything from everyone she interviewed. "So, how exactly, can you tell us, do you collect the honey from the bees?" she'd ask, dusky and smooth. Other times she held forth for the entire hour herself, discussing organic gardening and how to build your own cider press, quilting and the medicinal benefits of ginseng. Once, she'd played "Turkey in the Straw" on her dulcimer for all of northern Minnesota to hear and then read from a book about American folk music. Recently, she had announced how much money she'd spent on tampons in six months and then proceeded to describe other, less costly options: natural sponges and cotton pads that she'd sewn herself out of Joshua and Claire's old shirts. She'd actually said that: *Joshua and Claire's old shirts.* Claire was off to college by then, leaving Joshua alone to wallow in humiliation the first week of his senior year of high school.

Marcy pushed her way back into the kitchen through the swinging door, holding a stack of dirty plates with uneaten edges of food and wadded-up napkins. She set them on the counter where Joshua had just finished cleaning up and then reached into her apron for a cigarette. Joshua watched her, trying to appear not to, as he scraped off the dishes. She was in her late twenties, married, with two kids, short and big-breasted, which made her look heavier than she was. Joshua spent a lot of his time at work trying to decide whether he thought she was pretty or not. He was seventeen, lanky and fair, quiet but not shy.

His mother was talking to a dowser named Patty Peterson. He could hear Teresa's animated voice and then Patty's quavering one. Marcy stood listening, untied her apron, and tied it again more tightly. "Next thing you know your mom will go down to Africa and teach us all about it. Maybe the way they go to the bathroom down there."

"She would like to go to Africa," Joshua said, dumb and steadfast and serious, refusing to acknowledge even the slightest joke about his mother. She *would* go to Africa, he knew. She'd go anywhere, she'd leap at the chance.

"They got an African over in Blue River now. Some adopted kid," Vern said from the back door. He had it propped open with a bucket despite the cold. Marcy was the owner's daughter; Vern, the night cook.

"Not African, Vern. Black," said Marcy. "He's from the Cities. That's not Africa." She adjusted the barrette that held her curly hair up at the back of her head. "Are you trying to freeze us all to death in here?"

Vern shut the door. "Maybe your mom will interview the African," he said. "Tell us what he has to say for himself."

"Be nice," Marcy said. She went up on her tiptoes and pulled a stack of Styrofoam containers down from the top shelf, clenching her cigarette in her mouth. "Nothing against your mom, Josh," she said. "She's a super nice lady. An *interesting* lady. It takes all kinds." With great care, she tapped the burning end of her cigarette on a plate, then she blew on it and put it back into her apron pocket and buzzed out the door.

Six years ago, when his mother had first started the show, Joshua hadn't felt ashamed. He'd been proud, as if he had been hoisted up onto a platform and was glowing red-hot and lit up from within. He believed his mother was famous, that they all were—he and Claire and Bruce. Teresa had made them part of the show; his life, their lives, were the fodder. She made them eat raw garlic to protect against colds and heart disease, rub pennyroyal on their skin to keep the mosquitoes away, drink a tea of boiled jack-in-the-pulpit when they had a cough. They could not eat meat, or when they did they had to kill it themselves, which they did one winter when they'd butchered five roosters that as chicks they'd thought were hens. They shook jars of fresh cream until it congealed into lumps of butter. His mother got wool straight off a neighbor's sheep and carded it and spun it on a spinning wheel that Bruce had built for her. She saved broccoli leaves and collected dandelions and the inner layers of bark from certain trees and used these things to make dye for the yarn. It came out the most unlikely colors: red and purple and yellow, when you might have expected mudlike brown or green. And then their mother would tell everyone all about what the family did on the radio. Their successes and failures, discoveries and surprises. "We are all modern pioneers!" she'd say. Listeners would call in to ask her questions on the air, or would call her at home for advice. Slowly at first, and then overnight it seemed, Joshua didn't want to be a modern pioneer anymore. He wanted to be precisely what everyone else was and nothing more. Claire had stopped wanting to be a modern pioneer well before that. She insisted on wearing makeup and got into raging fights with their mother and Bruce about why they could not have a TV, why they could not be normal. These were the same fights Joshua was having with them now.

"You're going to have to clean the fryer too," said Vern. "Don't go trying to leave it for Angie."

Joshua went back to scrubbing, turning the hot water on full blast. The steam felt good on his face, opening the pores. Pimples bloomed on the rosy part of his cheeks and the wide plain of his forehead. At night in bed he scratched them until they bled, and then he would get up and put hydrogen peroxide on them. He liked the feeling of the bubbles, eating everything away.

"You hear what I told you?" Vern said, when Joshua shut the water off.

"Yep."

"What?"

"I said I did," he said more harshly, turning his blue eyes to Vern: a gaunt old man with a paunch and a bulbous red nose. One arm had a tattoo of a hula dancer, the other a hooked anchor with a rope wound around it.

"Well, answer me, then. Show some respect for your elders." Vern stood near the door in his apron and T-shirt, which were caked with smudges the color of barbeque sauce where he had wiped his hands. He opened the door again and tossed his cigarette butt into the darkness. Outside there was a concrete landing, glazed with ice, and an alley where Joshua's truck and Vern's van were parked along the back wall of Ed's Feed.

Joshua lifted the sliding hood of the dishwasher, and the steam roiled out. He slid a clean rack of flatware out and began to sort the utensils into round white holders as he wiped each one quickly with a towel.

"Running behind tonight, ain't you?"

"Nope." On the radio he heard his mother laugh, and the well-witcher laughed too, and then they settled back into their discussion, serious as owls.

"Ain't you?"

"I said no."

"Maybe you're gonna have to learn that when a man's got a job, a man's gotta show up on time, ain't you?"

"Yep."

"I seen you left the lasagna pan for Angie last night. Don't go thinking that I don't see. 'Cause I see. I see everything your shit for brains can think up about two weeks before you get to it. And I knowed you're always thinking things. Trying to see what you can get away with. Ain't you?"

"Nope."

Vern watched Joshua, slightly bent from the waist, a cigarette smoking between his lips, as though he were trying to come up with something else to say, running down the list of things that pissed him off. Joshua had known Vern most of his life, without having known him at all. It wasn't until they worked together at the café that he even knew that Vern's name was Vern — Vern Milkkinen. Before that, he'd known him as the Chicken Man, the way most people in Midden did, because he spent his summers in the Dairy Queen parking lot selling baby chicks and eggs and an ever-changing assortment of homemade canned goods, soap, beeswax candles, and his special chokecherry jam. It had never occurred to Joshua to wonder what the Chicken Man — what Vern — did to occupy his time in the months that he wasn't selling things until he walked into the kitchen at the café and saw Vern standing there, butcher knife in hand.

On that first day working together, Vern did not indicate that he remembered Joshua, seemingly unconscious of the fact that he'd actually watched him grow up, from four to seventeen, laying eyes on him during those fourteen summers at least once a week, first as a child, when Joshua would go with his mother to purchase things from the Chicken Man, and

13

then later when he was sent on his own. The DQ parking lot was the closest thing Midden had to a town square because it also shared its parking lot with the Kwik Mart and Gas, and Bonnie's Burger Chalet. Every week he and the Chicken Man would exchange a nod or the slightest lift of the chin or hand. Once, when Joshua was ten, the Chicken Man asked him if he liked girls, if he had a girlfriend yet, if he'd ever kissed a girl, if he'd preferred brunettes or blonds.

"Or redheads. Them are the ones to watch out for. Them are the ones with the tightest pussies," Vern had said, and then roared with laughter.

Vern had shown Joshua his anchor tattoo and asked him if he'd ever heard of the cartoon *Popeye the Sailor Man.*

"Yes," Joshua said solemnly, holding out the money his mother had given him.

"That's me. That's who I am," Vern said, his eyes wild and mystical, as if he'd been transported into a memory of a time when he'd been secretly heroic. "Only I'm the original one, not a cartoon." And then he laughed monstrously again while Joshua faked a smile.

It had taken Joshua several years to fully shake the sense that Vern *was* Popeye, despite the fact that Vern's real life was on obvious display. He had a son named Andrew, who was older than Joshua by twenty years. At work, when Vern was in a good mood, he would tell Joshua stories about Andrew when he was young. Andrew shooting his first deer, Andrew and his legendary basketball abilities, Andrew getting his arm broken by Vern when he'd caught him smoking pot in eighth grade. "I just took the little bugger and twisted it till it snapped," Vern said. "I woulda pulled it clean off if I could. That's how he learned. I don't mess around. Messing around's not how you raise a kid. You mess around and then they never get toughened up."

Joshua hardly knew his own father. He lived in Texas now. Joshua and Claire had gone to visit him there once when Joshua was ten, but they hadn't lived with him since Joshua was four. They didn't live in Midden then. They lived in Pennsylvania, where their father was a coal miner. They moved to Midden without ever having known about its existence until shortly before they'd arrived on a series of Greyhound buses, their mother having secured a job in housekeeping at the Rest-A-While Villa through the cousin of a friend.

Marcy came back into the kitchen and sat on an upturned bucket that they used as a chair. "I'll have the pork tenderloin tonight, Vern. With a baked potato. You can keep the peas. You got a baked potato for me?"

Vern nodded and closed the door he'd opened again.

"Is it thinking about snowing out there?" she asked, looking at her nails.

"Too cold to snow," he said.

All three of them listened to Teresa ask Patty Peterson what she thought the future of dowsing held and Patty told her it was a dying art. The radio show wasn't Teresa's real job; she was a volunteer, like almost everyone who worked at the station. Her real job was waiting tables at Len's Lookout out on Highway 32. She'd started there after the Rest-A-While Villa closed down ten years before.

Marcy grabbed the baseball cap off of Joshua's head and then put it back on crooked. "Tell Vern what you want for dinner so we can get the hell out of Dodge when it's time. I'm gonna go sweep."

"Onion rings, please," he said, and loaded up another tray of dirty dishes. On the radio, his mother asked what year the showy lady's slipper was made the Minnesota state flower.

"1892," said Vern. He opened the oven drawer and took out a potato wrapped in foil with his bare hands and dropped it onto a plate.

At the end of each show, his mother would ask a question and then would tell the listeners what next week's show would be while she waited for them to call in and guess the answer. She practiced these questions on Joshua and Claire and Bruce. She had them name all seven of the dwarfs, or define *pulchritudinous*, or tell her which is the most populous city in India. The people who called in to the show were triumphant if they got the answer right, as if they'd won something, though there was no prize at all. What they got was Teresa asking where they were calling from, and she'd repeat the place name back to them, delighted and surprised. The names of cold, country places with Indian names or the names of animals or rivers or lakes: Keewatin, Atumba, Beaver, Deer Lake.

"1910?" a voice on the radio asked uncertainly.

"Nooo," Teresa cooed. "Good guess, though."

Vern stepped in front of Joshua holding the fryer basket with a pair of tongs and flung it into the empty sink. "That's gonna be hot."

"1892," a voice said, and Teresa let out a happy cry.

Vern switched the radio off and Joshua felt a flash of gratitude. They wouldn't have to hear where this week's correct caller was from, wouldn't have to hear Teresa say what she said each week at the end of her show. "And this, folks, brings us to the end of another hour. Work hard. Do good. Be incredible. And come back next week for more of *Modern Pioneers*!"

"Your bud's out there," Marcy said to Joshua when she came back into the kitchen. She put her coat on. "I locked the front so whoever leaves last go out the back."

"It'll be this guy," Vern said, pulling his apron off. "'Cause it sure as shit ain't gonna be me."

Joshua changed out of his wet clothes in the kitchen when Vern left and took his plate of onion rings out front, where R.J. was playing Ms. Pac Man.

"I learned how to work it so we can play for free," he said, once all of R.J.'s players had died.

"I don't wanna play no more. Can I have some pop?"

Joshua poured them each a Mountain Dew from the dispenser. The café was peaceful without the overhead lights on, without any people in it but him and R.J. All the chairs sat upside down on the tables. R.J. wore jeans and a big sports jersey that wasn't tucked in, his body a barrel. His dad was Ojibwe, his mom white. Like all the Ojibwes who lived in Midden, each fall he received free Reebok shoes from the Reebok company, which meant the guys at school sometimes dragged him into the boy's bathroom, shoved his head into the toilet, and flushed it. Despite this, he and Joshua had been best friends since fifth grade.

"I got something if you ever wanna stay up all night." R.J. pulled a glassine envelope, the kind that stamps come in, from his pocket. "Bender gave it to me." Bender was his mom's boyfriend.

"What is it?"

R.J. gently opened the envelope and shook the contents into his chubby palm. Gray crystals the size of salt fell out. "Crystal meth. Bender made it," R.J. said, and blushed. "Don't tell anyone. Bender and my mom did. Just to see." His eyes were dark and bulbous. He resembled his father, a man whom R.J. seldom saw.

"Let's try it," Joshua said. He smoked pot often but hadn't done anything else. R.J.'s mom and Bender kept all of Midden supplied with marijuana, growing it in a sub-basement under their front porch that only R.J. and Joshua and Bender and R.J.'s mom knew existed.

"Right now?" R.J. poked the meth with one finger.

"What's it do?"

"Wakes you up and makes you hyper."

Joshua licked his finger and dabbed it into the crystals and then put it in his mouth.

"What are you doing?"

"Rubbing it on my gums. That's what you're supposed to do is wipe it on your gums so it gets into your system," Joshua said. He didn't know this for a fact, but he vaguely remembered hearing something like this, or seeing it in a movie.

"You're supposed to snort it," R.J. said. "Bender told me."

Joshua ignored him and sat down at a booth and closed his eyes, as if he were meditating.

"Are you a total fucking head case?" R.J. asked.

"You're the head case," Joshua said, keeping his eyes closed. "I'm letting it get into my system, you dumb fuck."

"What's it taste like?"

"Like medicine."

"What's it feel like?"

Joshua didn't answer. He felt a small swooping sensation but couldn't tell if it was a real feeling or if his desire to feel it had brought it on. He opened his eyes and the sensation went away. He said, "Let's go drive around."

R.J. carefully scraped most of the crystals back into the envelope, and then licked the rest of the meth from his palm.

Joshua drove. They drove through town without passing another moving vehicle. Ten P.M. was like the middle of the night. They drove past the dark storefronts—Ina's Drug, the Red Owl grocery, Video and Tan, past the Universe Roller Rink and the Dairy Queen and the school and the Midden Clinic that sat in the school parking lot, a converted mobile home, double wide—and past the two places that were open, the Kwik Mart and Punk's Hideaway, where Joshua knew that Vern would be —he went there every night. On the way out of town they went slowly by the Treetops Motel, where they could see Anita sitting on a flowered couch in the front office, which was also her living room, watching the news. They drove out Highway 32, past Len's Lookout, where Joshua's mother worked, and continued east for fifteen miles so R.J. could see if Melissa Lloyd's car was in her driveway, and then they drove fifteen miles back to town to R.J.'s house, and then Joshua drove himself another

17

twenty-six farther south to his own house. When he was alone in the car he realized that his jaw ached, that he'd been clenching it without his being aware. He tried consciously to let it hang, as if it dangled from the rest of his face. He did not feel high so much as acutely aware of the edges around him and within him, and he liked that feeling and knew that he wanted to feel it again.

When he pulled into the driveway and got out of his truck, he could hear Tanner and Spy barking their hello barks from inside the house, pushing against the front door to greet him. He hurried in and tried to get them to hush up so he might avoid waking his mother and Bruce. He didn't turn any lights on and walked quietly into the kitchen and opened the refrigerator to look inside, though he wasn't hungry. He took an apple and bit into it and then regretted it, but continued to eat it.

"Josh," his mother called to him.

He could hear her getting out of bed. "I'm home," he said, irritated, not wanting her to. He considered bolting immediately upstairs. He loved his room.

"You're late," she said, appearing in the kitchen, wearing her long fleece nightgown and fake fur slippers. The dogs went to her, forced their noses into her hands so she had to pet them.

"We closed late. Three tables came in right at the end." He tossed the apple at the garbage bin and could tell by the sound it made that he'd missed, but he didn't go to pick it up. "We don't have school tomorrow anyway. It's teacher workshop day."

"You're supposed to call when you're later than ten. That's the deal we made when you took the job."

"It's only eleven."

He poured himself a glass of water and drank the whole thing in one long chug, aware that his mother was watching him. "*What?*" he asked, filling the glass again, running the water hard.

"I'm not tired anyway," she said, as if he'd apologized for waking her. "You want some tea?" she asked, already putting the kettle on.

"Did you see the moon driving home?" she asked.

"Yep."

She took two mugs from their hooks above the sink and placed the tea bags into them without turning any lights on.

"The chamomile will help us sleep."

The kettle began to whistle. She picked it up and poured the water into the mugs and sat down at the table.

18

He sat too, sliding his hot mug toward him.

"It's that I worry when you're late. With the roads being icy," she said, gazing at him by the dim light of the moon that came in through the windows. "But you're home safe now and that's what matters."

She blew on the surface of her tea but didn't take a sip, and he did the same. He wore his headphones around his neck. He ached to put them on, to blast a CD. Instead, he imagined the music, playing a song in his head, its very thought a beacon to him.

"So, you were busy tonight?"

"Not really," he said, and then remembered his earlier lie. "Until just before closing and then the place filled up."

"That always happens." She laughed softly. "Every time I'm about to get out of Len's a busload of people shows up."

She'd tried to quit her job there once. She started up her own business selling her paintings at flea markets and consignment shops. Scenes of northern Minnesota. Ducks and daisies and streams and trees and fields of grass and goldenrod. Most of them were now hanging in their house, much to Joshua's chagrin. His mother had taken R.J. on an unsolicited tour of them once, telling him her inspiration for each painting and their titles. The titles embarrassed Joshua more than the paintings themselves. They were indicative of all the things that irked him about his mother: fancy and grandiose, girlish and overstated — *Wild Gooseberry Bush in Summer Marsh, The Simple Sway of the Maple Tree, Birthland of Father Mississippi* — as if each one were making a direct appeal to its own greatness.

Joshua took a tentative sip of his tea and remembered a game he and Claire used to play with their mother called "What are you drinking?" She'd make them drinks out of water with sugar and food coloring when she didn't have enough money for Kool-Aid and then she would ask them to tell her what they were drinking, smiling expectantly, and they would say whatever they wanted to say, whatever they could think up. They would say *martinis,* even though they didn't know what martinis were, and their mother would elaborately pretend to put an olive in. They would say *chocolate milkshakes* or *sarsaparilla* or the names of drinks they'd invented themselves and their mother would add on to it, making it better than it was, making the water taste different to them too. This was before they met Bruce, after they'd just moved to Midden, when they lived in the apartment above Len's Lookout. The apartment wasn't really an apartment and the town didn't yet feel to them like a town, so outside of it they were that first year, not knowing a soul in a place where everyone else knew each other. Their apartment was one big room, with a kitchen that Len had devised for them along one wall, and a shower and sauna and toilet out back. There was a couch that they pulled out into a bed, and they all slept on it together and usually didn't fold it back up, so that the apartment was really a giant bed, an island in the middle of their new, Minnesota life.

In the afternoons when Claire and Joshua had returned from school and their mother was home from work they would lie on the bed and talk and play games they'd made up. They would say that they could not get off the bed because the floor was actually a sea infested with sharks. Or their mother would close her eyes and ask, in a snooty voice that she used for only this occasion, "Who am I now?" and Joshua and Claire would shriek, "Miss Bettina Von So and So!" and then they would transform her. Softly, they touched her eyelids and her lips, her cheeks and her face, all the while saying which colors they were applying where, and from time to time their mother would open her eyes and say, "I think Miss Bettina Von So and So would wear more rouge, don't you?" They would rub her face for a while longer and then she would ask, "What on earth are we to do about Miss Bettina Von So and So's hair?" and they would rake their fingers through her hair and pretend to spray it into place or tie it into actual knots. When they were done, their mother would sit up and say, in her best, most luxuriously snooty voice, "*Darlings!* Miss Bettina Von So and So is so very pleased to make your acquaintance," and he and Claire would fall onto the floor in hysterics.

Joshua remembered these things now with embarrassment and something close to rage. As a child he'd been a fool. He wasn't going to be one now.

"What are you thinking?" his mother asked suddenly, suspiciously, as if she knew what he was thinking.

"Nothing."

"Do you have a girlfriend?"

He could hear that she was smiling and—he couldn't help it, he didn't know exactly why—he wanted to obliterate her smile.

"Why?" he asked bitterly.

"I wondered if that's what made you late."

"I *told* you. We got tables that came in."

The dogs sat between them and laid their paws on their laps every once in a while and then withdrew them when they got petted.

"Plus, if I had a girlfriend, I would be more than an hour late."

"I suppose you would," she said, thinking about it for a moment and then breaking into a long deep laugh. Despite himself, he began to laugh too, but less heartily.

She took off her wedding ring and set it on the table and went to the sink to pump lotion onto her hands and stood rubbing it in. He could see her silhouette in the dark. She looked like a friendly witch, her hair pressed up scarily on one side of her head, from how she'd been lying on her pillow.

"Here," she said, reaching out to him and sitting back down. "I took too much." She scraped the excess lotion from her hands onto his and then massaged it into his skin, onto his wrists and forearms too. He remembered when he had had colds as a child she would rub eucalyptus oil onto his chest and chant comically, "The illness in you is draining into my hands. All of Joshua's illness is leaving his body and will now and forevermore reside in the hands of his poor old mother." He had the feeling that she was remembering this too. He felt close to her all of a sudden, as if they'd driven far together and talked across the country all night.

"Does that feel good?"

"Yeah."

"I love having my hands rubbed more than anything," she said.

He took her hands and squeezed once, then let go.

"How was your day?" he asked.

"Fine. I went to Duluth actually. Bruce and I went. We ate at the Happy Garden." She took a sip of her tea. "There's something I want you to do for me, hon. It's a favor I want. Claire's coming home tomorrow and I want you to have dinner with us so we can all have dinner together as a family."

"I work."

"I know you work. That's why I'm asking now. You'll have to take the night off."

"I can't. Who's Angie going to find to cover for me?" He held his mug. It was empty, but still warm.

"It's a favor that I'm asking you to do," she said. "How often do I ask you for something?"

"*Often.*"

"Josh."

He petted the top of Tanner's head. He tried to keep his voice calm, though he felt enraged. "What's the big fricking deal about Claire coming home anyway? I see Claire all the time. She was here two weeks ago."

"Don't say fricking."

"Why?"

"Because I'm your mother and I told you not to say it." She looked at him for a while and then said quietly, "It's a stupid word. Say *fucking*, not *frigging*. And don't say that either."

"I didn't say *frigging*. I said *fricking*. There's no such thing as frigging."

"Look it up in the dictionary," his mother said gravely. "There *is* such a thing as frigging. It's just not the best choice, comparatively speaking."

He tilted himself back in his chair as far as he could, so far he had to anchor himself underneath the table with his knee, but his mother didn't tell him to stop, didn't even appear to notice. He let it fall back onto all four legs and said, "Ever since Claire went to college it's like she's the queen bee."

"This isn't about Claire." Her voice shook, he noticed. "It's about doing something that I asked you to do. It's about doing me a fucking favor."

They sat in silence for several moments.

"Okay," he said, at last. It was like someone walking up and cutting a rope.

"Thank you." She picked up both of their mugs and went to the sink and washed them, then turned toward him, drying her hands. "We'd better get some sleep."

"I'm wide awake."

"Me too," she said in a hushed voice. "It's the moon."

He stood and stretched and raised his arms up, as if he were about to shoot a basketball; then he jumped and swatted at the ceiling, landing in front of his mother. He patted the top of her head. He was taller than her by more than a foot and now he stood up straighter so he would be more so. The cuckoo clock that Bruce built poked its head out and cooed twelve times.

"Is everything okay?" she asked when the clock was done.

"Yeah," he said, a wave of self-consciousness rushing through him, remembering the meth. His mother had a way of detecting things.

"Good," she said, pulling her robe more tightly around herself. "And everything's *going* to be okay."

"I know."

"Because I have given you and Claire everything. All the tools you'll need throughout life."

"I know," he said again, uncomprehendingly, feeling mildly paranoid about seeming high, especially that now in fact he suddenly felt high.

"You *do* know, don't you?"

"Yes," he said insistently, not remembering what he knew. He felt simultaneously disoriented and yet also in full command of himself. The way he felt when he'd gone to a movie in the bright light of day and emerged from it and found the day had shifted astonishingly, yet predictably, to night.

"And I've given you so much love," his mother pressed on. "You and Claire."

He nodded. Out the window behind her he could see the silhouettes of three deer in the pasture, their heads bent to Lady Mae and Beau's salt lick.

"You know that too, don't you?"

"*Mom*," he said, pointing to the deer.

She turned and they both looked for several moments without saying anything.

And then the deer lifted their heads and disappeared back into the woods, which made the world right again.

3

THE AFTERNOON WAS SUNNY. Ice hung from the trees, shining, and then fell from their branches suddenly in great heaps. Claire sat near the window in the back of Len's Lookout, gazing at the balsam fir and blue spruce, the Norwegian pines and the poplars, with her coat still on, her scarf still wound around her neck, not knowing that she was looking at balsam fir and blue spruce, Norwegian pines and poplars. Not knowing anything. Not even that she didn't know.

She was twenty, tall, with blue eyes and dark blond hair that went to her shoulders and another, longer rope of hair that was streaked electric blue and was woven into a thin braid with dull silver bells embroidered into it. Despite this, she looked like a farm girl—*a big farm girl*, her boyfriend, David, had said once, grabbing onto her naked hips, meaning it nicely—though she did not want to look like this and didn't believe herself to look like this. Her fingernails were painted black, her toes a glimmering, morose green. The flesh on the right side of her nose was pierced and bejeweled with a fake sapphire stud. She twirled it in its tender hole and sipped her drink. Her brother sat across from her and sipped his drink too, looking out at the trees. Neither of them spoke for long stretches of time, feeling alone and yet together, enclosed in the crowd of the bar as they had been when they were children and waited here for the same reason they did now: for their mother to get off of work.

Claire sucked the last of her drink through her red straw until it made a hollow rasping sound and then she set her glass down. "Any more booze in your little stash?" she asked, stabbing her ice with the straw. Joshua had discreetly added tequila to the orange juice their mother brought them from a tiny bottle he had in his coat pocket.

He shook his head and took the plastic monkey that clung to the edge of her glass and put its tail in his mouth, letting the rest of it dangle. So delicate it was, Claire noticed, a sculpture more lovely than glass. For years they'd collected these monkeys in every color, and also the mermaids and the sharp miniature swords and the paper parasols that stretched open, taut and graceful, at the end of toothpicks. Now Claire wondered what had happened to them, this collection—their collections, his and hers—that they'd begged and bribed and battled to build.

"I should get up and help Mom," she said, without moving. She knew what to do. As a teenager, she'd worked here.

The place was packed, a Friday during ice season. People they didn't know occupied most of the tables, their glossy snowmobile helmets tucked beneath their chairs, their SUVs crammed every which way in the parking lot. People from Minneapolis and St. Paul—"the Cities"—and the suburbs. *City apes*, the locals called them, not necessarily meaning harm.

"Mom seems perfectly fine to me," Claire said, unwinding her scarf.

They both looked at her charging smoothly across the room, clutching the necks of three beer bottles in one hand and two plates of food in the other.

"Who said she wasn't?" Joshua asked.

"*She* did. The tone of her voice did. I *told* you. She sounded like someone died."

"And she said we need to talk?"

Claire nodded, sucking on an ice cube. She had to wait for it to melt before she could speak, her eyes watering from trying to keep the ice from touching her teeth.

"I already told you what I think," Joshua said, with the monkey still in his mouth. "It could totally still happen, you know."

Now Teresa stood near the small opening at the bar where the cherries and limes and lemons and olives were kept in a compartmentalized bin. She carefully set drinks on her tray one at a time, the strings of her green apron in a sturdy knot at the back of her waist. When she turned she saw them watching her and smiled and held up one hand to signal that she was almost done and then disappeared into the throngs of people, away from them.

"Trust me," Claire said. "It's not that. Her tubes are tied." She looked out the window again. There was a canoe there that Len and Mardell used as a trough to feed bears in the summertime, buried now, a hump of snow. "As in *fallopian* tubes," she continued, switching her eyes back to Joshua.

"I think I know what fucking tubes are."

"I'm just telling you."

"How stupid do you think I am?" he asked.

She didn't answer. She'd convinced him to eat dog food once, assuring him that the hard pellets were a new kind of snack mix. She took the book of matches that sat in the empty ashtray between them and lit one and watched it burn and then blew it out the moment before the flame scorched her fingers.

"Don't fight with me, Josh. Not now," she said, gravely, though she didn't feel that things were grave. She felt mildly elated, as if something exciting were about to happen. Driving up from Minneapolis she'd felt just the opposite. Filled with dread for four hours, imagining what could possibly be wrong, playing over and over in her head the words that her mother had spoken to her on the phone the night before when she'd called and commanded her to come home first thing in the morning, parsing them to bits in an effort to determine where exactly the danger lay. Bruce had cut off the end of his thumb with his table saw once. Another time, he'd fallen from a roof and crushed three vertebrae and banged his head so hard that he'd forgotten who Claire and Joshua were for almost a month, remembering Teresa only dimly. Claire knew that these things happened. She'd felt gripped by the enormity of it as she drove north, the vents of her Cutlass Supreme blasting hot air onto her face with the force of a desert wind. The fan had broken to the extent that it was either off entirely or on full blast and so she went from hot to cold and back and forth again, freezing and then roasting, never getting it right. She imagined Bruce unconscious in a bed with his limbs suspended from a ceiling contraption like the time when he'd broken his back. He wasn't her father, or anybody's father, but she loved him as one, and as she drove she imagined the things that she would say about him at his funeral, and she had cried so hard thinking about it that she thought she would have to pull over to the side of the road. But she gathered herself and blew her nose into a gob of napkins from Taco Bell that she'd found crammed into the crease of the seat. She turned on the radio and felt calmed and refreshed for having wept. She remembered, from this new, more reasonable vantage point, how the phone call that told her of Bruce's accident had been much like the one from her mother yesterday:

bossy and eerie and horrifically vague, but immediately identifiable as life-changing, although Bruce's accident had not ultimately changed his life, once he was able to identify them as his family. Now he just had a bad back. And from the accident with the table saw, a shortened thumb with a new pink tip that was as shiny and smooth as the skin of a bell pepper.

By the time that Claire had turned into their driveway, she'd worked herself up into a high state of anxiety again. Their house sat on top of a hill deep in the woods, a mile from the nearest neighbor. Bruce and Teresa had slowly built the house themselves, with weary, sporadic help from Claire and Joshua when they were too young to be of any use. Claire walked through the front door with her heart racing for fear of what she would find, but once she was inside she saw Joshua sitting bare-foot on the couch in sweatpants, methodically eating a giant bowl of a hideous concoction he loved composed of apple sauce, sliced bananas, wheat germ, walnuts, a ground-up chocolate bar, and milk, as if nothing was happening at all. She'd been enraged at the sight of him, at the real-ization that her mother was at work and so was Bruce. That nothing was the matter after all. She insisted they drive to the Lookout, to see their mother.

"So why does Mom have to talk, then?" Joshua asked.

Claire held her braid in front of her, examining it, fingering the bells, then looked up. Her face was as white and unmarked as a new bar of soap. "Don't say that word anymore, okay? It's freaking me out."

"What word?"

"*Talk*. If we have to talk, fine, let's talk. I don't know why I'm sitting here watching Mom run around if we have to talk so badly. We can talk on the phone, you know." She sat back in her chair, one arm stretched out on the table. "I know precisely what's fucking going on. It's just some ploy to get me to come home. It's Mom wanting attention."

She considered getting into her car and driving back to Minneapolis, to her apartment, which she shared with David in the bottom half of a house. He would be happy and surprised to see her, wanting to know what had been wrong, why her mother had needed her to come. *Just to fuck with me*, she'd say, and they'd laugh, and he'd make his Turkish coffee for her, and they'd stay up into the wee hours listening to reggae.

Leonard—the owner of Len's Lookout—appeared with a plate of French fries in his hand. A few cascaded onto their table when he stopped suddenly in front of them. "Hey, kiddos. Your mom's almost done. I thought you'd like a snack." He set the plate down between them and then kissed the top of Claire's head. Leonard wore cowboy boots no matter what the weather and a gold-colored watch that strained against the flesh of his fat wrist. His skin was sickly yellow in some places, a damp pink in others. Joshua and Claire considered him to be something like an uncle, and his wife, Mardell, an aunt, though they were closer in age to their grandparents.

"I hear Mardell's going to Butte," Claire said.

"Butte?" asked Joshua.

"Off to see her baby sister," he called to them, already returning to his place behind the bar. He had a passion for James Michener novels, which he lined up on a rickety shelf in the office behind the kitchen and read over and over again. As a girl, Claire would go into his office on the Saturdays when she came to the bar with her mother. There was a desk with an adding machine with a long tape that curled out of it and a statue of a naked lady with her dress around her ankles and, above it, the hide of an Angus cow nailed to the wall. Throughout her adolescence, Claire had read all the James Michener books one by one as she sat on a stool at the bar waiting for her mother to get off from work. In between the Michener books, she'd read books she'd checked out of the mobile library when it came to town. Optimistic instructional manuals about how to be a cheerleader and how to prevent pimples and how to determine when it was the right time to lose your virginity. She read novels about girls her age who'd run away from home and turned into prostitutes, or other girls who got to rent ponies for the summer, or who were going mad and were sent to therapists in New York City and then recovered fully by the time school started back up. Joshua always sat beside her while she read, spinning himself as fast as he could on his stool until it began to make a rumbling sound like the seat was going to break off and his mother told him to stop. He set his plastic cowboys and Indians out on the bar or his G.I. Joes and he made them fight viciously with one another, buzzing to himself, or making sounds as if he were blowing things up.

Men sat next to them at the bar. The same ones usually, the same ones who were there now. Mac Hanson, Tom Hiitennen, the Svedson cousins. "Your brain's going to melt from all that reading," Mac would say to Claire, his eyes loose and red and wet as a hound dog's. He'd get her to tell him the story of her book and then he'd discredit it jovially. "All those people think they got troubles. What they need is a good kick in the arse or an honest day's work." He held a cigarette between his thumb and forefinger a few inches from his mouth, his elbows resting heavily on the bar. "Just ask this guy," he'd say, jabbing a finger into his own chest, stewing while Claire returned to her book. "He'll tell you a few stories."

Other men came to talk to Claire as she got older. Men who'd happened in from other places, or men who rarely came to Len's Lookout, but got drunk when they did. They touched her hair. They tried to see what color her eyes were and then they said that she was in trouble because blue-eyed women were the worst kind when it came to men. They told her what they thought she'd look like when she was eighteen. They said they'd like to see her then. They warned her not to get fat, and then pinched her sides to test if she already was. Her mother would appear then, asking the men about their wives and kids if she knew them, the weather if she didn't. She spoke in a different voice when she worked at the Lookout, higher-pitched and smooth, and in another voice on her radio show, deep and somber and satisfied, and in an entirely different voice at home.

"It's hitting me," said Claire, gazing out the window. The sun had disappeared now, the sky clouding over. She turned back to Joshua and silently watched him squeeze a mound of mustard onto a napkin. "This thing about Mom being pregnant. You could be right. They can untie your tubes these days and maybe that's what she did." Joshua ate the fries two at a time, dipping them into the mustard. "And for the record, I think it's ludicrous. I think it's rather late in the game for her to be having a baby. I mean, what happened to college?"

"I'm going to Vo Tech," he said.

"Not *you*. *Mom*." She picked up an unusually long fry and dragged it contemplatively through the lake of mustard.

"She's going to college?"

"*Hello, Joshua?* You're the one who lives with her. What else has she talked about for the last year? Going to college once you graduate. Did you think she was planning to be a waitress all her life?"

"She's a painter."

Claire stared at him with disgust, then looked away. Her hand went to her necklace, a stone that protected her from everything. "I'm talking

29

about what she wants to have for a job. For money. Or maybe she wants to actually *study* painting. Did that ever occur to you?"

Joshua didn't answer. Their mother stood across the room before a table of people. She held a metal pitcher of water, her hip cocked to one side and her elbow resting on it, to help her hold the water. Claire couldn't hear her mother from this distance, but she knew what she was saying. All the things they were out of. *Tell them what they can't have first,* her mother had advised her when she trained Claire to be a waitress. *That way they won't have time to be disappointed.*

Joshua took a pack of cigarettes from his coat and shook one out and then lit it up.

"Since when do you smoke?" she asked.

"Since when is what I do your business?"

"Fine. Die then," she hissed, and then, more coolly, "It's not that *I* care. It's that Mom will see you and *she'll* care." She looked around the room, hoping their mother would see. On the walls there were enlarged black and white photographs taken decades before and set in rough wooden frames. Men who stooped down to grasp the antlers of deer they'd shot, or stood on the corpses of coyotes and wolves stacked like logs, or who held pipes and the halters of shimmering horses or the dull posts of fences.

Joshua took a long, intentional drag and then held the cigarette with his hand resting on his lap under the table. "I hate when you come home," he said quietly, not looking at her.

"Thank you," she said in a shrill voice. "I hate it too." She stood up and put her coat on with exaggerated dignity, and took her scarf and mittens and purse from the table.

"Where are you going?"

"Away," she said, half-thinking she meant it. Before Joshua could say anything, she walked out of the bar. In the parking lot, she remembered that she couldn't drive back to Minneapolis even if she wanted to. Joshua had driven them to the Lookout in his truck. It had begun to snow, the flakes falling in lazy swirls, already collecting in her hair. She took a long time winding the scarf around her neck and assumed the posture of someone who was content to be taking a stroll.

She stopped at the edge of the lot, where a hard heap of snow sat, pushed there by the plow. Behind her she could hear someone coming out of the bar. If it was Joshua, she would not speak to him. Her back became very erect in preparation for this, but then she heard a squeal and she turned and saw a boy gathering handfuls of snow and throwing it at another boy and then that boy crouching behind a car and scooping up his own snow to throw back.

She gazed up at a window above the bar. The curtain that covered it was the same curtain that had hung there when they had lived in the apartment. It was from the same fabric as a dress she used to wear, powder blue, with the smallest of red cherries scattered in a loose pattern all over it. Her mother had made the dress first, then the curtains with what was left over. She walked through the snow toward the two small buildings behind the bar. One they referred to as the shed, the other the bathhouse. Leonard and Mardell kept the mower and the rakes and shovels and a broken pinball machine they'd meant to get fixed for several years in the shed. The bathhouse had a sauna, toilet, and shower, which they had used when they lived in the apartment above the bar. She and Joshua had worn a path around it, chasing each other. When the snow was gone you could still see its trail. She sat down on the bench behind the bathhouse facing the woods and the canoe that Leonard and Mardell used for a bear trough and the blackened barrel they used to burn the garbage in. If Joshua looked out the window now, he would see her. The canoe had not been there when they lived in the apartment. It had been added later, to attract the bears, which attracted customers. In the summertime Leonard and Mardell placed a wooden sign out front that said SEE LIVE BEARS HERE! and then filled the canoe with leftover food and grease from the fryer. People sat inside the Lookout along the big picture windows and watched the bears from their tables. But when Claire and Joshua were kids, they would come and sit on the bench outside, even though there was nothing between them and the bears except for a clump of weeds on a small mound of dirt that had formed when the parking lot had been graded.

If the bears looked directly at them, they ran and screamed, though they knew that this was exactly the wrong thing to do. The bears ran too, frightened by the sound, lumbering away like agile old women, back to the trees. They'd turn and look for a while, swaying their thick heads from side to side, then slowly return to the trough to eat, moving with an indolent grace. They made a grunting sound as they ate, the same sound over and over, righteous and dignified. The black of them was a dark so dark that it took on a quality of light and contained colors other than it-

31

self, of blue and violet and green. The bears made Claire think of God, though she'd had no religious schooling. She'd been to church only a few times — confused and irritated, not knowing when to stand up or sit down or how to find the songs in the book or what she was supposed to say when certain things were said to her — but God is what she felt. She felt the same when she looked at fields of goldenrod or alfalfa, or pieces of the sky, or trees, not every tree, but particular trees, trees small and alone, new and fragile, or ancient trees, grand oaks that would kill you if they fell.

She stood up and walked through the parking lot, thinking she'd go back inside, but then continued walking past the bar and out onto the road, toward home. Her footsteps made a trail in the new snow. The wind was stronger on the road, and she bowed her head against it, pushing her chin into the scarf, instinctively looking for things in the ditch as she and Joshua had done when they'd gone out on their expeditions as kids. Over the years they'd found a collection of unmatched shoes, oil-covered T-shirts, cracked pens, and burned-out lighters. Once they found a ten-dollar bill. Once they found a Foghat tape, which Bruce and their mother still listened to from time to time. Once, mysteriously, they found a Canada goose, recently dead, and Joshua picked it up by its feet and spelled out his name and then her name in the gravel with the blood that ran in a steady stream from its beak.

She stopped walking and considered turning back when she saw her mother's car approaching and then pulling off onto the shoulder.

"Hey, jelly bean," Teresa said when Claire got in.

"Where's your truck?" Claire asked Joshua, in the back seat, but he didn't answer, his headphones blasting.

"The battery died — he left the lights on," Teresa explained.

Claire buckled her seat belt, and her mother pulled back out onto the road.

"Can you please tell me what's going on?" She noticed that her mother had applied a fresh coat of lipstick — frosted pink — as if she were on her way to work instead of coming home from it, and this seemed like something of a hint. "Is it that you're pregnant? Josh thinks that you're pregnant. I told him that's impossible. It's impossible, right?"

"*Claire.*"

"*Mom.*"

The snowflakes landed on the windshield and then melted instantly.

Teresa turned the wipers up to the highest speed. "I suppose the roads'll get bad now," she said. "They say it's going to snow six inches and then get cold."

"What about going to college? What happened to that?" Claire asked.

"Oh, for goodness' sake." She looked at Joshua in the rearview mirror, though he could not hear her. "You're both being silly. We'll talk when we get home. Until then, you're going to have to relax."

"I *am* relaxed," Claire said, trying to make her voice sound relaxed. She sat quietly for a while, staring at the road ahead of them, and then took off her mittens and got a tissue from her purse. "It's just that I think I have the right to know," she said, dabbing at her nose with the tissue. "I think driving two hundred miles like a maniac to get here gives me the right."

"I didn't tell you to drive like a maniac."

They passed the Simpson farm. Becka stood with a shovel in front of the house and waved.

"Honk the horn, Mom. There's Becka."

They were silent then, riding home. Trees streamed past, their trunks encrusted with snow, and behind them, not visible from the road, flowed the river, the Mississippi. Claire could feel everything they passed without having to see it, every weed and rock, every patch of bog and tree; even if it were dark she would feel them, so familiar they were to her. She watched herself in the cracked side mirror, remembering how she used to make faces at herself when she drove for long days with her mother, when she was in junior high school and her mother had worked for a short time as a Mary Kay lady. They'd driven all over Coltrap County, holding parties and trying to convince people to buy Mary Kay makeup. Teresa had a folding table that she'd cover with a pink cloth and a cardboard Mary Kay stand-up display. When the women at the party were ready, Teresa would have Claire sit in a chair in the center of the group and make her up, explaining what she was doing while she worked with gentle, emphatic strokes. Claire felt glamorous and important, though she pretended just the opposite, carrying herself as if she were submitting to something not quite distasteful, but approaching that. "Beauty is a few simple steps away," her mother would say when she'd finished applying the makeup, the roomful of women all beaming at Claire. Her mother didn't believe, though, that it was beautifying. Afterward, when they'd left the party and were back in the car, she would push herself up on the seat to look at herself in the rearview mirror and wipe away what she could with a tissue and the cold cream that she kept in her purse. Then she'd hold a clean tissue up to Claire and say, "Here. Get that junk off your face."

"So how've you been?" Teresa asked. "How's David?"

"Okay."

"How's school?"

"Fine."

They saw a deer standing at the edge of the woods in the ditch. Teresa let her foot off the gas and they coasted past him.

"How are things with you?" asked Claire. She turned to her mother, who looked tired but pretty, her hair pulled into a braid the color of toast. "Have you lost weight?"

"I don't know. I don't think so," Teresa said, and touched her face with one of her gloved hands. "Do I look like I have?"

"A little. It looks nice, Mom."

Claire turned on the radio. Only one station came in, KEBE, out of Grand Rapids, where her mother had her show. Now it was the classical music hour, an explosion of flutes and violas and violins.

"Bruce is making dinner," Teresa said loudly. "He's making his mac and cheese."

Claire switched the radio off. "Just tell me one thing. Is there even a *reason* that you had me come home?" She stared at Teresa, who concentrated on the road. "Because if there isn't, I am going to be pissed." She sat quietly, waiting for her mother to say something, but when she didn't she added, "For your information, I have a life and I can't be told to come home whenever you feel like I should."

"I know you have a life," Teresa said.

"I'm not a child anymore, you know."

"You're not *a* child, but you're *my* child. You always will be. Both you and Josh."

"That has nothing to do with what we're talking about," Claire said. She turned to Joshua behind her. "Did she tell *you* what was wrong?"

He stared at her for several moments and then clicked his CD player off.

"Did she tell you?" she asked him again.

"Are you pregnant, Mom?" Joshua asked, astonished.

34

"Claire! Stop, okay?" Teresa looked in the rearview mirror. "I'm not pregnant." And then she said, her voice quiet, "I have some news. That's all."

"*News?*"

"What kind of news?" Joshua asked, but Teresa didn't answer.

"Why are you torturing us like this?" Claire asked.

Their mother slowed the car and pulled to the side of the road and then put it in park but left the windshield wipers going.

Joshua asked, "Did something happen to Bruce?" He pushed his headphones off and let them hang around his neck.

"Bruce is fine." She turned the ignition off and removed her gloves. "Everyone's fine. It's just . . ." She hesitated for several moments, then continued, as if talking not to them, but to herself. "It's okay."

"*What's* okay?" Joshua asked savagely.

"Tell us!" demanded Claire, the tears rising in her eyes, more angry than sad, more frightened than angry. She believed that when her mother spoke again it would be like the moment in a fairy tale when a spell is broken and whatever had been horrible moments before was suddenly lifted and everyone was released from damnation.

But her mother didn't speak. She put her hands on the steering wheel, as if she were going to start the car and drive away. The three of them gazed silently out the windshield for several moments, at the carcass of a dead raccoon, flattened on the road, fine tufts of its fur blowing in the wind.

"What is it, Mom?" Claire whispered gently, as if trying to persuade a child.

The engine began to tick—for several moments there was no other sound—and then it stopped ticking and, aside from the wind, it was silent altogether.

Teresa turned in her seat so she could see both of them and smiled. "My babies," she crooned suddenly, and reached out to touch them.

Claire didn't have time to think about it, what she did the moment she felt the weight of her mother's hand. How she shifted, delicately, away.

4

THE SUN BEAT WARMLY against the sheets of plastic that covered the porch screens, and the flies, which had appeared to be dead that morning in the sills of the screens, stirred. They spun in mad circles on the backs of their wings, their legs black wires spindling frantically in the air, until some of them, by will or by luck, wrenched themselves at last upright. They beat themselves against the thick plastic until the dim January heat died behind the clouds and with it, them.

Bruce sat in the cold rocking chair on the porch and listened to the flies buzzing. It was all he could hear, that buzz, interrupted occasionally by the dogs, who scratched the door, wanting to be let in or out, from the house to the porch, from the porch to the yard, and then back again. But mostly they sat with him and snapped at the flies.

Bruce rolled a cigarette and then smoked it. He rolled another one and held it without lighting it. He wore a navy blue hat with earflaps that could be buttoned under his chin or on top of his head, but he'd not buttoned them at all, so they hung loosely over the sides of his face. He was a bony man, but strong, his limbs long and hard and pale as the bleached poles of a dock. His hair was blond and wispy and tied back always in a low ponytail that snaked thinly past his shoulders. He was freezing, but he didn't want to go inside, so he stayed sitting in the wooden rocking chair and stared at his truck in the driveway.

He considered getting into it and driving back to the job, back to the cabin on Lake Nakota where he was renovating a bathroom for a couple from Minneapolis. He'd spent the morning there, tearing the room apart with his hammer and crowbar and his own hands, ripping the sink out and the tub and shower stall and linoleum from the floor. None of it wanted to come out, all of it almost brand-new. And now tomorrow he would begin to install the bathroom the couple wanted, composed of the old things they'd found in antique shops and specialty hardware stores: an enormous iron bathtub with silver clawed feet, a porcelain sink shaped like a tulip, and tiles for the floor that looked precisely like packed mud.

He could be laying those tiles now. He'd driven home after lunch, thinking he'd find Claire and Joshua there, thinking he'd spare Teresa the grief and go ahead and tell them the bad news, despite what he and Teresa had decided—to tell the kids together that evening after dinner —but when he'd arrived the house was empty and Joshua's truck gone.

He stood and the dogs stood and they all went outside, where it had begun to snow. He turned his face up to the sky like a boy. All the times he'd gazed there, looking for things, finding things, knowing things and pointing them out to girls, or at other times to his father. The Milky Way and Pleiades, the Aurora Borealis and Orion. And all those times he'd felt he'd known the sky, yet now he felt that he knew nothing, or rather that he knew nothing except for what he felt, which was his body cold inside and out and the snowflakes tumbling softly onto his face. Wet fingerprints they were, no two the same, miracles that arrived and then melted.

It was too early to feed the horses, but he did it anyway. Then he fed the hens, huddled already into their beds of hay and shredded wool in the dark of the coop, their feathers brown against their beautiful bodies. He cooed to the first of them, cooed her name, though he could not be sure which name exactly was hers, never able to tell them apart. Teresa knew their names. She'd named them herself—Miss Pretty and Prudence Pinchpenny and Flowers McGillicutty and Mister Bojangles— though of course there was not a mister among them, her idea of a joke. He slid his hand under their rumps and found two warm eggs and put one in each pocket. He had to duck to keep from hitting his head on the ceiling of the coop. It was an A-frame hut that had once stood at the end of their long driveway so that Claire and Joshua had shelter while they waited for the school bus. Now that the kids had no use for it, he'd made it into a chicken coop—a thing that he did often and well, changing one thing to another, according to need. Changing station wagons into pickups, stumps into birdbaths, metal barrels into wood stoves.

He walked out the door of the coop, where the dogs waited for him. The snow, falling in earnest now, gathered on their shiny black backs and then wafted off when they moved. He trudged to the porch and lit the

cigarette he hadn't lit before, having carried it all this time pinched between his lips. He'd already prepared dinner and laid it all out in a bak-
ing pan and set it aside to go in the oven when it was time. He looked at
his watch. It was three o'clock and moving toward dark already. His insides felt heavy, weighted with guilt about not being where he should be
at this hour on a Friday afternoon. He closed his eyes and a list formed
there of all the work he had to do. He and Teresa had agreed that despite
everything they would continue to work. He would work. She would
work.

"There's nothing else we can do," she'd said to him the night before
as they lay together in bed, having gone there early, exhausted from their
day in Duluth. She didn't say it and neither did he, but they both knew
why it was so very important that they had to work: money. She said,
"We'll work every minute of every day that we can."

"Not you," he said. "Me. Your job is to get better."

She didn't reply, but he could feel her mind ticking. On Monday she
would start radiation treatments, but she could keep working. She'd
been able to schedule her appointments late enough that she had time to
work lunch and then drive the hour and a half to Duluth. Joshua would
take her after school. He'd have to take a leave from his own job. These
are the things they'd decided already, things they'd gone over, lying in
bed after trying to make love but then not being able to go through with
it because they were too sad. He had felt her going over it all as he held
her hand beneath the covers and rubbed the soft side of her hip with the
back of his hand. Even her hip had seemed to be thinking.

"Everything's going to be okay."

"I know," she said, and rolled onto her side, facing away from him.
He shifted onto his side too, and cupped her body into his. "Be careful,"
she whispered sharply.

"I am." He gently clutched the small mound of her stomach. She
wore a bra and nothing else. She had to wear the bra to protect the bandage that was taped to her breast to cover the stitches she'd gotten that
day, when she'd had a biopsy of a lump that the doctor had found. It
turned out to be benign, unlike everything else. He kissed her shoulder,
leaving saliva on her skin, and then he kissed it again where it was wet,
where it had already gotten cold.

They were one person, he thought, *not two*.

"Don't," she said. She sat up on the edge of the bed, her back very pale in the light of the moon, accentuated by the black straps of her bra.

"I don't want to go anywhere," she said, after a long while, as if he'd asked. "I mean, Paris or Tahiti or anywhere. I thought you were supposed to want to go where you'd always dreamed of going when you found out you're going to die."

"You're not going to die." His words barely came out, as if he were saying them from the bottom of a canoe, a fucking liar. Her body shifted infinitesimally, icily, and he remembered the words that had been spoken to them earlier in the day. Ordinary, happy words that had become suddenly daggers of fire. *A month, a year, perhaps by summer.* He imagined her dying next month, in February, and then he pushed the idea immediately from his mind, scorched by it. He imagined her dying a year from now —a whole year, an entire blessed year—and it seemed so very far and it seemed that if he knew it were true, that she would live for one more year, he could bear it. More than that, he would do anything for it, give up everything he had. He thought, *September.* September at least. Another spring, another summer. He could live with September. September suddenly made his chest open with joy. And then he thought, *there's always a chance.* What was the chance? Ten thousand to one? A hundred thousand to one? Whatever it was, it was there—the chance that she would live, go on living, and the cancer would languish and disappear and they would grow old and laugh about it or shudder when they remembered this awful winter of cancer, but they would also be thankful for it. How much it had taught them. How close it had brought them— Claire and Joshua and Bruce and Teresa. And they would understand how deeply they loved one another, how intricately bound they were to each other, how every conflict or division or thought in any such direction was nothing—petty folly—in the face of love, and not just their love for each other, but love in the world. Love for every man, woman, and beast, and even God, not just one God, but all gods, because now they knew the meaning of life because it—*life!*—had come so close to being taken from them.

Or the other option was that he would die before she did, no matter when she died. The knowledge that he could die tomorrow, that anyone could suddenly die at any moment of anything, seemed to him consoling, almost a complete relief. And then it came to him, what he would do when she died: die too. The thought was like a hand cool on his forehead.

"It's funny, but I thought of Karl," Teresa said, still sitting on the edge of the bed. "Whether he'll try to get in touch with the kids. You know, *afterwards*."

"How would he know?" asked Bruce.

"I don't know. If somehow word got to him."

Bruce didn't like to think about Karl, Teresa's ex-husband, Joshua and Claire's so-called father—a man they'd seen only once since their parents had divorced. When Bruce first met Teresa he said he was going to drive to Texas and find Karl and kill him on her behalf, because when they'd been married he'd broken her nose. He'd broken other bones too, at other times over the course of their marriage, but the nose Karl had tried to make up to her by buying her a new one, which was the nose she had now, the only nose that Bruce could imagine on her. Her nose had a name: Princess Anne. She'd picked it out herself from a stand-up display with several rows of noses that had names printed beneath them like paint samples. She'd almost chosen one named Audrey or another called Surfer Girl. She told Bruce about her nose and the other noses when they were first falling in love, and he'd said she possessed the most beautiful nose on the earth, and she'd burst into tears. She'd been working at the Rest-A-While Villa then, making sure that the residents took their pills, cleaning out bedpans, changing and washing sheets, whatever needed to be done. Bruce's Aunt Jenny had lived there. He'd visit her every couple of weeks, bringing her bottles of Orange Crush and the black licorice she liked, sitting with her in the community room to watch TV or play cards.

The first time he saw Teresa she was mopping up a pool of tomato juice that had spilled from a rolling cart in the hallway. "Hello," she said, and laughed lightly. The second time he saw her she was standing in the front door of the Rest-A-While Villa in the heat of summer holding a screwdriver, its handle, pale yellow, barely transparent, like honey gone hard. Later, he learned that she carried it with her wherever she went so she could open and close her car door by jamming it into the space where the handle had once been. "Hello," she said for the second time. Her earrings were real feathers that fluttered up into her hair as she walked past. The third time he saw her they spent an unexpected hour in the Rest-A-While Villa parking lot together while he fixed the handle on her car door.

They fell in love then. Languidly, secretly, during the hours that

Claire and Joshua were in school. She hadn't allowed him to meet them for months, and once they'd decided to live together—neither of them believed in marriage—they'd had a ceremony, a nonlegal wedding, which bound Bruce not only to Teresa but also to Claire and Joshua. The ceremony involved vows they'd written together and then the four of them each chose a lilac frond from the same bough and took turns letting it go in the Mississippi River to symbolize their bond as a family. Bruce Gunther to Teresa and Joshua and Claire Wood. That night Teresa had given Bruce a painting that she'd painted herself—*The Woods of Coltrap County*—three trees in the snow, one big, two smaller ones. It hung now on the wall at the foot of the bed, and he'd slept and woken to it every morning and night for the twelve years they'd been together.

He asked, "Do you want Karl to know? Should I call him when the time comes?"

"No," she said, turning slightly toward him, but not enough to face him. "Not unless Josh and Claire want that. I don't even know exactly where he lives anymore."

He stroked her back with the tips of his fingers and then he remembered that she didn't want to be touched and stopped, but left his hands near her on the bed. He felt a burning tightness in his center, down low, in rut and ache, wanting her, wanting to do everything to her, to push and pull and lick and hump and enter and suck and pinch and rub. He felt other ways at other times and he knew that she did too. Sometimes they'd had to almost will themselves to fuck, their bodies clacking together good-naturedly, as familiar and expected as water to the mouth. During those times, they got each other off expertly, lovingly, and kindly, but without urgency and without lust. Sometimes when she walked through the room naked he was no more moved by the sight of her than if the cat had sidled in, but now he felt the opposite: that he could make love to her again and again for days without stop.

"Josh is late," she said.

"He'll be along. Why don't you get some sleep?"

"I will," she said hoarsely, without moving.

He heard the rumble of a pickup making its way down their road, ice-glazed gravel and packed snow, with more snow coming on. He knew as it neared that it was neither Teresa nor Joshua, knew in fact that it was Kathy Tyson. He was mildly surprised when he heard her engine slow and then saw her truck turn into the driveway. The dogs barked and he tried to quiet them to no avail, and he walked off the porch and into the yard to greet her. He'd known her all his life, without actually ever truly coming to know her in anything but a neighborly way. She'd graduated high school a few years behind him and joined her dad in his business, inseminating cows. She lived on their road, another mile and a half on, in a cabin midway down a long driveway that continued up a hill to her parents' house, where she'd grown up.

"Afternoon," she called happily, rolling her window down, but not getting out. He walked up to her door. "I didn't expect to find anyone home this time of day."

"I'm headed back out now. I just stopped home to get some tools."

"The roads are icing up." Her eyes were brown, the same color as her hair. "I wanted to bring some things by." She handed Bruce an empty mason jar. "Thank Teresa again for the apple butter. And this came to me somehow." She handed him an envelope.

"Thanks." He looked at the envelope: nothing but junk mail, addressed to him in computer-generated cursive handwriting, a trick disguised as something real.

"You got any big weekend plans?" she asked.

"Not too much."

She shifted her truck into reverse. "Tell Teresa hi for me."

"You do the same with your folks," he called out to her as she rolled backward into the turnaround. He opened the envelope and read the letter that tried to persuade him that he needed to replace all the windows of his house. He ripped it in half and put it into his pocket, where he found one of the eggs he'd placed there earlier, cooler now. The snow had already laid down a fresh two inches. He ran his glove over the trunk of Claire's Cutlass, swishing the snow off of it, clearing it away for no actual reason, and then he stood staring at its maroon rump, the only color in sight.

He opened the back door of the car and got in and lay down on the seat, his knees bent, his feet crammed onto the floor. Snow covered the windows all around him, making the inside like a cocoon. The car had belonged to his parents, who'd died a few years ago, his father first, then his mother a couple months later. Bruce had given the car to Claire when she moved to Minneapolis to go to college. By the time his parents owned the car, Bruce had been living on his own, so he hadn't ridden in it all that much, but being inside of it made him feel as if he were in the presence of his mother and father again. His parents had died old, nearly eighty. Bruce was their only child, conceived late, after they'd given up hope. The car smelled good, the way all cars did to him, like his whole life pressed together in a room. A combination of metal and gas and bits of food and velour and vinyl and fake pine needles and plastic where people had been, where their hands had touched and touched again. There was a long rip in the fabric that covered the ceiling of the car, causing the whole thing to sag. He closed his eyes, and soon the dogs started up their ecstatic barking, hearing Teresa's car approach. Bruce stayed in the back seat as she turned into the driveway and made her way up the hill. He kept his eyes closed and a list formed again, not of the work he had to do, or the money he had to make, but of what he and Teresa were going to do now, what they'd decided to say, and how.

The engine stopped and he heard them get out; none of them said a word, not even to the dogs. He was going to sit up and get out in a minute, but something held him there. He heard them walking through the snow, up onto the porch. It occurred to him that he could stay in the car. They would think he was in the barn. How long could he stay there before they went looking for him? His hands were numb from the cold. He sat up, slowly, and one of the eggs in his pocket rolled out onto the seat. He put it back into his pocket and got out of the car. When he shut the door all the snow that had clung to the windows fell off like a large curtain.

The outside light went on, and Teresa stepped out onto the porch without her coat on. "There you are," she called to him, and stood waiting for him to come to her.

They hugged without looking at each other, and she held him for a very long time, then stepped back and said, "They know. I told them on the way home. I couldn't wait." He could see that she'd been crying. She looked down and then turned and went inside, and he followed her, straight into the living room without taking his boots off, where Joshua and Claire sat on opposite ends of the couch. Shadow was on Claire's lap. She stroked her as if she were concentrating very hard on following precisely the same line each time, tears falling quietly down her face.

"Cancer means a lot of things these days," said Teresa encouragingly, and sat down between them. "It can do different things. We don't know what mine will do."

43

Simultaneously Claire and Joshua began to weep, each of them scrambling to sit on the floor at Teresa's feet, their heads pressed into her corduroy-covered knees. Bruce pursed his lips, to keep his mouth from quivering, but then his jaw began to tremble and he coughed into his hands. He gazed at the gold-colored towels that sat always on the arms of his stuffed chair, to cover the places where the fabric had worn away. He smoothed the towels down with his rough hands, straightening them back into place, and tried to make his mind go blank as Teresa continued to speak, her voice like a band playing a march, reciting the numbers, the dates, the seasons, the estimations and the speculations and the calculations, the Septembers, the Marches, and the maybe-not Mays.

At last she stopped talking and Bruce watched her stroke Claire and Joshua's hair while they wept, stroking it in all the different ways that he had seen her stroke their hair over the years. Rubbing it like it was cloth, raking through it like it was leaves, then taking it in tiny tendrils and pulling delicately on it, as if she were playing the strings of a harp. His insides leapt and were still and then they leapt again as he thought of what to say but he said nothing. Pain washed through him in waves at seeing the sorrow of his children, and solace washed through him as well, for precisely the same reason.

"We're going to get through this," he said at last, his voice ghoulish and tinny, an echo from afar. Teresa looked at him gratefully, her eyes aflame and at the same time calm, as if she'd arrived at the scene of an accident and had come prepared to help. With their eyes they said things to one another, domestic and romantic, grandiose and mundane, but mostly they said, without any surprise, *Cancer. Cancer. It's truly cancer now.* The realization crackled starkly between them across the room. Bruce felt as if he were seeing it—the word itself—and understanding it for the first time. Fraught with horror. And beauty now too, because it lived in her, like a fish that swam or a sapphire of coal that burned. "We're going to get through this," he repeated, suddenly giddy, believing it, that if cancer could be beautiful, she would live. "We *are*."

"We are," Teresa agreed quietly, stilling her hands.

And then she turned away from him, as if all alone in a room, and rested her head back against the ruined velvet of the couch.

PART II

Good

The face of this love was quiet and feral. It was a ruthless act, but not a guilty one. A waterfall, a flood, is neither guilty nor not guilty. It simply drowns the people in its way.

—Mary Lee Settle, *Charley Bland*

5

THE CLOCK on Bruce's side of the bed was relentless. Two twelve, its terrible little red face said. Teresa reached for the cold mug of peppermint tea on the shelf beside her, pushing herself up to sit, and took a big sip. She'd fallen asleep, but then woken from a dream about a mass of brown goop attaching itself inextricably to the front of her shirt. *Cancer,* she thought now. Her first dream of cancer.

"Bruce?" she said quietly, her voice a drop of water, not really wanting to wake him. His breath remained unaltered, so deep and sure. She set the mug of tea back on the shelf and then lay down, the side of her arm just barely grazing Bruce's body under the covers. It was late Sunday night, actually the wee hours of Monday morning, the day on which she'd drive to Duluth for her first radiation treatment.

She closed her eyes and concentrated on relaxing her body, letting its weight sink into the bed, feeling how the blood moved through her, but then she opened her eyes, unable to feel anything. She felt that she was made of air and cold peppermint tea, her body a vessel that held only those two things. She stared at the shadows on the ceiling and remembered the other dreams she'd had: a cat in the median of a freeway that she had to rescue, and another in which she was dusting a gong. She realized that perhaps they were about cancer too, that, from now on, all of her dreams would be.

She would have to ask her brother, Tim. He believed that he knew everything about dreams—what it meant when something was pink, what it meant if you were on a train or a ship. Sometimes she agreed with his analysis, other times she thought it was a bunch of New Age crap. She seldom spoke to him anymore. As children they'd been fierce friends and as adults they had various things in common, but not much to say to each other about them. When they talked, they talked about their parents—Tim lived near them, so he gave her updates—how their health was, what insulting thing they'd said about Laura, Tim's girlfriend of twenty years. Tim and Laura owned a rock shop together. They dealt in crystals and agates, semiprecious stones, things Claire and Joshua had gone wild over when they were younger. She supposed Tim knew by now—his baby sister has cancer—thankfully, her parents had volunteered to tell him. Telling *them* had been all that Teresa could bear to do. Tim knew everything about what stones meant too, what curative powers they had. He would send her one by express mail, she knew. A rock to carry around in her purse or pocket or wear around her neck.

Teresa reached for the necklace that hung there now—a seashell on a leather string—and held it in the dark, a habit of hers when she was thinking. She hardly ever took the necklace off. Joshua and Claire had found the shell and given it to her the one time that they'd gone to the ocean. It was readymade for a necklace. Small and lovely, with a tiny hole bored through the top. They'd gone to Florida; somehow she'd scratched together the money. She tried now to recall how she'd gotten the money: her tax return. Usually she'd spent it on something more practical. Clothes for the kids or a new used junk heap of a car, but that year—the first year after she'd finally left their father—she wanted to take Claire and Joshua on a vacation, so she did. They rode a Greyhound bus for thirty-some hours from Minnesota to Florida, to the beach, to a forlorn-looking campground called Sea Scape, near the town of Port St. Joe. They set up the tent she'd borrowed from a friend. She'd borrowed everything—the sleeping bags and the Coleman stove, the flashlights and the tarp, even the enormous suitcase on wheels that she'd packed it all into. They stayed for almost a week, going to town only once to get more food, hitching a ride with an elderly couple who'd been camped near them in a ramshackle RV.

At night they played Old Maid and Go Fish, sitting at the picnic table, holding the flashlights to see. Teresa had been twenty-four, Claire almost seven, Joshua, five. This was their first real vacation.

They spent the days on the beach. It was beautiful, desolate; almost always they had it to themselves. Strange sharp reeds grew where the sand ended, a kind of ocean swamp that kept people from building houses there. They walked the beach up and down, finding shells and chunks of glass that had been worn and polished by the sea. The kids did gymnastics, yelling for her to watch every time. Cartwheels, backbends, tricks they'd practiced as a team, then performed. Each of them could do a complete back flip, somersaulting in the air from a standing position and then landing in that same position. "Do it again," she'd say, amazed each time. But then, after a while, she commanded them to stop. They were doing it too much. Surely they would tire and falter and land on their heads and break their necks and die. She had a precise image in her mind of what her children would look like with broken necks. She clutched their shoulders and forbade them from jumping when not in her sight. They laughed at her, giggling and giggling. Her kids were always giggling, as if a pair of invisible hands were tickling them, and also they hopped, up and down, down and up—so much hopping and giggling she thought she would go insane at times.

When they ran ahead of her on the shore she walked intentionally slowly so that she could pretend for a while that she was a normal person, not a mother. That those children in the distance belonged to someone else. That she was a woman on the beach contemplating things, letting the day go, or greeting it with calm, thinking ahead or back, instead of the endless present tense in which she lived. Or thinking nothing at all, thinking, *I wonder if God exists?* And then the kids ran toward her giggling, hopping, shrieking, "Mom! Mom! Look what we found!"

Joshua offered her his palms full of wet sand, and he and Claire told her to dig into it, to get her surprise, and she found the shell with the hole bored naturally, perfectly through it. She would wear it around her neck for the rest of her life.

"Thank you," she said, the tears rising in her eyes.

"What's wrong?" they both asked, in a chorus, walking back to the campground.

"Nothing," she answered, though she began to cry harder. "It's that we're so happy," she said at last. She put her hands on their heads. The three of them had the same hair. Not blond, not brown, but something in between: the faded yellow of grass where an animal had slept.

On the way back to Minnesota they got off the bus in Memphis to visit her parents. When they arrived, tanned from Florida, tired from the ride, her parents were so overjoyed to see them that they all five grabbed onto one another in one big embrace. Her parents weren't rich, but Claire and Joshua thought they were, running victoriously through the house, not used to such things. Cars without rust, walls without cracks, rooms with beds that no one slept in, things in the cupboard like bags of

49

Doritos and Chips Ahoy! cookies that hadn't been immediately ripped open and consumed. Teresa had not grown up in Memphis, but this is where her father worked now. They had moved all over the country when Teresa was a child, following her father's job selling a special kind of paint that held up when exposed to extreme heat. The last place she'd lived with her parents was in El Paso, when she was seventeen and pregnant, a few days out of high school.

Her parents had disapproved bitterly when she decided to continue with her pregnancy. They said she was going to be the worst kind of mother—a *teen* mom, a *single* mom—but then when she eloped with Karl they'd also disapproved of that, because Karl was a coal miner who'd dragged her off to Pennsylvania to live in a trailer. They disapproved when she left him the first time and the second time and the third and the fourth, because when you get married you stick it out no matter what; but they also disapproved when she went back because how could she continue to be married to such a loser of a man. They disapproved when she left him for real the fifth time and moved across the country to a remote town that didn't even appear on the map, because how was she going to make it on her own, and then later, they disapproved when she met Bruce and committed herself to what they called a "hippie charade of a marriage."

Against this backdrop, she lived her life. She hated her parents at times, loved them at other times. She talked to them each Sunday on the phone and often after they'd hung up she decided to never speak to them again, but then she would call the next Sunday. She was a slave to Sundays.

How are you? Good. How are you? Good. How are the kids? Great.

Her mother would be on one phone, sitting on the aqua bedspread that covered her parents' king-size bed, her father on the other phone, standing in the dining room with a grandfather clock ticking nearby.

Several times a year they sent her boxes of things they wanted to get rid of. Things they said they thought she could use. Old towels and impossible kitchen equipment that performed only one simple task: shredding cheese or mashing fruit. Or hideous swaths of fabric that it took Teresa several minutes to figure out were curtains—as opposed to other hideous swaths of fabric that she had first *thought* to be curtains, but turned out to be pants her mother had worn in the seventies. But every once in a while, in the midst of all the crap, there would be a shirt she loved and wore and wore and wore. Her parents took out life insurance policies on Claire and Joshua, just enough to cover their funerals, but wouldn't give Teresa a dime. Not at Christmas, not for her birthday. When she'd married Karl they told her that she was an adult now. When she left him, they said she had to weed the garden that she'd planted.

And she did. She weeded her garden. She had a million jobs. As a waitress, a nurse's assistant, a factory worker, a janitor. Her million jobs were always doing one of these four things, but the place changed a million times. It turned out that Claire was smart, good in school, good at math and reading, good at tests, her mind like flypaper. She would go to college and be famous somehow. She would be rich and buy her mother a house in Tahiti, they said, without any of them being exactly sure where Tahiti was. She would be the first woman president of the United States. *Imagine that!* They did. She won a scholarship to the University of Minnesota. A full ride and off she went, majoring in political science, in dance, in Spanish, and in English, and then a combination of all four things.

Joshua was not as much of an overachiever, but kind and good-hearted, hardworking and honest. He'd had some trouble with his ears in first grade—couldn't hear what the teacher was saying—so they put him in the front row. Teresa took him in for a procedure. Tubes. He was mildly dyslexic, wrote *gotfor* instead of forgot. He liked to imagine things, that they had a swimming pool or a pet giraffe named Jim. He excelled at drawing automobiles meticulously, beautifully in pencil, perfectly to scale. He knew everything about cars and trucks—the models, years, makes. Like Bruce, he was a Chevy man, and everything made by Ford sucked. He could fix cars too. His hands a gentle pair of tools taking things apart, then putting them back together again, better than before.

One Sunday on the phone her father said, "It's a shame that the brains got wasted on Claire. If only one person in the family gets the brains, you hope they go to a boy. It's just like with you and Tim, the brains got wasted on you."

She set the receiver back into its cradle without a word, but quietly, not slamming it down. Who *were* these assholes? What had happened to them? Her childhood had been filled with a reasonable amount of joy. Barbecues and birthday parties, pushing a pin through a paper plate and holding it up to the sky in their backyard to see the solar eclipse.

She called the next Sunday and nobody mentioned the Sunday before.

Years passed. She was thirty, then thirty-five. Slowly, stingily, she forgave them without their knowing about it. She accepted the way things were—the way *they* were—and found that acceptance was not what she'd imagined it would be. It wasn't a room she could lounge in, a field she could run through. It was small and scroungy, in constant need of repair. It was the exact size of the hole in the solar eclipse paper plate, a pin of light through which the entire sun could radiate, so bright it would blind you if you looked. She looked. And something astonishing happened: she loved them, felt loved by them, all the love traveling back and forth through that small shaft. She saw her parents in their most distilled form, being precisely who they'd always been. The people who sent her garbage in the mail. The people who made her cry each Sunday. The people who would gladly give their lives to save hers. The only people who would do that. Ever, ever. Her mom and dad.

She'd told them about her cancer the previous morning. It seemed better, somehow, for her to tell them in the morning. She'd allowed only a few tears to escape when she told Claire and Joshua, but when she'd heard the voices of her parents, she cried hard enough that it took her several minutes to get a single sentence out. "I . . . I . . . I have . . ."

Her father got calm and her mother got hysterical, the way they'd been for as long as Teresa could remember. Her mother pounded against something, on the bed frame or a table, Teresa could hear it over the phone. She claimed she was going to leave the house at once and get on a plane to fly to Minnesota. Teresa's father emphasized that this was just the beginning, that cancer was easily cured these days, that she was young and she should not—that he would not—get too worried yet. By the time they hung up it had been decided that they would come in one month. That they would call Tim and tell him and ask him to come too and they would all be together again for the first time in ages. She hung up the phone feeling slightly giddy and sick to her stomach, the way she always did at the prospect of a visit from her parents.

In bed she lay awake, thinking about what she would feed them when they came. They were meat and potatoes people; she and Bruce and the kids were vegetarians. This always caused an uproar, even though when her parents visited she cooked them beef, chicken, pork—some kind of meat each night.

Bruce rolled onto his side and let out a small groan.

"Are you awake?" she asked, sitting up.

He didn't answer and she sat silently watching him, pondering whether she had the energy to get out of bed to get herself something to drink. She stared at the painting of the trees that hung at the foot of the bed. She'd painted it herself. Three trees, winter trees, not a leaf among them. Bare and black and big as boys against a landscape of snow. One tree represented love, another truth, the other faith. She couldn't remember which was which now, though when she'd painted it she'd gone to such pains, such excesses to paint those trees. Which way the branches should reach, how thick the trunks should be, making small imperfections to show where an animal might have come to scratch or chew the bark. She stared at the painting so long in the dark that she began to see strange things in it: the silhouettes of glum faces, a tall spindly boot, the backside of a man who carried a candle in a sconce.

"I can't sleep," she said loudly to Bruce.

He inhaled sharply and reached for her hand and held it under the covers.

"I had a dream and then I woke up thinking about it and now I can't fall back asleep," she said. She lay down again, nestling into him. "I dreamed there was this brown goop attaching itself to me. And then I dreamed of a woman I used to work for—Mrs. Turlington—I was her housekeeper. Not in the dream, in real life I was her housekeeper when I was a teenager. I would go after school. She had this gong that had supposedly belonged to some emperor at one point—some emperor in Japan. I had to dust it every day with a feather duster. And that's what I dreamed—that I was dusting this gong."

She was silent then, considering whether she should tell him the dream about the cat in the middle of the freeway.

"She fired me in the end. I can't remember why. I moved away anyway. I got married." She lay staring at the ceiling. "She gave me a ceramic rooster with a head that came off and had lotion inside."

"For being fired?"

"For getting married."

He patted her leg. "Let's sleep. You need your rest. Tomorrow's a big day."

She closed her eyes, then opened them again, wild with anger about the rooster. "It's ridiculous when I think about it. Why would she fire me and then give me a rooster?" Her voice wavered and then she sat up and cried.

He tried to pat her back but she shook his hand away. She went to the bureau and took several tissues from the box and blew her nose. Her head was stuffed up from talking and crying and consoling everyone all weekend.

"I'm sorry," she said. "It's okay. I'm just thinking all kinds of things right now."

"That's the past," said Bruce, wide awake now. "That's not what you should be thinking about."

"I'm not thinking about it," she said.

"You just had a dream."

"I know." She crouched down, feeling around in the dark for the socks she'd taken off before she went to bed. "Go back to sleep," she said. She sat on the padded bench along the wall and pulled the socks on.

"I can't sleep if you can't sleep."

"Yes, you can." Through the window, she could make out Lady Mae and Beau standing close to each other just outside the entrance to their stalls, keeping each other warm.

When Bruce began to snore, she walked quietly out of the room. The house was dark, but it felt alive, the way houses did to her when no lights were on and she was the only one awake. Claire and Joshua were asleep upstairs. In the morning Claire would drive back to Minneapolis. Teresa felt that Claire's departure would mark a new era in their lives: the era in which she actually had cancer. At the moment she felt almost nothing—that cancer could not be real because her body was not real. She felt numb and stuffed and fuzzy, weightless and yet weighted. As if her veins had been filled with wet feathers. She'd felt that way all weekend, hazy and deeply sad, yet laboring to reassure Joshua and Claire and Bruce that she was actually just fine.

She walked through the living room, where Spy and Tanner lifted their heads from the couch and flapped their tails. In the bathroom, she shut the door, turned the light on, and saw herself—a wreck—in the mirror. Her eyes were swollen, her skin craggy and pale with a patch of rough bumps across her cheeks. She turned on the cold water and let it run full blast till it was ice cold. There was a space heater in the room and she plugged it in. She held a washcloth under the running water and wrung it out and pressed it to her eyes, and then lay down on the floor, on a hooked yarn rug she'd made herself, and set the washcloth over her eyes. There had been a time when she'd done this often, when Karl had beaten her up. She remembered that now, the way a body remembers, with precision, though she scarcely remembered Karl himself at all. Her life with him, in memory, felt like a play she'd seen years ago. The first time he had beaten her they'd been married for three days. It was never going to happen again. It happened again. Her nose, her collarbone, a tooth. He had his good days and he had his bad days, and so did she, so did they. She had Claire and Joshua to think about and Karl had never hurt them—not directly. Once, Joshua cut his foot, having stepped on a dagger of plastic from a shattered radio that Karl had thrown against the wall. And Claire had to have stitches in her lip when her highchair was knocked over during one of their scuffles. But they did not remember these things. Years later, Claire had asked, "How'd I get this?" She pulled her lower lip out, examining the scar on the soft flesh inside.

"In the tub," Teresa said, smooth as butter. "You slipped when you were a baby."

But they did remember other things—there was nothing Teresa could do about that. They remembered Karl choking her almost to death and having to run barefoot to wake the neighbors in the middle of the night. They remembered being driven around while they slept and how Claire had to get dressed for school in the car. They remembered the things that clothing could not conceal—gashes and bruises and welts. But she got out, and that's what mattered in the end. She was setting a good example now, in her relationship with Bruce. They would know what a good man was, what love was, what they should not accept.

But Karl had left his mark. Claire had written a paper about him in a women's studies class her freshman year. *My mother was a battered woman, my father was a batterer. What does this make me? A survivor,* the first lines said. Teresa's stomach had flipped when she read this and her mouth felt funny, as if it were filled suddenly with blood, as if a lie were being told about her, as if the truth had not occurred to her until that very moment.

"What's this?" she asked.

"It's none of your business, that's what it is." Claire ripped the paper from her hands, then tore it viciously in half. Teresa had unknowingly picked it up from a nest of papers and books on Claire's bed.

"I would say it's precisely my business," she said, trying to sound conciliatory and motherly, superior but kind, though she felt that she'd been struck. "Honey, you shouldn't dwell on those kinds of things." She sat on the bed, on the quilt she'd made Claire for her thirteenth birthday, composed of patches of clothes she'd worn throughout her childhood. She looked down almost shyly and ran her hand over a brigade of dancing vitamins that at one point had been Claire's favorite pants. "All in all, you had a very happy childhood, wouldn't you say?"

She wouldn't say. She pulled her hair back into a ponytail and told Teresa that she felt her childhood had been "mixed."

"*Mixed?*" Teresa asked. Things came into her mind, a series of things, most of them involving wanting to lock Claire in the house until she admitted that her childhood had not been "mixed."

"Oh—I always knew you loved me," she conceded, then added, "But there was Dad. That was hard. There was having to worry about you all the time and feeling responsible. I was completely parentified by the age of, like, six."

"Parentified?"

She nodded. "It's where a child who is still a child doesn't get to be a child entirely because he or she has to take on things that children shouldn't have to take on. It's very common in single-parent families— where the child has to look after younger siblings, cook meals, and stuff like that." She looked at her mother sweetly. "I don't blame you specifically."

Teresa sat without moving a muscle. Sometimes she hated Claire.

"I thought you liked to cook," she said in a shrill voice.

The years with Karl had been difficult, she'd grant Claire that. Their life was nightmarish at times. She couldn't honestly say she'd ever truly loved him beyond their high school infatuation, but they had made a family, they were companions of a sort. There were times when they'd tried to be happy. They had kids together, rented apartments together, ate dinner, went to parks, made love. This, despite the fact that Karl was a madman. When she left him for good, half of her believed he would kill her, the other half believed he would kill himself. He did neither, though their parting was not without its drama. He broke into and ransacked her new apartment across town from where she had lived with him. He tried to kidnap the kids. He became convinced that Teresa was sleeping with a sad man named Ray, who cooked in the restaurant where she worked as a waitress. Once, on Ray's day off, Karl went to his house and beat him up and then drove to the restaurant and dragged Teresa out into the parking lot by her hair. He beat her while all of her customers looked on from a distance, indignantly yelling, "Hey!"

Of course she hadn't been sleeping with Ray. Sex was the furthest thing from her mind. She was never going to touch another man. She would stay single and celibate forever. But she saw that Karl would never leave her in peace, so she thought about where she could go. A friend had a cousin in Minnesota who was quitting her job in a town called Midden, somewhere in the woods a couple of hours west of Duluth. She made a few phone calls and within a week she and the kids were on a bus with a suitcase and a pillow apiece.

They rode for days, meeting people. Good people who told her their life stories and helped her accommodate the kids. Smelly old men and enormously fat women who allowed Claire and Joshua to stretch out and sleep on their laps and when they woke gave them treats, licorice and peanuts and sticks of Juicy Fruit gum. Teresa felt more like their big sister than their mother during that trip—during that entire time in their lives really—so intimidated she was to be out in the world alone. She became sick from the motion of the bus and had to vomit into a plastic bag that had once held beef jerky. She stared out the window, watching Ohio roll by, then Indiana, Chicago, and Madison, contemplating Minnesota, feeling Minnesota waiting silently, darkly, like a giant iceberg that would rip a ship in two, so cold it was. That's all she knew. How cold Minnesota would be.

But when they arrived it was hot, August. She took off her sweater, which she'd worn because of the air-conditioning on the bus. They'd been dropped in the gravel parking lot in front of a bar called Len's Lookout, about a mile outside of town. She stood next to their suitcases, looking around. They'd driven through the town—Midden—just moments before. It was smaller than she'd imagined. The sign on the highway had said "POPULATION 408" and she thought what she always thought when reading such a preposterous number: *Who were the eight?* The town consisted of a brick school and several houses and businesses in low buildings and a water tower with a giant *M* painted on it, jutting above everything else, but mostly, it seemed, of the trees and grasses that surrounded the town on all sides, as if the wilderness were gaining on the town, as if it had arrived more recently, rather than the other way around. Len's Lookout itself was in the wilderness, the only building in sight.

Joshua and Claire ran back and forth, from her to the doorway of the bar. They asked if they could go inside, if they could have a can of pop. She stared at the bar, her hand raised above her eyes to shield them from the glaring sun. The front windows were plastered with papers — advertisements for Labor Day festivals, the Lion's Club Corn Feed, something at the VFW, someone who would do your taxes, another someone who would trim your horse's hooves — with neon beer signs above.

She walked toward the door, dragging the suitcases behind her. The man who greeted them was named Leonard, he told them immediately, and by the way he stood Teresa knew that he'd been watching them since they'd gotten off the bus. He owned the place with his wife, Mardell. His parents had owned it before he had. It was named after his father, the original Leonard. He gave them each a Shirley Temple and wouldn't let Teresa pay for them. He gave the kids a bowl of peanuts and offered Teresa a bowl of her own, which she refused. She asked if there was a paper she could buy.

"Paper?"

"Yeah — a newspaper," she said, sipping her drink.

"Oh." He laughed. "There's the *Coltrap Times*. Comes out every Wednesday, but mostly you just gotta ask whatever you want to know because by the time it's in the paper, it's over and done with."

She told him about her job at the Rest-A-While Villa, about needing to find a place to live. He stared at her for a long while, leaning on the wooden bar, so long that she thought he wasn't going to say anything and she'd have to leave.

"Let me show you something," he said. "Then you can tell me what you think."

They followed him back, behind the bar, through the small kitchen, past surprisingly jumbo-sized cooking equipment, out the back door, and up a flight of stairs that went up the side of the building to an apartment. Empty boxes were stacked haphazardly around the place. Near the door sat a giant mixer that looked broken. The apartment was one big room and not much else. There was an alcove with a half-sized refrigerator and stove and a closet beyond that was bigger than the alcove. Teresa walked around contemplatively, swatted a mosquito that had landed on her bare shoulder. Joshua touched the blade of the mixer with one finger.

"Don't touch that," she snapped, almost reached to slap his hand the way she had when he and Claire were younger, before she'd read that hitting your kids in even the most minor ways taught them that violence was the way to solve problems. There were small things like that that she regretted, things she'd do differently now. There were a few years during which she fed Claire and Joshua mostly canned soup and Hamburger Helper and a ghastly amount of a certain kind of cheese spread that wasn't manufactured anymore.

"Is there a . . ."

"The bathroom's out back," Leonard said. He gestured out a window to a shed in the yard.

"It's a bathhouse. There's a shower and a toilet and a sauna. Mardell and I heat up the sauna about once a week and we have some folks over too. You're welcome to join us anytime. Or you can light one yourself whenever you want. Our son, Jay, keeps us in wood."

The bathhouse was white, wooden, with a shingled roof the color of a ripe peach. Beyond it civilization ended and became dense woods that dipped down to a river that she could see in small glimmers.

"It's the Mississippi," said Leonard, as if he'd read the question in her mind.

Without asking, Claire and Joshua ran out the door and down the stairs toward the bathhouse.

"I can let you have it for two hundred a month, including everything," he said. "You'll be able to walk to work when it's not too cold—it's just a mile—and if you need a bed, Mardell and I got a couch that pulls out we can loan you."

"Perfect," she said.

Packages arrived at the post office that she'd mailed to herself from Pennsylvania. Blankets and pots and pans, forks and spoons and her good knives. The apartment was lovely in the afternoon when the sun shone in, and in the morning it smelled like the cakes and pies Mardell baked in the kitchen below. The bar never got too loud and Teresa rather enjoyed the sound of the music from the jukebox as it filtered up through the floor anyway.

Everyone was curious about why they'd come and who they were. It seemed that nobody had moved to Midden for eighty years, but eighty years ago is when everyone who wasn't Ojibwe had arrived. They came from Finland mostly, a few from Sweden, a few from Denmark or Norway. At the Rest-A-While Villa, Teresa heard stories about things that had happened years and years before—blizzards and fires, trains and dances, marriages and deaths and births—while she mopped the floors or scrubbed pots or went into the residents' rooms to change bedpans. The residents were mostly women with names like Tyme and Hulda, with last names Teresa couldn't pronounce if she read them on a page. The women had dozens of photographs taped to the walls behind their beds. Pictures of children, grandchildren, great-grandchildren. They were sorry to hear that Teresa did not have a Finnish bone in her body, but relieved to hear that at least her children's father was a Swede. Being a Swede was better than nothing. They told her that she was nice for someone who was Irish, though it had never occurred to her until they asked that Irish was what she was.

Winter came and she forgot about not having sex again. She met a man named Larry, who didn't live in Midden, but came several times a week to deliver things to the Rest-A-While Villa. They had sex in his delivery truck. They had sex in the bed above Len's Lookout while Claire and Joshua were at school. They had sex on a blanket in the grass near the river that ran several yards behind the bar, back in the woods. One day Larry said he didn't like the idea that she had kids.

"Idea?" she said, laughing coolly, pulling her shirt back on. "They're a bit more than an *idea*, Lar."

They fought, and he apologized and claimed that actually he was crazy about Joshua and Claire. He bought them a stuffed purple gorilla to prove it. The gorilla was as big as a chair. Aside from the couch, it was the only place in the apartment to sit and Claire and Joshua fought over whose turn it was to sit in his lap. They named him Little Larry and had it for years—long after the real Larry had disappeared—until one day tiny white balls started coming out in the place where his big leg met his crotch and Teresa threw him out.

After Larry, Teresa dated a man named Killer and didn't ask him how he got the name. *Killer*, it said on his arm in a cursive tattoo. He was a beautiful, skanky man with an incredibly thin and sinewy body. He liked her version of tuna casserole. He liked it so much they didn't call it tuna casserole anymore, but Killer casserole. He was good in bed, the first man who could honestly make her come. She took him back to the river too, on a trail that started behind the bar, worn by Joshua and Claire in the daytime. She went back at night, while the kids slept, feeling somewhat guilty to be leaving them alone in the apartment, but also gloriously free. She left a light on and she could see it just barely through the trees when she crawled up onto a big rock that sat near the bank of the river. Seeing the light made her feel reasonably assured that everyone was safe inside. Killer sat on the rock next to her and they smoked a joint and fucked and smoked another joint and she felt like maybe this was her life now, that he was her man, though in the light of day she knew this was not remotely true. He drank too much, smoked too much weed. He was a biker and he bought her a leather lace-up top for her birthday that she was supposed to wear when she rode on the back of his bike.

There was a long spell of nobody, and then she met Bruce.

Bruce Gunther, Bruce Gunther, Bruce Gunther. His name was like a cure that had taken her a century to find. She was twenty-seven and so was he. She'd noticed him at the laundromat, drinking a can of Coke. She saw him again at the Rest-A-While Villa, visiting his Aunt Jenny. "Hello," he said. "Hello," she said. His eyes were so pale and blue and kind; his hair so fine and blond, like a doll's. He fixed the handle of her car so she didn't have to use a screwdriver to open it anymore. He was a carpenter, an only child, and the year before she met him he'd broken up with a woman named Suzie Keillor, who worked at the school. Teresa wouldn't let him meet her kids, wouldn't even take him back to the river in the middle of the night. She'd become more careful again, wary of men, not wanting to get anyone's hopes up, so she and Bruce kept their relationship a secret until they were truly in love. Finally, she invited him to dinner, to meet Claire and Joshua. He was not to touch her, or to act as if they were anything but friends. When he pulled up in his truck, the kids ran down the stairs to greet him. She stood on the landing, watching from above.

Instantly he began playing a game with them, teaching them a song. She finished making dinner, hearing her children shrieking with joy through the open window. He chased them around the bathhouse on the path they'd worn. He didn't come up to the apartment to see her until she called them all in to eat. They sat on the couch, all four of them, Little Larry sitting across from them against the beige wall. The kids could hardly eat, so besotted they were with Bruce.

Afterward, when he stood to leave, the room became smaller with his standing. He shook their hands with a special handshake they'd made up outside. He shook Claire's hand, then Joshua's hand, and then hers, but she grabbed him and kissed him instead.

The kids hopped and giggled, giggled and hopped.

"Bye," she called ecstatically, as he descended the stairs.

There, she thought, *there you are.*

She woke with the wet washcloth draped over her face. The bathroom was as warm as a sauna from the space heater humming on high. She realized that there had been a knock, and that's why she'd woken. She sat up and looked at the closed door.

"Ter?" Bruce said from the other side.

She opened the door, reaching awkwardly for it, still sitting on the rug with her socks and bra on, her robe laid out beneath her. "I fell asleep," she said when he came into the room, squinting at the light. "What time is it?"

"Four something."

"Why aren't you sleeping?" she asked, standing up.

"I am. I just had to pee."

She examined her face in the mirror while he urinated. "I think I'll take a bath," she said. She took her bra off and felt a tight pulling sensation where the stitches strained against the weight of her breast. Slowly, she tugged the tape that held the gauze bandage in place, covering the stitches from her biopsy. "I can take this off now."

"Here," Bruce said. "Let me." He stood in front of her and pulled the tape off more gently than she had, peeling it away bit by bit and then removing the gauze. There were pink lines on her skin from the elastic of the bra, and other, meaner-looking marks where the tape had been. The air felt cool and damp on her newly uncovered skin. There was a small bruise at the center, where the stitches were, and the skin yellowed as it circled out away from them. She got into the tub and ran the water without putting the stopper in the drain. She wetted the washcloth and patted the stitches with it, then turned the water off and leaned against the back of the empty tub. Bruce sat on the floor beside her and stroked her arm, kneading the muscles.

"Would you please stop?" she asked, sharply. "I can't stand all this rubbing. I don't want to be rubbed, okay? It's like you're my fucking massage therapist all of a sudden."

He let go of her. He wore boxers and nothing else. The slit in the front was gaping open, his soft penis in a nest of hair just inside. She looked away from him to the end of the tub, at her feet braced on either side of the faucet. "I want it to be the way it's always been. That's how I need you to treat me."

She turned to Bruce. He'd been looking at her all the time, hadn't taken his eyes off of her, and now she gazed back at him with the same intention. She would not look away. He would not look away. They were children playing a game of wills and then they were hostile enemies. She felt enraged by him and then mad with love. Their eyes did this, said this, shifting from one thing to the next like a baton being passed off.

He crouched over her, leaning into the tub and then bent to press his tongue against the stitches on her breast. Pain shot all the way back to her collarbone and then down through the channels of her body, going everywhere, growing enormous, filling her entirely, and also staying small, as if her whole being were centered on Bruce's mouth. His tongue was a knife or a flame that opened her up.

She pulled him into the tub on top of her and wrapped her legs around him, moaning low and soft into his chest, and then she shifted and he was inside of her and she rocked against him. Her head knocked rhythmically against the rim of the tub and then she pushed herself up onto her elbows and they fucked that way until Bruce's knees couldn't take it anymore and they laughed and climbed out of the tub and tumbled onto the rug, where they fucked some more. Hard and soft and slow and fast. Not like she had cancer. Not in any way differently than they had fucked each other for the past twelve years. Joy filled them, then ecstasy. Out in the living room the dogs lifted their heads. Upstairs Claire and Joshua woke momentarily to roll and shift before falling back to sleep in their beds. Shadow jumped up onto the back of the couch and gazed out the window at the deer who came to the salt lick each night, and then she turned abruptly and listened intently as the cuckoo clock sounded five times.

Teresa and Bruce were asleep by then, their bodies intertwined on the bathroom rug, their eyes closed against the light overhead that they'd both been too tired to reach up and switch off. So bright it was, and yet they hardly seemed to notice it, the way it beat down on them without mercy.

6

WHAT DOES THE FUTURE HOLD *for me? What are my career interests? What do I look for in a spouse? Will I have children? How will I balance the demands of career and family?* Joshua sat staring at the questions on the blackboard and let Lisa Boudreaux—his so-called wife—do the work. She wrote the questions in her notebook and then took Joshua's notebook and wrote them in his. Now they were supposed to discuss these questions, desk-to-desk, like all the other "married" couples around the room, making compromises like real couples did.

"What if one wants to be a farmer and the other a Broadway star?" Mr. Bradley had asked them, smiling, pretending to be confounded. "What if one hates snow and the other is a dog musher? What if Cindy likes to party and Jimmy wants to bake bread?" He paced, then stopped suddenly and looked at them with the expectant air of a TV talk show host. His own wife—his actual wife—was a teacher at the school too, in math. He set his stick of chalk down dramatically on the metal rim that ran the length of the board and then turned back to face them. "Welcome, ladies and gents, to 'Life and Love and Work.'"

Joshua stared at his forearm. It was covered with an intricate blue pen drawing he'd made of a spider web. They'd just completed the unit called "Life and Personal Values." When they were done with "Life and Love and Work," they'd move on to "Life and Money," a sort of light-at-the-end-of-the-tunnel project, in which they'd each be given an imaginary five thousand dollars to invest in the stock market. The class itself was simply called "Life." Everyone had to take it in the last semester of their senior year in order to graduate from Midden High School, even the kids in special ed.

"What do you want to be?" asked Lisa, once they'd arranged their desks. Her pen had a pink feathery furry thing at the end of it, and she swished it contemplatively along her pale cheek.

"An astronaut," he said, after thinking for a while.

Lisa wrote this down in her notebook. "I'll be an astronaut too. We'll make, like, a ton of money." She took Joshua's notebook and wrote *We are both astronauts!*

"We could get on the same flights together or whatever," she said. "We'll be like this total *couple in space*." She put her fluffy pen down and took a cherry Ricola from her purse and sucked on it while still holding it in her fingers. Together they glanced around the room. Joshua knew he'd gotten lucky. At least they were at the same level, socially. Not extremely popular, but not unpopular either. Many of the couples had not been so fortunate. People in drama and band and Knowledge Bowl had been paired up with heavyweights like Jordan Parker or Jessica Miller, who sat looking mortified. And Tom Halverson and Jason Kooda had had to agree to be married to each other, thanks to a shortage of girls.

"How many kids should we have?"

"Six."

"No," said Lisa, bobbing in her chair. "Like ten." And then she wrote *ten* and underlined it twice.

He smiled at her. She was basically a cool, sweet, hot girl. Not perfect, but hot. Her body was one long noodle, tall and thin and flat, and all the clothes she wore accentuated that. It was not so unlikely that she was his wife. In seventh grade she'd been his girlfriend for two weeks, his longest relationship until he went out with Tammy Horner for six months last year. He and Lisa broke up because she thought they were getting too serious too fast during their afterschool, before track practice make-out sessions in the back of the dark band room where everyone went to make out, where Tammy Horner and Brian Hill had allegedly *gone all the way* a few months ago. Brian Hill was a pussy as far as Joshua was concerned, and nothing made him happier than the fact that Brian had been the biggest victim of "Life and Love and Work," having been forced to draw a straw along with Tom Halverson and Jason Kooda and not only be married to someone who was not a girl, but in fact to someone who was Mr. Bradley.

"Okay, so seriously, we have to kick ass on this, Josh. I totally have to get an A." Lisa opened the classified section of the *Star-Tribune* that they'd been given. They had to find a place to live that was financially feasible in relation to their professions and number of children. Then they'd cut the ad out and paste it to a page and write all about why they chose that house and where it was located—they could say it was anywhere they wanted—and how much they paid in rent or mortgage and what percentage of their income that was, and how it met the needs of their family.

"I think we have to live in Florida, don't we?" Lisa asked. "That's where they take off."

"Take off?"

"The astronauts—you know—the launching pad for the rockets is there."

Joshua began to draw a spider with his pen onto his arm, onto the web. Without looking up he said, "We could live in Port St. Joe."

"Where's that?" asked Lisa, carefully ripping a jagged square out of the newspaper.

"Florida. I went on vacation there one time."

Port St. Joe, he wrote in his notebook and then took hers and wrote *Mr. and Mrs. Wood live happily ever after in Port St. Joe.*

"Hey, who said I was going to change my name?" Lisa asked, punching him in the arm. He grabbed her scrawny wrist and held on to it just hard enough that she couldn't pull away. "Mr. Bradley! My husband's abusing me," she yelled. Her wrist was so soft, almost unreal. "*Mr. Bradley!*" she shrieked again, though he ignored her, engrossed in a conversation with Brian Hill. "I want a divorce," she said, hitting Joshua with her free hand until he let her go.

Tammy Horner turned and rested her eyes on them for a moment and then turned away. Joshua's heart lurched and then slowed and he cackled loud enough so she could hear, knowing that she would know the cackle was meant only for her. He had loved her once, but he hated her now. Sometimes he drew a pen tattoo of her name on his hand and then washed it off.

"So we live in Florida?" Lisa asked.

He nodded. In real life Lisa was engaged to Trent Fisher. He was older, twenty-six, a logger. Technically, since she wasn't yet eighteen, every time they did it, it was statutory rape, but nobody cared. They'd been dating since she was in eighth grade. She wore his class ring wrapped with yarn so it would fit.

"Are you going to change your name to Fisher?" he asked.

66

"Probably," she said hesitantly, readjusting the clip in her hair. "Why?"

"Just curious."

He took the fluffy pen from her desk and examined it to see how the feather thing stayed attached. It smelled like a combination of perfume and bubble gum, which is what Lisa Boudreaux smelled like too.

During seventh period he walked through town, not caring who saw him or that he was supposed to be in study hall. It was Monday, the first day of the last week that he would have to drive his mother to Duluth for her radiation treatments. He'd driven her for the past two weeks, Monday through Friday, going home immediately after school instead of to the Midden Café to wash dishes. He walked past the café now and saw Marcy through the front windows, but she didn't see him. He thought about going inside to say hi—it was Vern's day off and Angie would be there too—but he didn't, afraid of how they would act when they saw him. At school he was still fairly safe. Only a few people knew about his mom having cancer. The streets were empty, all the kids still in school. He wished he were going to work, though he usually went there with a mild dread, bracing himself for Vern's bullying and blathering, and a monotonous night scrubbing pots. When he'd told Marcy and Angie about needing to take three weeks off, they cried and told him he could take four. He wouldn't, though. He'd go back as soon as his mother's radiation was done with and her cancer eradicated. He would work and save money. Money for June, when he graduated and could move to California and escape Midden, which he considered barely a town. The library was not a library, but a milk truck painted green and parked two days a week in the Universe Roller Rink lot. The mayor wasn't a mayor, but Lars Finn, whose real job was at the feed store. The firefighters weren't firefighters, but anyone who volunteered, guys with big guts and a lone woman named Margie. Even the clinic was a sham; no actual doctor worked there, though whoever did was referred to as a doctor anyway. Dr. Minnow, Dr. Glenn, Dr. Johansson, Dr. Wu—a string of ever-changing people who came to fulfill a requirement to become a nurse practitioner and in exchange got a break on their student loans. They were mostly women. One came to school and talked to them about birth. She told them about how, before the baby came out, a woman's cervix dilated to ten centimeters, and then she took a large protractor with a piece of chalk fitted into it and drew a perfect ten-centimeter circle on the board. It stayed for weeks, the circle itself, and then the ghost of the circle, still visible though it had been erased from the board.

Joshua recognized that his mother was not so unlike these women, so open about various things. She had told him all about sex already, about women's bodies and men's. She felt that it was important to know what she called "the facts of life." She told him that she had lost her virginity at seventeen, and advised him against it until he was twenty-one. He did not tell her it was too late, that he'd been sixteen, with Tammy Horner. During this discussion he sat silently, looking anywhere but at his mother, and she told him to always use a condom no matter what urges he felt, because of AIDS, and then she gave him a box of condoms —handing it to him in its little paper bag with the receipt inside. He buried it in a drawer beneath his T-shirts.

On their drives to Duluth and back she'd asked him questions about Tammy Horner, whether he loved her still, whether he was interested in someone else. He hadn't been alone with his mother for such extended amounts of time since he was little—before he'd started school, when Claire was away at school all day—but mostly they didn't talk at all because his mother was too sick. On the drive home the first time they went, his mother had asked him to pull over so she could get out and vomit, holding on to the side of the car. He shut the engine off and got out, walked to the back of the car to see what he could do. "Leave me alone," she'd said. "I don't want you to see this." And then when he stayed, watching her, she hollered, "Go!"

Within a few days she didn't mind vomiting in front of him. She took a plastic milk jug in the car with her, with the top cut off but the handle still intact, to vomit into while he drove. They had dozens of these jugs around the place to use as scoops for the dog food, the corn for the chickens, oats for the horses. By then his mother had had to stop working at Len's. He didn't know what was next for her, and neither did she. "What we're going to do is wait and see," she'd say, wiping her mouth, forcing herself to drink another sip of Gatorade.

Despite the fact that the radiation made her sick, it would shrink the tumors that grew along her spine and ease her pain. The nurse named Benji had explained this on the first day they went. Before Benji radiated Teresa, he had shown them both around the radiation room.

"This is where it all happens," he said, waving his hand. There was a silver table and, hovering over it, a metal contraption that culminated in an arm that reached out with a dumb round eye, wide and conical like what Joshua imagined an elephant gun would look like. On one side of the room there was a wall that was not actually a wall, but rather a special kind of glass through which they could see the people in the waiting room, without being seen by them.

"That way Mom can keep an eye on you," Benji said, swatting Joshua's shoulder. "To make sure you're not flirting with the girls."

He looked out into the waiting room and didn't see any girls. He saw a number of gray-haired people who wore brightly colored coats and ratty boots made of rubber and fake fur, and a woman with a cast on one foot, rocking a baby in a plastic carrier with the other.

His mother came up beside him and tapped on the glass. "Yoo-hoo," she called, testing it out, to see if she could get anyone's attention, but nobody moved or looked.

"I guess I'm safe," she said, and laughed.

"*Very*," Benji said, handing her a gown.

In the waiting room, Joshua sat near a tank of fish, then stood to gaze into it, feeling that his mother was watching his every move. From this side, the wall of glass was pure black. He pressed his face in close, making a tunnel around his eyes with his hands to block out the light of the waiting room.

"Did you see me looking in?" he asked her when they were driving home.

"Oh—did you? No. I wasn't turned in that direction most of the time. What could you see?"

"Nothing."

They drove in silence for a while. This was day one, several minutes before his mother would have to tell him to stop the car so she could vomit into the ditch. He could sense that she was waning as she rested her head back against the seat.

"So, did it hurt—the radiation?"

"No. Radiation doesn't hurt, honey, it's just . . . I don't know . . . like powerful rays of light."

"What did it feel like when it was shooting in?" he asked.

She thought about it for a few moments, fanning her face with her gloves.

"Nothing."

.   .   .

69

When he saw all the buses driving through town to line up at the school, he blended in with the kids streaming into the parking lot, to avoid being noticed, and got into his truck. Before he started the engine, he saw R.J. walking toward him. He waved, and R.J. got in.

"You're so fucking busted," he said. "Spacey saw you leave. She was standing right by the window when you took off."

"I don't care," Joshua said. "What are you doing now?"

"Nothing."

When they pulled up to R.J.'s house, Joshua got out too.

"Don't you have to go to Duluth?" R.J. asked, and blushed. He couldn't even allude to Joshua's mother being sick without blushing.

"Pretty soon."

Inside, R.J.'s mother, Vivian, was sitting on the floor with her elbows propped on the coffee table, rolling joints. A pile of them was stacked neatly like logs inside a tin container. "My boys! How are my boys?" she asked.

"Fine," Joshua said, sitting down in a chair near the stereo. R.J. went into the kitchen and came back holding a tube of cookie dough he'd sliced open, gouging out chunks to eat with the blade of a knife.

"You want some?" he asked, holding a slab of dough out to Joshua, who took it and ate it in one big bite.

"You want some, Mom?" R.J. asked, turning to Vivian.

"That's why you're so fucking fat," she said. Her hair was parted in the middle, shoulder-length, feathered into brown sheets on each side of her head.

She finished rolling a joint, then lit it up, inhaled, and handed it to Joshua. He was high already—he and R.J. had smoked on the drive from school—but he took a couple hits anyway and passed the joint to R.J., who passed it back to his mother without smoking.

"This is good stuff," she said, smoke coming out of her mouth. "Bender's special batch." She gave it back to Joshua. "I'm all done."

"Me too," he said.

"You can keep it," Vivian said, sprawled back on the couch. Her fingernails were freshly painted red, so long they curved in toward her palms at the ends. "My little gift to you."

Joshua gently tamped the burning end out in an ashtray that sat on the arm of his chair. He tucked the rest of the joint in his coat pocket.

"So did R.J. tell you about our little plan?" she asked Joshua.

"It's not our plan," R.J. said. "I told you I'd think about it." He held the tube of dough in his lap, sitting in a chair that was the twin to Joshua's, an itchy brown plaid.

"Bender and I thought we'd let you sell to your friends and whatnot. Dime bags and loose joints. Whatever they want." She lit a cigarette and sat back, smoking and gazing intently, but dreamily, at Joshua. "We figured you two could use the money, with graduating and all, and our place wouldn't be like Grand Central Station. It's making me fucking paranoid, you know? All the people coming in and out. And half of them are your friends anyway."

"They're not our friends," R.J. said, holding up the remote, trying to turn the TV on. He banged it on his chair and then it worked.

"Well, they're your *peers*. They're people you know." She flicked the ash from her cigarette. "What do you think, Josh?"

"I think it sounds cool," he said, looking tentatively at R.J. "If we keep it low-key."

"Completely," said Vivian. "No way would we be anything but low-key. Everything is totally mellow. It's not on the level of dealing. It's on the level of just having mellow connections with people and you guys making some extra cash."

"I don't need any cash," R.J. said.

Vivian looked at him for a while, then crushed her cigarette out. "What are you talking about?"

"I'm talking about how I don't need cash," he said quietly. He turned the TV off.

"You don't need cash, my ass. Who you think's gonna buy the food you stuff into your big fat face? Huh? You think it's gonna be me for the rest of your life? Well I got news for you, porky pie. I got news the day you turn eighteen."

R.J. stood up. "I got news for you the day I turn eighteen too," he yelled as he went back into the kitchen.

"What's that?" she asked tauntingly, smiling at Joshua. "I'm just *dying* to hear your news," she yelled, then fell onto her side on the couch laughing.

Joshua stood up and stared at a newspaper flyer that sat on the floor, advertising the things on sale at Red Owl—Granny Smith apples, an economy pack of paper towels.

"I gotta go," he said. Then hollered, "I gotta take off, R.J."

"I'll go with you," he said, walking back into the living room.

Joshua didn't want R.J. to come but was afraid to say anything that would get him in trouble with Vivian again. "Okay," he said, and they left.

He dropped R.J. off at the bowling alley, where he would play pinball and then walk down the street to the Midden Café, where he would play Ms. Pac Man. He did this almost every night.

Once he was alone in his truck, Joshua drove away slowly, convincing himself that he had time. Plenty of it. A full half-hour before he and his mom technically needed to be on their way to Duluth. His house was a twenty-minute drive from town when the roads were good. He told himself these things, watching the clock that he'd glued to the dash of his truck, but a strange panic rose in him anyway. Why had he wasted his time after school? Why hadn't he come home during seventh hour instead of walking around town? He became aware of the fact that he missed his mother, ached for her in his gut. The thought that maybe when he arrived at home his mother would be dead entered his mind and would not leave. He tried to make himself relax by imagining her doing what she was most likely doing now: lying on the couch, storing up her energy for the trip to Duluth. He imagined himself walking in the door and taking her hand. He imagined her saying what she said every day to him when he got home: "How was school?"

"Good," he'd say, like he always did.

But when he walked in the door his mother was alive and well and standing in the kitchen drinking a glass of water. He didn't go to her and take her hand.

"How was school?" she asked.

"Good," he said, standing in the door, keeping his voice flat and disinterested. "Are you ready to go?"

She was dressed in a manner that she called "funky" or sometimes "all hipped out," in an outfit that embarrassed and repulsed him: cowboy boots and grape-colored tights, a black miniskirt and a slim lilac sweater that ended at her waist but had a cascade of yarn tassels that came down almost to the edge of her skirt. Her legs in the tights looked bony and taut, like those of an adolescent girl.

"Well, I had a pretty good day myself. I raked the stalls. I'm not so nauseous. I think it's thanks to the weekend being off radiation." She wore lipstick the color of rust; the rest of her face was bare, which made the rust of her lips even more striking, her eyes more blue. She put her hat on, another funky thing, velvet leopard print, a get-well gift from her friend Linea.

"I'll be in the car," he said.

"Wait, hon. I'm coming right now."

Spy and Tanner wagged their tails, pushing up to Teresa as she put her coat on. "Oh, you think you're going with us, don't you?" she said in her baby voice, bending to let them lick her face. "You're saying, 'We want to go too!' You're saying, 'Where are Mommy and Joshie going?' Aren't you? Oh, yes you are."

"Mom, they're not saying anything, okay? They're dogs."

"Spy thinks that Joshie is grumpy today," she said in a baby pout voice.

"Don't call me Joshie," he said savagely. "I told you. Don't ever call me that again."

He walked out and slammed the door so hard the dried-flower wreath that hung on the front fell off its nail. He hung it back up crooked. He didn't know what he was doing. All he knew is that everything about his mother enraged him, especially her habit of reporting what the animals were thinking and saying, as if her mind were the conduit of all things. For hens and horses and dogs and cats his mother delivered a steady stream of translation to anyone who would listen—even to R.J. or Tammy or whoever he had over.

She stepped outside. "What's wrong with *you* today?"

"Nothing's wrong with me, Mom. It's what's wrong with *you*. Did you ever think of that? That maybe it's *you*? That maybe you don't know what the dogs are thinking? Or maybe that you don't know everything in the universe?"

"Oh, but maybe I *do*," she said like a sorceress, smiling, impervious to his mood.

This enraged him even more. He got in the driver's seat and turned the engine on.

She got in next to him, buckling her seat belt. "So, how'd Mr. Bradley's class go today?" she asked happily, tapping his knee. "Who's your wife?"

At school the next morning Ms. Keillor intercepted him before he went to class.

"Mr. Wood," she said dispassionately. "You're to come with me."

"Why?"

She turned and began to walk away from him.

"I didn't do anything," he said, but then followed after her, down the hallway, past the bathrooms and drinking fountains, one low, one high, through the gym doors and through the glossy, peaceful, honey-colored world of the empty gym, to the door at the back that had a warning, EMERGENCY ALARM WILL SOUND WHEN OPENED, emblazoned across it, though the alarm never sounded when Ms. Keillor opened it with her key. She wore the key on a yellow bracelet that looked like a telephone cord. The principal's office was in a trailer out behind the school, and Ms. Keillor's job was to escort students there, to take papers back and forth, and to keep track of the accounting in the cafeteria.

"After you," she said, holding the door open for him, but then walked ahead of him once they were outside. She was barely five feet tall, slightly plump all over, like a teddy bear.

"You don't have to take me. I know the way," he said, but she ignored him. He unwrapped a stick of Big Red gum and put it in his mouth.

There were two trailers out back—both had small patio porches in front that had been built by the students taking shop. One trailer was for the principal and his secretary and the copy machine and teachers' mailboxes, the other was where the special-ed and developmentally disabled students had their classes. Beyond the trailers was the playground for the elementary kids and beyond that a football field and bleachers, all of it covered in snow now. Ms. Keillor went up the stairs to the door and then turned to him. "Dr. Pearson is expecting you. You can tell Violet."

He nodded, waiting for her to step aside so he could go in.

"I wanted to say that I heard about your mom and I was sorry to hear that."

He nodded again, less perceptibly this time, chewing his gum, the cinnamon so fresh in his mouth it almost hurt. What did she expect him to say?

"You all don't eat meat, do you?"

"What?"

"Your family. You're vegetarians."

He was used to this. He nodded again.

"We thought we'd make a dish and send it home—the ladies in the school would like to do something. We thought a pan of scalloped potatoes with something instead of the ham. Maybe peas or carrots."

He couldn't bring himself to look at her. He concentrated instead on her white Adidas.

"Which would you like better?"

The wind picked up and a wooden cardinal that was hanging on a fishing wire from the eave banged rhythmically against the outside wall of the trailer. He reached up and stilled the wooden bird.

"That's not your property," Ms. Keillor said.

He let go.

"So why'd you feel the need to skip seventh hour yesterday?"

"Because I felt the need to walk to the river and get high."

Deep pink splotches appeared on her face, then spread like a rash down onto her throat. "Why are you saying that? Why would you do that?"

He shrugged, blushing too, surprised at his own admission.

"You know there are people who you can talk to about this, Josh. There's Mr. Doyle. That's exactly what he's here for. Those social-problem-oriented issues." She put her hands into her coat pockets. "The brain does not do well on drugs, I don't think I need to tell you." Her face was slowly going back to its normal dough color. "Okay. You'd better get inside. And I'll tell the cooks that scalloped potatoes would be fine. Which do you prefer, carrots or peas?"

He didn't prefer either, but told her peas.

"That's what I thought too," she said. "Peas are awfully nice for color. And we wanted to help. I know that at a time like this, every family would need some help."

They stood together for a moment on the porch. Joshua put his hand on the doorknob. He didn't know what to say. *Goodbye? I look forward to having scalloped potatoes?* His mind was blank.

"Thank you," he said, and walked inside.

He had to eat his lunch in detention, going to the cafeteria to get it at 10:45, before the rest of the students arrived. He saw Lisa in the empty hallway as he walked back to the detention room.

"My husband's a prisoner," she said. Her face was pale against her hair, as black as a crow's wing, French Canadian.

"Spacey won't even let me sleep," he said, holding his tray. They both looked down at his food, chow mein, covered with a waxy brown sauce that had formed a skin on its surface.

"Did you write your rough draft?" she asked him.

"What rough draft?"

"The one that's due today." She looked at him, irked, but smiling. "We were supposed to write our dreams and share them with each other to see if they match. Didn't you pay attention? What am I going to do today when you're not in class?" She held a block of wood the size of a rolling pin with HALL PASS written in red marker on all four sides.

"I'll write it now," he said.

"But how are we going to discuss them if you're not in class? They have to match or it won't work out." She took a slice of apple from his plate and ate it.

"What are your dreams?" he asked. "Just tell me and I'll say what you said."

He felt like they were very alone and intimate, sharing food. Her shirt was nearly as black as her hair, the sleeves translucent and speckled with glitter.

"Well. We have the dream about being astronauts and having lots of kids. I wrote about that. And the importance of having a good relationship," she looked at him. "Those are my dreams."

"They're my dreams too," he said.

"Joshua!" Mrs. Stacey yelled from a doorway down the hall.

His desk in the detention room had its own little cubby, half walls rising up on three sides. He ate his chow mein and the rest of the apple sections and drank two cartons of milk with his back to Mrs. Stacey.

"How's your sister?" she asked when he was done eating, walking over to get his lunch tray.

"Fine." Teachers often asked him about Claire. She was something of a local legend. Aside from getting the scholarship to attend college, she'd been the valedictorian of her class, the queen of Snowball, voted by her classmates the "Most Likely to Succeed," and also "Girl with the Prettiest Peepers," a distinction that had instigated what seemed to Joshua hours of Claire gazing at herself in the bathroom mirror. "Do *you* think my eyes are pretty?" she'd asked him, ignoring his pleas for access to the bathroom. "No," he'd answered, dragging her out the door. He'd been bullied, throughout his childhood and adolescence, to tell her whether she was fat, whether she should get highlights in

76

her hair, whether her butt seemed hideously large, or her thighs too squat. Whatever he said, she never believed him or took his advice; she simply presented the same questions to him all over again the next time.

"I wondered if she was coming home, to help out and all," Mrs. Stacey said, blushing. Everywhere he went now people alluded to his mother's cancer and then went red in the face, embarrassed to have to mention it at all.

"On weekends," he said. "She's got college."

"Of course she does. She'll go far, I'm sure." She looked down at him, still holding his lunch tray, as if seeing him for the first time. "The two of you look like twins—just like your mom too. Like triplets."

Joshua nodded, feeling humiliated but unable to disagree. He'd been told this all of his life: same eyes, same hair, knobby noses that were variations on a theme.

A bell rang, and he could hear the low roar of students out in the hall, going to lunch. He ached to be among them. "Can I take my tray back? I mean, so you don't have to do it."

Mrs. Stacey smiled at him, bemused. "I don't know, *can* you?"

He stared dumbly at her for a moment, then asked, "*May* I?"

"No," she said matter-of-factly, turning from him. "You may not. But I will do it for you." When she left, he went to her desk. Her purse sat in an open drawer. Inside he could see a glasses case and a small spiral-bound address book and a fat red leather wallet. He went to the doorway. The hallway was empty, but he could hear a dim commotion in the direction of the cafeteria. He began to walk, not thinking of what he was doing until he was doing it, going calmly but quickly toward the side doors at the end of the building, and then out into the parking lot, past his truck.

He crossed the street and his insides jumped, giddy to be free. He walked past the motel, through the bakery parking lot, past a metal FOR SALE sign that blew and squeaked quietly in the wind, onto the highway. He walked south, toward Len's Lookout, but veered off the road and into the woods before reaching it, not wanting Leonard or Mardell to see him. Through the snow he followed a path he'd worn all winter down to the river, to the spot on the bank behind Len's that he and Claire had claimed as their own when they were kids. The river wound through town, going under roads, past houses and buildings, past countless towns, to Minneapolis and St. Paul, and farther south, all the way to the Gulf of Mexico, but this spot of the Mississippi was their spot—Claire and Joshua's—and when they talked about it and said *the river*, each of them knew precisely what the other was talking about. He didn't come back here with Claire anymore, but he came often on his own, and sometimes with R.J.

He climbed onto a rock that sat near the frozen river's edge. He could hear the water beneath the ice, gurgling, as if it were going down a giant drain. He smoked from the one hit he had in his pocket and walked to the river. Several holes had melted through the ice, and he could see the water raging by. He put his hand in to see how cold it was—freezing—then shook it and put it, wet, into his coat pocket.

The three towns of Coltrap County were all situated on the river. Flame Lake was twenty miles to the north of Midden, Blue River thirty to the south. The river started out so narrow that even in Midden it was still more stream than river, with not a hint of what it was, or would become: "The mighty Mississippi," his mother would say, "the father of all waters." Blue River had a festival each year in the Mississippi's honor, as if the river were theirs, as if the river were blue, as if it weren't the color of mud three hundred and sixty-five days a year, as if it didn't flow through Flame Lake and Midden first. When Claire and Joshua lived above Len's Lookout, when the river was their main playground, they had a game called Blue River Piss Off! Claire had started it one day, standing in the river.

"You're peeing!" Joshua yelled, swimming frantically away from her, kicking his feet to splash her.

"Shhh . . ." she said. "I'm doing something. I'm saying, 'Blue River Piss Off!'" Her face was serious, concentrating, and then it became wild and frenzied and she spun and shrieked and dove upstream.

From that day forward, whenever one of them peed in the river they would chant "Blue River Piss Off!" and laugh like hyenas. When the river was too cold or too fast to go in, they would throw things in it, orange peels and apple cores, pieces of string and blades of grass, and yell "Blue River Piss Off!" letting the water take it, watching it go. They felt a surge of power, a sense of righteous rage. Blue River had a Burger King, a hospital, a jail. There was the courthouse with a broken clock, a park with a gazebo painted white. The people who lived there thought they were better than all the rest of the people in Coltrap County, thought themselves more stylish and smart.

Joshua picked up a stick now, a branch the length of his arm, and set it into the water, in a place where the ice had melted. "Blue River Piss Off," he said.

The branch caught on the ice, half of it in the water, the other half jutting up. He threw a rock at it, but it wouldn't budge. He wished Claire would come home, though when she did they fought. She'd been home each weekend since their mother got cancer and on the other days she called several times. When their mother wasn't feeling well enough to talk, she spoke to Joshua. "How is she?" she'd ask, serious as an actress in a movie, suddenly grown up.

"I don't know. Okay I guess," he'd say.

"*Okay?*" she'd ask. "Define *okay*."

"Okay as in fucking OKAY, okay?" he'd yell, wanting to hang up. Sometimes, ultimately, he did hang up, but then she would call back, angrier than before.

He wondered what he should do now. It was just past noon. He stared at the river and saw that the branch he'd thrown into the water had freed itself from the ice and disappeared.

Bender was home. His semi was parked in the driveway out front. He'd be gone for days at a time and then inexplicably be home for weeks.

"Did they let school out early?" Vivian asked, opening the door. Joshua followed her into the kitchen, where Bender sat eating a taco.

"You can make one for yourself," he said to Joshua, waving to the bowls and dishes of food on the table. Joshua picked up a taco shell and piled it full of cheese and salsa and ate it standing up.

"Where's your sidekick?" Bender asked.

"At school. I had detention, so I thought fuck that."

Bender nodded. He was a small man with an elfin face. In the silence, Joshua could hear his mother's voice murmuring from the radio on the counter, saying something about natural cures for insomnia. The station was playing reruns until she got better. The volume was turned so low he could almost keep himself from hearing it if he tried. He heard her say, "Now let's talk about homeopathic remedies. Are there any you can recommend?" He cleared his throat to drown her out.

"Vivian told me about your mom," Bender said. "That's a shock."

Joshua nodded. "She's getting better. She's having radiation."

"Tell her hi from us," Vivian said, and tapped the ash of her cigarette into an empty can of Coke.

"I will."

"We were just listening to her show," Bender said, gesturing toward the radio.

"She's taking a break until she's done with radiation," Joshua explained. "She's only got three more days of it."

"I always liked that show."

"It's very informative," Vivian said.

Joshua turned the radio off. He wasn't usually so bold, but he wasn't able to keep himself from doing it. He said, "So, Viv was telling me about maybe me and R.J. selling for you."

Bender laughed. He was tan, despite the fact that it was winter, but his face turned red from the laughing. "Sure, I got plenty to sell," he said. "I got some new things too. We're branching out. R.J. said he showed you the meth I made."

"Where'd you make it?"

"Out in the garage," Bender said. "There's more money in meth than there will ever be in weed."

"It's not just anyone we would trust, Josh," Vivian said. "I hope you know that. Because if you fuck with us, your ass is grass."

"I know."

"Good," she said, putting her hand on Bender's shoulder. "'Cause you're just like a son to us."

He went to school the next day acting like nothing had happened the day before.

"Well, hello there," Ms. Keillor said when she saw him in the hall. And then added, "Come with me" before he had time to say hello in return.

They walked out to Dr. Pearson's trailer without a word. When they got to the door, Ms. Keillor opened it and said, "I've got a dish to send home with you. I'll send it up to Mrs. Stacey by the end of the day."

He walked into the trailer, over the plush cream carpet, to Violet's desk. Before she looked up from her computer screen, Dr. Pearson appeared in the open doorway of his office.

They entered without speaking. Joshua sat down on the varnished wood chair he'd sat on the day before, and the week before that.

"You're skipping school," Dr. Pearson said. "And now you're skipping detention too." He stared at Joshua, as if waiting for the answer to a question he'd posed. Joshua tried to meet his gaze, but then looked away at a row of metal balls that hung on wires from a stand on the desk. He reached for one of the balls and then let it go, so it hit the other balls and they all swung and banged into each other.

"Do you have something to say about that?" Dr. Pearson asked.

"Not really," Joshua said, trying to sound polite. He didn't mean anything personal against Dr. Pearson and he considered telling him that.

"Pardon me?"

"I said, no. I don't. I have no explanation for skipping school."

"And skipping detention."

"It was boring."

Dr. Pearson smiled. "Well. That's a shame. I'm sorry to know that we didn't keep you well enough entertained."

"I wasn't saying you had to."

They sat in silence again.

"You know what's next, don't you?"

Joshua shook his head.

"I think you're lying to me. I think you know full well what's next. In fact, I know you do because I told you yesterday."

Joshua waited.

Dr. Pearson leaned against the back of his chair so that it rocked away from the desk. He took his glasses off and set them on his knee. His brown hair grew only in a ring that ran around the sides of his head.

"You did this to yourself, do you understand?"

"Yeah," Joshua said.

"You're to sit in detention the rest of the day, all right? And it doesn't matter if you're bored. I don't give a rip. You're to stay there. And then tomorrow you don't come at all. You don't come until next Thursday. You're not welcome here. You understand? You're being suspended for one week. Those are the consequences, Josh. You know that full well."

Dr. Pearson stared at Joshua for several moments, then put his glasses on and stood up. "Ms. Keillor will send a letter home to your folks and it will tell you what work you need to do while you're out. Being suspended doesn't mean you aren't responsible for the work you miss. You do all the same work. Violet will walk you back."

Joshua spent the morning drawing engines, carburetors, air filters, and cans until Mrs. Stacey saw what he was doing and took all of his paper away. He read for a while, *The Norton Anthology of Poetry*, poems he was supposed to have read three days before. He went down the list, checking them off as he read, twenty-six in all, poems by Stevie Smith, W. H. Auden, and HD. He had no idea what they were about. At least most of the poems were short. He shut the book and wrote PORNO in pen on his forearm and then, next to it, drew a man with a long beard and horns.

When the last bell of the day rang Mrs. Stacey came in with a casserole dish covered with aluminum foil. "Ms. Keillor asked me to give this to you." And then when he took it from her she said, "You can bring the pan back next week when you come."

He walked out in the crowded hallway, mortified to be holding the pan. He hesitated, considered setting it on top of the pop machine and walking away. Kids laughed and talked and ran and screeched all around him, happy to be done with school. He spoke to no one, carrying the pan, his silence almost making him feel invisible. He went out to his truck in the parking lot. R.J. was nowhere in sight. Maybe he had skipped seventh hour. Just as he drove out of the lot, Trent Fisher pulled in. He saw Lisa Boudreaux in his rearview mirror, running from the school doors to Trent's Camaro.

"I brought something from Ms. Keillor and the cooks. Scalloped potatoes," he said to his mother when he walked in.

"That's nice," she said, lying very still on the couch. "That's what you can have." If she moved, if anything moved, if the light in the room changed, it hurt her. He could see that.

"How was school?" she asked, with her eyes closed.

"Good," he said. "Are you ready to go?"

She didn't answer for a long while and then she opened her eyes, as if she were startled to see him.

"Are you ready?"

"Oh—I thought I said—we don't have to go today. They decided I should take a day off because the radiation is making me so sick."

He sat down on the floor next to her, next to the dogs. He rested one of his hands near her hand, near where Shadow was sleeping, curled up like a lima bean against her hip.

"I thought the radiation was supposed to make you better."

"It will, honey. It just takes a while to kick in."

She turned to him. "Bruce is working at the Taylors' place—he's got so much work—but he wants to finish up there tonight. He's not going to come home until it's done, so he'll be late. You can go ahead and have what you brought for dinner."

"Okay," he said. Shadow's tail waved slowly up and down, grazing lightly against his hand.

"You got the application from the Vo Tech today."

"I saw."

"I know how well you'll do. You don't even have to go—you know so much about cars already—but they like you to have your degree, the places that hire now."

He took his shoes and socks off. "I heard your show today."

She didn't reply or make any indication that she heard him.

"It was the one about not taking sleeping pills. About how you can do things like drink chamomile tea instead." She'd done that with them for years, made them chamomile tea before bed. She grew the chamomile herself out in the yard. "Do you want some tea?" he asked, though it seemed she was already asleep.

"No thanks." She opened her eyes. "Aren't you hungry?"

"Kind of."

"Well, then, you should eat. But help me to bed first. I think I'll just spend the night in bed to get my strength back. I need you to arrange the pillows right." She stood up and he followed her into her room.

Once she was settled he sat on the couch eating the scalloped potatoes, picking out the peas. Even the dogs wouldn't eat the peas. He washed his plate and then dried it immediately and put it away, trying to be helpful. He got a glass of water to bring to his mother, to set on the shelf near her bed so it would be there when she woke, but then he couldn't make himself go into her room, feeling strange and shy all of a sudden. He could see her bare feet poking out from under the blankets from where he stood in the hallway. It struck him how familiar her feet were to him, even the calluses on the insides of her big toes. His stomach hurt, and he was acutely aware of all the sounds she made, the small moans and shallow coughs, her body shifting in bed. He went back into the living room and sat down on the couch in the nest of blankets his mother had left behind. He wished they had a television. He would never forgive his mother and Bruce for denying him that.

It was silent except for the damper of the wood stove clicking the way it did when the fire began to die down. He got up and stoked the stove and went to the phone. Why hadn't anyone called—Claire or Bruce? He dialed Claire's number and David answered, told him Claire was at work, that she worked until midnight, but would be "so glad to hear he'd called." Hearing David say this made him want to rip the phone out of the wall for a reason he could not comprehend. What did David know about him and Claire? What did David know at all?

"Do you want me to have her call you when she gets in—is it urgent?" He could imagine David sitting there with a little pad and pen, waiting to write down whatever he said. He said no thanks and hung up. He called R.J. and R.J. picked up.

"What are you doing?" he asked.

"Nothing," R.J. said. "What about you?"

"Nothing."

"Did you tell your mom and Bruce about getting suspended?"

"Nope." There was a corkboard near the phone and Joshua rearranged the thumbtacks so they formed a *J*.

"What are you going to do tomorrow?"

"Nothing," Joshua said.

When he hung up, he turned the lamp off and lay down on the couch. The moonlight cast shadows on the walls, on the outlines of the furniture and his mother's paintings. He sat up and looked out the window for a while at Lady Mae and Beau, who stood in their pasture, and then lay back down, covering himself up with the blankets.

A couple of hours later he woke with a start. He realized that his mother was up, that she was in the bathroom with the door open, its light beaming out in a bright rectangle on the floor several feet away from him. She coughed and then vomited into the toilet and he sat up, listening, wide-awake.

"Mom?" he said, without getting up to go to her.

She didn't hear him, but continued to vomit, roaring now, and then choking and roaring again. When she was done he heard her crying softly, still leaning against the seat of the toilet, her voice echoing against the bowl.

Incrementally, he lay back down and closed his eyes, pretending so fiercely to still be asleep that he began to believe it himself, not so much that he was sleeping but not present—the way he believed himself to be invisible to Claire when he was very young and they would play hide and seek, even when he was standing in full view.

At last his mother stopped crying and blew her nose. He could hear the squeak of the cold-water faucet and the water running, his mother lapping it into her hands and splashing it onto her face several times, and then finally she turned the water off and called his name.

He didn't answer. He stayed so still he hardly allowed himself to breathe. He willed himself to relax his hands, which were clasped tightly on his chest, releasing them bit by bit, trying to make them look like the hands of a sleeping person.

"Joshie," she said again. Then, "I'm sick, honey." Her voice wavered, squeaked, gave way to tears. "I'm just so, so sick, and I need your help."

He was asleep. He could not help her because he couldn't know she needed it. She would walk into the room and see that any minute. He clamped his eyes shut, waiting for her, willing her to come. He breathed through his nose, concentrating on allowing the breath to go further than just to the tops of his lungs. He would never go to her. Nothing in him would. She would gather herself, he knew, and then walk into the living room and see him on the couch and he would pretend to wake up in response to her presence and she'd say, "Why don't you go to bed?" and he would stumble past her, up the stairs, a pattern the two of them repeated at least a couple of nights a week.

But she didn't. With new vigor she said, "Josh, I need you to go get Bruce. I need to go to the hospital. I'm too sick. I'm very, very, very sick."

Delicately, without moving his hands, with one finger, then another, he applied pressure to his chest, as if he were playing a keyboard. It calmed him. He pressed harder and harder against his rib bones, with one finger, then the next.

"Oh, God," his mother whimpered. "Just one thing. Just don't let me die. I don't want to die." Her voice cracked and she sobbed. He'd never heard her sob like that. Nobody had ever sobbed like that. With such velocity, at such length. She sobbed so hard that Tanner and Spy rose simultaneously from where they lay near Joshua and went to her, their nails clicking along the floor, and stood and barked at her.

"Shhh . . . " she said finally. He could imagine her hands. How they went to her face to brush her tears away, how she would push her hair back behind her ears, collecting herself, and then he heard her scratching the dogs' necks the way they liked it, so robustly that he could hear the metals on their collars jangling.

"It's okay," she said in her baby voice, sounding exactly like herself now. "You're worried about Mommy, aren't you? Mommy made you upset, but now it's okay. Mommy's fine. And now you have to be quiet. You have to be good dogs. You don't want to wake Josh."

7

AT FIVE IN THE MORNING Claire took a long bath. She closed her eyes and almost dozed off, then woke, confused, believing for an instant that she was in her apartment in Minneapolis. But she had been home, in Midden, for two weeks, shuttling back and forth to the hospital in Duluth to sit with her mother, trading off shifts with Bruce. He took the nights; Claire, the days. In the dark of each evening she'd return home exhausted, but then she would not be able to sleep. She would walk through the house turning on lamps in rooms she wasn't using, and then walk through them again turning them off. She cuddled with the dogs; pulled with mock enthusiasm on the knotted ropes they'd offered her to play tug of war. She'd wish that Joshua would come home and talk to her, though on the couple of occasions he did come home, she wished he'd leave.

She got out of the tub and dressed by the light of the candle that burned from an old wine bottle on the edge of the tub. Several minutes before, she'd heard Bruce's truck driving up the driveway, and then she heard him come into the house. Joshua was home too, still asleep. She switched the bright light on and watched herself in the mirror, solemnly brushing her wet hair. She thought of her mother, alone at the hospital, an unbearable thought. Usually Claire tried to be at the hospital by now, but this morning she had trouble making herself get out of the tub.

"How is she?" Claire asked when she walked into the kitchen.

"The same," said Bruce.

It was dawn, but dark still. She opened the refrigerator and took out a carton of eggs. "As when? As yesterday?"

"As yesterday." He sat at the table drinking coffee from the small metal cup that went with his Thermos.

She made scrambled eggs and toast and put it on two plates and set

87

them on the table. Bruce made a sandwich with his and dug into it hungrily with big bites, his elbows resting on the table.

"So, when you mean the same as yesterday, how do you mean?" she asked, not touching her food. "Because actually she was fine when I left last night, though she'd had some rough patches during the day."

Bruce set his sandwich down. He looked at her and his face got tight as though he were about to say something, but then he didn't, and instead he reached over and rubbed Claire's shoulder.

"She's very tired," he said after a while.

Yesterday Teresa had begun to say strange things, to see people who were not there, to insist the phone was ringing when it wasn't. One of the doctors had asked Claire to go out into the hall with him so he could tell her "it didn't look good." She had gotten into an annoying conversation with him that centered around her trying to get him to define his terms. All of them. What did *it* mean? What did *look* mean? What did he mean by *good*? Teresa had been admitted into the hospice section of the hospital a couple of weeks ago not because she was dying, but because all of the beds in oncology were full, but now that there were beds available, the doctors had decided that there was no use in moving her.

Joshua came into the kitchen dressed, but hardly awake, his hair poking out in different directions. "Morning," he said.

"There are eggs for you," Claire said, gesturing toward the stove.

Joshua got himself a plate and scooped the eggs from the pan and sat down at the table.

"You can go with me today, Josh. Mom will like that."

He slowly chewed his toast, which was covered with chokecherry jam that Teresa had made last fall. "I was gonna go and see Randy about that truck."

"You can go and see Randy later," Claire said. She looked at her brother steadily while he continued to eat. "Please," she said. "Pretty please." And then when he kept eating without saying he would go, she said viciously, "Some things are more important than trucks. Mom is more important than a truck."

"I need a truck. I *told* you yesterday. I'll go to be with Mom tomorrow." He looked at her for several moments, trying to out-stare her. Her earrings were silver hands that turned, caught in her hair.

"Your mom would want to see you," Bruce said lightly.

"Which is why I'm going tomorrow."

Claire put a bite of eggs into her mouth, but had to force herself to swallow them, like a handful of soft pills. She was aware of the fact that though she was eating, she seemed like a person who was pretending to eat. She stood and scraped her plate into the dogs' dishes. Spy and Tanner rumbled into the room and the eggs were gone in an instant.

"I'm going," she called, putting her coat on.

"I'll see you around eight tonight," Bruce said.

"Yep."

"I told you I couldn't go today, so don't be acting like this," Joshua said.

"I'm not acting like anything," said Claire. Sometimes she hated Joshua's guts. She considered telling him this: *I hate your guts.* They had said it to each other before, when they were kids. She'd put her coat on in a huff, but now she pulled her boots on in a calmer fashion, as if to demonstrate that she wasn't going to let him get to her.

"Your car been running okay?" asked Bruce.

"Yeah." She walked to the door and opened it. "Bye," she hollered back.

"The roads'll be slick," Bruce said.

"Tell Mom hi," said Joshua as she shut the door.

It took ninety-five minutes to drive to Duluth in March. Claire had it timed. Seven minutes to the blacktop, thirteen to Midden, then an hour and fifteen minutes straight east to Duluth. Mostly she was the only one on the road. When a car drove by she waved to whoever it was and they waved back, and as she got closer to Duluth more and more cars passed her and fewer and fewer people waved until she was in the light morning traffic of downtown and she didn't wave at anyone at all.

She parked her car near St. Benedict's Hospital. When she approached the doors, they whooshed open with a hot gust of air. She passed the information kiosk, the flower shop, the coffee cart, and the gift store, and went straight to the elevators that took her four floors up to her mother's room.

"You look pretty," Teresa said when Claire walked into the room. "You look like Little Red Riding Hood." Her eyes were open and clear. Now that her mother was on morphine, Claire never knew what to expect. Teresa could be in a near stupor and then shift back to her old self within an hour.

"I wore your coat." Claire stood at the end of the bed and rubbed the tops of her mother's feet. It was the only place she could get at freely, without the tangle of tubes and plastic bags of fluid and tall carts holding the machines that sat near her head.

"That was always my favorite," Teresa said. "I wore it ice-skating when I was a teenager."

Claire pushed her hands into the pockets of her mother's old coat, red wool. The room was packed with flowers in vases and it smelled like them, black-eyed and exuberant, angular and bright.

"You wore it other times too. I remember you wearing it all the time."

"I wear it to feed the chickens. And the horses. It's my barn coat."

"I know," Claire said, afraid now, thinking that her mother was becoming delirious again, despite the fact that everything she said was true. Yesterday she'd sworn that someone named Peter had attempted to shave her legs. Claire sat down and took the coat off and picked up a book she'd been reading and removed a pressed leaf from the page where she'd left it to mark her place. She twirled the dry leaf by its stem and held it up. "What's this?" she asked, to test her mother's mind.

"A leaf."

"Yeah, but what kind of leaf?"

Teresa took a deep breath and held it, as if she were doing yoga, and then she let it out slowly. "Aspen," she said, looking at Claire and not the leaf. Her arms were utterly unmoving on the bed, her wrists swaddled in gauze to keep the IV lines secured. "Otherwise known as poplar."

"Correct," Claire said, although she did not know whether it was an aspen leaf or not, having never bothered to learn such things.

"*Populus tremulus*," Teresa said in Latin, dragging the syllables out. On *Modern Pioneers*, she'd done a whole show about the botanical names of common northland trees and grasses. She'd quizzed Claire and Joshua and Bruce on several of them the week before the show. Claire tried to remember one now, to demonstrate to her mother that she'd been paying attention, but she couldn't.

"Where's Bruce?"

"He left a couple of hours ago, Mom. He has to go to work. Don't you remember?"

"Oh," she said. "Now I remember. I thought I dreamed it. Where's Josh?"

"He said hi. He'll be coming tomorrow."

She began to straighten the objects that sat on the little table so she wouldn't have to look at her mother. A tube of lip balm, a box of Kleenex, a cup of warm Gatorade. It had been two weeks since her mother had been admitted to the hospital and Joshua had not come to visit even once.

"I brought something for you," she said after a while, searching through her backpack. She pulled out a lollipop made of honey and ginger that she'd bought at the health food store, and handed it to her mother.

Teresa hadn't eaten for three days. The radiation treatments had started decomposing her stomach and she vomited pieces of it up into a yellow pan that was clipped to the side of her bed.

"Thank you," Teresa said. She held the lollipop, shaking, and brought it slowly to her mouth. Large blisters had formed on her lips, burnt by the acid of her stomach. "Maybe this will make me feel better. Ginger is what you should have when you're pregnant, by the way. It's a natural cure for nausea."

"I know." And she did know—that, too, had been on *Modern Pioneers*. "So is peppermint," she said and Teresa smiled in recognition. Claire pushed an IV stand back toward the wall so she could stand near her mother and stroke the top of her head. Her hair was sharp and dry like the weeds that grow flat along the cracks in rocks.

"Oh," Teresa moaned. "Don't touch me. It hurts. Everything hurts. You wouldn't believe the pain." She closed her eyes; held the lollipop. "Let's sit and not say anything. That's what I want more than anything. To be together and rest."

Claire took the lollipop from her mother's swollen fingers. She held it for a while and then began to eat it herself.

Teresa lay with her eyes closed. Her face was flushed, feverish-looking. At other times it was as pale as snow. Claire considered singing a lullaby, but she didn't know more than a few words of one or two. Her mother hadn't sung lullabies to her and Joshua that she could remember. She'd sung other songs, funny songs, songs with lyrics she made up as she went along. Or sad songs by Joan Baez or Emmylou Harris. Claire didn't think her mother wanted to hear these songs now, so she stood at the foot of her bed and sucked the lollipop and listened to her breathe, waiting to hear the breath that meant that she was sleeping. When this breath finally came, Claire watched her mother's face for signs of relief, which did not come. Her face had an expression of permanent tension. Claire could not discern whether this was a new thing, because of the cancer, or if that expression had been there all along, masked by the ordinary light of day. Teresa's chin hung slack, making the flesh beneath it baggy, but her mouth was strangely alert, puckered, and faintly streaked with vomit. Claire thought of the TV commercials of starving children, how the flies gathered at the corners of their eyes, but the kids were too weak to swat them away. How unbearable it was to see that, more so than anything else, more so than all the other things, lack of food, lack of water, lack of love, which were so much worse.

She got a washcloth and wetted it and delicately wiped her mother's face.

"Thank you, honey," Teresa said, without opening her eyes, without moving or giving any other indication that she was awake. And then she said, "I was thinking about a lot of different things last night. Like that time that I locked myself in the bathroom."

"What time?"

"You remember the time." Teresa opened her eyes and looked at Claire.

"I don't remember any time."

"I was furious with you and Josh. You were about five. I don't know what the two of you did. Probably a combination of things."

She smiled at Claire. Her beauty, even then, was like a Chinese lantern hanging in an oak tree.

"It was just before I finally left your father. Anyway. Nobody tells you how it will be. I was so furious that I wanted to hurt you. I mean, *do you physical harm*. Well, I didn't *really*, and I wouldn't have, but right then and there I felt *capable* of it. They don't tell you that when you become a mother—and nobody wants to talk about it—but everyone has a breaking point, even with children. *Especially* with children." She laughed softly. "So. I went and shut myself into the bathroom to calm down."

"That was probably good," Claire said passively. She was sitting on the vinyl couch, the damp washcloth next to her.

"Oh, were you ever mad! Just seething. You couldn't bear that I wouldn't let you in. You hurled your body against the door with all your might. I thought you would hurt yourself. I thought you were going to break a bone. I had to come out so you wouldn't."

She kept a smile on her face, gazing at Claire for a long time. After a while she said, "Sometimes I would think crazy thoughts when you and Josh were babies. Things I wouldn't do, things that would come into my head from out of nowhere."

"Like what?"

"Like awful things. Like I would be chopping vegetables and I would think I could chop your heads off."

"*Mom!*"

"I wasn't going to do it, but the thought came into my mind. I think it's natural. Nature's way of helping me adjust to the responsibility."

Claire laid the washcloth to dry on the wooden arm of the chair. She said, "When Shadow was a kitten and I would carry her around, I would get this feeling that I would drop her and it would freak me out until I set her down."

"Yeah. It's sort of like that. Not what you *want* to do, but what you *could* do."

Claire picked up an envelope. "The people from the radio station sent you a card."

"That's nice."

"Do you want me to read it to you?" she asked, tearing the envelope open.

"Maybe later."

Claire stared at her mother as she slept or tried to sleep. The longer she watched her, the more foreign Teresa seemed to her, as if she hadn't known her all her life. She'd felt the same peculiar dislocation years before, when it had been explained to her how babies were made. It wasn't the facts that had confused her, not the mystery of sex or birth or creation, but the question of why. Why should there be people at all? Or fish or lions or rats? Now she felt a new wonder washing over her. If there were to be people and fish and lions and rats, then why should they die? And why, most of all, should her mother die? She stood up in order to shake the feeling off and walked softly across the room to the window and gazed out at the street below. She stood perfectly still and erect and was acutely aware of her stillness, her erectness. Grief had suddenly, inexplicably, improved her posture. It had also, more understandably, made her thin. She felt as though her body had become something brittle, like the branch of a tree or a broomstick.

She turned away from the window and picked up the card from her mother's friends at the radio station. On the front there was a sepia-toned photo of a woman sitting on the seat of a Conestoga wagon, pulled by a pair of oxen. Inside there was a constellation of messages, each saying practically the same thing: *Get well soon.* She propped the card on the sill of the window and walked out of the room past her mother asleep in the bed.

Claire had become familiar with the hospital's hallways and rooms, the small places she could go for privacy or entertainment. The nurses smiled politely as she passed. Each day she went to the gift shop and lingered over shot glasses and key chains, smiling clocks and teddy bears. There was a bin of small toys and she became obsessed with one in particular, but wouldn't buy it—a little plastic tray of letters on cubes that shifted to form words. Every word had to be four letters long. She stood in the gift store and played the game, spelling *wand, toss, pond, burn, bask, piss, fish,* and so it went, until the woman who worked there seemed annoyed and she set the game down and left. She would take the long corridors to the maternity ward, through several sets of doors, up an elevator, past cardiology and radiology and neurology, and over an indoor bridge that spanned the street below. The babies were tiny and not beautiful, but inspiring nonetheless. She watched them through a wide glass pane, not wanting them, but wanting desperately to hold them. They smelled good to her, even through the glass, like raw vegetables when they were still dirty.

"Are you an aunt?" everyone would ask her.

"No. Just visiting!" she'd say too jovially.

And then she would leave, taking a roundabout way through the day clinic, back through oncology, and into the hospice. There were only a few patients here besides her mother, another woman about her mother's age and several old people. She caught glimpses of these people as she walked past their rooms and came to know them the way one knows the houses along a familiar street. The lady with the hole in her throat, the endlessly sleeping bald woman, the thrashing man who eventually had to be tied by all four limbs to his bed, the other man who beckoned and yelled, "Jeanie!" to everyone who passed, until finally one day Claire stopped.

"Jeanie?" he asked. His voice sounded young, but he was old. Old old, like most of the others—people who were so old nobody knew them anymore, or if they did, they came to visit only on Sundays.

"Yes," Claire said. She stayed in the hallway, peering at him through his open door.

"Jeanie," he said, relieved.

"Yes."

"*Jeanie?*"

"Yes." She twisted her hands into the wrists of her sweater.

"You ain't Jeanie," he said at last, gently, as if he were sorry to hurt Claire's feelings. "I know my Jeanie and you ain't her."

A nurse appeared then, carrying a lunch tray, pushing into the door past Claire. "Is he hassling you?"

"No," Claire said.

"Just ignore him," the nurse said.

"Ah, Christ," the man said and sat up in his bed, his feet dangling off, oddly bruised-looking, his toenails in need of a trim.

"You just gotta let it go in one ear and out the other," the nurse said, and laughed uproariously.

There was a room at the end of the hall reserved for the relatives of the people who were patients in the hospice wing. On the door there was a painted wooden sign that said FAMILY ROOM in puffy letters. Inside, the same artist had painted a giant rainbow on the wall, and at the end of it, a pot of gold and a fat elf doing a jig. There was also an orange couch, a refrigerator, a microwave oven, a coffee pot, and a water dispenser with one spout that was hot, the other cold.

Claire went there to drink herbal tea from a pointed paper cup and to read the bulletin board. There were signs advertising groups for people with AIDS, with chronic fatigue, for parents of premature babies or twins, for drug addicts and anorexics. She read these things each day, as if she'd never read them before. There was a television in the room, but she didn't have the heart to turn it on. Usually she had the room all to herself. One day a man had walked in.

"Hello," he said. "I'm Bill Ristow."

"I'm Claire. Claire Wood." She shook his hand with one hand and with the other held on to her empty paper cup. It was as pliant and soft and wet as the petal of a lily.

"My wife's down in four-ninety. She's got cancer." He scratched his head with a pinkie finger. "You must be new here."

"Kind of. We've been here—my mom's been here—for two weeks. We didn't know anything. I mean, about the cancer. She had this bad cold that wouldn't go away. And then all of a sudden she had cancer everywhere." She paused and glanced up at him. His eyes were hazel, sunken. She smiled, stopped smiling, went on. "Anyway. It's just been a little more than a month that we knew she had cancer and now there's nothing they can do." She stared at the absurdly rugged leather reinforcements on the toes of her shoes. She didn't know what she would say or not say. She didn't feel like she would cry. She had no control over either.

"Christ," Bill said, and jingled the coins in his pocket. He was making coffee. The water fell one drop at a time into the pot. "Well, kiddo, I hate to say it, but in a way you're lucky. It's no vacation to drag it on. Nance and I—we've been doing the cancer dance for six years."

He was older, but not old, her mother's age. She thought he might have been a wrestler in high school, his body wide and dense, like a certain kind of boulder; his face too—primitive. He wasn't good-looking. He wasn't bad-looking. He took a mug that said WYOMING! from the cupboard and another one with a chain of vegetables holding hands and filled them both with coffee. He handed Claire WYOMING! without asking if she wanted it.

"You and me have a lot in common," he said.

She didn't say anything. She didn't drink coffee. She didn't like coffee, but she held it anyway, the mug cradled in her hands. With pleasure.

In the afternoon she called David from the pay phone near the nurse's station. She dialed his number—*their* number, though in the short time since she'd been gone, she'd suddenly felt as if she didn't live there anymore. As she waited for him to pick up, she became aware of the fact that a woman was standing behind her. When she turned to look, the woman smiled and waved animatedly, as if she were standing far off instead of uncomfortably close.

"Hi," Claire whispered, still holding the telephone receiver to her ear, the line ringing and ringing.

"I'd hoped to catch you," the woman said, putting her hand out. "I'm Pepper Jones-Kachinsky. I'm the grief counselor here. I met your father . . . your stepdad . . . Bruce."

"Oh," Claire said, and hung up the phone. "Hello."

Pepper stepped closer and took her hand, shook it, and didn't let it go.

"How are you?" she asked. Her eyes were sad, glimmering. "You know, Claire, I want you to know—oh, it's *terrible* about your mother—

and I want you to know that my door is always open if you ever want to talk about all that you're experiencing. Twenty-four seven, as they say!"

"Thank you," Claire said politely. She didn't want to be consoled. She wanted one thing and one thing only—for her mother to live. "It's just that I don't know what good it will do." Pepper kept her eyes locked on Claire's face, still holding her hand. "I mean," Claire stammered, "not that I couldn't *talk* to you."

"Oh, I would like that. I would like that very much," Pepper said. She had two gray braids rolled into buns and pinned to the sides of her head.

"But I can't. That's the thing. I'm busy all day. Being with my mom." Claire's hand felt hot and damp. Infinitesimally, she tried to extricate it from Pepper's grip.

"I don't have a schedule. I'm at your beck and call. There's no nine to five for me." She put a finger to her lips, her crow's feet crinkled in thought. "Let's see. What about now? Why don't we pop into my office this very minute?"

"Um," Claire said, pointing to the phone. "Actually I was about to call someone . . ."

"Oh," Pepper said, disappointed, as if she hadn't noticed that Claire had been on the phone in the first place.

"But *maybe*," Claire said. She didn't want to hurt Pepper's feelings. Perhaps, if no one went to talk to her, she would lose her job. "Briefly."

"Fair enough!" Pepper exclaimed, and led the way to her office.

First they talked about Joshua. How he was never around. How he wouldn't come to see Teresa at the hospital. How whenever Claire saw him he was high on marijuana. Pepper said this was called disassociation, Joshua's version of coping. They sat on twin rocking chairs, wooden, with multicolored afghan blankets slung over the backs. Claire rocked steadily in her chair and then stopped.

"So what about you?" Claire asked shyly, when there seemed to be nothing more to talk about.

"Me?"

"Well . . . I mean how long have you worked here?"

Pepper said that she was an ex-nun, married now to a man named Keith, a nurse, whom she'd met on an Indian reservation in New Mexico. She told Claire how Keith had become addicted to gambling after his first wife left him. "Everyone has their own way of grieving," she explained. "And that was Keith's way. Joshua has his way. You have your way. There is no right way. There is no wrong way. All ways lead to the mountaintop."

"What mountaintop?"

Pepper didn't answer. She leaned back and folded her hands on her lap and looked magnificently amazed, which is how, Claire had noticed, Pepper always looked. As if she held a giant ruby. As if cool rain were falling softly on her hot, grateful head.

Without warning, Claire began to cry. She simply inhaled and when she exhaled she was weeping—gulping and choking and bawling loudly. Embarrassed, she reached for a tissue from the table between them and blew her nose and then took another one. To gather herself, she concentrated on the row of cornhusk dolls that stood along the edge of Pepper's desk and went up onto the sill of the window that looked out into the nurse's station.

Finally Pepper said, "God is with you, and God is with your brother. God is with your stepfather, and God is with your mother. He is standing right next to each one of you and holding your hands whether you know it or not."

"I don't think so," Claire squeaked. She was taking small puffing breaths, trying to get ahold of herself. "Maybe for you, but not for everyone."

Pepper stayed looking like she did. Happy and holy and amazed and gazing directly into the eyes of whoever was looking at her, which made it impossible for Claire to look back at Pepper for any length of time. She took the afghan from the back of her chair and wrapped it around her shoulders even though she wasn't cold.

"You don't choose God. God chooses you," Pepper said, and Claire began to cry again, but softly now, gushing silent tears. "You are chosen by God. *You*, Claire. I know in my heart that you are and that your mother is too."

"Well, *I* don't know it," Claire said sharply from behind the tissue she held pressed to her nose. "I mean, I don't feel his presence. I don't even feel whether it's actually a *him*. It could be a woman, you know. Did you ever think of that? Or it could not even be a *person*. And isn't God supposed to *help* you or protect you or something? I don't feel at all protected. And what use is God if you don't feel *that?*" She cried in a few small gasps and then collected herself again and blew her nose. "It all just seems so *indirect*. And I need more than that."

98

Pepper smiled kindly. "God is not a hotline," she said. "You don't get to just dial Him up. No. The problem is that you—oh, me as well, all of us, every last one of us—we expect happiness. God has a plan for each and every one of us and perhaps for you, perhaps right now for you, muffin, happiness is not in the plan. We are at the *mercy of the Divine*. Every last one of us!" She sat looking sadly at Claire and then crossed her legs and smoothed the fabric of her pants on the tops of her thighs. "Now look at that," she said, "my shoe's come untied," and leaned forward to tie it.

Claire didn't say a word. Her tears fell thicker and came down her face in hot streams and dripped off of her chin while Pepper sat quietly watching and then she sprang up out of her chair and bent to hold Claire.

"Oh, angel. Oh, sweet child. I know it's hard. I *know* it is." She held the sides of Claire's face and then kissed her forehead and sat down on the floor and rubbed her ankles, then leaned back on her hands and told Claire about her life as a nun. Being called, knowing, knowing since she was ten that she wanted to be a nun, despite the disapproval of her parents. Her family owned a paper products manufacturing giant. They'd been the wealthiest family in Duluth for a century. Roads were named after them, ships, parks, and a museum that Claire had visited on a field trip in sixth grade. Pepper had given this all up and had been a nun for thirty-two years, from the ages of twenty-two until fifty-four. She lived in Chicago and then Green Bay. But most of the years she lived in El Salvador running a goat farm with three other American nuns and three Salvadoran nuns until one day a gang of men raided their house and kidnapped all of the nuns except for Pepper, who happened to be out back feeding the goats when the commotion started. She jumped into an oat bin and stayed there for two days, trying not to make a sound or think about water. Meanwhile, the other nuns had been taken away and gang-raped, tortured with a pair of scissors, several cigarettes, and an electric cattle prod, shot in the head, doused with gasoline, and set on fire.

Claire wiped her face with the balled-up tissue. She got the hiccups and listened hard. It was immensely helpful.

"So now you're friends with the Bible thumper," her mother said the next morning. And then, before Claire could answer, "To think it was me who raised you."

"Pepper isn't a Bible thumper. Anyway—who said we're friends? I talked to her once. I wouldn't call that friends."

"I'm not going to say a word about it," Teresa said. She tapped her feet together. "Far be it from me to tell you what to do. I always raised you to think for yourself. You want God, go take a walk in the woods. Read a book. Read Emily Dickinson! What are you reading these days? Don't tell me it's some religious blather."

"*Mom.*"

Claire told Teresa about Pepper almost being murdered by a right-wing death squad, about the Navajo reservation, and about her new husband, Keith.

Teresa scratched her arm, softening. "It isn't that I am against faith," she said warily. "I'm against the thinking that says that humans are shameful and bad. I know all about that, thank you very much. Had it shoved down my throat for breakfast, lunch, and dinner for eighteen years, but I kept you and Joshua from all that."

"Why'd you have us baptized then?"

Teresa turned to Claire, alarmed, like an eagle with its feathers ruffed up.

"I was weakened by childbirth, for your information. I was in a maternal daze. It was what you did with babies then, smarty-pants. Plus, in case all that mumbo-jumbo about going to hell turns out to be true, you'll have me to thank later. I was safeguarding you against eternal damnation."

"Well, you can't have it both ways, Mom."

"Fine. I'm a terrible mother. I did everything wrong. Forgive me."

"I'm not saying that. I'm saying that Pepper is not a Bible thumper."

"Apparently not," Teresa said grimly.

"What?"

"I said okay!"

Claire sat in the wide bay of the windowsill.

"What's it doing out there?" asked Teresa.

"Snowing."

They sat in silence for several minutes and then Claire said, "It's nothing, Mom. I just talked to Pepper. I'm not going to be a Jesus freak now."

"I know, honey." Her voice lilted from the morphine in a way that

Claire had come to recognize. "I don't mean to argue. I understand you perfectly. You're just exactly like me. A seeker."

In slow increments, she turned her head toward Claire sitting in the window.

Once her mother had fallen asleep, Claire walked down the hallway, but differently now, self-consciously trolling, looking for Bill without allowing herself to believe that. She passed his wife's room, keeping her gaze straight ahead and then after a while she heard her name being called.

"You want to grab some lunch?" Bill asked, coming toward her. His face was marked with creases on one side, as if he'd been lying down.

They walked to a place a couple of blocks from the hospital called the Lakeshore Lounge. The bar was dark, windowless, lit with dim yellow light bulbs and Leinenkugel beer signs. They ordered vodka and grapefruit juice and sat down in a booth. The only other person in the place was the bartender, an old lady with painted-on eyebrows who sat on a stool and watched television.

Bill told Claire that he'd grown up in Fargo and had joined the Navy and spent most of two years on a ship in the Middle East. He'd married his high school sweetheart, a woman named Janet, before he went into the Navy and by the time he'd returned Janet had a tattoo of a fire-breathing dragon on her ass and was running around with a man called Turner, who was the leader of a Manitoba motorcycle gang.

"Such is life," he said, sipping tentatively from his drink. It meant something to him that they had the same kind of drink. Initially, he'd asked for beer. "Let me ask you this. You got a tattoo?"

Claire shook her head. Bill rolled his sleeve up and showed her the inside of his forearm: a cougar, ready to pounce.

"Take my advice and don't. It's a bad idea, especially for women."

"I've thought about it. Maybe a chain of daisies."

"Anyhoo," he said. "After all that with Janet, I took my broken heart to Alaska to work in a salmon cannery. Now that's good money. But that's work. That's not like what passes for work with some of these guys. These white shirt types. That's where I met Nancy. She worked at the cannery too—women do it too—but that's not where we got together. Where we got together is about five years later when I moved to Duluth to take a job—I schedule the ships that go in and out of the harbor—and I thought, Who the heck do you know in Duluth? And I had never forgotten about Nancy, you know. I met her and never forgot her and I knew she was from Duluth, so I looked in the phone book and thought, Why the heck not call her up? The rest, as they say, is history."

Bill asked Claire where she lived, who her family was, whether she liked the Minnesota winters or not, if she'd ever been to California. He wanted to know what her favorite movie was, if she believed that life existed on other planets, if she ever wanted to have children.

"We were planning on kids, but then *boom* — Nancy has cancer." He looked around the room. There was a row of video games across from them repeating a display of wrecking balls and exploding rockets, automobile crashes and little hooded men wielding axes. "So are we going to have lunch or not?" he asked.

"I'm not hungry anymore."

"Me, neither," he said. "You want another drink?"

"I don't know," Claire said. She could feel the one drink running pleasantly through her. She had the sensation that everything was going to be okay, that her mother was not as sick as she seemed, and if she was, Claire could accept that fact with calm and reason. "I could go either way. I'll have one if you do."

"I don't need one," Bill said, and they sat in silence together.

A woman with a rash on her face came into the bar with a bucket of flowers and asked them if they would like to buy some and they said no, but then Bill called her back and bought a bouquet after all. Red carnations with a tassel of leaves and baby's breath. He set them beside him on the seat.

"It's nice to talk to you, Claire."

"Yeah."

"There aren't many people you can talk to. People in this situation, so to speak."

"No."

"Nobody wants to hear it. Oh, sure, they want to know what they can do for you and so forth. That's nice. But no one really wants to hear about it."

"No," Claire said. She was sitting on her hands. She rocked forward every few moments to sip from her straw. "I know exactly what you mean about all that." People had carved messages and names into the table. *Tammy Z.* it said in front of her, *cunt*.

Bill coughed into his fist, then asked, "You got a boyfriend in Minneapolis?"

Claire told him about David, about what he was studying in graduate school—a mix of political science and philosophy, literature and history, but none of those things solely.

"I know the kind of thing you're talking about. The humanities," Bill said, coughing some more. "You go to bars much?"

"No. Not too much. Actually, I just turned twenty-one a few weeks ago."

"No kidding," he said, and fished an ice cube out of his glass and tossed it in his mouth. "You seem older. I'd've guessed twenty-five. You strike me as a sophisticated lady. You've got a way that's very grown-up."

He had a small, firm belly and a thick bush of graying hair on his head. Tufts of hair sprang from his eyebrows and nostrils and the backs of his hands. His ears were red and burly and sat like small wings. He reminded Claire, not unkindly, of a baby elephant, in a lordly, farcical way.

Claire crossed her legs under the table. She rattled her ice. "We should be getting back. My mom is probably waking up now."

"Well. It was nice to get away. Everyone's got a right to that from time to time." He raked his hands through his hair, as if he were waking from a nap.

Claire was acutely aware of his body across the table, of her own pressing luxuriously back against the ripped-up vinyl. "Where do you live?" she asked.

"Not far from here. About a mile."

He set his hands on the table and knocked on it with his knuckles. She reached out and set her hands lightly on top of his. He stayed still for a moment, then turned his hands over and laced his fingers into hers.

"Shall we?" he asked, after a while.

"Yes," she said. "We shall."

Bill's house was white, surrounded by a picket fence, and cloistered in a thicket of pines. It sat a few steps below the street, but above everything else—the buildings of downtown Duluth, the lake. Claire could see the roof of the hospital far off and she pointed it out to Bill. It was freezing. Claire was shaking but impervious to the cold.

"The snow is sparkling like diamonds," she said, idiotically.

"Diamonds?" Bill smiled at her curiously.

"I mean, the ice crystals. They're sparkling," she said, and blushed. "I like the word *sparkle*, don't you? It's one of my favorite words. Sometimes I'll just be attracted to a certain word for no reason at all, but that it sounds nice. Or it looks nice on the page."

"I can see what you mean," he said, guiding her onto the porch. "Sparkle has a ring."

They stepped into the house. Claire felt slightly dizzy, but alert, not at all like she'd had a drink and no lunch in the middle of the day. She took her coat off, and her gloves. She wanted to take everything else off as soon as possible so she'd stop being nervous. She wore jeans and a shirt that exposed a sliver of her lower abdomen, despite the cold, and boots that echoed loudly against the wooden floors as she followed Bill from room to room, on a tour.

"It's lovely," she kept saying, and it was. Every room was painted beautifully, a different color, but none of the colors clashed. She reached for the earring that she usually wore in her nose—often she twisted it when she was nervous—but it wasn't there. More and more, she'd been forgetting to put it in before leaving for the hospital. She held her little braid instead, pulling on one of the tiny bells as he showed her the cabinets that he'd built, the place where there had once been a wall that he and Nancy had knocked down to let more light into the dining room, the hardwood floors they'd sanded and refinished themselves.

In the bathroom, where Bill left her alone at last, there was a bowl of stiff rose petals on a narrow shelf and a photograph of Bill and Nancy —both of them completely bald—with their heads tilted toward one another. Claire washed her hands and face with a bar of green soap that smelled like aftershave and then went into the living room.

"You like Greg Brown?" Bill asked her, holding a record, blowing on it, putting it on the turntable.

"I love him," Claire said.

"This is some of his older stuff," he said, and the music began.

"You never see records anymore."

"I collect them." He opened a cabinet with several shelves of albums. "I've got all kinds of music—anything you could want. Country, rock, classical, bluegrass, you name it."

"Me, too. I mean, that's what I like. All kinds." The skin of her face was tight from the soap. She sat down on a blue couch and instantly stood up again. "So . . . come here," she said, smiling like a maniac.

He took her hair by the ends and pressed it to his nose and smelled it. He wound it around his fingers, pulling her toward him, and kissed her. His mouth was cool and shaking and strange, but nice, nicer to her than anything. She shoved her hands into the back pockets of his jeans and felt his ass.

"I'm glad I met you," he said.

"Me too. Take this off," she said impishly, tugging at his shirt. He gathered her wrists in his hands and pulled her into the bedroom. The walls were the same color as the comforter on his bed. Amber, with an edge of smoke.

"Now," he said, unbuttoning her shirt. They laughed awkwardly, pawed at each other. He bent to kiss her breasts, biting her nipples tenderly, and then harder. They teetered, finally onto his bed.

"Do you have a condom?" he asked her.

"No."

But they went ahead anyway. It seemed impossible that she would get pregnant, that anything at all could be transmitted or take root or live in them. She knew it. He knew it. This didn't make sense, but they were right.

Claire watched Bill's face while they fucked. It was haggard and tense, as if he were concentrating on something either very far or very near, as if he were attempting to remove a splinter or thread a needle or telepathically shatter a glass in France. He saw her watching him and then his face became animated again, wide-eyed and carnivorous, until it crumpled as if he were about to sob in agony, and he came.

"That was nice," he said after a while, looking up at her, straddled over him. She rolled off of him and lay down beside him. A mobile of fat chefs dangled overhead, and farther, down near their feet, a birdcage without a bird. He turned onto his side and placed his hand delicately on her stomach. He found her birthmark and petted it and outlined it with his finger, as if he'd known her all of her life.

"Was that weird for you?" she asked.

"I wouldn't say that."

"What was it like?"

He stood up, jerked his jeans on. "Like a million bucks."

"There's a lady down the hall who's a high school teacher," Claire said to her mother, even though she appeared to be sleeping. She was standing by the window, looking out at the street below, from where she'd just come. There was a long silence, and then her mother's low voice.

"What's her name?"

Claire turned and went to stand by the bed, near her mother.

"Nancy Ristow."

"Is she a visitor or a resident?" She smiled, a small glorious smile.

"Resident. She's a history teacher."

It was nearly four. Claire had had a panicked feeling when she and Bill had rushed back to the hospital, but when she'd entered her mother's room, it was as if she'd never left.

"Ask her what she thinks happened to Amelia Earhart."

"Who?"

"This teacher. Nancy."

"Why?" Claire snapped.

"You said she teaches history, right? History interests me. I'd be curious to know if she has a theory, since she's in the know. I always liked Amelia Earhart." She opened her eyes and tried to push herself up to a sitting position against the pillows, the tubes swaying around her. "I think of her going off like that. Can you imagine? I mean, *can you imagine?* Having no idea what would happen? Imagine how brave she was. She was one of my personal heroes."

"Is."

"What?"

"Is, Mom. She *is* one of your personal heroes."

"Yes," she said. "Is."

She sat looking carefully at Claire. "Where have you been?"

"Nowhere. You were sleeping. I walked around."

She continued to look at Claire. Her face pale, drained, regal. *"What?"*

"You've been somewhere."

"I *told* you."

"You're different."

That night, back at home, she called David.

"How are things?" he asked. "How's your mom?"

"Hard. It's . . . horrible." She began to cry and he listened to her crying over the phone. She could hear music playing in the background. "She seems to be getting sicker. Every morning when I go in, it's worse.

I can see the difference. And Josh is still being an ass—he came home last night. I saw him this morning, but he squirmed out of coming to the hospital with me."

"That sucks," David said.

Claire sat at the kitchen table, pulling the phone to reach from the wall. She drew arrows and triangles and spiraling lines on the back of an envelope that had been sitting there. She hadn't talked to David for two days, yet now she couldn't think of what to say to him.

"You seem far away," she said.

"I am," he said, and laughed.

"No, I mean, actually *far.* Like Russia or something. I don't even feel like I'm on the same planet with you."

"We're on the same planet," he said irritably.

"Not just you and me, but me and everyone else. Like I'm on this other planet. Or in a dream, a nightmare. That's what everyone always says, 'It was like being in a nightmare,' and that's totally how it is. Like I'm going to wake up."

"I'm here for you," David said. The music had stopped and now she could hear a remote crackling on the line, a mysterious, celestial sound that made her feel even lonelier.

"Do you hear that?"

"What?"

"The phone. It's making a sound. It's creeping me out. Say something. Talk to me."

"I love you," he said.

She thought that she loved him too, but she didn't have it in her to say it anymore, the way they'd always said it, every day, back and forth, a Ping-Pong of words. *I love you. I love you too.* Sometimes, she couldn't help it, she wished that one of his parents were sick or dead or long gone from his life. It didn't seem fair to her that he should have two loving parents, still married and madly in love with each other, perfectly alive and well, even though they were fifteen years older than her mother.

"I could read to you," he said. That was something they did at night, one book at a time.

"Okay," she said glumly. And he began. She found herself listening to his words in a way that she'd never listened to anything before: with all of her attention, and yet also forgetting each detail the moment it registered—who was married to whom, for how long, and why the characters were where they were. It didn't matter. The story lulled her into something like a trance.

After they hung up, she walked into her mother and Bruce's room and turned on all the lamps and lay down on the bed sideways, her feet hanging off. She wished her brother were here. She thought maybe he would come home in the middle of the night and then in the morning she could talk to him, convince him to come to the hospital with her. The phone rang and she waited for the answering machine and listened to her mother's voice saying *hello, please leave a message,* and then the somber voice of their neighbor, Kathy Tyson, offering to look after the animals if they needed it. On impulse, Claire lunged for the phone, but by then Kathy had hung up. She'd had the idea that maybe Kathy could come over and have a cup of tea with her and distract her from her sorrow. They could talk about men and how few eligible ones there were in Midden, the way they had the year before, at Gail Nystrom's wedding reception, when they'd been assigned to sit next to each other at the singles table because there were too few men to go boy-girl. Kathy had confided that she'd posted a listing on a Web site for singles who liked country living, that the very next day she was driving to Norway to meet a man who'd answered her ad.

Claire didn't know her number and to look for it seemed too much of an effort, so she hung up the phone and stood. She realized that she was still wearing her mother's wool coat, not having taken it off for the nearly two hours she'd been home. She pushed her hands into the pockets and instantly found the cassette tape she had put there earlier. She pulled it out and looked at it for the first time. *Kenny G,* it said. She'd taken it that day, from Bill's house. She didn't know why. It sat next to the tune box in his bedroom among a scattering of other cassettes that Bill and perhaps Nancy had been presumably listening to recently. Instinctually she'd reached for a cassette and shoved it into her pocket. She sat up now and opened the drawer of the small table beside the bed and tossed the cassette in and then shut the drawer.

She met Bill twice the next day. Once just after ten, and then again in the late afternoon. Both times they went to his house and had sex in almost precisely the manner they had the day before. They already had a ritual: afterward they would dress and sit in the kitchen, drinking warm apple cider and eating toast with peanut butter. They told each other stories about the lovers they'd had. Claire's list was short, only four men long, Bill being the most interesting, the one least like her. Bill's list was long and complicated, grouped mostly into categories, rather than individuals. He told her about losing his virginity with Janet in a closet where his mother stored cleaning supplies; about prostitutes he had slept with in various ports during his Navy years; a series of alcoholics in Alaska; and then Nancy. He told her about how they'd gone to Puerto Rico for their tenth wedding anniversary. They'd lolled in bed and made love and ate a bag of plums they'd bought on the street. In jest, Bill put one of these plums into Nancy's vagina and it sucked itself up inside of her and they couldn't get it out.

"Well, it came out eventually," he said, laughing, rubbing his face, laughing again, laughing so hard that his eyes filled with tears.

Claire sat with him and smiled. She nibbled her toast.

"Now there's something," he said, finally getting ahold of himself, wiping his tears away. "There's something you don't do twice."

She didn't see him the next day at all. Her mother had become so ill that Claire hardly left the room.

"You're interrupting me," she'd said as soon as she saw Claire that morning, a new edge to her voice.

"What?"

"That's what you do. You interrupt." Teresa swung her head in Claire's direction. Her eyes blue, beloved, uncomprehending as a buzzard.

"*Mom*."

Bruce was still there, asleep in the cot, and he sat up, startled and confused.

"Why is she here?" Teresa demanded, banging on the rails of her bed so hard the yellow pan that was clipped onto it fell off.

Bruce reached out and stroked Teresa's shoulder. "It's Claire, Ter."

"It's *me*, Mom. What's wrong?"

Teresa sat quietly for a while and then closed her eyes.

"Mom. It's me, okay? Do you understand that?"

She opened her eyes, soft now, back to normal. "I understand that. It's you. I'm glad."

"Stay awake with me, Mom."

"Okay," Teresa said, then closed her eyes and slept. She slept all

morning and into the afternoon, and Claire sat next to her bed, not reading or watching TV, not doing anything but watching her mother. She
said the beginnings of prayers silently to herself but then petered out,
not remembering how they went. "Our Lord, who art in Heaven, hal-
lowed be thy name . . ." and "Now I lay me down to sleep . . ." When the
afternoon sky began to darken Claire could not keep herself from it anymore. She shook her mother hard until she opened her eyes and kept
them open.

"Hello," she whispered.

"Hello," her mother said back to her, as if she were hypnotized.

"I miss you."

Teresa said nothing.

Claire held out her fingers; on one there was a mood ring that belonged to her mother. "What does it mean when it's red?"

"That your hands are cold," Teresa answered, then closed her eyes.

Claire shifted the ring. When she pressed on its little oval surface, it
became a purplish green. "I've been going through things. Remember
the macramé feather earrings you made?"

Teresa didn't answer or open her eyes, but turned her head toward
Claire.

"I found them. And also that skirt you made out of your jeans."

"You can have them. Take whatever you want."

"Okay," she said, though she had already—taken what she wanted—
a lion figurine, a shawl made of string. She'd felt compelled to search
through her mother's things since she'd been admitted to the hospital, like
a child left home alone for the afternoon, not knowing what she'd find,
but then knowing everything she did find, being shocked over and over
again by the excavation of her mother's life. The things she'd remembered
and forgotten: garish beads that had fallen from necklaces, a square of
lace, a photo of an old boyfriend of her mother's named Killer. All these
things she'd found and more, none of it mysterious, all of it astonishing in
its familiarity, as if they had been embroidered onto her skin all along.

"Also, I found this." She touched the pewter belt buckle she now
wore. It was perfectly round, etched with an image of a woman with
flowing hair who held a feather, a relic from her childhood. The buckle
was attached to a braided leather belt that her mother had made herself.

"You can have it," Teresa said, and then appeared to instantly fall
asleep.

Claire stood, watching her mother, running her fingertips over the engraving on the buckle. Since her mother got cancer she'd become superstitious. She believed that everything she did was in direct relation to the survival of her mother, that wearing the belt would save her. As a child she'd believed that the pewter woman with the flowing hair who held a feather on the buckle *was* her mother. This made some sense on a practical level. Teresa's hair had been flowing for a time. She'd worn necklaces, earrings, halter-tops made of feathers. But this isn't why Claire believed it. She'd believed it because her mother was that omnipotent and omnipresent, her power over Claire absolute. She believed it again now, or perhaps she had believed it all along.

Her mother: Teresa Rae Wood. Anything she said would be true.

After several minutes Claire rose and silently walked to the Family Room to make a cup of tea. Bruce would return in an hour or two, perhaps Joshua would be with him. She let her fingers graze against the wall as she walked, as if to help her keep her balance. Her body felt weightless, like she was not walking but floating down the hall, a pretty ghost. She didn't see Bill as she passed by Nancy's room, its door closed, but she imagined Nancy behind that door, lying on her side, her thin hip a triangle, her blond frizzy hair matted into a flat nest at the back of her head. Claire thought of that plum. Imagined it warm inside Nancy, as if it were still there: a thing she would not release. Purple, red, and black. Sweet and soft and bruised.

The door to the Family Room was also closed, but she went inside. Bill was there, emptying his part of the refrigerator, clutching a paper bag.

"Hey," he said dreamily.

"Hi," she said, wiping her face with her hands. It was only six, but it felt like the middle of the night. Her life always was the middle of the night now.

"It happened," Bill said, turning to her. "She died."

Claire shut the door behind her and locked it. She felt shocked beyond words, as if death were an enormous surprise. She hugged Bill and the paper bag. "Oh my God. I'm so sorry," she said. "I'm so, so sorry."

"It isn't what I expected," he said.

"What did you expect?"

He set the bag on the floor. "I'm not taking these. They're those frozen dinners. You can have them if you want."

"Okay," Claire said gravely. Bill's face was pale and puffy. He smelled like worn-out peppermint gum and French fries. She hugged him and cupped her hand around the back of his neck, and he pressed into it the way a baby who can't hold his head up does.

"Look," he said, almost inaudibly. "I feel that I should apologize."

"For what?" She let go of him, took a step back.

"For what's gone on with you and me."

"There isn't anything to be sorry about."

"I feel that I behaved badly."

"No." She peered at him. "Nobody behaved badly."

He took several deep breaths, panting almost, his hand on the counter. "I didn't want to leave the room. They took her—her body— out after a couple of hours. People came to see her, to say goodbye. Her folks, her brothers, and a couple of her best friends. And then they took her away and I didn't want to leave, you know. The room."

"That's understandable," Claire said gently. She was holding herself, her arms crisscrossed around her waist. "I can see wanting that."

He sobbed. He made small whimpering noises, and then he found a rhythm and his cries softened. Claire rubbed his shoulders. He let her do this for a while, and then he went to the sink and leaned deeply into it and rinsed his face and dried it with a hard paper towel from the dispenser.

"Anyway, you know something? I never cheated on Nancy up until now. That's the God's honest truth. Maybe you don't know that, but thirteen years plus and I never cheated. I almost did once or twice, but I never followed through. That's normal human temptation. That can happen in any marriage. But I didn't do it. I honored the vows." His voice quavered and he tried to breathe deeply again. "The vows meant something to me once upon a time." He paused. "And don't get me wrong. None of this is your fault. I hold you responsible not one iota. You are a beautiful girl. A top-notch young lady. I was the one married. It has nothing to do with you."

The bag of frozen dinners shifted without either of them touching it.

"It didn't take anything away from what you had with Nancy," Claire said. "I never thought that."

"No. Definitely not. My allegiance was always with her. No offense. I think you're wonderful. You're one very pretty girl. And smart too.

Kind." He clutched the edge of the counter. "And what am I when Nancy needs me most? I'm a pathetic old man."

"You aren't old."

"Not old. But to you I am. I'm too old for you. I lost my morals."

Claire stared at the floor. A spoon had fallen there, crusted with hair and what looked like bits of dried chocolate pudding.

"Plus, what was I doing gallivanting around and meanwhile she's dying?"

"She was sleeping. She didn't even know you were gone."

"Oh, she *knew*. She *knew*." He put his hand to his forehead and pressed hard.

"We weren't gallivanting anywhere. We were at your house."

He kept his hand pressed to his forehead. Claire bent to pick up the dirty spoon and set it soundlessly in the sink.

"Well," he said. "I wish you the best. I'm hoping for a miracle for your mom."

"Thank you." She touched his hand on the counter and they looked at each other, their eyes as serious as animals. He took her hand and kissed it and then pulled her into him and held her hard against him. His breathing was heavy and she thought he'd started to cry again, but when she looked at him his eyes were calm and dry.

"Claire," he said, but didn't say anything more. His fingers began to slowly graze her throat, down over the top of her chest, over her breasts, barely touching her. He grabbed her face with both of his hands and kissed her fiercely and then stopped abruptly. "What am I doing?" he asked sadly, and then pulled her back to him and squeezed her hips, her ass, her thighs.

"Stop it then," she said. She unbuckled his belt, unzipped his jeans, got down on her knees.

"This is completely wrong."

"Stop me then," she hissed. She took his cock in her mouth. She had the sensation that he was going to hit her; that he was going to smack the side of her head or yank her away from him by the hair. She also had the sensation that she wanted him to do this, though she had never wanted this from a man. She wanted something to be clear, right, and she wanted him to be the one who made it that way.

"Jesus," he whispered, and leaned back against the wall and gripped onto it to keep him up.

She smelled his man smells, his cock smells: a sour salt, a sharp sub-aqueous mud. He came without a word and she sat back on her heels and swallowed hard. She touched the hairs on his thighs, kissed one knee.

He reached for the sides of her face. "Oh," he moaned. "I can't stand up."

"Something about you sitting in that window reminds me of when you were little," Teresa said to Claire as the sun rose through the windows. "Sometimes I see your face and I can see just exactly what you looked like when you were a baby and other times I can see what you'll look like when you're old. Do you know what I mean? Does that same thing happen to you?"

"Yeah. I know what you mean," Claire said, turning from the window to her mother, grateful that she had spoken at such length. "Are you feeling better?" she asked. "We were scared. You hardly woke up all yesterday. You slept for like twenty hours straight. And then you were weird."

"I needed my sleep," Teresa said. "Where's Bruce?"

"Getting coffee. It's about six, Mom. In the morning."

"Where's Josh?"

"I don't know," she snapped, then caught herself and continued more gently, "He'll be here in a little bit." She got down from the windowsill and pulled a chair up next to her mother, coiling her way through the IV lines.

"Yes. Come sit with me," Teresa said, her words slurred from the morphine. "That's what I'm glad of. That you're here with me. I'll never forget you were here with me during the hardest time. And sitting the way you were in the window, it made me think of that, of all the things, of you and Joshua being little and now being grown-up."

"We're not grown-up."

"Almost. You almost are."

Claire tugged on a thread that dangled from the edge of the blanket that covered her mother; it caught, still attached.

"It was the same way when you used to sit in that window in Pennsylvania. Do you remember the window seat in the apartment in Pennsylvania?"

Claire shook her head.

Teresa smiled. "Oh, sure. You were too small then. You wouldn't remember. But that was *your spot*. You liked to sit in that window seat and wait for the mail to come." She paused, as if a wave of nausea were about to overtake her, but then continued. "You liked to see the mailman come and put the mail in the box and then you wanted to be the one to go and take it out. You *had* to be the one! You always liked to be involved with things, to be a helper, to be at the center."

"I don't remember," she said, and leaned forward to rest her head on the bed, the top of her head pressing into her mother's hip.

"Well, that's how you were," Teresa said happily. "It's how you are."

"How's that?"

"The way I taught you to be. Good."

Teresa lifted her hand from the bed. Softly, she stroked Claire's hair.

8

BRUCE DID NOT WONDER. He knew. He had not a single doubt about what he would do after Teresa died. It played in his mind like a movie with him as the only character, its solo shining star. He knew *before* she died—seven weeks to the very day, it turned out, to everyone's sorrow and surprise. The knowledge of what he would do did not come to him immediately, in the moment they learned that she had cancer, but later on that night, in the wee hours of the next morning, after they'd left the hospital and gone—amazingly—to eat dinner at a Chinese restaurant, and then driven home and lain in bed thinking they would make love, but then not been able to make love because they were weeping so hard and Teresa's back hurt.

Her back did more than hurt.

Hurt was too small a word to contain what was going on in her back. It was *killing* her, she'd said before they'd found out about the cancer. Once she'd said it afterward too, about a week after they knew about the cancer, when the reality had hunkered down and stayed. "My back is killing me," she'd muttered, turning to him in the kitchen, holding two glasses of water, one for each of them, in the short window of time they had when a thing such as holding two glasses of water did not seem to them an utterly Herculean task. He looked at her and for a moment they both hesitated, as if taking a breath in unison. They'd been balling their brains out since noon. Her back *was* killing her, they realized, and then they almost fell onto the floor laughing in hysterics. The water was dropped. The glasses were shattered. Their house was a madhouse from that moment on. Nobody gave a fuck about a glass.

It felt like a zipper, she'd explained to the doctor that day they'd found out. That her spine was a zipper and someone was coming up behind her and zipping it and unzipping it mercilessly. She'd almost cried saying this, almost seemed to grovel and beg. It pained him. He rose and went to stand behind her chair and rubbed her back uselessly. The doctor nodded his head, as if he'd known about the zipper all along, as if people marched through his door every day to complain about mechanical devices embedded in their spines.

Later, they learned her spine *was* a zipper, the cancer pulling it apart, stitching it back together in a way that it was never meant to be. Her lungs were also a zipper, and likewise her liver, and ovaries, and parts of her body they didn't even know were there. It was like a root that went on and on, blocking the way no matter where they dug. Even the doctor used these words. The zipper. The root. Nothing was a metaphor. With Teresa's cancer the most absurd things were literal.

And so Bruce, by necessity, was literal too. He wasn't kidding when he decided that after Teresa died he would kill himself. He had not, in his life, in his *before Teresa has cancer* life, been the type of person to say, "I would just die" or "It made me want to die" or anything along those ridiculous lines, the way people did when they in fact had no intention or desire to actually die—when they thought they were being funny or needed to exaggerate a point.

Bruce was not a man to exaggerate. He would truly, absolutely, cross-his-heart die.

He would live through the funeral and then he would act. He reasoned this would give Joshua and Claire a moment to catch their breath, but not enough time to even begin to accept their reality. Reality for Joshua and Claire would be that, in one horrible week, they lost their mother and then their father. Not what they called their *real father*, a man named Karl they scarcely knew, but their stepdad, their *Bruce*, the guy they'd loved as their father since they were six and eight. Of course they would grieve their mother harder. Bruce did not begrudge them that, but still he knew his death would be a mighty hard blow. It did not make him happy to think of them and what they would do all by themselves; in fact, it pierced his heart. But the pain of that was not as great as the pain of having to go on living without their mother, and so his mind was made up. If this was to work, he could not afford compassion and he could also not afford pity. Not for Claire, not for Joshua, not for Teresa.

Regrettably, he had promised Teresa things on which he was simply not going to be able to follow through. At the time that he made the promises, he had not lied. The promises had been made dry-eyed and immediately, while they ate that first night in the Chinese restaurant, before he'd known what he would do. Of course he said he would raise her children, who were essentially both already raised.

"But they still need their mother," Teresa had crooned, almost losing it entirely. Years before, she had told him that her secret way of collecting herself was to think of things, things that had nothing to do with anything. Often, she kept herself from crying by thinking *can of beans, can of beans*, again and again. In the Chinese restaurant, while she had gazed at the goldfish, he wondered if she was thinking *can of beans*. She didn't seem to be. She seemed to be honestly concerned about the fish. Out loud, she wondered if they were hungry and looked around, as if for food, and then her eyes latched back onto him.

She told him she wanted to discuss this issue once and right away and then they would never speak of it again.

Yes, he would be there for Claire and Joshua, Bruce told her. Yes, he would be both mother and father. Neither of them at this point had actually absorbed the information that she was truly going to die soon. They'd been told, but they didn't believe. For that blessed hour in the Chinese restaurant his future life as a widower played before him sweetly as a benign dream. It was the movie that played in his mind before the movie of him killing himself supplanted it. He would comfort Joshua and Claire in their grief. He would hold them and weep and remind them of all the things their mother had said and done. He would tell them things they hadn't known—how their mother used to think *can of beans* when she didn't want to cry. The three of them would go on a camping trip—perhaps they'd canoe down the Namekagon River like they'd done several times as a family—or to Florida, to Port St. Joe, where they'd been with their mother, before they knew him. This trip would heal their grief. They would laugh, they would weep, they would return home stronger and better and basically okay. They would take this trip annually, to commemorate the anniversary of her death. When they married he would walk them down the aisle and give them a special flower that represented their mother. Their children would call him *grandpa* or maybe simply *papa*, the name he'd called his own dad's dad.

At the Chinese restaurant, Teresa had put her hands over his on the table. "I wasn't questioning you. I hope you know that," she said. "I know how much you love them. It's just that I needed it all to be spoken out loud."

She took her hands away and looked again into the pond and it was done.

There was nothing administrative to take care of. She had not written a will, but why should she? She had no life insurance policy. The land and the house would of course someday go to the kids. This, they hadn't even thought to say.

Later that night almost everything he'd promised was washed away by his new plan. He decided he would live five, maybe six days without her. They would have the funeral and he would wait a day, letting everyone get a good night's sleep, and then he would make his move.

Once the idea came to him it took about five minutes to make up his mind between rope or gun. He chose the rope. He was not a hunter. The gun in their house had been used for only three purposes: to scare away the raccoons that came on occasion to harass the hens, to scare away the porcupines that came to gnaw the wood of their front stairs, and to teach them all how to shoot the gun so they, when necessary, could scare away the raccoons and the porcupines. If he used the gun, there was a chance he would botch the job. He knew how to tie a knot. He knew how to tie *seventeen* knots, each perfect for one task or another. This, he owed to his mother, whose father had been a sailor on the Great Lakes and who had insisted that he learn all the knots that her father had taught her.

First he imagined the exact knot he would use, then he imagined the exact tree. It was a maple. It grew in the place on their land they called "the clearing"—a small meadow, the only meadow on their forty acres amid the trees—a good spot to die. The place calmed him. He and Teresa and Claire and Joshua had had many good times there. When he could honestly picture himself hanging dead from the maple tree in the clearing he was more sorry than ever about Claire and Joshua. But in this he had to be selfish. He knew what he could do and what he could not do and he could not go on living without Teresa no matter how much he loved her kids.

He hoped they wouldn't be the ones to find him. But then, who else would? He imagined them trudging through the woods calling his name —at the time he decided to kill himself he didn't know how quickly Teresa would die, so he could not know whether there would be snow in the woods or not—but for all of their sakes, he imagined there would be snow. Not this year's snow, but next year's snow. Snow that hadn't even been formed yet, snow that wasn't even remotely thinking about falling, snow that would be made in the sky and let drop to the ground in the farthest reaches of the time that the doctor predicted Teresa could be expected to live. One year. And so, in next winter's snow Claire and Joshua would be trudging through the woods calling his name. When he had first met them he had told them his name was not Bruce. They had been waiting for him in the parking lot of Len's Lookout, but when he finally pulled up, they ran, frightened as wild animals who were instantly tamed once he called their names. "Are you Bruce?" asked Claire, giggling and hopping on one foot. "No," he'd said, "I'm Bruce, Bruce-Bo-Buce-Banana-Fanna-Fo-Fuce . . ." They shrieked with delight when he was done and begged him to sing it again. Then he taught them the song using their own names. They scared him a little, how fast they loved him, how they clenched his hands with theirs as they sang, how later, at dinner, they did not want to sit beside him but on him, fighting with each other over his lap.

These children whom he had met when he was twenty-seven, these children who had been born in a state where he'd never been, these children whom he had bossed and cajoled, kissed and scolded, grounded and applauded and taught how to drive a stick shift, they would be his search party of two.

He did not think they would make a big ruckus. At first they would believe that he was sad and had simply gone out to chop wood. He was a worker, they'd always known him to work, and they would assume that it was to work he turned in his grief. Slowly, dimly, they would wonder why they didn't hear the chain saw, the ax. They would stand first on the porch and call his name, and then in the driveway. Finally, before dark, they would go out to look for him. Claire would most likely be wearing the scarf her mother knitted for her, red, soft wool, with a white star near each end. Her nose would run and, along with the mist from her breath, the whole mess would freeze on her chin and on the scarf that pressed against it. She and Joshua would stop walking and listen for him, then hearing nothing, holler his name. They would look at each other and then into the trees despairingly. Possibly, Joshua, on some gut instinct, would be carrying the gun.

He attempted to keep from imagining their faces in the moment when they actually came upon his body hanging in the tree, but he could not keep the image from surfacing in his mind and the grief that shot through him as he lay in bed beside Teresa was so great that he almost decided to live.

Then it dawned on him that he could write a note.

Of course he could, and he would. The note would be left in the middle of the kitchen table and they would find it well before beginning to wonder where he was. In the note he would strongly discourage them from going into the woods themselves. He would *forbid* them from going into the woods. He would command them to call the sheriff. This was precisely the kind of thing the sheriff was for. He would write that he was sorry and that everything he owned belonged to them. His truck, his tools, the house and land. He assumed they would assume this, but since they were not related by blood or in any way legally bound to him, he did not want them to have any trouble. His note would serve as his will. He would tell them other things they already knew but would need to hear one last time. That he had loved their mother and he loved them like his own children since day one. He would write that they should stick to-gether and take care of each other—they only had each other now—and that someday in many, many, many years they would all be together as a family again, reunited in heaven. He did not necessarily believe in heaven, and they knew this, but neither did he *not* believe in it, and he hoped they knew this too. For the sake of Joshua and Claire he would become a believer in heaven. Heaven would soften the blow.

In bed that first night beside Teresa, and then later, while he sat next to her hospital bed or lay in the cot the nurses had set up for him in her room, he wrote his note to Claire and Joshua in his mind over and over again. He scanned for other details, things he might have overlooked. He pictured himself hanging in the tree. And then the dogs came run-ning up, right into the picture. Thank God he was planning ahead. He would have to leave Spy and Tanner inside—shut into a room—so they wouldn't dash out when Joshua or Claire entered the house and go di-rectly to the clearing to howl frightfully up at him hanging in the tree, causing Claire or Joshua to follow them, inevitably drawn, curious and entertained, before having noticed the note.

He would see to it that they absolutely noticed the note. This was his solemn vow, his version of keeping his promise to Teresa. Her chil-dren would never have to see their "father" dangling by a rope, with a broken neck, dead in a tree.

At the very end, Bruce confessed his plan to Teresa while she lay in her bed in the hospice wing of the hospital, but she made no response. Her skin was the texture of dust, her body like that of a paper doll. He pinched her arm hard then—he had to do that sometimes, just to keep his sanity—and she opened her eyes like a drunkard and closed them and fell instantly back to sleep. They'd reached the point where her morphine dose needed to be so high that most of the time she slept or when she woke she spoke of things that made no sense—not even to her, when pressed to explain—though on occasion she was as conscious and lucid as if she'd simply arisen from a long, restorative nap.

"I'm going to kill myself," he almost shouted, and then he put his head on the bed, too exhausted to weep. Again she did nothing. It was almost midnight. He'd just gotten off the phone with Claire, who'd called to report that she'd be there in the morning and at last—they believed —she'd have Joshua with her. They would arrive in the morning and then the long wait would begin, the vigil that the three of them would keep night and day in the hospital until it was—*the words were ridiculous*, Bruce thought, *he didn't even want to use them*—over. Earlier in the evening a doctor had asked Bruce to come out into the hallway and informed him that Teresa was "actively dying."

Afterward he hadn't returned to her room. Instead he began walking, not knowing where he was going. The hallways were lit dimly, soothingly, good lights to die by, lit only by the glowing lights of vending machines, and punctured by the bright lights that spilled occasionally from patients' rooms or the nurses' station, a beacon at the center of everything. He passed the room of an angry hippie man who didn't seem to be dying because he spent the better part of each evening dragging his IV to the third-floor patio where patients were allowed to smoke. He passed the room of an old man who was strapped into his bed by all four limbs. He passed the room of a frizzy-haired blond woman and noticed that she wasn't there anymore, her bed now made with a clean white sheet, the room empty. Bruce had met her husband once. Bill. He imagined that Bill's wife was dead now. He imagined it and didn't feel a thing. Nor did he feel anything for the angry hippie man or the old man strapped in four places to his bed. In the smallest, hardest part of him he didn't care if any of them suffered or died. He was sorry, but he couldn't. To pity them would be to doom his wife.

He seemed to have no control over where his feet carried him. They carried him to the stairwell and then down five flights of stairs, each flight turned back on itself, until he had followed them as far as he could go. He went to the door that led back into the hospital and pushed it open.

Now he was in the basement, where the light was entirely different

122

from the hospice wing. Brutal and fluorescent: a comfort to him. He walked down the long hallway. There was no one in sight. *Maybe this is where the morgue is*, he thought. Farther down the hall, in an industrial-sized kitchen, a black woman dressed in white stirred a giant pot of something with a paddle. He passed several orange, windowless doors, all of them closed. His earliest sexual fantasies had involved these sorts of mysterious doors that occupied public, yet seemingly forbidden, spaces. At the age of nine he'd been told by a friend's older brother that gangs of beautiful naked women waited behind such doors, harems of sex-starved beauties, locked in, yearning for a man to walk through. He hadn't thought of this for years, and a remote, perverse ache thrummed through him. He walked past a pay phone and then stopped and went back to it and dialed his home phone number. Claire didn't pick up until the answering machine had and he'd spoken into it.

"Bruce," she said, her voice sounding clogged, as if she had a cold, though he knew she didn't.

"What's happening?" he asked.

"Nothing . . . Josh—he's allegedly out ice fishing with R.J. That's what Vivian said. I'm waiting for him to come back and then we'll come first thing in the morning. What's happening there?"

"Things have . . ." How was he going to say it? He decided to say what the doctor had first said to him. "It seems as though this is it." He wasn't going to say what the doctor had said second. That she was dying. *Actively.*

"It?" howled Claire. She made a noise, like she was choking, gasping for air, but he pushed through it.

"So you should come with Josh as soon as you can."

"But Josh is out ice fishing," she said through her tears, her voice high-pitched and jagged. "And I'm afraid my Cutlass will get stuck if I drive out to the ice house to get him."

"Well, then just wait until he comes back. We have some time, Claire. Come when you can."

"Okay," she said intently, as if he'd just given her a complicated list of instructions, and then hung up the phone without saying goodbye. He hung up too and then began to walk down the hall again, in the same direction he'd been heading, still not knowing where he was going or why. Maybe he would find a door that led out into the parking garage. He'd go there and look at cars.

"Excuse me," a woman's voice called from behind him.

He turned. He felt that he was being busted for something. Like trespassing.

"I could use a hand if you don't mind."

It was the woman who'd been stirring with the paddle in the kitchen. Before Bruce could move or reply, she turned and disappeared back into the doorway from which she'd emerged. He walked quickly down the long length of the hallway until he came to the kitchen again and he entered, weaving his way past enormous cooking machinery, until he got to where she stood.

"I need some muscle," she explained. The woman's hair was covered with a translucent plastic cap. She wore gold earrings shaped like turtles with little green gems for eyes. "I don't know if they told you, but the guys in maintenance usually help me out when I need it since I'm here by myself for a couple of hours."

He followed her to the gigantic pot that she had been stirring. It was full of a green liquid: Jell-O before it set.

"I've got to get this from the pot into these pans." She gestured to more than a dozen pans lined up on a long wooden counter. "It's real heavy, so it takes two."

She gave him a pair of silver insulated mitts, burnt in places along each thumb. Bruce put them on and then gripped the handle on one side of the pot and the woman took the other handle and together they poured the liquid into the pans, working their way carefully down the counter, filling each one.

"Thanks," she said, after they'd set the empty pot down. She took off her mitts and wiped the sweat from her forehead with the back of one hand. "How do you like it so far?"

"Like what?"

"Maintenance," she said. "Aren't you the new guy?"

He put his hands in his pockets and shook his head. "I was just taking a walk."

"Oh!" She laughed deeply, throwing her head back. "All right, then. Well, I guess you fooled me," she said, waving him away, turning back to her Jell-O. "I guess you're just a Good Samaritan."

He stood there for a few more moments, watching her slide the pans onto a cart that held each of them in racks, one on top of the other. She began to roll the cart, pushing on it with all of her weight, and he stepped forward to help her.

"I got it," she said, pushing harder, so the cart pulled away from his hands. She opened a door that led to a walk-in cooler and then guided the cart in. "Happy St. Paddy's Day," she called to him. She came out of the cooler and slammed the door shut behind her. "It's tomorrow. That's why I made green."

But by then he was already gone.

When he returned to Teresa's room, Pepper Jones-Kachinsky was sitting next to her, holding her limp arm, two fingers pressed against Teresa's wrist.

"I'm checking her pulse," she whispered, without looking up.

Bruce watched her for several moments, the silent concentration of her face as she counted his wife's heartbeats. Teresa didn't stir or give any indication that she was aware of Pepper by her side, or of his presence in the room. She'd never met Pepper, technically speaking.

"It's an ancient Chinese practice," she said when she was done. "A holistic method. They believe you can learn everything you need to know about the condition of the patient from the pulse, and then you respond accordingly."

He nodded. He didn't have the heart to ask her what she had divined. He wanted only to be alone with his wife. Pepper came in the evenings to visit Bruce, and he imagined she'd been of some comfort to Claire in the daytime. He supposed he was grateful for that. Pepper meant well, and yet whenever he was in her presence it was as if a wasp were loose in the room.

"How *are* you?" she asked, standing up, coming to him. She took both of his hands and squeezed and looked directly into his eyes and would not look away. She did this every time she looked at him.

"Okay." He turned to Teresa, and then Pepper did too. Teresa's face in repose was as delicate and tranquil as a shell.

"Why are you here so late?" He gestured for her to sit on the vinyl couch and he sat in the chair across from her.

"I felt like coming down. I thought of you and I felt that I should come. That maybe you'd like to pray." Immediately she closed her eyes and began, "Dear Lord . . ."

He bowed his head and lowered his eyes without closing them entirely and listened to her pray in a steady murmur while gazing at her shoes. Lavender Keds with clean white bumpers shaped like half-moons.

He didn't believe in God and neither did Teresa. Or at least not the version of God that Pepper seemed to be promoting, but he didn't have it in him to say no. Certainly praying couldn't hurt, even if it did make him feel remotely like a hypocrite, and remotely like the boy he'd once been, who'd been made to go to church each Sunday, to confession every time he'd sinned. Pepper prayed for Teresa's health and recovery, for her peaceful passage if health could not be restored, for Bruce's strength in the face of this suffering, and for that of all the people who loved Teresa. She asked God to watch over "all the children of the world and most especially Claire and Josh" and followed that with a formal prayer, something rote and vaguely familiar to Bruce, and then she crossed herself and reached out with her eyes still crushed shut and clutched his knee.

"Amen," he said and she whispered amen too, saying it fiercely, almost savagely, without taking her hand from his knee.

When a decent enough time had passed, he said, "I appreciate it — you coming in. But you don't have to. Actually . . . I thought I should tell you that my own beliefs," he glanced at Teresa, "*our* beliefs — I mean, in God — are not that firm. We were both raised Catholic, but we didn't stick with it. We aren't in any way religious. So prayer . . ." He didn't know how to continue without offending. Out on the street far below, he could hear a car horn blare for several seconds and then stop. "Prayer," he continued, "is not going to be of much use to us."

Pepper didn't say anything. She went to the small table in the room, where they'd propped all the get-well cards, and picked one up and read it. It had a sepia-toned photo of a Conestoga wagon on the front. He wanted to rip it from her wrinkled hands.

She looked at him abruptly and put the card down, careful to prop it precisely as it had been. "Would you like a doughnut?" she asked, glancing toward a long box that sat near her coat and purse. She walked over to it and carried it to him, hoisting it up so he could choose.

He wasn't hungry, but he hadn't eaten since breakfast, so he took one — the first one his hand landed on, a glazed twist — and chewed it dispassionately as a beast in a field. When he was done he reached for his coffee, cold now, and took a swig. The coffee was strong and he intended to drink it all night. He didn't want to sleep. Ever again.

"Thank you," he said, setting his mug down. It said WYOMING! across the side; he'd taken it from the Family Room down the hall.

"They're left over from my group that meets Monday nights." She sat on the couch again and gestured for him to join her, and he did. "Speaking of which, that's something you should know, Bruce. For afterwards. We have a group, 'The Loss of a Loved One and Other Life Changes.' It's a family group. It meets once a week. You can all come together. We find that it—" she interrupted herself, a look of realization overtaking her face. "You know, we just did something that you may be interested in. In fact, it's something I'd very much like to share with you."

She stood and went to her purse, knelt to rummage through it, smiling at its contents, searching in the dim light of the room in each of its pockets and sections. She had an incredibly fit body for a seventy-year-old. She wore jeans with an elastic waistband and a sports bra that gathered her breasts into one firm bundle. She seemed constantly on the verge of turning a cartwheel.

"Here it is," she exclaimed. "Heavens, this purse. All the doggone things I cart around!" She stood and came toward him, holding what he could now see was a purple marker, and took the cap off. "It's a little exercise we did. Bow your head," she said, as if she was about to perform a party trick. She parted his hair with her free hand and before he could agree or disagree, she pressed the tip of the marker to his scalp.

"Now," she said, stepping back, replacing the cap on the marker. "I want you to remember that dot when you're feeling sad or lonely. You can't wash it off. Once it's there, it's there for life. It's a reminder that you're a special person. That you're a child of God, which means that you're never alone, Bruce. Not for a minute. It means that you are a beloved man who lives in the light of God's love, as we all do."

"How are the animals?" Teresa asked suddenly, her voice clear as a spoon against a jar.

They turned to her, startled. Bruce rushed to the bed.

"The animals? Fine." He put his hand on her shoulder. "Did you just wake up? They miss you—everyone does. The dogs are staying at Kathy Tyson's now, until we can all be home."

"Kathy Tyson?" She lifted her eyes to him. They appeared younger, bluer now because the rest of her had become so old.

"So they won't be lonely. With us gone all the time they don't have company."

She smiled at him and her smile was like her eyes. The only two parts of her that were still that way.

"Would you like to pray?" Pepper asked from the foot of the bed, still holding the marker.

"Actually," he said irritably, "we'd prefer if you'd—"

"Yes," said Teresa, keeping her eyes on Bruce.

That night, despite the coffee, Bruce slept. Then woke. Then he flickered back to sleep and woke again, and again and again, as if a dumb but persistent hand attached to a stick was prodding him. At last he woke entirely, instantly, and sat up in his cot as if the hand had slapped him. He knew exactly where he was. Never in all of this did he forget where he was. The room was quiet, but recently so. The silence had a luxurious quality, as if in the wake of the terrible sound that had preceded it. Teresa was asleep, bathed in the gentle lights of the machines that were stationed around her head. He watched her face and then the noise came again—the noise he presumed had woken him in the first place—and he went toward it, a horrible high pitch from one of the machines. He pressed the flat buttons on the panel covered with numbers and indecipherable commands until the noise stopped. He stood staring at the display. Whatever he had done to silence the noise had caused the screen to rhythmically flash a series of zeros.

"You're awake," the nurse said as he glided into the room. His name was Eric. He carried a tray with a plate on it, covered by a dome-shaped lid. Teresa ate no matter what the time of day—or rather they tried to get her to eat, a thing that had become next to impossible. The evening before she'd allowed Bruce to spoon a sliver of a canned peach into her mouth and then chewed it obediently without seeming to taste it at all. The nurse set the tray down on the table beside Teresa's bed and edged in next to Bruce and pressed several buttons on the panel and the zeros disappeared. "You were snoring like a baby when I came by here last."

Bruce gazed at him dreamily, as if unable to comprehend what he was saying. His waking life had taken on the quality of dreams, his dream life, the quality of reality. "How's your car running?" he asked after several moments.

"Fine," Eric said. He was a chubby kid barely out of nursing school. Bruce had come to know and like him over the weeks of nights he'd spent at the hospital. Eric's presence was undemanding and, most importantly, unconcerned. He hadn't tried to talk Bruce into counseling, hadn't told him how sorry he was, or how there were people "there for him," or that his wife dying so quickly was actually for the best because now she wouldn't suffer. Eric scarcely acknowledged that Bruce was having any trouble at all. In fact, he'd burdened Bruce with his own problem —a car that wouldn't start on occasion or made a knocking sound upon acceleration when it did. Twice Bruce had gone down to the parking lot with Eric on his breaks to investigate the trouble with the car.

"Has she woken up?"

"No." Then, "Once. About ten thirty, but just briefly. Maybe five minutes."

Eric took Teresa's wrist to check her pulse, watching the clock.

Bruce sensed that it was snowing. He felt that he could hear it falling outside or maybe he could smell it. He went to the window, drew back the curtains, and looked out.

"How's her pulse?" he asked, turning back to Eric.

"Good."

"There are these doctors. They base everything on the pulse. How to cure diseases and so on."

Eric nodded pleasantly and wrote on the clipboard that was kept in a bin bolted to the wall by the door.

"They're Chinese. That's the kind of thing my wife's into. Alternative things. I was thinking maybe I'd look into it, to see if they could help."

Eric began to change Teresa's catheter bag. Bruce turned back to the window and stared out the opening in the curtains. He'd been right. It was snowing, though spring was only a few days away. The wee hours of March 17, perhaps an hour before sunrise. Teresa's parents and brother would be arriving that afternoon—they'd planned the visit weeks before, not knowing how sick Teresa would become, how quickly.

"I mean, you never know. I figure it's worth a shot." He pushed his hands into his pockets. He was fully dressed, in jeans, shirt, boots. He'd slept that way for the past sixteen nights. He became aware once more of the purple dot on his head that Pepper had made. It felt wet, as if it would smear if he touched it. And also slightly weighted, as if he were balancing a book on his head. After Pepper had left that evening he'd gone into the bathroom and attempted, uselessly, to get a look at it in the mirror. Of course he couldn't see it. But it was there. It would stay. He felt it bore into him, a bullet from a soft gun.

He smoothed a hand over his hair and turned to Eric. "I'm not going to work anymore. I'm staying right here until all of this gets resolved. The kids are coming too." He thought about Claire and Joshua, driving to Duluth now, he hoped. He ached for them.

"So you'll need two more cots?" Eric asked.

Bruce nodded.

"I'll submit a request form before I leave." He placed the clipboard back in its bin and then removed his gloves, peeling them off from the inside out so that no part that had touched Teresa would touch him, and then walked out the door.

Bruce opened the curtains, wanting the light to wake Teresa when it came, feeling already how fierce it would be, the morning sun cutting against the new snow. He sat down in the chair beside her and opened the drawer of her nightstand and took the phone book from it. He had no idea where to begin, so he turned first to *Chinese*, though he knew that was ridiculous. Then he turned to *Physicians* and flipped through the pages, overwhelmed by the long list. He sat thinking for several moments and then paged through the list of doctors, scanning each name for anyone that sounded Asian and found a Dr. Yu. It was five o'clock in the morning, but such things didn't deter him anymore. He dialed the number. "I need a healer," he was going to say. Just like that. Maybe the Chinese doctor would know. Maybe he had a friend who would come and check Teresa's pulse. The phone rang and rang, so long that the ringing finally stopped and there was an almost-silence that contained almost-sounds—faint crackling, glimmers of voices and conversations on other lines. He put the phone down and sat gazing at Teresa, who, though silent, had opened her eyes.

He said her name, shaking her a little. She remained perfectly still.

"Wake up, baby," he said, shaking her harder. He put his hand to her face and at the very last moment she blinked. Though her eyes were open, she was neither looking at him nor not looking at him. She reminded him of one of those old-fashioned dolls with movable eyelids that close when you tilt them back and open when you put them upright. His mother had had one named Holly that he was forbidden as a child to touch without supervision, though he'd rarely cared to touch her, so deeply she'd creeped him out. He took the pillows from his cot and shoved them behind Teresa's back, propping her up, so now she was staring in the direction of her feet instead of the ceiling. Her lower jaw hung slack, leaving her mouth slightly ajar. He pushed it closed, but when he let go it fell open again.

"The kids are coming," he said. "Josh too—he was out ice fishing. And your parents and Tim, they'll be here by three."

If she would just make the smallest sound, the slightest motion, the most remote indication. Then he would be happy. All these days he'd been waiting for her to open her eyes and for her to keep them open, and yet now that she was doing that he wished she would close them. He placed his hand over her eyes, but they stayed open beneath it.

"You ready for breakfast?" He lifted the lid from the tray that Eric had brought in. A square of green Jell-O sat alone in a small bowl on a plate. He scooped some onto a spoon and held it to her mouth. "I made this for you, Ter. Open up. Honestly, it was so funny. I went for a walk and I ended up downstairs and then there was this kitchen and—"

She blinked.

"Here," he said, and pushed the spoon into her mouth. "You've got to eat. If you don't eat, how're you going to get better?" Streaks of green liquid began to ooze from her mouth, dripping down her chin, but he wouldn't look at her. He filled the spoon again and pushed another bite into her mouth, then turned to refill it again, but stopped himself and instead threw the spoon against the wall behind Teresa's head with all of his strength. It ricocheted onto the wall at their side, then clanged to the hard floor beneath the bed.

After several minutes he took the cloth they kept nearby and wetted it in the sink and returned to clean her face with it, wiping the green stains from her chin and throat. He opened the tube of lip balm that sat on the table beside her bed and applied it to her slack lips.

"What do you want?" he asked, smoothing her eyebrows with his thumbs the way she liked.

She coughed once and her eyes fluttered shut, then opened again.

"Do you want me to say it's okay if you die?" Pepper had told him this, that Teresa might need permission. That dying people will often wait until the people who love them encourage them to let go. "Because it isn't, Ter. It's *not okay*. You have a life to live, and we have our lives to live, and everyone needs you, so you can't just give up now. Do you hear me?"

She made no move or acknowledgment of him. He sat silently watching her until light began to filter into the room from the window, soft and pale, first purple, then blue.

He bent and took his boots off and then pulled off his jeans and unbuttoned his flannel shirt and tossed them both onto his cot and crawled into the bed beside her and arranged the blankets over them. She wore only her hospital gown, and he pushed it out of the way so he could feel her skin against him.

"Let's watch the sun rise," he whispered into her ear and then closed his eyes. He stroked her arm, tracing his fingers down to her wrist until he found her pulse. It was strong, like he knew it would be. And fierce and small and fast. Like a force that could not be stopped or changed or helped or harmed. Like a woman who would live forever.

PART III

Mud
Days

...there is really no such thing as youth, there is only luck, and the enormity of something which can happen, whence a person, any person, is brought deeper and more profoundly into sorrow, and once they have gone there, they can't come back, they have to live in it, live in that dark, and find some glimmer in it.

—Edna O'Brien, *Down by the River*

9

EIGHT DAYS AFTER TERESA DIED, Bruce woke in a field.

He was still alive. It took him several moments to understand this, as he lay numb from the cold under the blue morning sky. The horses hovered over him, making chuffing sounds with their warm brown noses, and he listened to them without opening his eyes. For those moments he had no past, no life, no dead wife. He was no man in a no man's land, and reality was a glimmering series of pictures in a dream that went back no farther than the night before. How he'd stood on the front porch drinking the bottle of Jack Daniel's. How it had felt as the flesh of his cheek opened against the rock in the field where he fell. How Teresa was. How she had come to him. Silent, but there. Her eyes were the stars, her hair the black sky, her body the trees at the edge of the field, her arms the whiplike saplings that surrounded him.

He grabbed one of the saplings now with both hands and pulled on its wire stem with all his might, making a growling sound that spooked the horses, so they ran, stopping to watch him from a distance. He pulled so hard that he rolled over onto his belly with the effort, as if he were not pulling on the sapling, but it was pulling him. He let it go and it sprang back to its upright position, rooted in the frozen ground.

When he opened his eyes, a shard of glass seemed to cleave through his head. It was his life coming back to him. Beside him was a patch of vomit, congealed and almost frozen solid. Very slowly, he pushed himself up. When he made it to his knees he had to lean forward onto his hands and vomit again. Afterward, he sat back on his heels and wiped his mouth with his sleeve. He touched his face with his numb fingers, tracing the scab that had formed there.

At last he stood and staggered a few steps. The horses had begun to graze, but now they lifted their heads from the grass and stared at him expectantly until he called their names, and immediately they came to him and pressed their noses into his hands, as if he were holding apples.

The three of them began to walk home, following the path that the horses had made; the path Bruce had no doubt followed the night before, though he could not remember it. When the barn came into view, Lady Mae and Beau trotted ahead and stood in their stalls, waiting to be fed. He gave them oats and then went to the hens to get the eggs, but found none.

When he walked in the house he saw that Joshua had not come home the night before. All the lights that Bruce had turned on were still on, and the radio played fiddle music so loudly he thought he would have to vomit again before he reached the stereo and turned it off. Now that he was inside he realized how cold he was. He began to build a fire in the wood stove. Joshua had slept over at his new girlfriend's house, he assumed. Claire had gone back to Minneapolis the afternoon before—she had to go back to her job and, Bruce hoped, eventually school. Both she and Joshua were meant to graduate in June, Claire from college, Joshua from high school. In the course of their mother's dying, both of them had stopped attending school. Teresa had not been aware of this, and Bruce, though dimly aware, hadn't been able to muster up enough energy to be concerned. He'd needed Claire. What would he have done with her away at school? They would go back soon, he figured, and left it at that. They needed time to get over things, another reason for him to act soon on his plan to kill himself—he hadn't forgotten his plan—so they could grieve and get on with it.

The kindling began to burn and the heat of the flames felt good on his face as he stooped near the open door of the stove. The gash in his cheek began to pulse. It was two days after the day he'd hoped to be dead. Last night he'd been willing to die, but now he realized that drinking and then half freezing himself to death was not how he wanted to do it. It lacked dignity, but more, it could be misconstrued as unintentional. He would do what he intended to do and nothing less. He had the rope all ready to go, tied into its knot and coiled in the trunk in the barn where they kept the tack.

But today was not the day to die, he decided. So far, each day had been like that. It was one thing and then another. The day after the funeral, which was originally to have been his last day on earth, Joshua's truck broke down and he needed Bruce to help him fix it. There was a part they'd ordered that wouldn't come in for five days. Plus, he could not very well have hung himself while Teresa's parents and brother were still there visiting. In the days after the funeral he'd done his best to be a good host, despite the circumstances. He took them to Flame Lake to visit the Ojibwe Museum, to Blue River to eat walleye at the Hunt Club. They'd had a horrible shock when they arrived at the airport in Duluth, what with Pepper waiting to greet them instead of Bruce and the kids.

"There's still enough time to see the body," Pepper had told them when they got off the plane. They stood in a corner of the airport near a sheet of windows with the sun beating brutally through. "The *body!*" Teresa's mom had shrieked, then ran off not knowing where she was headed, bogged down by the huge purse she carried, and stopped eventually by a giant potted plant in her path.

Teresa's parents and her brother had not wanted to see the body, unlike Bruce and Claire and Joshua, who protested angrily when told at last by a curly-haired nurse that they would "have to say their goodbyes." They'd spent four hours in the hospital room after Teresa took her last breath, which all of them had missed. Claire and Joshua had been racing to Duluth after having spent hours trying to get Claire's car unstuck from the snow and slush that it had become mired in on the ice in the middle of Lake Nakota. When Bruce had woken up beside Teresa he had gone to get a cup of coffee. It sat now, its half-and-half forming a skin across its wretched surface, in the mug that said WYOMING! on the windowsill of the big window in the room. Four hours was an unorthodox length of time to stay with a dead body at St. Benedict's Hospital, but they had Pepper on their side, plus they had the excuse of Teresa's parents arriving soon.

They did their best to be unobtrusive. After those first rounds of uproarious weeping, they muffled their cries by pressing their faces into pillows or one another or, most often, into the body of Teresa lying dead on the bed. She was still warm when Claire and Joshua arrived. They held on to her through her blankets, and then slowly the warmth receded, became only an island on her belly and then that cooled too and they touched her no longer.

When Bruce had entered the room with his coffee, he had not realized she was dead. Minutes before, he'd been in bed with her. Her eyes were open but seemed unchanged. He'd said a few words to her about the weather, which was cold but sunny, March but still winter. The same snow that had fallen when, as far as anyone knew, Teresa didn't have cancer still sat frozen into layers on the ground. He went to her then and took her hand, hot and swollen from all the needles attached to it, but then he looked at her and what he saw—the not thereness of her—made him fall hard and, without his being aware, from his feet onto his knees.

While they sat with her and waited for her parents and brother to arrive they cooperated with the nurses as best they could. Teresa had wanted to be an organ donor, but because of the cancer, her eyes were all they could use. Until they were surgically removed, they needed to be preserved, which, Pepper kindly explained, called for ice. They agreed to keep the bags of ice on Teresa's eyes forty-five minutes of each hour, and Bruce agreed to be the one to keep the time. He took his watch off and set it on the bed near her hip to remind himself of the task.

Finally, the curly-headed nurse stepped in to tell them that Teresa's parents and brother were waiting for them in the lobby and did not care to come up. After their initial resistance, Bruce and Claire and Joshua knew they had to go. Bruce and Joshua approached Teresa solemnly one by one, each of them bending to kiss her cold lips. Claire began sobbing hysterically all over again, even more loudly than she had when she'd first walked in and seen her mother dead. She pushed Bruce and Joshua violently away when they tried to comfort her, batting her arms at them. Then she quieted and told them without looking up that she wanted a few minutes alone with her mother.

Bruce stood silently with Joshua outside the closed door, and then together they walked to the end of the hallway, where there was a window from floor to ceiling. Joshua looked out over the streets of Duluth, and then beyond them, to the lake. Bruce looked at Joshua. He hadn't seen him for days. In the brief minutes of each day that he and Claire had not been consumed by what was happening with Teresa, they had been consumed by the whereabouts of Joshua. He had left messages on the answering machine, he had left notes on the kitchen table, but he had not appeared. Over his absence Bruce had raged, Claire had wept, Teresa in her delirium had cried out his name: *Where is Joshua? Where is Joshua?* until, in the last days, she had intermittently believed him to be right there in the room. Bruce still didn't know where Joshua had been and now he didn't care. He was only glad that Claire had brought him here.

He knew that Joshua was also asking the question, *Where was I? Where was I when my mother died and where, because of me, was Claire?* He wanted to say to Joshua that it was okay, but something stopped him. *It's okay* kept forming in his mouth, then turning to mist.

"Your mother, she thought you were with her all yesterday," he said, which was fairly true—she'd hallucinated his presence the day before, as well as Claire's, and a dog they used to have named Monty. "She believed you were right there sitting in the chair."

Joshua turned his pink eyes to Bruce for a moment, then he shifted them wordlessly back out to the streets.

Bruce reached over and began to massage Joshua's back, the way he'd done in countless attempts to ease Teresa's pain.

"Oh," Joshua said, leaning into Bruce's hands. "That feels so good."

When Bruce woke on the ninth day that Teresa no longer lived on the earth he knew that now was his chance. He could feel the quiet of the house around him; so quiet it was as if he weren't inside of his house but rather lying again in the field where he'd woken the morning before. He opened his eyes but felt unable to move, the weight of his sorrow pinning him to the bed.

"Shadow," he called in a high-pitched voice. "Kitty kitty. Kitty kitty." He heard her feet land on the floor above him, in Claire's room. After several moments she appeared in the doorway. "Come here," he implored sweetly, though she did not move from her place by the door. He lay in bed gazing at her. She had known Teresa as long as he had. She had been on the bed sometimes when they'd made love, making a space for herself in the farthest corner as long as they didn't cause too much commotion.

He closed his eyes and said out loud, "I'll be dead soon." And then he wept in several short yelps and fell back to sleep.

At noon he woke with Shadow's weight on his chest.

He put his hands on her warm body and instantly she purred. Usually the weight to which he woke did not have a form. Usually it was a series of pictures too wonderful or terrible to bear. Images of Teresa either very happy or very sad, very healthy or very sick, each of them torturing him in their severity. Sometimes a question would occur to him with such ferocity that he felt his body grow unbelievably heavy, as if the weight of him in that instant would break the bed. *Why had he not quit working immediately when they learned she had cancer? Why had he not spent every minute of every day and night with her from the moment he met her?* And then darker questions would come, questions that were not actually questions, but bullets from a gun that implicated him in her death. The doctors believed her cancer had started in her lungs. *Had it been the wood stove? Had it been the insulation he had scavenged from a job and used?* It could have been anything, the doctor had told them, uncurious when they'd asked. But anything was anything — it did not exclude Bruce. It encompassed him and all the things he'd made for her and touched and delivered to her for almost twelve years.

He sat up and put his bare feet on the floor and then stood carefully, unsure of his legs, as if they'd recently been released from casts. He had a mission. Two missions. He was going to get the dogs from Kathy Tyson — she'd been taking care of them since days before Teresa died, and with the funeral and the comings and goings of so many people in their house, they had not yet picked them up — and then he was going to come home and kill himself.

He considered not going to get the dogs. It would make sense logistically, but he decided against it for two reasons. One, the dogs would be a comfort to Claire and Joshua and if he didn't go get them now, there would be the next funeral to deal with and the dogs would remain at Kathy's for at least another week. And two, he wanted to see them one last time.

First, he shaved. He had not shaved since the morning of the funeral and a shaggy beard was starting to grow in. He felt the least he could do if he was going to kill himself was to shave. He also dressed in a good shirt — not a flannel one like he normally wore, but in the white shirt with turquoise snaps that Teresa loved. When he wore it she would croon her rendition of a cowboy song, which she had likely made up herself, probably the moment she first saw him in that shirt. He tried to recall how the song went, but for the life of him he couldn't. He would never hear it again, he realized, unless, of course, there was a heaven after all and then she would be there waiting for him and happy that he was wearing that shirt. She would be wearing her hospital gown with nothing on underneath, or perhaps she'd be wearing the blouse and skirt that Claire had picked out for her to wear in the casket, over her best underwear and bra, the outfit she'd worn also into the incinerator. Bruce allowed himself to wonder for a glimmer of a moment about the person who had loaded her into the incinerator. Whoever it was would have been the last person to lay eyes on her. But then he remembered that was not true. She had been burned in her casket, a state law, and the last person who saw her was Kurt Moyle, the owner of the funeral home, who stepped forward and reached up his hand and softly lowered the lid on her just as they sang the last line of "Amazing Grace."

Like her death, Teresa's funeral had not been the funeral Bruce had imagined seven weeks before when they had first learned of Teresa's cancer and he'd allowed the movie version of her funeral to play in his mind. Bruce didn't behave the way he'd thought he would. He didn't take anyone's hands in an attempt to either console or be consoled. He didn't say anything about how his wife was in a better place now. What he did was try his best not to look at anyone. Looking at people made the strength in his legs disappear. He held on to chairs, walls, at one point even to Teresa's coffin, to keep himself up. When he looked at her parents a phrase came instantly into his mind: *stampeded by grief.* Teresa and her parents, in her adult life, had not been terribly close. Still, at their daughter's funeral they howled and pawed with their hands, mussing each other's clothes. They were not howlers; never had he imagined that they would paw. Claire and Joshua were the opposite, moving from the chairs to their mother's coffin, from her coffin to the drinking fountain, from the drinking fountain to the little stand where they'd put the book where people could sign their names. They seemed to both know to keep moving in this circuit, apart from each other, but in synchronicity, swooping like owls on a night hunt, wide-eyed and silent. When they passed Bruce their eyes lashed on to his like ropes for climbing that landed, dug in, then gripped and grew taut. He looked away from them as quickly as he could, though he was forced to appear to be looking at other people. Manners dictated that.

"I'm so sorry," they said, each of them, over and over.

"Thank you," he croaked. Those two words like the pits of plums he sucked the fruit from and then spit, sucked and then spit. He wondered if it were possible to add up all the people he'd thanked over the course of his entire life, whether that sum would be equal to the number of people he thanked on the one day that his wife's body was to be sealed in a wooden box, shoved into an incinerator, and burned, at an extremely high temperature, to ashes.

. . .

Kathy Tyson expected him. He'd called the night before and she said he could come by at any time. It took him several minutes before he could speak to her because Spy and Tanner were so glad to see him, jumping up like they were trained not to do, almost knocking him over when he stooped down to their level.

At last he was able to move from the porch into the house, the dogs pushing in with him. Kathy's house was a cabin, all one room, with a loft for her bed and a tiny bathroom just beyond the kitchen nook. Her parents' house was hidden behind a stand of trees a few hundred yards farther up the driveway. Kathy's grandparents had lived in the cabin years before, while they built the bigger house up the hill.

"How about a cup of coffee?" she asked, and poured some into a mug without waiting for him to answer. They sat down at the table. A stick of incense burned on the shelf behind her, a tendril of sweet smoke rising above her head.

"We're very grateful to you for taking care of the dogs."

"I don't mind a bit," she said, looking around for them. They lay near his feet under the table, both of them licking their private parts. "I'll miss them. They're good dogs."

"They *are* good dogs," Bruce said. A couple of weeks ago, Teresa had asked him to give Kathy a jar of jam that she had made, as a thank-you gift, but at the last minute Bruce left it on the kitchen table, feeling it was too valuable to give away, not for its contents so much as for Teresa's writing scrawled across the label on the lid. *Raspberry, June.*

"What happened to your face?" she asked.

He pressed his fingertips to the scab on his cheek. "I slipped."

She nodded. The bowl that sat between them on the table held a single tangerine.

"How's work?" he asked. She was a cow inseminator like her father. He didn't know whether cows were inseminated year-round or what she was doing home on a Wednesday at noon.

"Good," she nodded. "We keep busy." She stood up and refilled both of their mugs. She wore jeans and a purple shirt and a cluster of crystals and beads and stones around her throat and wrists and fingers. Once, Teresa had chatted with her about having her as a guest on *Modern Pioneers* to discuss the art of reading tarot, Bruce remembered now, though nothing had come of it. He had known Kathy all of his life, though, sitting here in her house, he realized he hardly knew her at all.

They'd gone to school together, she four years behind him, and then when he bought his land they were neighbors, and they helped one another out in a neighborly way. He remembered that she played softball, not in high school, but now, for the Jake's Tavern team.

"Spring's on its way," he said. "It's already here, I guess."

"Yep," said Kathy. It had officially been spring for nearly a week. They both looked out the window at the snow, which was melting, the weather having warmed to the low forties.

"So that means you'll start practicing soon."

"Practicing?" she asked.

"Softball."

"Oh, yeah," she said, blushing a little. A lock of her brown hair had come loose from her ponytail, softening her face. She pushed it behind her ear. "I don't know if I'll do it this year. It's very time-consuming."

"It keeps you busy," he said.

"It's not only practice and games, but I'm also the secretary."

Bruce nodded. He wondered what the secretary of the softball team would have to do.

"You could play with us. We could certainly use some men. It seems like only the women in this town want to do anything. To join in."

"I would want to play for Len's Lookout," he said sternly.

Her eyes flickered from her hands to his eyes and then back to her hands. "I can understand that," she said, a little breathless.

"Len's . . . what are they?"

"The Leopards."

"Len's Leopards," he said quietly, ridiculously, without any intention of joining a softball team. Teresa had waited tables at Len's Lookout. Everyone had loved her there. Leonard and Mardell, the customers from Midden and from the Cities. Mardell had taped Teresa's obituary to the wall at the bar, along with a picture she'd taken of Teresa at the annual Christmas party. People had left flowers beneath it and notes and votive candles that burned until they burned out. He hadn't been there to see it himself, but Mardell had called and told him about it, how the notes and flowers were piling on the floor and covering the pinball machine that sat nearby.

"It's almost his name," Kathy said.

"What?"

"Leopard. It's almost Leonard. Only one letter is different."

143

"Oh. I never thought of that."

She reached back to her ponytail and draped it over her left shoulder. "It would be a way of honoring her perhaps."

"Perhaps," agreed Bruce, without committing himself. Now that they were on the subject, he hoped she would not say how sorry she was. She'd already said it at the funeral. He cleared his throat and then coughed hard, as if to free something caught in his lungs.

Her phone rang, but she did not answer it. When the machine clicked on, the person on the line hung up. "It's my mom," she explained. "She never leaves a message. That's how I know to call."

He gave her a small smile. It seemed that he should leave, but he didn't want to. He didn't feel happy, but he didn't feel sad either. He felt a glorious sense of safety from the rest of his life in Kathy's small house. It was not like the way he'd felt before Teresa got cancer, before he knew there was anything he needed to feel safe from. It was an entirely new sensation, and it filled him up like a drug.

"So I was thinking, I wanted to tell you, if you ever want to take a walk or talk on the phone or whatnot, I wanted you to know that I'm here. I mean, if you ever need an ear, I'm just right down the road."

She got up to stoke the stove.

"I should go," he said, standing. "But thank you again."

"I enjoyed it, being of assistance." She walked him to the door and then stood on the porch as he drove away with the dogs beside him in the cab.

He drove past his house and out to the highway, to Len's Lookout, where he parked and shut the ignition off. He sat waiting, as if for Teresa to come out, as she'd done when he came to pick her up after her shift. It was just after one: several people were inside eating lunch, their cars and trucks were in the parking lot. He recognized almost all of them. He started the engine again and drove to Norway and back, a sixty-mile roundtrip that took him a couple of hours because he avoided the highway and took the long way, on mostly dirt roads, for no reason at all.

When he got home Joshua was there, and together they cooked up a pound of hamburger, pressing it into four patties. They covered the patties with ketchup and ate them without buns. When Teresa had died they had all abruptly, inexplicably, without having mentioned it, stopped being vegetarians. It was one of the first things that changed. As Bruce did the dishes, Lisa Boudreaux pulled up into the driveway and Joshua went out to greet her. Fifteen minutes later they walked into the house and Lisa handed Bruce a card.

"This is from my mom," she explained almost inaudibly, without looking at him.

"Thank you," he said. He could not think of who her mother was. Lisa he recognized from school functions over the years, and also Teresa's funeral, though she had not spoken to him then, which meant she had not said she was sorry, a fact he now found himself strangely resenting.

"Would you like a burger?" he asked, though they'd eaten all the beef.

"We're going upstairs," Joshua said curtly. Teresa had not been a strict mother, but neither had she allowed her high school–age children to sleep with their romantic partners in her house. Bruce watched them walk up the stairs and didn't see them for the rest of the day.

On the morning of the tenth day he woke from a dream in which he was murdering Teresa by beating her to death with his fists. He lay on his side, staring at the line of small yellow circular stains that a leak in the roof had made last year where the ceiling met the wall. He heard Joshua and Lisa in the kitchen. Almost immediately Lisa began to laugh, rather loudly, he thought, given the fact that she was in someone else's house at nine o'clock in the morning and it was obvious that he was not up. Usually by nine Bruce would have been up for three and a half hours, but he'd been sleeping late since Teresa died. He was on a vacation from work—which would actually become permanent since he would soon be dead.

"Josh," he hollered out from his bed three times before receiving a sullen, almost vicious, "What?" in return.

"Will you feed?"

Joshua said he would and then, without another word, the front door slammed shut. Bruce listened until he heard them drive away. Once the sounds of their engines faded, the house took on the quality of quiet he'd felt the morning before—that he was not in a house, but a field. He lay there in it, his eyes not shut but merely lowered as if to shield against the sun.

It came to him then: he was not going to be brave enough to kill himself.

It came whole and solid, like a fish that swam up to him, the same way it had when he'd decided the opposite. He wailed, and then wailed and wailed, so loudly that all the animals came and jumped up to be near him on the bed—Spy and Tanner and Shadow. The dogs licked his face and throat and arms and hands, as though he were a plate, and then a new sound emerged from him, one he'd never made before or witnessed anyone else making: a kind of whimpering and peeping and coughing and hooting all at once.

When he quieted he became aware of the fact that he was encased by animals, the dogs lying against him on either side, Shadow above him, pressed up against the top of his head. He was surprised that Shadow in particular had stayed so near, in the midst of such horrible noise. He reached up and stroked her with both hands, the tears dripping silently at last, off his face and into his ears and neck and hair.

He knew something else then. That in some way he already was dead, that *his life was killing him*, and worse, that he would not ever be able to kill his life.

Once he had heard a terrible story about a man in New York City who had slipped and fallen into the path of a train, but only half of this man's body had been run over, the other half, his top half—either blessedly or not blessedly, depending on how you looked at it—had remained above, on the platform, conscious and fully alive. He could talk, he could listen, he could recite the Pledge of Allegiance. He could do everything but move from precisely where the train pinned him to the platform from the waist down. The rescue people came and soon it was determined that the man would die the moment they moved the train, but in the meanwhile he was kept alive by the train in its stillness, holding his organs together, his blood inside.

Bruce, in bed on the morning of day ten, remembered that man. He *was* that man.

An hour passed while he stared at the ceiling and did not move. When he sat up it was only to reach over to rummage around in the drawer of Teresa's nightstand, looking for tissue to blow his nose, but he found a cassette tape instead. He lay back down with it in his hand and stared at it for several moments before he could make out that it was by Kenny G. He had never listened to Kenny G. He had never known Teresa to listen to Kenny G. He had no idea how the tape had found its way into the drawer on the side of their bed or why a grown man would call himself "G" instead of simply using his full last name. He leaned over and popped the tape into the player that sat on the shelf behind his head. When one side ended he switched it to the other side, and he did it again and again. He played it and played it, and it told him his whole life story, and hers. It pinned him beautifully, all day, to the bed, and though it made him weep, it also managed to shout down the other sounds that had pinned him to the bed before—the voice that hissed the questions that all began with *why*.

At four the phone rang. He assumed it would be Claire, who had called him three times that day already, leaving messages for him in her new sad voice. He picked it up, ready now to possibly drag himself out of bed.

"Bruce. It's Kathy," the voice said, then added, "Tyson."

"Hi." He reached over to click off Kenny G.

"How are you?"

"Fine," he said, clearing his throat.

"I was wondering if you wanted dinner. I made chili. I could bring it over or you're more than welcome to come here."

"I can't. But thank you. Claire's coming home," he lied. She wouldn't be there in time for dinner. She wouldn't be there until past ten.

"Oh," she spoke quickly. "I meant that you could bring the kids too. If they would want to come." She paused. "But it sounds like you're all set."

"I think Claire has something planned. She already bought the food."

"Well, anyway, before dinner . . . I was thinking of taking a walk."

He agreed to meet her at the stream, the midway point between his house and hers. He wasn't so much interested in seeing Kathy as he was in getting out of his bed, and miraculously, the house. He walked the three quarters of a mile slowly, feeling strangely feverish and out of breath. He passed one cabin and then the other one—both stood empty most of the time, belonging to city people. No one lived between his house and Kathy's, which he'd known all along, but hadn't thought of specifically until today. When he saw her in the distance he waved, and Spy and Tanner lowered their tails, thinking Bruce was leaving them again.

"Greetings," she called in response to his wave. She did not walk toward him, but instead gathered her poncho in more closely around herself, and stood waiting in the part of the road that covered the culvert through which the stream flowed, the official spot where they'd agreed to meet. When he was near enough to her, they shook hands awkwardly and walked to the edge of the road and looked at the water.

"So," she asked, solemnly, as if out of respect. "How was your day?"

"My day?" he asked, surprised at what he would tell her. "Hard."

When Bruce returned home Claire was sitting in the kitchen drinking coffee.

"There you are," she said.

"You're home early. Since when do you drink coffee?" he asked, pouring himself a cup.

"Since the hospital, I suppose. Where were you? I worried—your truck was here and I didn't hear your chain saw. And I called you today. Did you get my messages?"

"I thought coffee made you sick."

"It doesn't anymore," said Claire. "I lost my sensitivity and now I'm addicted." Her hands gripped the cup, bony and hard-looking and pale. She seemed suddenly older to him than she was, and he realized that this had probably, recently, become true. In the course of Teresa's dying and death, Claire had been less his daughter and more his comrade in arms. Together they had tended to Teresa, together they had searched for Joshua, together they had sat businesslike with Kurt Moyle and told him what they wanted—which casket, which flowers, which program, which songs. Alone, she wrote the thank-you cards, in one long day, signing all of their names.

"Did you ever meet that guy named Bill?" he asked.

"Bill?"

"At the hospital. He lost his wife."

She stared at him for a few beats and then stood up. "No. Why?"

She got the coffee pot and refilled both their cups. He noticed her hand trembled as she poured.

"You're still sensitive," he said.

"What?" She set the pot down too hard.

"To the caffeine. It's making you shake."

"Oh," she said, sitting down. She pushed her hands between her legs as though she were trying to warm them up.

"So, this Bill. I thought of him the other day. I only talked to him once or twice, but he seemed like a good guy. We had a lot in common. His wife was about your mom's age and she died a couple of days before her—her room was a few rooms down from your mom's. Anyway, I wondered how he was."

Claire nodded coolly. "I'm sure it's difficult for him just like it is for us." She took a sip of her coffee and swallowed hard, like she was taking a pill. "Where were you?"

"I took a walk."

She combed her hair with her fingers. It was longer than it had been for years and tinted a faint, unnatural red. She wore lipstick that was the same color as her new hair, the rest of her face bare.

"What happened to your braid?" he asked, noticing for the first time that it was gone. He'd teased her about it, but he'd always liked how the little bells tinkled when she moved. It had reminded him of a cat entering the room.

"I cut it off." Her hand went to where the braid had once rested on her neck. "Did you work today?"

He shook his head. "But I will Monday. I figured it's time. What else am I going to do? I'm broke."

"I could loan you money."

"No."

"Well, if you need it, just ask. 'Cause I have it. My tips have been good." She was now waiting tables full-time at the restaurant where she'd worked part-time before she dropped out of school, before her mother got sick.

"So, how are you doing?" Bruce asked.

"I'm hanging on," she said, giving him a twisted little smile. "I can't sleep much. I keep waking up with nightmares. And I still can't eat anything yet."

"What do you dream?"

She propped her chin on her hand, thinking of what to tell him, which dream. "I dream that I have to murder her," she said. "That she forces me to do the most horrible things like beat her to death with a bat or tie her to a tree, pour gasoline on her, and light her on fire."

"That's probably normal. It's your way of saying goodbye."

"No, it's not," she snapped, and looked angrily at him. "I'm not saying goodbye, Bruce. I'm *never going to say goodbye*, so don't say that, okay?"

"Okay," he said gently. He put his hand on top of hers, but she pulled it away.

He looked at her for a long time, so long that he could see the effect of his gaze. How it opened her, softened her, broke her. Tears came into her eyes and dripped silently down her face. He reached out and with his thumbs he dabbed them away. He remembered how she used to gallop around with her arms swinging in front of her and whinnying, pretending she was a horse.

"How about you?" she asked. "What do you dream?"

Teresa's face flashed into his mind, the dream face that had come to him that morning, in the moment before he punched her. How she cackled at him with her bloody mouth and demanded that he do it again, and how, helplessly, he did it. Again and again and again.

"So far," he said to Claire, "nothing I can recall."

On Monday morning he got into his truck and started it up and sat in it, letting it run for several minutes. He had a kitchen to remodel. The people who had contracted him to do it—a couple from the Cities—had been patient, waiting months past when he said he'd have the job done, knowing what he'd been through. He drove the twenty miles to their cabin without turning the radio on. When he shut his truck off in their driveway he sat staring at the cabin, a log A-frame. Finally he got out and took his tool belt with him. He made it as far as the porch and sat down. He took out a cigarette and smoked it. The day was gray, rainy, and there was a chill in the wind, a good day to be working inside. It was day thirteen without Teresa, and he realized that enough days had passed by now that he could document the time without her in weeks. He would say, *My wife died two weeks ago* to anyone who asked, though no one yet had. And then eventually he would have to say three, or possibly he would skip past three and jump ahead to months and then years, though years he could not imagine, not even one.

When he'd smoked his second cigarette he stood up and got into his truck and drove home and spent the afternoon in bed listening to Kenny G, which he also did the entire next day, not even attempting to work, managing only the briefest conversation with Joshua when he appeared. On the third day that Bruce stayed in bed and listened to Kenny G and cried until it got dark, Kathy Tyson called to see if he wanted to come over for dinner.

150

He said he did.

She served him what she called "Mexican quiche" with a salad that had tortilla chips poking decoratively out of its edges. She thought he was still a vegetarian.

"It looks delicious," he said, standing near the table.

Kathy wore pants that had so much fabric he first thought they were a skirt. Her hair was held back by an enormous beaded barrette like the kind he'd seen for sale at the annual powwow on the reservation in Flame Lake. Every year Teresa broadcast a live edition of *Modern Pioneers* from there.

"Some wine?" she offered, struggling to get the cork out of the bottle. He took it from her and opened it, and then poured the wine into the glasses she held, feeling vaguely awkward. Usually he drank milk with his dinner, and when he drank alcohol he drank beer or the occasional rum and Coke.

"Here's to you," he said, raising his glass, and a surge of joy seized his heart. It had the same effect sorrow had had on him when it was sorrow he had not been used to—as if it had the power to stop him from breathing. It felt like it could, though it never did.

"No," she said, "here's to *you*."

"Here's to *both* of us," Bruce said.

"To us," she agreed, and they clinked their glasses. They each took a sip, and then Kathy looked at him gravely, expectantly, and set her glass down. "So. How was the weekend?"

They had bonded on Friday's walk after he'd confided in her about crying in bed all day and lying to her about Claire being home in time to make dinner. Kathy had been kind to him, had listened and said things that made sense and then had given him a big hug when she said goodbye.

"The weekend was okay, but sad, of course," Bruce said.

"*Of course*," said Kathy. She was going around the room lighting candles, and then she went to the stereo and put a CD on. It wasn't music so much as it was sound. Falling rain, chirping birds, pounding thunder, and the whoosh of what Bruce presumed was the ocean. The radio station played this kind of music each Sunday evening at ten, on a show called *Audioscape*. He and Teresa had mocked it whenever it came on.

"We were all together all weekend—even Josh stuck around. We made a plot for Teresa—for where we're going to put the ashes, her *grave*, I suppose you can call it. We're going to make this flower bed, where we'll bury her ashes and then plant flowers and put her gravestone when we get it—it won't come for a while, but we ordered it." Kathy nodded, listening; she'd already consumed a third of her wine. Bruce noticed this and took a sip of his. "It's nice to have the kids around, but then it's also tough. They remind me of everything."

"Of course they do! They're your whole history with Teresa." She squeezed his arm and then stroked it, the way Pepper Jones-Kachinsky used to do in an attempt to console him. It felt different when Kathy did it, though. It consoled him. "Claire and Joshua are a huge part of your past, Bruce. With them, there's no escaping the reality of what's happened. The three of you are going to have to find a new path in order to move forward."

"I'm not saying it's bad. I mean, I like having them around."

"I know," she said. "Of course you do."

That night he drove home with a spot on his neck that felt like a burn. It was the place where Kathy had pressed her lips. It had not been an actual kiss. He had not, in return, kissed her on the neck. In fact, even his hug had kept her at bay. She had kissed him when they said goodbye, after she reached to give him a hug the way she had a few days before. Women had given him kisses such as this before, kissing hello, kissing goodbye, kissing him in this way hundreds of times right before Teresa's eyes, but now, driving home from Kathy's he felt that he had done something terribly wrong. He wiped the place where her kiss had landed, rubbing it until he felt he had rubbed it entirely away.

When he turned into his driveway, he saw that Joshua was home, almost every light on inside.

"Where were you?" he asked, sitting at the kitchen table, when Bruce walked in. Joshua, who himself was rarely home, was almost never accountable for his whereabouts.

"I went and had dinner." In one hand he carried a pie that Kathy had baked for them. He set it down on the table.

"Where?"

He gestured in a southeastern direction, and then, seeing that would not be enough, said, "Over at the Tysons'."

Joshua nodded. Bruce knew he thought *the Tysons'*—Kathy's parents

—not Kathy herself. Inexplicably, he allowed him to think that. "Because I made dinner," Joshua said. "I made hot dogs and Tater Tots."

"Thank you," Bruce said, sitting down. He looked around. "Is Lisa here?"

"Nope."

"Is everything okay? I mean, with you and Lisa?"

"Yep."

"She seems nice."

"I love her," said Joshua with real emotion, his eyes flaring as they did on occasion, which allowed Bruce to glimpse the Joshua he used to know, instead of the one he saw most of the time now, who kept his eyes dim and impossibly private.

"Is that where you've been staying so much? At her mom's house? She has that trailer, out past the dump, right?"

"But her mom's hardly ever there. Her boyfriend's John Rileen, and they stay over at his place most the time."

Bruce remembered who Lisa's mom was now. Short and plump with very blond hair, she worked back in the kitchen of the deli at the Red Owl. "Pam Simpson," Bruce said. "That's her mom." Joshua nodded. Bruce had not yet opened the card that Lisa had given him. It sat on top of a pile of other unopened cards on Teresa's old desk. "I didn't really know her in school. She's a few years older than me."

"I know. She told me."

"So you and Lisa—tonight you decided to take a break?"

"Not a break," Joshua said, irritated. He held an empty bottle of Mountain Dew in front of him, pulling its label off in wet shreds. He so closely resembled his mother that, at times, Bruce had to look away.

"You just decided on a night apart," he said.

Joshua's eyes flared, then dimmed and became private again. "I wanted to hang out with you."

It had been years since he had expressed an interest in spending time with either him or Teresa. "Well, I'm sorry I missed it."

"You didn't."

"What?"

"You didn't miss it," Joshua said. "It's only ten."

"True."

"You have something on your teeth."

Bruce rubbed his front teeth with his finger and loosened a piece of black bean and swallowed it. "What would you like to do? We could play cards."

Joshua sat thinking, as if considering whether he was in the mood for cards, then he said, bitterly, "Cards are boring."

They sat together not doing or saying anything for ten minutes. Bruce got two beers from the refrigerator, wrenched the caps off, and handed one to Joshua. He got the tune box that had the Kenny G tape inside of it from his bedroom and plugged it in next to the toaster. When the tape started, Joshua looked at the stereo uncertainly, as if about to object—he was adamant about his music—but remained quiet.

Bruce shook two cigarettes from the pack he had in his shirt pocket, lit them both up, and handed one to Joshua, who took it without a look of surprise. Who was he to say the kid couldn't smoke? Cancer, it seemed like lightning to him. It wouldn't strike twice.

They went outside and stood on the top stair of the porch without their coats on, leaving the front door open so they could hear the music filtering out to them. After several minutes, the tape came to its end and clicked off, and they stood in the silence, looking at the sky.

"What are you going to do now?" asked Joshua.

"Now?"

"I mean, now that Mom's dead. What are you going to do?"

Bruce almost said *live*. He almost confessed that his plan had been the opposite—that he had planned to die—but he stopped himself. He almost said, *I'm going to do my best to have a happy life because that's what your mother would have wanted.* Or, *Push on. As we all will do.* He almost asked, *What do you mean, what am I going to do? Do I have a choice in the matter?* And he almost reached out and put his hand on Joshua's shoulder and said, *Suffer for a while, but then we're going to be okay.*

But he said none of those things. He wasn't that man. Not in this instant. He was a man so alone that he could not speak. He remained silent for so long that the silence seemed to absorb the question entirely, so that it would have been stranger to answer than to leave it be. He heard the flapping of the plastic that covered the porch screens, where it had come loose from its staples. He found a loose edge and pulled the whole sheet off, popping the staples one by one. Joshua did the other side and then they balled the plastic up into a bundle and tossed it onto the porch so it wouldn't blow away in the night.

Bruce picked up his bottle of beer and took the last swig. "Can you smell that?"

Joshua nodded.

"That means it's spring."

It was the smell that came to Coltrap County about this time every year, when the ground remained frozen, but whatever lived above it had finally begun to thaw. The smell of old snow mixed with something alive but slightly rotten, like the stems of cut flowers left too long in a vase. A sudden wave of wind came up and hit their faces, so they smelled it even more. The wind was cold and it pushed into their collars and blew through the thin cotton of their shirts, but they didn't move to protect themselves from it. They stood in place, still as statues, until they couldn't take it anymore. Together, they shivered.

10

THE APARTMENT ABOVE Len's Lookout was penitentiary now that no one lived there. An oven hulked in the middle of the room, detached from everything, and a gathering of objects sat in the corner: a rolled rug with gnarled tassels, a chair from the bar downstairs that was missing a leg, a box taped shut that had Mardell's writing on it: *Christmas things*. On the wall hung a perfect mirror. Joshua held his lighter up to it. His face was ghoulish in the yellow slash above the flame, so much so that he scared himself and had to turn away. His thumb grew hot, but he kept it pressed down on the little button of the lighter anyway as he walked around the apartment on that first night. From then on, he brought candles.

After sleeping undetected for seven nights in the apartment, Joshua decided it was safe to change one thing. By then his mother was in the hospital, so he could have gone home — being home no longer entailed having to hear his mother's comings and goings throughout the night, her cries and moans and suffering — but he'd begun to prefer the apartment over anywhere else. The thing he changed was the oven: moving it from its place in the center of the room would make the apartment more pleasant, and he doubted Leonard and Mardell would notice. It was too heavy for him to lift by himself, so he squatted and wrapped his arms around it, clutching it into a bear hug, and walked it from edge to edge until it sat against the wall.

He hadn't had to break into the apartment. The key was still in the place his mother had designated years before, when they'd lived there — in the snout of the iron pig that sat at the bottom of the stairs. In the summertime violets bloomed from a flower box that filled its body, cascading down the pig's sides. Joshua was careful never to arrive before midnight, before the bar had closed, and each morning he left by ten, before Mardell and Leonard arrived to set up for lunch. Each night he parked his truck in town, in his old spot behind the Midden Café, and walked along the highway carrying his things—candles and sleeping bag, notebook and pens and headphones and CDs. When cars approached he stepped into the darkness of the ditch so they wouldn't stop to ask if he wanted a ride.

Most mornings he didn't go straight to his truck. Instead he followed the trail that went through the trees behind the Lookout to the river, to sit on the rock there and smoke from his one hit. Since he'd been suspended from school he hadn't bothered to return, so there was nowhere he needed to be all through February while his mother was so sick that he could not bear to look at her, and into March, when she began to die and then did. And all through April, when she was dead and gone and nothing would bring her back.

On occasion he made an appearance, showing up at home a couple of times a week for Bruce or Claire so they wouldn't worry, and at least once a day he saw Lisa Boudreaux. But mostly he liked to be alone, in silence, or listening to his music as he lay on the unfurled rug in the apartment or sat by the river on the rock, not remembering where the world was. Remembering it, but willing himself not to. Often this meant that he could not allow a single thought into his mind, and he got good at it, forcing his mind to go separate and blank, imagining himself not human, but rather an animal that hibernated or went into torpor. He became a beaver, a hummingbird, saving his energy up, breathing slow and shallow, allowing his heart to beat only so fast. He brought his notebook and pens, but drawing made the world come back, the one he was trying to keep at bay, so he couldn't use them. The world he could tolerate was the apartment at night or the rock by the river in the day, where no one knew to look, and in that world he felt safe and secret and powerful the way he had when he was a child and built a fort in the woods or burrowed into enormous nests in the high summer grass, where he could peep out onto everything without everything peeping back.

The apartment was his and no one knew it, and so was the rock by the river, and so was the river, the mighty Mississippi, and so were the cattails and milkweed that grew in the bog on the other side of the river, which he watched when he sat high up on his rock in the mornings. In February and March their stems had poked up through the snow, so brittle and frail it seemed that it was the snow that was holding them up. But then, by April, the snow melted and the cattails and milkweed remained standing and Joshua saw that they'd been standing on their own volition all along.

When the wind blew they knocked against each other and made a clattering sound like tiny seashells rolling in a jar.

One morning Mardell came to work early and found Joshua sitting on his rock. He leapt from it the moment he saw her emerging from the trees, thinking in a flash that he would run, but he remained still.

"What a surprise!" she exclaimed, not actually appearing to be surprised at all. She wore yellow sweatpants and a matching sweatshirt that had a rabbit on the front. Before the bar opened she would change into jeans, but the shirt she would wear all day. "I didn't see your truck."

"I walked from town."

"It's a nice morning for it," she said, standing before him now, a bewildered expression on her face. "Don't you have school?"

His cell phone began to play the national anthem. He reached for it but didn't answer it, knowing who it was. Vivian or Bender, wanting him to pick up some bags. He pressed a button and the phone went silent.

"Would you get a load of this mud?" Mardell asked, looking at the ground.

"Yeah. Bruce got stuck on our road. It's real muddy out our way. We had to get the Tysons' tractor to drag him out."

"It used to be you couldn't go nowhere this time of year," Mardell said with her hands on her hips. She was a plump woman with a big rear end. "It would be a week or two where you just stayed put and that was that. School was cancelled. Everything. That was back when none of these roads were paved, you know, so everyone was affected. We called it mud days. And then I go off to the Cities, you know, after graduating, and that's when I hear all about this spring break. All the city people taking their spring break. Spring break, I said. All's I got was mud days. Can you imagine?" She laughed so hard then that Joshua could see the work she'd had done at the back of her teeth until she covered her mouth with her hand, self-conscious. She was shy, but not with people she knew. When she finished laughing she took her glasses off and rubbed her oily eyelids and cleaned the glasses with the edge of her sweatshirt and then put them back on. "Heavens, I miss your mom," she said suddenly, and grabbed him.

Joshua allowed himself to be hugged, to be folded into Mardell's arms without folding her into his own. He could feel the cool swath of plastic that formed the rabbit like a placard on the front of her shirt and her plush breasts beneath it, pressing against his chest.

She let go of him and took several steps toward the river, looking out across it into the bog. "Well, I said to Len last night, I said, I wonder when we'll see the first of the bears. They usually show their faces about now. We'll start putting the food out for them any day now, I guess, though Len always likes to wait and see them first. I said, Len, why do you think they're going to come if we don't got food out to entice them over?" She looked at Joshua, as if it had been him, not Leonard, who had disputed her about the bears. Mardell and Leonard had been married to each other for more than forty years, but they were always haggling good-naturedly, pulling whoever was around them in to their disagreements.

"I don't know," he said.

"Well, you tell Len that. He won't listen to me." She laughed and squatted to get a closer look at something in the mud. "You know, your mom used to say that it's good luck whoever sees the bears first. Whoever among us, I mean, not counting the customers. Whichever one of us sees them first, it's good luck."

"That sounds like my mom," he said. "She believes in things."

Mardell turned abruptly toward him and then looked back down. Years before she had taught him how to make a whistle out of a blade of grass held between two thumbs. "What'd you find?" he asked.

"Some kind of bug. The little devil looks like he's got his wings all mucked up." Very delicately she picked the bug up by one of its legs and set it on a patch of ground that was drier, and they watched as it limped back toward the mud.

Mardell stood and patted the dirt from her hands. "Why don't you come up to the bar and I'll make you some breakfast," she asked, though she did not say it like a question. "Len'll be there by now. We drove separate today 'cause I got a hair appointment at three."

"I can't. I've got to get into town."

"What am I thinking?" she smiled. "I forgot all about school. In fact, you should be there right this minute. Come on up and I'll drive you."

"I want to walk, but thanks."

Before she could say another word he began to make his way along the path he'd worn when he'd come here all winter to skip school.

"Do me a favor and come for dinner one night. All of you, the next time Claire's up," she called after him.

He waved one hand in acknowledgment, without looking back.

His phone rang the moment he turned it on, only this time it wasn't the national anthem, but a sound that seemed to him what the wave of a magic wand would sound like if there were such a thing as a magic wand and it made a sound. It was Lisa.

"Where are you?" she asked.

He'd known her most of his life, and for most of it she'd been nothing to him, but now everything had changed. Now he got a certain feeling inside whenever he saw her or heard her voice, like a swarm of bees had been let loose in his stomach, like someone had walked up behind him and said *boo*.

"In town. Almost in town." He stopped walking so he could get better reception. "I'm by the bakery." He knew she assumed that he was in his truck, driving; like everyone else, Lisa didn't know about the apartment.

"What are you wearing?" she whispered in a tone of mock seduction, and then burst into laughter. She was at school, using her cell phone, which was forbidden there, her head tucked into her locker so no one would see. Joshua could tell by the way her voice echoed.

"Come and meet me."

"I can't!"

"Behind the café. In five minutes."

"Josh. Just 'cause you're not in school."

There was a FOR SALE sign hanging on a metal frame a few feet away from him, rusted now after having hung there all winter long. He put his hand on it.

"Well then, after."

"Of course," she said. "Okay. I gotta go. *I miss you.*"

"Me too."

"I love you," she said, her voice husky and serious, almost sad with the weight of what they had between them now.

"Me too."

He clicked off his phone and began to walk again. He hadn't meant to fall in love with Lisa, but now that he was in love with her he couldn't believe he'd lived any other way, or that she had; that a couple of months before she'd been engaged to Trent Fisher. Lisa had been the one to start things up. She called him one night to discuss the assignment they had to do together for their class, but then after he told her he wouldn't be doing it, that he'd dropped out of school, she didn't want to hang up. She talked to him about an argument she'd had with her mom, about how she sometimes had to go to Bemidji to visit her dad's parents even though she had met them only the year before, about whether she should go out for track or not. He was in his apartment when she'd called— she'd gotten the number of his cell phone from R.J.—and he lay in his sleeping bag listening to her in the dark of a Sunday night, which was really the wee hours of a Monday morning, well past when either of them should have been asleep. She told him that she couldn't sleep when her mom was gone, that her mom was gone three nights a week, staying over at the house of her new boyfriend, John Rileen. His mother was gone too by then. In the hospital, two weeks away from dying, though he didn't know it then. Lisa talked and talked that first night, roaming her house, taking the phone with Joshua on the other end of it wherever she went. She sat on the edge of her bathtub and shaved her legs while they talked. She played music and held the phone up to the speaker so he could hear her favorite parts of songs. By the time they got off the phone they were in love with each other, though they didn't say it for weeks, until after they'd spent several evenings in Lisa's bed together and Lisa had worked up the courage to break it off with Trent Fisher.

When Joshua entered the alley behind the Midden Café he saw from a distance that there was a note on his windshield. His face flushed, thinking that it was from Lisa, but when he opened it he saw that it was from Marcy, asking him to stop in and see her before he left. He went up the back steps of the café, pounded hard on the heavy door, and stood for several moments waiting. He went around to the front door, which was locked. He saw Marcy inside, removing chairs from the tops of the tables. He tapped gently on the glass, and she looked up and took two more chairs down from a table before coming to let him in.

"Lock it," she said, walking away. "If you don't, we'll have someone trying to come in every other minute. We don't open until eleven thirty now. Did you hear?" She looked at him for the first time, her eyes were hard, and then they softened. "We don't do breakfast anymore. Not enough people coming in. Everyone goes out to the Kwik-Mart now, ever since they put that breakfast buffet in and they got a cappuccino machine too. It's all this prepackaged shit, but I guess that's fine with people these days."

He sat down at one of the chairs that Marcy had set near him. He hadn't been inside the café since the last time he worked nearly four months ago, the night before he learned that his mother had cancer. Since then, he'd avoided the café and Marcy and Angie and Vern, the same way he avoided most of the people and places he knew before his mother got sick.

"I suppose you're getting by," Marcy said. Her eyes flickered away from his. "I mean, with . . . everything."

He nodded and looked away from her, to the Ms. Pac Man machine in the corner, silently displaying its lights.

"Your friend still comes in every night to play," she said. "R.J. Jesus, he loves that game. He's not half bad at it, either." She reached for her cigarette, burning in an ashtray on the counter. "You don't want your job back, do you?"

"No, that's not why I came —"

"I know, I know. I mean, I hope you don't want it back because it's gone. We would have had to lay you off anyways, with no more breakfasts. Your leave was good timing." She took the last drag of her cigarette and crushed it out. "Oh, well. You won't be needing this job anyway. You'll be graduating and then you're off to Florida."

"California," he said.

"California," she echoed, looking at him meaningfully, like she was about to divulge a secret. Then she turned away and said, "Lucky you."

Clyde Earle appeared in the front door, pressing his face up against the glass with his hands tented around it so he could see inside.

"We're closed," yelled Marcy, and then yelled it again, more vehemently the second time. But Clyde remained where he was until she went to the door and gestured in an exaggerated fashion to the sign that listed the new hours. When he left she came back to her place by the counter. "The Indians are on the warpath about us being closed for breakfast. They used to have their little gatherings here every morning. Never ordered anything but coffee, and then they wanted ten refills apiece. And now everyone wonders why." She shook another cigarette from her pack.

"You got one of those for me?" he asked, though he had a fresh pack in his pocket. She slid the pack down the counter toward him and he took one and lit it up.

"So hi," she said softly, sitting down on a stool.

"Hi."

"It's good to see you." She reached up to adjust the clip in her hair. "I've missed you. My little buddy."

"How's Vern?" He'd despised Vern when they worked together, but now he felt a kind of longing for him, and for the feelings and smells and sounds of the café kitchen at dinnertime.

"We had to put him down to two nights, but at least summer's coming and he's got his things to sell at the DQ. It's just me and Mom now. We can't be paying anyone else." She set her hair clip on the counter. It was brown and shaped like a butterfly. "Mom doesn't come in until noon when it gets busy. Since it's just us two we try to only have both of us here when we need it."

"I could come in to help," he said. "I mean, for free. If you ever need a hand."

"That's sweet, Josh." She bowed her head and put the clip back in her hair and then picked up her cigarette again. They both sat silently with the smoke coiling around them, hanging blue in the air.

"How's Brent and the kids?" he asked.

"Fine," she nodded. Her arms were thinner than they had been, he noticed, her chest flatter. He realized now, after all those months of working with her, that he'd had a crush on her, though he couldn't admit it until this very moment, now that he no longer did.

"I should get going," he said, rising.

Marcy stood too. Something urgent flashed across her face. "Isn't there something that . . . you have for me?"

When he looked at her curiously, she took the dishrag that hung on a hook and began to wipe the counter.

"Vivian Plebo," she blurted, without glancing up. "She told me she called you."

In the weeks since he'd begun selling for Vivian and Bender, he'd come to believe that he'd moved beyond being surprised about who used drugs in Midden. There were the people he'd always assumed, of course, but then there were those he'd never have guessed—Anita at the Treetop

Motel, Dave Collins, whose wife worked at the school, teaching fourth grade—but Joshua never expected to be selling crystal meth to Marcy. He hadn't been able to bring himself to look at her as he'd taken it from his pocket, neatly rolled into a piece of plastic by Vivian the day before. He quickly set it on the counter, and just as quickly Marcy's hand was on it, pulling it toward her, then she ducked behind the counter and zipped it into the inside pocket of her purse and gave him the money she had ready, folded in half. *What are you doing?* he'd almost asked, suddenly schoolmarmish, but instead he took the money, tucking it into his pocket. He pulled on the door, forgetting it was locked, and then unlocked it and let himself out, hearing Marcy's voice behind him telling him not to be such a stranger.

Vivian's car was parked in its spot when he pulled up in front of her house. No sign of Bender's truck. He liked it better when Bender was home, though that was rare, because he was usually on the road, driving his semi to Fargo and Minot and Bismarck and back.

"Where the fuck have you been?" Vivian asked when she opened the door, already disappearing back into the house. He followed her down the dark hallway and into the living room. "I called a bunch a times. Did you get my messages?"

"Yeah," he lied. It was Vivian and Bender who had given him the cell phone and paid for half the bill each month, so they could get in touch with him whenever they needed him to deliver or pick up. He sat on the arm of the brown plaid chair. "I got the one about Marcy and I brought it to her, but then that's the last I had. I need to get more before I do the other stuff."

"What other stuff?"

"The other deliveries."

"There aren't any," she said, looking at him for the first time, a bitter smile coming across her face over having busted him. "I only called about Marcy. She was calling me every fifteen minutes and she didn't want to call you directly—she was too shy or embarrassed or something. She's always been like that, you know? As long as I can remember, like she was better than everyone else."

"Marcy?"

"She's stuck up," Vivian said, as if there was nothing more to say about it, then opened a tin cookie container, took out four baggies of marijuana and another four of crystal meth, and tossed them in his direction. They landed on the cushion of the brown chair. He picked them up and put them one by one into his jacket pockets. Some he would sell whole, others he would divvy up into whatever amounts people wanted. "You need to go by the oven factory when they let out for lunch. John Rileen wants one and Eric Wycoski wants another. After that you need to drive out to Norway to Pete and Autumn's house. You know where they live at?"

He nodded. She looked at him for several moments, as if silently assessing whether he was telling her the truth and then, peaceably, she lit a cigarette. "You got my money?"

He counted the cash onto the coffee table between them, all of it, stacking it neatly into piles, and then he took back a quarter of what was there as Vivian watched, his cut of whatever he sold. It was good money, better than washing dishes, better than any job he could get in Midden.

"R.J. said you're going out with Pam Simpson's daughter," Vivian said.

"And?"

"And I hope you kept our deal about keeping your mouth shut."

"She wouldn't tell."

"Well, her mom sure as shit would. Trust me. You don't want that getting around, kiddo. That Pam's one to watch out for. I used to work with her and I know."

"I didn't tell anyone," he said, trying to pacify her, though in truth he had told Lisa, at least a scaled-down version of what he was doing. "Plus her mom's boyfriend buys weed from me. John Rileen's her boyfriend. Did you know that?" he asked.

Vivian's expression shifted, telling him that she didn't know, though she didn't admit to this. "That's a different story. It's the difference between your boyfriend doing something and your daughter doing something."

"She doesn't care," said Joshua, though he didn't know for sure whether Pam cared. Usually she let Lisa do whatever she wanted to do, like the two of them were friends, more than mother and daughter.

Vivian picked up a pizza box that sat on the floor, its bottom stained with grease. "Are you hungry?" she asked, holding it out to him.

He ate two slices of Vivian's cold pizza while he listened to his messages in his truck parked in the parking lot of the oven factory, waiting for the workers to be let out for lunch. The first message had been received early that morning, before he'd even left the apartment. He'd seen his sister's number flashing across the screen and heard the familiar ring, but hadn't answered it. Now he listened to her telling him that she would be coming home that night and would stay all weekend like she always did and she hoped that he would come home too. He deleted it, along with the three from Vivian telling him to go see Marcy at the café, and then listened to Bruce say almost exactly what Claire had said, only in a less direct, less bossy tone. He would go home so they would be happy and then they would leave him alone for a few weeks. They'd both been shocked that he possessed a cell phone, and even more shocked that he hadn't told them about it or given them the number all those days and nights that his mother was sick and dying and they had no way to reach him. And then, when Claire had at last reached him, it had been too late. She'd thought he was out ice fishing, that he was spending nights in his ice house, and so on the last night of their mother's life she'd driven out onto Lake Nakota to get him, but he wasn't there. As she drove back, her Cutlass snagged on a tree that had fallen and frozen in the ice. It was only by coincidence that Joshua and R.J. had come across her just as the sun began to rise, uselessly revving her engine, her back tires wearing deep ruts in the snow. When Claire saw them approaching she got out and stood silently. She never so much as glanced at R.J. Instead she bore her eyes solely into Joshua. He called out to her, asking her what she was doing there, and in reply she screamed at him so loudly that he could feel her anger beating him like the wind, tearing into his chest and hair and face.

R.J. had turned back by then, off to the ice house to get a shovel, which turned out to be of no use, and then he walked to the shore, to Bob Jewell's, to ask him to come out with his tractor and a chain and pull Claire's car out. Joshua had waited with Claire while R.J. was gone. They sat in the front seat and ran the heat and she told him in a maniacally calm voice that their mother was about to die. He reached over and put his hand on her shoulder and he could feel the way her body was as hard as a board.

"We're going to get the car out and then we're going to drive to Duluth and then we're going to see her," Claire said like a zombie. She said it over and over again, no matter what he said to her, no matter that he said he was sorry about not coming home or going to the hospital or being at the ice house when she thought he was. When she was done repeating it they sat together in silence. He thought of his mother, of parts of her he had never thought about before, of her lungs and her brain, her heart and her hands. He thought of the parts of his mother lying on a bed he'd never seen in a room he'd never entered in a hospital in Duluth where he hoped he'd never have to visit.

"So how is she?" Joshua asked, after a long while.

"How is she?" Claire asked quietly. *"How. Is. She?"* she said, as if each word were a new discovery. "How *is* she?" she spat savagely. She turned her entire body to face him. She wore a hat that their mother had knitted, red, with a white star and a white pompom that wasn't there anymore. She took the hat off and looked at it in her hands, then looked back up at Joshua, her eyes bloodshot and glassy and rabid. "Dying. *Dying*, okay? Do you understand that? She's not ever coming home."

"We've got to keep up hope," he whispered.

"I hate you," she whispered fiercely back, still looking directly into his eyes. "I'm going to hate you for the rest of my life for leaving me alone through all of this." And then she sobbed, making horrible yipping sounds like a pack of coyotes after they've made a kill, and he cried too, the way he always did, seeping and silent.

After several minutes she reached over and put her hands on his cheeks and pulled his face to hers, and he reached up and held her face too.

"I'm sorry," she said. "I'm so sorry."

"Me too."

"What are we going to do?"

"It's going to be okay," he said. "Mom's going to get better."

She let go of him and blotted her face with the hat and looked out her window. There was nothing in sight but the snow on the lake and the trees half a mile away on the shore. "Josh, Mom's not getting better. You need to understand that." She handed the hat to him and he pressed it to his face and wiped his tears away.

"But we have to keep the faith," he said. "She's not going to die. She wouldn't do that. I know it for a fact."

"You do?"

"Yes," he said, believing that he did. That whatever he decided firmly to be true would be true. That their mother would not die, not now, or ever.

"Promise?" Claire asked, like a child, turning to him.

"I promise," he said, then buried his face in the hat again.

John Rileen tapped his fist against the hood of Joshua's truck and then went to sit in his car, parked in the corner of the lot. After a few minutes, Joshua walked over to John's car and leaned in the window like they were talking, though in truth they were trading money and marijuana. Joshua had dozed off in his truck as he waited and had been startled awake by John, so the exchange had a dreamlike quality from which he didn't entirely emerge until he was at Pete and Autumn's house in Norway.

It was nearly three by the time he got back to Midden. He parked his truck in the alleyway that bordered the school's property. He parked here at this same time almost every day, pulling in just as the yellow buses began to line up, so that kids could purchase whatever they wanted once class let out. A couple of days a week, one of the bus drivers ambled over to Joshua's truck, under the guise of taking a stroll, and bought a bag. The alleyway bordered the football field and the baseball diamond and the narrow dirt path that circled around each of them, where the track team practiced. At 3:05, Joshua watched Suzy Keillor escorting the special-ed kids to their buses, as she did most days. Every time he saw her, he remembered that he hadn't returned the pan she'd given him with the scalloped potatoes.

His cell phone chirped like a cricket: Claire.

"Hey."

"How are you?" She sounded like she had a cold, though he knew without asking that she didn't, that she'd been crying.

"Good."

"I was thinking about how your birthday is coming up in a couple of weeks. Are you getting excited to be eighteen?"

"Not really," he said. She remained silent, wanting him to say more. *Talk to me!* she'd recently shrieked. "I mean, I suppose it'll be cool," he said, "being an adult and everything."

"Yeah," she said remotely, as though he had said something profound, and then they were silent together for almost a full minute. Joshua watched the drops of water on his windshield turn to rain, making jagged streams down the glass.

"So, what's new?" he asked at last. She didn't answer, but he sensed that her silence was distracted and occupied. "What are you doing?"

"Sewing," she said very carefully, as if at just that moment she were threading a needle, and then her attention shifted back to him. "I found these amazing buttons in Mom's sewing cabinet. I don't know where she got them—they're sort of Asian-y. They have this kind of tarnished copper gold color and then there are these little engravings of temples. Anyway, I'm putting them on my jean jacket."

"I thought you were coming up."

"I am. I'm leaving as soon as I'm done. I just wanted to call and see if you'll be home tomorrow."

"I will," he said. He watched Suzy Keillor run through the rain to the school.

"I'll make dinner."

"You don't have to do that."

"I want to," she said sharply. "Won't it be nice to have dinner?" Her voice trembled, as though she might burst into tears.

"I suppose," he said. "Is David coming up?" Claire had not brought David home with her since their mother's funeral. Joshua had never been very close to him, though he'd liked him well enough.

"No."

"Are you guys getting along?"

"Yeah—kind of. I don't really know anymore," said Claire.

"What don't you know?"

"I don't know, ever since Mom died I've been different. I've been thinking all kinds of things. Like how monogamy can just be this crock of shit."

"Why do you say that?" he asked, trying to remember what monogamy meant.

"Because it's a system that's set up to self-destruct!" she exclaimed, as if he'd accused her of something. He could tell that she'd set her sewing aside. More calmly she said, "I don't expect you to understand. Not now that you're on this whole new love fantasy spaceship with Lisa. But, Josh, it's true. It's all like a fairy tale and fairy tales are not real. And you know what's wild? I never saw it—I mean I *thought* I saw it—but I never really saw it until Mom got sick. I was walking around just completely believing in these archaic, sexist, ridiculous notions about love and life and then Mom got sick and died and *boom* — the whole truth is revealed."

"About what?" he asked.

169

"Everything, Josh. *Everything.*"

He didn't know what to say. He barely understood what she was talking about, which was true about half the time that she went off on one of her new theories of life. But if he tried to ask her about it in a way that seemed even to remotely disagree, they'd get into a fight. Since their mother had died, he'd entered a phase of avoiding fights with his sister. He had been wrong that morning as they sat in her Cutlass on the frozen lake waiting for Bob Jewell to come with the tractor to get them out. Their mother had died. And she'd done it without waiting for them. *I'm sorry,* he'd said to Claire later. Sorry for being gone all those weeks, sorry for making it so Claire was not with their mother when she died. But whenever he spoke the word *sorry* in her direction, Claire held her hand up, and her breath became labored and heavy as if she would pass out that very moment if he said another word. Except for the first time, when she'd looked straight into his eyes and told him that sorry was not enough.

"So," Claire said. "I was thinking—you could bring Lisa to dinner tomorrow."

"Why?" School had let out and people began streaming out the doors on every side of the building.

"Because I want to meet her."

"You already know her."

"Yes, but not *as your girlfriend.* Plus I barely know her. I know who she is. It's not like I've really ever talked to her."

"She has to work tomorrow." Lisa worked at the Red Owl, like her mother, mostly on weekends. He saw her now, walking straight across the muddy field, toward him. The rain had subsided to a light mist. When she saw that he was watching her, she waved. "I gotta go," he said to Claire.

"No," she crooned. "Talk to me longer."

"I can't."

"I'm bored," she said suddenly, then added, "and lonely."

"Why?" he asked, taken aback. As long as he could remember his sister had asserted that she'd never been bored or lonely—too interested in the world to be bored, too independent to need the company of others.

"I don't know," she said, on the verge of tears. "Why do you think?" He could hear her breath in the phone, the way she wasn't sewing buttons anymore, but focused now entirely on their conversation.

"Because you're boring?" he suggested, but she didn't laugh, even though it was her own joke. *Only boring people get bored.* "I really gotta go."

"So go," said Claire darkly.

She hung up before he said goodbye, but he sat with the phone still pressed to his ear anyway, watching Lisa take the last few steps toward him, to stand beside his window, smiling at him without saying a word. She reached out and pressed her hand to the glass, as flat and elegant as a wet leaf. He placed his hand on the window too, lining it up so perfectly that, beneath his, hers disappeared.

When Lisa got in the truck he didn't wait to see if anyone would come out to buy. He started the engine and they drove out of town, north, to Lisa's trailer, where they made love quickly before Lisa's mother came home from work. Afterward, Lisa got two Mountain Dews and a bag of barbeque-flavored chips from the kitchen and they devoured them in her room.

"How was school?" he asked, and his face flushed, realizing that the question seemed foreign coming from him—a question his mother used to ask him almost every day.

"Good." Lisa was perched on bed, Joshua on the floor beside it. "Oh, I handed in my final project for 'Love, Life, and Work.'" She looked at him with an amused pout. She'd had to finish it without him, pretending they'd divorced. "I can't believe it's just two more weeks, Josh, and then we're completely done. We're free."

"*You* are."

"You're *already* free," she said, wiggling her toes with their painted pink nails.

"Yeah, but I'm not done. I'll never be done."

She leaned off the bed and put her hand in his hair. "But you're getting your GED. That's the same thing."

They both turned, hearing Pam's car pulling up in the driveway. Lisa went to close her bedroom door. They listened to the jingle of Pam's keys as she tossed them into a wooden bowl on the coffee table. Joshua's heart raced, remembering selling to Pam's boyfriend earlier in the day, saying a silent prayer that he would never tell her.

"Leese!" Pam called.

"Yeah," Lisa replied reluctantly.

"I'm home." Pam came to Lisa's bedroom and tapped on the door. "What're you doing?"

"Studying," she said in a shrill voice, and then scrambled for a book. "With Josh. Josh is here too."

"Hello!" he yelled politely. Lisa made a gesture for him to look like he was studying too, so he grabbed what was closest to him, a copy of *Seventeen*, and began to page through it vigorously.

"Are you hungry?" Pam asked, still standing outside the door.

"We had a snack," said Lisa.

Pam pushed the door open and looked in at them, and they both looked up and smiled at her. In Lisa's tiny tin garbage can with Snoopy on the outside, the condom they'd used was wrapped up in a stream of toilet paper. "You staying for dinner?" Pam asked Joshua.

"I can't." He felt he should explain why he couldn't stay, but his mind went blank when he was nervous. He had more deliveries to make. The messages from Vivian had been stacking up, unanswered.

"Next time," said Pam. She turned and walked down the hallway, without bothering to close the door.

Lisa's bare foot hung lazily off the side of the bed. Joshua reached out and held it and then very silently he lowered himself to the floor and kissed it. She laughed without making a sound and then jumped from the bed and shut her door without allowing the latch to so much as click and returned to Joshua and pulled him into her closet, where they wedged themselves in between the wicker hamper and the clothes that were hanging there and made love again, crouched in an impossible position, knocking the hamper over, coming silently.

Out in the kitchen Pam was frying pork chops, their sizzle and aroma filling the house.

As Joshua drove through town, he saw R.J. walking down Main Street, his hands in his pockets. He turned as Joshua slowed and pulled up next to him, and then R.J. got in and Joshua continued driving, out of town, to the Lookout. They didn't get out of the truck when they arrived. They sat in the parking lot, in the spot behind the Dumpster, so no one inside the bar could see them waiting for Dave Huuta to pull up. Vivian had called and told Joshua that Dave would meet him there.

"What happened?" Joshua asked, gesturing towards R.J.'s face.

R.J. touched his cheek and traced his fingers along the scratch that went from his nose almost back to his ear, scabbed over now. "My fucking mom one night when she was trashed."

Joshua nodded and took out his one hit. They'd been over it all before, how Vivian could be. He loaded up the one hit, keeping it below the window, and handed it to R.J., who crouched and took a hit.

"I'm moving out anyways," R.J. said, after he exhaled the smoke. "In a couple a weeks, as soon as I graduate." He watched Joshua take another hit. "I was thinking of heading up to Flame Lake, to my grandma's." He blushed, knowing this would be a surprise. R.J.'s father's family lived on the reservation in Flame Lake, though R.J. hardly knew them.

"To the res?" Joshua asked.

"Yeah, I been talking to my dad, eh. He called me up one day. He's a born-again now, so it's God this, God that, but it keeps him from drinking, so it's not too bad."

"How long's he gone without drinking?" Joshua asked skeptically. He'd only seen R.J.'s father once, when he'd staggered drunk into the school gym to watch a basketball game that Joshua and R.J. were playing in, become disoriented about where the restrooms were, and urinated on the gym floor in front of everyone.

"I don't know. Like at least two months." He took his hat off and smoothed his hair and then put it back on. R.J. had the same name as his father: Reynard James Plebo. "I was thinking of going up to there to live for a bit, you know? Just to check it out and see what it's like living on the res, being a *nitchie*." He smiled at the word and blushed a little because he'd never used it, the nigger word for Indian. "Being Ojibwe," he continued, more seriously now. "Anishinabe," he said, with a strange flourish.

Joshua stared out his window at the canoe in the grass behind the bar. Something rose in this throat. He couldn't quite think what. He wished he were Indian. When he was a kid he had a shirt with beads sewn onto the front and when he wore it he let himself imagine he was. "But there's no jobs up there," he said after a while.

"There's no jobs down here, either," R.J. shot back.

"There's *this*," Joshua said, meaning what they were doing now, selling drugs. "I thought that was the plan, once you were done with school."

"That wasn't the plan. That was never the plan." His brown eyes were defiant and then apologetic, and his face flushed and Joshua knew that R.J. was remembering the same thing he was: that they had had a plan and it was neither staying in Midden to be small-time drug dealers, nor was it moving to Flame Lake. What they'd planned was to move to California together after graduation and become private mechanics for rich people and their fleets of fancy cars. Joshua still thought it was his plan, though now he had to admit that it had been set back by a few months.

"Anyways, I got a job up there," R.J. said. "I'm gonna work with my Uncle Don. Ricing. That's what my dad's doing too. The tribe has a whole operation now where they sell the rice to all these distributors and they might have a casino coming up there too pretty soon." He looked at Joshua hopefully. "If the casino happens, maybe I can get you a job there, and we could both be blackjack dealers."

Joshua didn't say anything, though he was silently considering the notion. He'd never been to a casino, but working at one seemed like the kind of job he'd like.

"Plus, I can't live with my mom no more, Josh. I can't have anything to do with her from now on until she gets her shit together."

"Like your *dad* did?" he asked, his voice full of a rage that surprised even him. "Okay, so your mom's not always the coolest, but she raised you, asshole. And now it's your dad who's this big hero . . . and why do you even call him your dad? He's not your *dad*. When did he ever even show his worthless piece-of-shit face? Not once." Joshua couldn't bring himself to look at R.J. He rolled his window down, leaned out, and spat and stared at it as it congealed on the surface of the gravel. His throat burned, his nose stung, but he wasn't going to let the tears rise into his eyes. He was stunned and outraged by his sudden emotion. He wanted to punch R.J. in the face. Instead he pushed his door open and got out and paced along the length of the truck. The sun had sunk below the tops of trees by now, the light soft and fading. He glanced up at his apartment, at the window with an old curtain pulled over it, powder blue, with cherries dappled every which way. He wished he could be up there now, listening to his headphones.

"He showed it," R.J. said from inside the cab.

"What?" He stopped walking and stood near the open window, looking in at R.J.

"My dad," R.J. pressed gently. "He showed his face. Once. In fact, he showed more than that, eh." He smiled and then looked away and Joshua smiled too, without wanting to, remembering R.J.'s dad peeing on the floor, though it hadn't been funny at the time. R.J. got out of the truck and came around to the side where Joshua stood and they both lit up a cigarette.

"The thing is that I got to get outta here," R.J. said, and coughed.

"Going to Flame Lake is not getting outta here," Joshua said. "Flame Lake is more here than here is. Flame Lake is Midden times ten."

"At least it's different. At least it's somewhere else."

"I'm going somewhere the fuck else too."

"Where?" R.J. asked.

Joshua stood thinking for a few moments, believing that he was still going to California and yet finding it hard to say the word.

"To California," he said at last, and killed a mosquito on his arm.

They didn't say anything for several minutes, swatting at bugs and making small concentrated rings with their smoke in a silent competition until the light faded entirely from the sky.

"There he is now," Joshua said, interrupting the silence, gesturing toward the highway. They watched Dave Huuta's truck slow and turn into the parking lot. The headlights swept hard across their faces, and then it went dark again. Darker than before.

11

GRIEF BECAME CLAIRE. Everyone saw it and said so, how good she looked these days, how thin since her mother got sick and died. Even Mardell noticed it, when Claire stopped in to the Lookout on her way home.

"Good heavens, look at you," she said, taking her glasses off. She was sitting on a stool at the end of the bar playing solitaire, done with her work in the kitchen.

"She looks just like she always did," said Leonard, disputing her, as usual.

"Well, I know she was always pretty, Len. But now she's downright glamorous-looking." She turned to Claire. "But you're getting too thin, hon, if you want to know the God's honest truth. I know that's all the rage these days, this gaunt look, but I like a woman with a little more meat on her bones. Len does too. Don't you, Len?"

"I think she looks fine."

Claire took a seat next to Mardell, relieved to be out of the car after the long drive from Minneapolis. It was a Friday night at nine, but there were only a few customers in the bar. "I thought Bruce might be here," she said.

"We don't see him an awful lot lately," said Mardell. "Though we try to get him to come in for dinner. I told him any time he wants, I'll cook for him. I know he's out there all alone during the week."

"What will you have, sweetheart?" asked Leonard.

She ordered a Diet Coke, and then, before he had time to get it, changed her mind, and asked for a cosmopolitan, a drink Leonard disapproved of, though he made it for her anyway, taking extra time to twist an orange slice into a fancy spiral along the rim of the glass. She'd had a horrible day, which had included getting stiffed by a party of five at work, an argument with David, and a traffic jam on her way out of Minneapolis. When Leonard slid the drink in her direction, filled to the brim, she leaned into it and took a long sip without lifting it from the bar.

"So, I suppose you'll all be celebrating Josh's birthday," said Mardell.

"On Sunday." Claire watched her flip a card and then another one.

"Well, you tell him we got something for him, but he has to come in himself and get it. He's another one that we don't see much lately." She looked up at Claire. "How's your friend?" Mardell always referred to David that way, never as her boyfriend. She didn't believe in boyfriends, she told Claire once. Only friends and fiancés and husbands and wives.

"Great," Claire said, attempting to sound more upbeat about David than she was. "He's coming up tomorrow, actually. He'd've come up tonight with me, but he tutors on Saturday mornings, so he's coming up after he's done."

"What's it he does again?" asked Leonard.

"He's a graduate student. But he also teaches—it's part of his deal, you know, with the department—and he does research so he can write his dissertation. Actually, he's done with the research part and now he's starting in on the writing." She took another sip of her cocktail and hoped they wouldn't ask again what his dissertation was about: an obscure Scottish poet who founded a community in the 1930s based on the belief that a mix of Marxism, free love, and daily artistic expression was the key to human advancement. This seemed like a perfectly legitimate and fascinating topic to Claire when she discussed it with David or her friends, but with Leonard and Mardell it became something different entirely. She'd explained it to them perhaps a half dozen times before, but each time, they could not be made to understand what it was David did, or rather, she could not make it seem to them that what David did was anything but an absurd and comical sham. It was the same with Bruce and Joshua, though they'd both given up on asking after the second time. Her mother had done the opposite, of course, taking an avid interest, as she did with almost everything, much to Claire's humiliation. She'd asked David to give her copies of a dozen poems by the Scottish poet—his name was Terrell Jenkins—and then she'd read her two favorites on her radio show, going on at some length about David's research and branching off into a discussion about Claire's studies at the university. Claire had settled at last on a double major in political science and women's studies—the latter another subject that Leonard and Mardell could not be made to understand, no matter how many times she explained it.

"So, he's a professor," said Leonard.

"Yes," she answered joyously, though it wasn't entirely true.

"Well, I'm glad he's coming up," said Mardell. "It seems like he never comes anymore."

Claire took another sip of her drink. Earlier in the day, she and David had fought over that very issue. Why she never wanted him to come to Midden with her—she hadn't brought him home since her mother's funeral. Why she never wanted to have sex with him—they hadn't made love since her mother got sick. He'd pulled her to him when she came out of the shower that afternoon, after she'd gotten off work from Giselle's, running his hands along her bare hips. She'd moved away, attempting to seem as though she'd only done so in order to more thoroughly dry her hair with a towel, but he hadn't been fooled.

"Fuck it," he'd hissed, and left the room.

"What?" she called after him, trying to conceal the guilt from her voice. She didn't know what was wrong with her, what kept her from him lately. She only knew that something had changed when her mother got cancer. She couldn't see David anymore in the light that she'd seen him before, and she didn't know whether this new way of seeing him had been distorted by her grief or unveiled by it. Whether her life with him was fraudulent or the best thing she had. She loved him and, in equal measure, felt sickened and swaddled by his love. At times, it rose in her throat, filling it like strep.

"Are you having an affair?" he'd asked that afternoon, coming back into the room.

"An affair?" She wore a robe tied with a sash around her waist, her wet hair bundled in a towel on top of her head.

"An affair, Claire. Are you cheating on me?"

Of Bill Ristow, David knew nothing. The thought of him finding out filled her with a dizzy panic and yet also a terrible hilarity. "Yes," she could say and, in that single word, her life would change.

"No," she said, and then made a crumpled, helpless gesture with her hands that she hoped would represent her innocence. In some ways, she truly did believe herself innocent. She hadn't spoken to Bill since a couple of days before her mother died, in another lifetime, really. It was as if

Bill had never existed, though in fact he often came into her mind. Not him entirely, but instead a flash of him. The hair that grew on his wrists, the way he would say "put that in your pipe and smoke it," the shape of his two jagged front teeth. He was the most ordinary man in all the world, and yet in her memory he'd become luminous, like the prince in a fairy tale.

"I would never cheat on you," she said earnestly.

"Never?" David asked morosely. He placed his hands over his face, as if he didn't really want to see or know, despite the fact that he'd asked, and then he removed them and looked at her. "Okay, so maybe you haven't acted on it, but are you interested in someone else?"

"No!" she exclaimed. "No," she repeated, more insistently now. She pushed her hands into the pockets of the robe. It had been her mother's —terry cloth, coming apart at the hem. Her mother had called its color "French pink," though Claire could not discern what was French about it. "No, no, no," she chanted softly to David. Even in the dim light of the room, she could see how deep and tender and open his eyes were to her, and she tried to make her eyes convey those same qualities to him. She was the first to admit that she'd been a terrible girlfriend in recent months. She'd taken to spending hours staring at the ceiling or sitting on the grubby cushion of the bay window that faced out onto the street, going too long without saying a word. She'd previously thought herself a romantic, believed that David was her future husband—they'd even gone so far, in a playful and yet serious way, to propose to one another the summer before.

"Do you promise?" he asked.

"I promise."

"I love you." He came to wrap his arms around her waist from be-hind.

"I love you," echoed Claire. Together they gazed out at the hedge that grew in front of their apartment, its jagged top in need of a trim so badly they could see it even at night.

It was then that David suggested he drive up to Midden on Saturday to spend the night with her and Bruce and Joshua. When she resisted, he'd become enraged. He reached for the ficus tree that she'd nurtured for five years and picked it up by the rim of its pot.

"What are you doing?" she asked, and then watched as he dumped it upside down onto the rug they'd purchased together at a garage sale.

The dirt and tiny bulbs that had hung from the tree's little branches since Christmas fell into a pile, first showering down, then coming all at once in a heavy clump. His anger was like that. Silent, and yet also grandiose. Sudden, and then gone.

"There," he said with his back turned to her, looking at the mess with grim satisfaction. After several moments, he raked his hands through his hair, a gesture that signaled to her that his anger had passed and he felt like a fool.

"I'm sorry," he said, turning to her. He tried to wipe a tear from her cheek, but she pushed him away and dabbed at her face with the sleeve of the robe. "I didn't mean . . ."

"No," said Claire and hugged him and held on. "It's my fault. I . . ."

"I'm so sorry," he said.

"I'm the one who's sorry," she replied, clutching onto him. He was her first true love. The day she met him they swam in a lake together and she went under and opened her eyes, the way she always had as a kid in the river, and he thought this was crazy and beautiful and wild and she convinced him to do it too, and they did—holding hands, though they were virtually strangers—which made them love each other. Until their recent troubles they'd had an easy, happy time of it, drinking herbal tea in the mornings, a bottle of wine at night. Going on hikes and bicycle rides and having long talks and a decent amount of fun in bed.

"We need to stop doing this—tearing each other apart," he said. He lifted the upturned ficus tree and set it upright in its pot, empty of dirt.

"We need to start over," she suggested, really wanting to.

"So how about this. How about we do that thing that Rachel suggested?"

"What thing?" she asked, suspicious already. Rachel was a therapist they'd seen once together—Claire had gone to her a couple of times alone before that.

"Write a contract. A sort of list of rules or guidelines for our relationship."

"Okay," she said tentatively, and David went immediately to get a piece of paper and returned with it, propped on top of a book on his knee. With a blue pen he wrote *Our Contract* across the top of the page.

"You first," she said, turning on the lamp. "What do you want me to do?" She waited expectantly, willing to do anything, and then she said yes to everything he said. She would allow him to accompany her to Midden that weekend to celebrate Joshua's birthday, she would be more emotionally available to him, which meant, oddly, that she would attempt to cry less over her mother—she'd been crying every day, alone in the bathroom or lying on their bed—and she would have sex with him again, and soon. She watched him as he wrote, her heart aching from the things she would do, wanted to do but couldn't, hadn't done but would, would do but didn't want to.

"Okay, so what about me?" he asked.

"You?"

"What do you want me to work on?"

"I wish you'd be better at cleaning the bathroom," she said.

"I clean the kitchen," he said, addled. "And I do the yard."

"I know. I'm just saying you don't seem to notice when the bathroom needs cleaning."

"You don't seem to notice about the kitchen," he countered.

"Look. You asked me what I wanted. Do you want to know or not?" She stood and stepped carefully around the mess of dirt and bulbs and ficus leaves on the floor.

"Okay," he said, softening. He wrote, *David will be more aware of the bathroom.*

"Of keeping it *clean*," she pressed.

He looked up at her. Around his neck he wore a macramé necklace with a single brown bead that she had made for him the year before.

"I think we should be clear," she insisted. "Saying that you'll be aware isn't enough."

To the end of the sentence he added, *being kept clean.*

"What else?" he asked.

She thought again, studying him as if his face would contain the answer. He was handsome in a classic Scandinavian way, his skin bronze already, in May. Each day he walked the mile and a half to the university and back, carrying his laptop computer and a backpack of books, to sit in a corner of the library and work on his dissertation. He'd been working on it for nearly the entire time Claire had known him—two years.

"I want you to be honest," she said, more darkly than intended.

"Honest," he said, writing it down instantly. "That's no problem at all." He took a swig from his water bottle. "Rachel would be proud."

A small huff of air escaped from Claire. Whenever she thought of Rachel, she went into a silent, private fury.

"What?" David asked defensively.

"Fuck Rachel," said Claire, though she knew he was right: Rachel would be pleased and also curious with a kind of craven and vulturous therapist's glee. She didn't know why she was angry, though she sensed it had something to do with the fact that David had horned in on her therapy. She hadn't originally planned to see Rachel with him. She'd gone on her own shortly after her mother died, not because she had much faith that seeing a therapist would actually alleviate her grief, but because so many people had pressed the idea upon her that it seemed like something she had to do. Plus, a small, hopeful part of her believed that therapy would do something to make it okay that her mother was dead. Her meetings with Pepper Jones-Kachinsky in the hospital had, to her surprise, been somewhat consoling. And it was Pepper who had given her Rachel's number and, when Claire had been reluctant, actually called to arrange the first appointment herself. When Claire wrote the time and date of her first appointment in her pocket calendar, a small glimmer of solace washed through her, a sweet tendril of optimism not unlike the feeling that she had in the hours immediately after her mother's funeral. For those hours she'd felt oddly pacified, remotely less sad, briefly convinced of what everyone had told her: that it would be *okay*. That her mother was in a *better place*. That her sorrow was a road that she would travel down, or a river or a sea. And that to her grief, like each of these things, there was another side, an end, a place to which she'd be delivered and there she could be happy again, content without her mother.

This did not prove to be true.

Instead, as the weeks passed and then turned to months, Claire's sorrow thickened, deepened. She came to see that her grief did not have an end, or if it did, she would not be delivered there. Grief was not a road or a river or a sea but a world, and she would have to live there now. The world was different for each person, for her and for Joshua and for Bruce. She couldn't say what Joshua's or Bruce's was, but hers was a place vast and wide. It was everywhere, went on forever. The sky at night in a place famous for its night sky: Montana or the Sahara Desert. And her face eternally tipped up to that sky.

Stars and stars and stars.

.   .   .

After finishing her drink at the Lookout, Claire drove the last miles home with a plate of baked chicken covered with foil on the seat beside her. Mardell had insisted she take it, despite Claire's protests. As she drove, she ate tiny bites of it, tearing pieces of it off the bone with one hand, while she steered her car with the other. It wasn't that she was trying to lose weight; it was that she seldom registered hunger anymore. Her sorrow had taken its place, filling her to the gills.

Bruce's truck wasn't in the driveway when she arrived, the house entirely dark. She went inside and walked from room to room turning lights on, with the dogs trailing behind her, pushing their noses into her palms. In the kitchen, she opened a cupboard door and gazed at the neatly organized dishes. The previous weekend she had taken each dish out and washed it and lined the cupboards with new paper. She reached inside and rearranged the glasses so they stood in a straight row. Since her mother died she'd made a project of the house, taking everything apart, putting it back together. Each Sunday she drove back to Minneapolis exhausted by the weekend's tasks, though they were things her mother had done on a regular basis without comment. Claire did these things in order to approximate some continuation of life as she and Joshua and Bruce had known it, and she did it willfully, almost gratefully, though often she felt resentful and underappreciated by Bruce and Joshua, who seemed not to care whether she cleaned or cooked, or in Joshua's case, that she bothered to come home at all.

She heard Bruce's truck pull in and she let the dogs out so they could run to greet him.

"Have you been here long?" he asked when he came inside, hugging her.

"No. Where were you?"

"At the Lookout."

"At the Lookout." She smiled at him quizzically. "But I was just there. I—"

"I meant Jake's," he corrected himself quickly. "Jake's Tavern."

"Jake's?" She blushed, feeling disoriented, as if she'd never heard of Jake's before, though, of course, she had. It was a bar in town. She'd been there a few times herself, though it struck her as odd that Bruce would go there instead of to the Lookout and even odder that he would get them confused, even momentarily. It occurred to her that he was lying to her, but that seemed impossible, so she shook the thought from her mind.

"So, I got a call today," he said, and sat down at the table. "From the hospital—the morgue at the hospital. Your mom's ashes are ready."

"*Ready?*" she repeated, alarmed by the word. It made it sound as if her mother had been prepared like bread or tea or roast for supper.

"That's what the lady who called said."

"Wow," she whispered. She sat down and stared at the newspaper called *The Nickel Shopper* in the center of the table. It didn't contain any news—only ads for used cars and trucks and old furniture and wedding dresses that had never been worn. It came every Tuesday and was Bruce's favorite thing to read. "Mom's ready to be picked up," she said contemplatively, like it didn't hurt at all. It occurred to her that in a way her mother *had* been prepared. Dressed and boxed and burned. She wondered what kind of container the ashes would be in. A Hollywood version of a genie bottle came into her mind—the kind you rub and get three wishes.

"It isn't your mom. It's her ashes."

"Don't say it's not my mom," said Claire. "It *is* my mom."

"I'm just being factual," he said gently.

"It's a piece of her, Bruce. It's all we have, so just let it be what it is."

He nodded. "We all grieve differently. I understand that."

"I'm not *grieving differently*," she said, exasperated. "You know who you sound like?" She paused. "Pepper Jones-Kachinsky." She said Pepper's name like she hated her guts.

He smiled, though she hadn't meant it as a compliment. It hurt her that he seemed to be healing. More so than it had hurt her to see him unable to rise from his bed in those first weeks after her mother had died. Tears came to her eyes from the realization now: how wretched she was, how cruel she was to want Bruce to be in pain, and yet she did, more than anything. If he wasn't, she would be alone.

"I'm sorry."

"For what?" Bruce asked.

"For saying you were like Pepper." She got up to make tea.

"So, we could go tomorrow. David won't be here till about five."

Bruce nodded, though Claire sensed a hesitation in him. "I was going to run errands tomorrow," he said, finally. "I've got to pick up some lumber for a job."

"We could run your errands and then go afterwards."

"Or we could wait and I'll go Monday," Bruce countered.

"Monday is Memorial Day," she said. "I'm sure they'll be closed."

"Or Tuesday."

"I'll go," Claire snapped.

"Are you sure you don't mind going alone?"

"I'm fine." She hadn't been to Duluth since the day her mother died, and she didn't think Bruce had either.

"Watch yourself on our road. I've been stuck in the mud twice already."

"I'm fine," she said again, and then looked at him accusingly. "I'm not going to just leave her there, you know."

"I wasn't saying we'd leave her there. I was saying Tuesday—"

She nodded but didn't look at him. If she looked at him she would burst into tears. There was something odd in his voice—sorrow edged with guilt—something odd about his entire being since he'd walked in the door and misspoke about where he'd been. It made her wary. Perhaps he *would* leave her mother's ashes at the morgue for days and days that turned to weeks and months. "Have you seen Josh?" she asked, wanting to change the subject.

"He was home a couple of nights ago. He's all hot and heavy with Lisa now, so he stays at her house most of the time."

"And that's cool with Lisa's mom?" She took a dishrag and began vigorously wiping the wall behind the faucet.

His expression told her that it hadn't occurred to him to care. "I suppose so."

"Huh."

"We should turn in." He came to her and gave her shoulder a squeeze.

"I'm not tired," she said. She rinsed the rag out and then twisted it and wiped the same spot again, though it was already clean.

"Good night," she called, several minutes after Bruce had gone.

Her mother came to her not in a genie bottle but in an ordinary cardboard box. It was light brown and taller than it was wide, as though it might contain an overly large football, though it was far heavier than that.

"Thank you," she said to the man who handed it to her. A couple of months earlier, Pepper Jones-Kachinsky had taken Claire and Bruce down to this very office, where the remains of those who died at the hospital were processed, so that when the time came they would know where to go. It was hidden at the back of the building, behind the elevators on the hospital's first floor.

"I need you to sign this," the man said, holding an electronic tablet and a special plastic pen out to her. He was young, Claire's age, and for this reason, she assumed, he was the one who had to work on Saturdays. She clutched the box of her mother's ashes with one hand and took the pen with the other and signed the tablet. Her name appeared on a tiny screen at the top of the tablet, sloppy and childlike.

"Have a nice day," he said solemnly, and held the door open for her.

She glided past him, carrying the box as if it were nothing at all. She walked past the places in the hospital that had become so familiar to her —the gift shop and the coffee cart, the information desk and the community kiosk—and into an area that had been cordoned off for construction when she was there last. It was an atrium composed almost entirely of windows, empty now, the air lush and warm and tropical. Palm trees rose high above her, anchored into pots embedded into the new floor.

She sat down on a bench and flipped the box over in her hands. *To the Family of Teresa Rae Wood* it said on a white sticker, in curly, old-fashioned typescript. She gasped and quickly sobbed, clutching the box to her chest. It was amazing. Her mother. The ashes of her mother's body, in her hands. She realized now that all these weeks that she'd been dead, Claire had held on to one image of her, to that of her mother the way she lay in the hospital after she'd died—altered, but intact—and in particular, the way she'd looked when Claire had been alone in the room with her, after Bruce and Joshua had left and she'd pulled the hospital gown from her body, stripping her naked, to get one last look at her mother: fleshy and solid and cold, but still there, still her mother. And in some way that image had reassured her, had made it remotely possible that her mother wasn't really dead at all, or that she was dead but would come back to her, back to life. That if her body still existed in such appalling glory, that indeed it could be true that at any moment she could appear in their living room, or when the phone rang, Claire could pick it up and it would be her mother, calling to see how she was.

This was gone now, vanished in a moment, the truth, a weight in her own hands.

Slowly she released the box from her chest and sat with it on her lap for several minutes wondering what to do next. She could take the elevator up to the fourth floor and see if Pepper Jones-Kachinsky was in and leave a note if she wasn't. She could have lunch at the Happy Garden, where she used to go with her mother when they came to Duluth. She could go home and wait for Bruce or Joshua or David to arrive. She could do all three in that precise order. But then another thought came to her, which immediately washed all the other thoughts away.

"Welcome," Bill Ristow said when he opened the door. His voice had the calm of a Zen master, his demeanor like that too—as if he'd not only been expecting her, but willed her, through weeks of meditation, to come.

"Hey," she said, and placed her hand on the side of her neck, a new habit of hers now that her blue braid with the bells was gone. She kept forgetting and reaching for it when she was nervous or attempting to seem nonchalant, or, unconsciously, trying to draw attention to the image that she felt the blue braid with the bells had bestowed upon her. She'd cut it off the morning of her mother's funeral and, that afternoon at the wake when she'd had a moment alone with her mother, she'd stuffed the thin braid into the pocket of the skirt her mother wore in the casket.

"Look at you," said Bill.

"Look at *you*," she parroted back to him. They embraced briefly.

"Come on in," he said. She followed him into the living room. "Sit," he said, and she did.

"I wanted to . . ."

"Shhh," he said, holding his hands up. "Let's just be together for a minute. I want a moment to see that it's really you."

"It's me," said Claire, but he held his hands up to silence her again. He sat smiling and staring at her for so long she wondered if he actually had become a Zen master since they'd last met, but then he rose and went into the kitchen and returned with two cans of Coke and an intricately made submarine sandwich that he'd just finished preparing when she knocked on his door. He cut it in half for them to share.

"So how are you?" he asked her.

"Fine. How about you?"

He told her a long story about how his truck had died so he had to get a new one and another long story about what was happening at his job with the Port of Duluth. Claire ate her half of the sandwich while he talked, hungry after having not eaten since having a few bites of Mardell's chicken the night before. From the couch she could see her car. The box with her mother's ashes was on the passenger seat and she felt it beckoning to her like a light.

"And I've been traveling too," Bill continued on. He took a long last sip of his drink. "Here's the places I've been since I saw you." He counted them off with his fingers. "Hawaii, Jamaica, and Maine."

"Wow. You've been busy. Which place did you like best?"

"Maine," he answered, without having to think about it. "It reminded me a bit of Alaska in a way. My youth."

Claire wondered about her youth. This was it, she supposed, and it seemed that it would go on and on and on. It wasn't a pleasant thought. It was like walking across a desert without a hat.

"Did you have fun?"

"I suppose so. More like I got to run away from my grief." He chuckled and looked away, out the window, at Claire's car. "You still got that Cutlass?"

She nodded and smiled.

"It's a good car," Bill said, still staring out at it. He went to the stereo cabinet and began sorting through his record collection. "What do you want to hear?"

"Greg Brown," she said. That's what he'd played for her the first time she was here, though now she could see that he didn't remember it.

"How about Billie Holiday?" he said, putting the record on without waiting for her answer. They listened to the music without saying anything. It was a warm day and the windows of the house were open. The breeze blew various things around the room: balls of dust and hair, an empty pill bottle that had fallen from a tabletop and rolled, pristine pieces of paper that had been lifted by the wind one page at time from a printer that Bill had set up in the corner of the room. All of these things felt familiar to Claire, the breeze and the things blown by it, as if she'd lived in the house for years. And Bill felt that way to her too—his very presence a balm.

"So what about you?" he asked after a while. He sat down on the coffee table so he could be closer to her. "Are you back in school?"

She shook her head. "I'm taking some time off. I figured," she twisted her hands together, "with my mom and everything."

He nodded.

"There's so much to do, getting things all settled at our house. And my brother needs someone to look after him. He's not graduating, but he's working on getting his GED."

He nodded again. She looked out at her car. It seemed to be both on fire and also frozen solid, a block of glimmering ice.

"You have to be a mother to him now," Bill said.

"In some ways." Her eyes went to his and then flickered away. "He'll be eighteen tomorrow, actually."

"A man," he said.

"Not really," said Claire. She thought of Bruce then, of how he didn't treat her and Joshua like kids anymore, ever since their mother died.

"What happened to your little braid?" he asked, reaching out to touch her shoulder where the braid used to sit.

"Oh." She reached for it and got Bill's hand instead. "I just wanted something different."

"Different is good," he said, still holding her hand, their fingers tangled awkwardly together.

She laughed a little, her other hand fluttering up to touch her neck. She wondered what he thought of her being there, if he'd slept with anyone since her. She considered telling him what she'd done with the braid, but then decided against it. He would think it was juvenile. She'd regretted placing it into her mother's coffin almost immediately after doing it. She thought that perhaps she should have written a letter and folded it up and put it in the pocket of the skirt her mother wore instead, or a photograph of herself, as Joshua had done, or a poem that both she and her mother had loved, as she'd initially considered doing. It had been too late by then, of course, as she sat in the front row of metal folding chairs at her mother's funeral, listening to the weeping and coughing and nose-blowing of all the people who sat in the rows of chairs behind her. She'd ached to turn and see who was doing what—who was weeping, who was coughing, who was blowing their noses—and silently she scolded this indecently curious part of herself. Instead, she sat as unmoving as a statue and ramrod straight, as she believed a woman should sit when sitting at the funeral of her mother. She'd had to do what she thought she was expected to do at her mother's funeral because she hadn't felt what she believed she was expected to feel. What she felt, after days of sobbing, was that she would never again shed another tear. That her body was now a piece of ice. She remembered the way she felt like an inanimate object during those long days at the hospital, and now, she realized, her transformation was complete. At her mother's funeral she felt she was inanimate not just in body but also in spirit and in mind. She stared at the ugly chandelier that hung above her mother's casket and felt in sympathy with it, felt some essence of herself emanating back to her from its small glass bulbs shaped like flames. She felt this way about the silver doorknobs on the doors as well, and the maroon carpet edged in cream. She listened as the minister spoke about her mother and life, death and grief, and the fact that that very day was the first day of spring. Claire bowed her head and stared at her lap. Mardell, who sat behind her, took this pose as a sign that she was crying and she placed a hand on Claire's back. Through the holes of her crocheted sweater Claire could feel a dime of Mardell's palm making direct contact with the flesh on her back and then the dime seemed to heat up and enlarge, and it crept like a rash all over her back, becoming a nickel and then a quarter and taking her entire body over until Claire couldn't be the chandelier or the doorknob or the carpet anymore and the tears seeped from her eyes. She shifted away from Mardell's hand and gathered herself by smoothing the pleats of her black skirt hard against her thighs.

She wasn't about to tell Bill all of this, though Bill would be the one most likely to understand. There were things she remembered about him more clearly now that they were in the same room, things she'd forgotten, and things she realized the moment he'd answered the door: that she wasn't in love with him, for one. Not now or ever. That to love him or to be loved by him had never been the objective. That with him she would both never and always be alone.

"It's good to see you, kiddo," he said.

In reply she squeezed his hands tighter and leaned forward so her knees were knocking against his.

"*What?*" she asked after several moments, smiling. He'd been staring at her, silent again, like he was a Zen master, like she was a marvel.

He got down on his knees and kissed her hands, taking them into his mouth, eating them up, and then he pulled her down to him on the floor and whispered into her hair the same thing over and over: "Thank God you came."

.   .   .

On the drive home, it occurred to Claire that she'd been driving on this very highway the moment her mother had died. She and Joshua had been about half an hour away from the hospital when their mother took her last breath. She concentrated on that now, passing billboards and copses of trees, rumbling over cracks in the concrete and past abandoned farms, thinking: *there? there?* A part of her believed she would recognize the place she'd been when her life had changed, but she was wrong. She didn't think about the cardboard box on the seat beside her, or why she'd had sex with Bill an hour before, or what she would say to David when she saw him.

"You're early" is what she said when she got out of her car. She looked at her watch; it was four.

"I packed this morning and left straight from work," he said, coming toward her. "Where were you?"

"Duluth," she answered, not ready yet to tell him about her mother's ashes. She glanced at the box in her car as she slammed the door shut. It would be safe there.

"Are Bruce and Josh home?" she asked as they ascended the porch stairs.

He shook his head and pulled her to him, nuzzling his mouth into her neck. He smelled like sweat and her expensive organic shampoo, which he swore he never used. "We could make use of our time alone."

"*David!*" She pulled away from him.

"What?"

She looked around the porch. "We're not going to do it *here.*"

"Not here. In your room."

"We can't do it in my room!" she said, scandalized.

"We've done it there before."

He was right. They had had desperately silent sex in her childhood bedroom with her mother and Bruce and Joshua sleeping a mere wall or two away several times, when he had come home with her in the past. But this was different, their future sex. It was intentional sex, sex with a purpose. It was the sex that would make it all good again between the two of them. It was sex that needed room, but not an actual room. She'd thought of something else.

"Let's pitch a tent in the yard and sleep out there." She looked at him encouragingly. "That way we'll have our privacy."

He smiled like a boy. He wore a T-shirt that bore the name of a volunteer fire department in Nebraska he'd never heard of and a pair of baggy shorts that went past his skinny knees. She touched his arm, studying it with her fingers, as if she were looking at it for the first time. Sometimes he was that way to her: brand-new. A sting of sorrow shot into her, or nostalgia, or regret. All three, she realized, each one truer than the one that came before. She wished she could go back and not sleep with Bill, or she could go back and love David the way she did before her mother died, or she could go back and never have fallen in love with David to begin with. All three, she realized, each one truer than the one that came before.

Before she and David lived together, he lived alone in an apartment on the fifth floor of a big building near Loring Park, and she thought of that now—thought, strangely, of it often. How she would take an ancient elevator and then walk down a long hallway to his apartment, excited to see him, passing by the sounds and smells that emanated from other people's doorways. How David would open his door and pull her inside. His apartment was clean and simple and orderly, with a futon lying on the bare oak floor, covered by a quilt he'd sewn in a class he took at the community college. It was those sorts of things that made her love him: the futon, the quilt, the bare wooden floor. She remembered herself now being that woman. The woman who walked down the hallway, passing the doors of strangers, curious and dumb and pure and sweet and kind and good. A daughter. Beloved. The girl who thought herself a woman. The woman who'd never loved anyone who'd died. The woman who arrived at her lover's apartment, full of joy and wonder, dressed in whatever she'd concocted from her day of thrift-store shopping, thinking she looked hot and intriguing and cool.

She was older than that now, she believed, with both remorse and relief.

"So, where's the tent?" David asked.

"In the barn." She saw her sunglasses sitting on the ledge where she'd forgotten them that morning and put them on.

"Let's go get it," he whispered, and pulled her to him again.

Her first impulse was to shake him off, but she remained still, her body a sculpture made of stone or glass, her face expressionless behind the blind eyes of her black sunglasses.

And so they would fuck. They erected the tent on the flattest spot they could find, on the grass just beyond the fence-line of the horses' pasture.

Her mother's rhubarb grew nearby, flourishing already, and beyond them, her tulips, the colors fading from their rims. All around them, the hens grazed and rooted, looking for bugs and whatever else interested them. They would be gone by nightfall, tucked into their coop. Claire shooed them away from the tent, feeling sick with calculation about the night's events. She realized that having sex in the yard was a more absurd prospect to her than having to be quiet in her room, but she forged ahead anyway, inflating the air mattress and spreading out sleeping bags and pillows. She lay down, staring at the tent's ceiling, happy to be alone for a moment. It was growing dark, and still Bruce and Joshua weren't home. It occurred to Claire that she and David could just go into the house and do it now, get it over with, but she didn't have the heart to propose it.

She crawled out of the tent and went to her car and got a bag from the back seat. David sat on the picnic table smoking a cigarette. He smoked one at the end of each day, his only vice. "Look what I got for Josh's birthday," she said, walking toward him. She pulled out a wide tin tray from the bag. When she opened it up, it fanned out like an accordion. On one level there was a neat row of colored pencils, on the next what looked like crayons, and on the last, fat markers.

"Cool," he said, smashing his cigarette in the metal dish that Bruce kept out there. "Can it be from both of us?"

"Sure. I figured he could use it, with all the drawing he does." She reached for one of the markers, a purple one, and removed the cap and pressed the tip to David's scalp, where his part was. Pepper Jones-Kachinsky had done the same to her the day before her mother died. It was meant to remind her always that she was a child of God.

"What are you doing?" he asked, swatting at his hair.

"Messing around," she said, more gravely than she'd hoped, and then she smiled, as if she really had been just messing around, and handed the marker back to him.

"Come here," he said, grabbing her wrist with mock violence.

"No," she shrieked, laughing.

He kissed her collarbone and she kissed his throat and then they both recoiled and spat, tasting the bug spray they'd recently applied, which burned their lips like poison.

"I wonder where they are," she said, looking toward the road. "It's not Joshua I worry about. It's Bruce. It's typical for Josh to not show up, but not Bruce."

"It's Saturday night. I'm sure he's just out having fun."

"I hardly think that's what he's doing." She felt heavy with dread over the idea that Bruce was out having fun. *Maybe he was at Jake's Tavern*, she thought.

David tugged on her arm. "Come here."

She laughed, unable to think of another way to say no, and followed him to the tent. It was dark inside, though the light hadn't faded entirely from the sky. David came in behind her and tied a small flashlight to a loop on the ceiling.

"It's glaring right into my eyes," she said, shielding them. She lay on top of the sleeping bags, wishing she'd had a shower. In the close air of the tent she could smell Bill on her.

David adjusted the light so it beamed onto her feet. "Better?" he asked, hovering over her.

"Better," she whispered. She felt almost shy, almost virginal. She reached up and pushed a lock of hair behind his ear and then pulled his face down to her. A lump rose in her throat as she kissed him, but she continued on. She had to do this or he wouldn't love her anymore, or she wouldn't love him anymore, she couldn't decide which was the truth, whether she would be his lover in order to go on living with him, or so she could go on living with herself. She pulled his T-shirt off and then reached for the button of his shorts.

"Do you want to do this?" he asked, taking both of her hands.

"*Yes.*"

They were silent for several seconds, listening to the engine of a truck out on the road to see if it was Bruce or Joshua. It was neither, going on past.

"Do *you?*" she asked accusingly, as if it had been David who had been the problem all along.

"Yeah, but only if you do, Claire."

"I do," she said furiously. She pulled her jacket off and then her shirt, as if to prove it. Sometimes she wished he were less kind. They were sitting up, facing each other in the dark, the flashlight, a dagger of yellow in the corner.

He kissed her gently and then more firmly.

She pulled away from him and put her hand on his chest. "But, there's one thing," she said soberly. "The thing is, there's something you should know. I slept with someone. A couple of months ago at the hospital when my mom was sick. This guy named Bill. His wife was dying too." She said it calmly, matter-of-factly, as if she'd rehearsed it in her mind, though she hadn't. The notion to tell David had just occurred to her that moment. She gripped the fabric of his shorts fiercely. "I slept with him a few times. We had . . . ," she hesitated, searching for the right way to phrase it, ". . . an affair. I know I should have told you when—"

"*Should* have?" David boomed, incredulous.

"I'm sorry." She leaned forward, wanting to push herself into his embrace, but he wouldn't have it.

"*Should* have told me?"

"Yes. I . . . I couldn't. But I'm telling you now." She couldn't see his face clearly in the dark. He unzipped the tent and got out. Claire lay down in the jumble of the sleeping bags feeling miserable and relieved and free. *Free to do what?* she wondered, and then sat up.

"David?"

"What?"

By his voice she knew he was ready to talk to her again.

"I love you," she yelled, and then waited for him to reply. When he didn't, she pulled her shirt and jacket on and got out of the tent. He was sitting on the picnic table, smoking a cigarette, his second of the day.

"I would *never* do that to you," he said, jabbing his cigarette in her direction. "I would *never* hurt you like that."

"It wasn't about hurting you."

"Fuck you," he snapped.

They both petted the dogs, who'd settled in beneath the table.

"Do you love him? I mean, was it a big deal or is it still going on, or what?"

"I didn't love him," she said. She tried to touch him, but he pulled away. "I haven't even talked to him for months," she lied.

"You *didn't* or you *don't?*"

"Don't *what?*"

"*Love him!*" David screamed.

"Neither," she said. "I didn't and I don't love him. I love *you.*"

"Bullshit!"

She didn't say anything for fear of making things worse.

"Did he make you . . . ." He waved his hands in a rolling motion.

"What?" she asked, pulling her jean jacket more tightly around herself.

"Did you . . . was it *fun?*"

"*Fun?*" She thought of Bruce then, wondering if David was right, that he was out having fun.

"Yes, fun," he said. "*Nice?*"

"It was . . . It wasn't like it is with us."

"Huh," he spat.

"It *wasn't!*"

"There *is* nothing with us."

She couldn't dispute this, at least when it came to sex.

"Did you come?" he hissed.

They heard the approach of another car on the road. They both turned toward it and back to each other, grateful that it wasn't Bruce or Joshua. *Maybe they're dead,* Claire thought. She thought that often these days, that if her mother could die, anyone could, and would.

"*Did* you?" he demanded.

It took her several moments to answer. She had. That very afternoon.

"Sometimes, but . . ."

"Fuck you," he shouted, standing. "I would *never* fucking do this to you. *Never!*" He began to walk away from her and then he bent over with his hands on his knees and sobbed. He'd left his cigarette behind, burning in the little dish, and she picked it up and took a drag, then crushed it out and stood up.

"I . . ."

"*Never!*" he screamed again.

She thought of his ex-girlfriend, Elizabeth. He'd cheated on her for nearly a year with a string of women, though she'd never found out about it. In the end, he'd been the one to break up with her, telling her he needed to focus on his dissertation, though, within a month, he was dating Claire. She almost reminded him of Elizabeth now but decided against it. She tried to think of what to say to make it all better again, or at least the way it was before she'd made her confession, though she didn't regret having confessed. Perhaps that was what had been wrong with her all along. Now that the lie wasn't between them anymore, maybe she could love him again. She placed her hand on his back, hoping this was true. He allowed her to inch one hand up under his shirt and then she kissed his neck and his lips and he allowed that too. He remained distant, not kissing her back or even seeming to notice that she was kissing him for several moments and then he relented and held her to him. He removed her jacket and shirt and they got down on the ground and took everything else off, making a bed of their clothes.

As they fucked, she could feel the copper button she'd recently sewn into her jacket digging into her, imprinting its mysterious Chinese symbol into her flesh.

"I want us to go away together," she said afterward, a fantasy playing in her mind. They would go live somewhere entirely different from here: New Mexico, Washington, Connecticut. The names of faraway places made her ache with an excruciating longing. *Here* was where she could never forget her mother. She wanted to forget her mother. The sudden clarity of it was like ice on her tongue.

"I think we need some time," said David, shifting off of her. He pulled his shirt from beneath her rump.

"Time?" She sat up and wrapped her arms around her legs to stay warm.

"To think about us. Whether there is such a thing as us." He was nearly dressed now, finding his clothes in the dark, pulling them away from hers.

"There's an us," she said.

"Not really, Claire," he said bitterly.

A hush came over her, inside of her. It hadn't occurred to her that David would break up with her. All this time that she'd been silent and sad and distant, without joy or lust, she'd expected him to stay, or perhaps, it occurred to her now, she'd been daring him to leave all along, taunting him to go. The truth took shape and turned solid inside of her: he would stop loving her. Of course he would. How easy it was not to love her.

"It doesn't have to end," she said. She began to get dressed, tugging numbly at her clothes. David's semen gushed out of her when she stood.

"Don't put this on me," he said, anger edging his voice again. "It isn't what I want. It's what *you* brought on, Claire. I want you to remember that. This is your own doing."

She nodded, not caring whether he could see her nod in the dark or not. Tears stung her nose, but she wasn't about to start crying now.

"I can go to Blake's," he said, as if he'd planned this out already, his escape. "His housemate is moving out and he needs someone." He reached into his pocket and took out another cigarette and lit it. "Don't worry about rent. I can still pay my half until our lease is up in August. I got that fellowship and—"

"I don't need your fucking money," she said savagely, though she did. It pained her that he could so quickly allow himself to think about the logistics, but then her mind went in that direction too—what he would take with him, what she would keep. Until her mother got sick, she and David had spent most of their weekends shopping at garage sales and thrift stores, buying things together: old coats they both wore and sets of dishes, magazine racks, and rickety tables that they had no actual use for. They purchased a set of glass jars, in which they'd planned to store foods that they were too busy or lazy to purchase, let alone make into anything that would actually become edible: dried beans and seeds, flour and sugar. They'd even bought a rocking chair with a wide comfortable seat. Claire had been fool enough to imagine herself in it, rocking their future babies to sleep.

"There's your dad," David said, turning toward the lights coming up the driveway. She reached for his cigarette and took a drag and handed it back. With that, they made a silent pact to pretend at least for this moment that they were still a couple.

"Bruuuce," she called when he got out of his truck, crooning his name like a song.

"I was hoping David would stay for the day. It's been a while," Bruce said the next morning. He seemed to be looking closely at Claire, suspecting more than she wanted him to.

"He had to get back to work on his dissertation. It's a lot, you know. The equivalent of writing a book." She stood near the counter with a spatula in her hand, frosting Joshua's birthday cake. She'd been up since five, when David woke her, enraged about Bill all over again. They'd fought again and broken up again, more certainly this time, whispering fiercely in the tent. They decided he should leave immediately for Minneapolis, to pack up his things so he wouldn't be in their apartment when she returned late that night. After he drove away, she'd come into the house and quietly baked the cake and then sat watching it cool until Bruce woke up.

"Well, I better get out and feed the animals," said Bruce, without moving from his place at the table. He gestured toward the ceiling, upstairs where Joshua was still sleeping. He'd come home last night after everyone had gone to bed. "I can probably get the stalls cleaned before Prince Charming wakes up."

"And then we'll have our little celebration," Claire said, without looking at him. She didn't want him to notice that her face was puffy from having wept a few hours before. While the cake baked, she'd pressed a cool washcloth against the lids of her eyes.

"So, how was Duluth?" Bruce asked.

"Fine." She set the spatula down and turned the cake from side to side to make sure she'd covered all the bare spots. It was their tradition to eat cake for breakfast on their birthdays. "Actually, it's there." She pointed to the box of her mother's ashes, which sat inside the curio cabinet. After David left, she had placed it there, among her mother's best things, among the breakables and fragiles that she had purchased at flea markets over the years and a few worthless family heirlooms. There was a collection of dinner bells and half a dozen porcelain birds and a single open fan, made of white feathers tipped in black, that had once belonged to a relative that Claire couldn't name. As a child Claire used to beg to be allowed to play with this fan and would sometimes be granted permission. She would twirl it before her face, then peep coquettishly over it, pretending to be a beautiful debutante at a ball, vigorously fanning herself with it until her bangs lifted from her forehead.

Bruce went to the cabinet and looked in, but he didn't open the door to touch the box.

"I was thinking we could spread the ashes next weekend," she said.

Bruce nodded and pulled his boots on and went outside.

Claire walked through the house, picking things up, wiping the surfaces of tabletops and shelves whether they needed it or not, arranging the pillows neatly on the couch. She stopped at the doorway of her mother and Bruce's bedroom—it was only Bruce's now, but still she thought of it as theirs—and looked in at the unmade bed. Dust had settled on all of the surfaces; this room and Joshua's were the only two that Claire left untouched each weekend. She stepped inside and lay down on the bed, remembering the nights she had slept there when her mother and Bruce were at the hospital and Joshua was God knows where. She had thought those were the worst nights of her life. But now she knew how wrong she'd been. How sweet they were, those nights when her mother was still alive, when in the mornings Claire could drive to the hospital and see her and say hello, to ask how did you sleep or did you have breakfast, or to be asked these things and to answer in return. She lay staring at the objects on the table on her mother's side of the bed—a green lamp shaped like a tulip, an alarm clock, and a tune box that Bruce had put there after Teresa died. Claire sat up and opened the little drawer beneath the table.

"What are you looking for?" Joshua asked, standing in the door.

"Nothing," she said. She shut the drawer. His face was still sleepy, his feet bare. He wore a T-shirt that had MIDDEN MONARCHS printed on the front, a relic from their childhood, back when the Midden school team was still the Monarchs, before the school in Two Falls closed down and all the students had to transfer to Midden and together they became the Pioneers.

"You're snooping around again."

"Not snooping. Looking."

"For what?" he said.

"For things," she said nonchalantly, though the question rattled her. *What was she looking for?* It hadn't occurred to her until this very moment that looking was what she'd been doing every weekend since her mother died. Searching for something she would never find.

"Mom had this vibrator thing that was like the size of a lipstick," said Joshua. He paused, waiting for Claire to react. When she didn't, he continued on. "I found it in a shoebox in the closet."

She turned to the closed doors of her mother's closet, stunned that Joshua had gotten there before her.

"I wasn't snooping like you, though. I just needed the box," he said, as if reading her thoughts. "It's all still there for you to explore."

She felt a strange gratitude. She had to keep herself from pulling the doors open this very instant, continuing the search.

"I thought David was coming up with you."

"He was. I mean, he did, and . . ." A temptation to tell him the truth pulsed through her, but then she waved her hand as if the story was too complicated to explain. "He had to get back to the Cities."

He nodded.

Claire looked at the painting at the end of the bed, the one their mother had done, *The Woods of Coltrap County*, and then Joshua turned to it as well. She didn't know if he remembered that the three trees represented the three of them—she and her mother and Joshua. She didn't know what he remembered or knew or what his life was like now. Until recently she'd always believed she'd known—what he did, what he thought, who he liked and didn't like. She hadn't had to work at knowing these things. They'd been, all her life, on full display, and in more recent years, when she hadn't looked closely, hadn't even really wanted to know who her brother was, it had been telegraphed to her through her mother and Bruce.

"Aren't you going to say happy birthday?" he asked.

"I did." She stood. "When you first came in. But happy birthday again," she said, thumping him on the shoulder as she walked past.

He followed her into the kitchen. It had begun to rain, and the house had grown dark though it was only ten in the morning, a storm moving in. Claire reached to close the window over the kitchen sink. Outside the tree branches were waving violently in the wind. "So what does it feel like?" she asked Joshua. "Being eighteen."

"Like normal," he said.

She wanted to say something meaningful about him being grown-up now, but she couldn't think of what exactly to say, so she said nothing.

Bruce came running in the door, wet from the rain and the dogs wet too, running in behind him. A loud clap of thunder sounded and then the rain began in earnest, beating hard against the roof. "Your tent's getting soaked," he said to Claire.

"What tent?" asked Joshua.

Together they went to the window and looked out. She'd neglected to zip the tent door entirely shut, she saw now. A pool of water was forming on its nylon roof. She thought of David in Minneapolis, packing his things. *Maybe he was watching this same rain, thinking about her,* she thought. Maybe he would be waiting for her when she arrived at their apartment tonight and they'd take back all the things they'd said. They'd pull their contract out and read it over, vowing to obey it this time.

"I'm ready for cake," said Joshua.

"Me too," said Bruce. "Happy birthday, by the way."

Claire got a tube of icing from the refrigerator to put the final touches on the cake.

"So guess what?" Bruce asked lightly as he poured himself a cup of coffee. "I joined the softball team. The Jake's team."

"*Jake's?*" Claire asked suspiciously, pausing in her work to look at him.

"Yeah."

"Since when did you like softball?" asked Joshua.

"I always liked softball," he answered, unconvincingly, stirring the sugar into his cup. "And Jake's needed more players, so I thought, well, it's something to do. I have to keep myself busy or I get depressed."

"What's wrong with being depressed?" asked Claire. "*Of course* you're depressed. Something horrible just happened. That's how we're *supposed* to be. Plus, you seem to be coping," she said. "You're back at work."

"Which is my point. If I stay busy, then I'm fine. Softball gives me something to do when I'm not at work."

"What about your knees?" asked Joshua.

"My knees are fine," he said defensively. "It's softball, for Christ's sake. Why would it hurt my knees?" He looked helplessly at each of them. "It's something to keep me occupied."

"Leonard is going to be pissed," said Joshua.

"That's what I was wondering," agreed Claire, assessing her cake. "What Leonard and Mardell will think."

"Why would they think *anything?*" he asked them, and then continued without waiting for a reply. "If you mean will he be mad about why I'm not playing on his team, I think you're being ridiculous."

Claire set the cake on the table and forced a smile onto her face.

"There you go, cowpoke," Bruce said.

The cake was covered with yellow frosting and on its round surface there was a giant smiling face, a black stripe for a mouth and two black dots for eyes. "I was going to write happy birthday," she explained, "but then I thought this would look more cheery."

"It does," said Joshua.

There was a long silence. Claire regretted now not having written *Happy Birthday Joshua* on it, the way they always had. She felt the presence of her mother so strongly now, even more strongly than before, as if the box that contained her ashes wasn't sitting in the curio cabinet but on her chest.

"With all this cake, it's too bad David isn't here to help us," Bruce said.

"I'll bring a piece home for him," Claire said.

"Is Lisa coming over?" Bruce asked Joshua. "I mean, later."

Joshua shook his head and tilted back in his chair. "She's gotta work."

"We could ask Kathy Tyson if she wanted to come over for cake," Bruce suggested, obviously straining to sound casual but trying so hard that Joshua and Claire abruptly looked up.

"Kathy Tyson?" Claire asked. She said the name distinctly, as if she'd never spoken it before, a sick panic filling her. Instantly, she remembered having sat next to Kathy at a wedding reception the year before. How eager Kathy had been to find a man. Claire had egged her on, giving her ideas, laughing and lamenting about men in the intimate way she did with her best women friends, though Kathy was almost as old as her mother. "Why would we invite Kathy?" She took a butcher knife from its block and set it near Joshua on the table.

"To be neighborly."

"What about the other neighbors?" Joshua asked.

"We could invite them too," Bruce said falsely. "It's that we have all this cake."

He had never worried about having too much cake before, Claire thought. She felt that Bruce was emitting a sort of heat that rose to a vibration, and it occurred to her for the first time that he was different now, that the Bruce without her mother would not be who the Bruce with her mother had been.

"Do you two have something going on?" she blurted, feeling tears rise into her eyes. She shook white candles from a tiny box onto the table and began to push them one by one into the cake.

"We've become friends," he said, too gently. "She's been very good to me."

"How so?" Joshua asked.

"She's been a friend, you know. She's there for me when I need to talk."

Claire could feel Bruce watching her, waiting for her to say something, to press the subject harder, so the entire truth would come out. To do what she now realized she always did with him, and with Joshua too, to ask and ask until he said whatever it was he was too afraid to say all by himself. But she wouldn't, she couldn't. This was going to be a normal birthday party. This was going to be like it had always been before. She concentrated on arranging the candles in a formation that went all the way around the rim of the cake, her hands trembling. Satisfied with the candles at last, she looked up. "Who has a light?"

With his lighter Bruce moved from one candle to the next until all eighteen were aflame, and then he turned off the lights. Claire pushed the cake toward Joshua, his face glowing above the candles.

"Are we going to sing?" Bruce asked.

"You don't have to sing," Joshua said.

"Absolutely, we're going to sing," roared Claire from the darkness. And immediately, she began.

PART IV

Company

All the conventions conspire
To make this fort assume
The furniture of home;
Lest we should see where we are,
Lost in a haunted wood,
Children afraid of the night
Who have never been happy or good.

—W. H. Auden, "September 1, 1939"

12

THE GIRL AT THE Calhoun Square Mall ear-piercing shop wore a low-slung apron with three large pockets in the front. In one pocket she kept a purple marker, in another a purple gun, and in the last was her cell phone, which trumpeted like an electronic elephant the moment she pulled the trigger against the fat lobe of Bruce's ear.

"Hey," she said morosely into the phone, holding the gun in the other hand. Her hands were chubby, unlike the rest of her. Bruce waited on his stool, staring, inevitably, at the bony features of the girl's bare abdomen. "Uh-huh," she said into the phone. "Yes. Yes. No," she said in the same monotone each time, with a contempt so entrenched that of all the people in the world the girl could possibly be talking to, Bruce knew it could only be either her mother or her father.

"Did it hurt?" Kathy asked, thumping on his back and then rubbing it, as if to warm him. The earring had been her idea.

"No," he said, though his ear throbbed with a small, focused pain. He examined it in the star-shaped mirror that was framed by tiny light bulbs. It looked like it felt, like it had a fever. He touched the fake diamond stud, but the girl saw this and waved urgently at him to stop.

When she flipped her phone shut, she soaked a cotton ball with a solution and then dabbed his ear roughly with it.

"Maybe I should get one too," said Kathy, though earlier she'd decided against it. She stepped up to the mirror and pulled back her hair so she could look at her ear. She had three earrings on one lobe and four on the other; each one represented something to her, she'd told Bruce, a passage in her life. "We're getting married today," she explained to the girl. "This is his wedding ring—instead of a *ring* ring. He can't have things on his hands. He's a carpenter. They get in the way."

"How romantic," said the girl, her face remaining impassive. Bruce wondered if he was supposed to tip her. He felt that he should. He reached for his wallet, but then Kathy pushed past him, following the girl through the store, and hoisted her purse up onto the counter near the register to pay the bill.

"Do you like it?" she asked, once they had left the earring store. "*I* like it," she said, without waiting for him to answer. She grabbed his hand and kissed it, leaving a plum-colored lipstick mark. "I think it's sexy."

He thought he liked it. He caught discreet glimpses of it as they walked around the mall buying clothes they would wear later that afternoon, when they would be married at the Minneapolis City Hall. He caught glimpses of his new ear in the mirrored walls inside the stores and in the glass of the display windows outside of the stores they passed. He had a series of sensations: that his ear was the largest part of his body, that it was not attached to him but was some hot object, balanced on the side of his head, and then he felt the opposite, that it was attached to him entirely, but also to something else that tugged with a small weight as he moved through the mall, like that of a fish caught irrevocably on a line. The girl had said that his ear would no longer be sore in a few days and in six weeks the hole would be healed entirely. In the meanwhile he was to take care of it. He carried a small plastic bag that held a bottle of solution that Kathy had purchased for four ninety-five, with which he was to bathe his ear daily.

Alone, he went to the jewelry store to pick up the ring they'd ordered for Kathy, a thin gold band, while she was off to buy white sandals. Everywhere he looked he saw himself, in the walls and ceilings covered with giant mirrors, and he realized that the earring made him look younger. At thirty-eight the thought of wanting to look younger had not yet occurred to him, but now that he saw that he looked younger, he felt that he'd become old without being aware of it and he liked the idea of at least partially reversing that.

When they were done shopping they had a cup of coffee at the café in the mall. They shared a slice of banana bread and watched the people of Minneapolis doing what they did in Minneapolis. Usually they saw the Minneapolis people in Midden: people who came up from the city on weekends to fish or hunt or relax on the lakes. Cabin people. City apes. Now that he was here Bruce felt not so different from them as he normally did, as if he and Kathy blended in, unlike the city people when they came to Midden. The city apes seemed to him more humble here on their own turf, less ignorant and less arrogant. He watched them go by with their shopping bags and children strapped into backpacks and strollers, balancing their lattes in cardboard cups. They didn't seem to Bruce the kind of people who should be called apes, despite everything.

A group of men dressed in bicycle regalia came into the café and took over several tables. They pulled over extra chairs all around them and then propped up their feet, their small bright shoes slim as slippers. They laughed and asked each other questions for which Bruce had no context. "Did you see it coming?" one of them asked three times, until finally he got an answer and they all shook their heads. Their legs were hard as stones, sinewy with muscle, and yet also fragile and as brittle looking as crockery, easily smashed.

From the bicycle men, they learned that it had begun to rain.

"And on our wedding day!" Kathy exclaimed so loudly that several people turned quizzically and smiled.

"Here's my something blue," she whispered to Bruce, after the people had returned to their own conversations. She opened a tiny pink bag and showed him a lacy edge of a pair of blue panties and then stuffed them back inside.

He leaned over and kissed her and then kissed her again, longer the second time. She smelled like chemical jasmine from the lotion sample she'd tried in one of the stores.

"Should we go?" he asked. He felt sad, knowing he shouldn't. He wanted to marry her, and yet also his heart ached for Teresa. He understood this was to be expected, another feeling to be gotten through, like all the other feelings he'd had since Teresa died. As they made their way silently through the mall it occurred to him that it was not too late to back out of marrying Kathy. They could continue dating. They could get married in a year. He took her hand, as if to speak.

"What's wrong?" She stopped walking and turned to him, sensing his thoughts.

"I was just thinking, whether we're sure this is the right time to do this."

"I *know* it is, Bruce," she said, her dark eyes flashing.

"I know too," he said uncertainly, not wanting to hurt her feelings.

"I know it *here*," she said, and held his hand against her heart. And she did. She'd consulted her psychic, a man named Gerry whom she called up whenever she wanted what she called "clarification." He claimed to have seen Bruce coming years ago, when he first predicted she'd marry by the age of thirty-five—and now here she was, barely a month shy of her thirty-fifth birthday.

"It's that it happened so fast."

She ran her hand along his arm and they began to walk again. "Sometimes that's how things happen, Bruce. If anything, for me at least, it's more proof that we're meant to be."

They'd decided to marry only the week before. No one knew, aside from Kathy's Minneapolis friends, Naomi and Steve, who would be their witnesses at City Hall. No one even knew they were dating. Claire had asked him about Kathy once, if there was something going on. He'd told her they were just friends, which was true at the time, though it had become untrue within days of him saying it.

In April and May they *were* friends. And in some ways, Kathy Tyson had been Bruce's only friend. He could not bring himself to socialize with anyone that he and Teresa had been friends with together. He'd become short with them on the phone when they called. He turned down invitations to dinner, nights out drinking, afternoon barbecues. Often he quit work early, by midafternoon, and he would drive to Kathy's house and they would go walking or sit on her tiny porch and drink coffee. By May she'd convinced him to join her softball team, and twice a week they drove together to practice in town and then, afterward, for a drink at Jake's Tavern. Kathy Tyson made him laugh, she made him talk, she made him dinner, she made him a braided-leather bracelet with a single stone in its center, and she made him—without knowing she was making him—play less and less often the tape by Kenny G that he'd become ridiculously attached to. Which is to say that she made him for hours at a time forget Teresa and the fact that he could not live without her.

Her cabin was the stage upon which their friendship played. His house was forbidden territory. They did not mention this, nor did they mention the fact that Kathy knew not to call on the weekends, when Claire was home. During the week if Joshua picked up the phone, she was vague and never left a message. But then something shifted and deepened and shifted again. Kathy Tyson rose in him cold like a flood. He loved her. He wanted her. He could not bear a day without seeing her. When he realized this, they had not yet made love. They kissed, painfully and awkwardly at first. Twice he'd had to sob in her arms, so powerful was the feeling that he was betraying Teresa. But then he recovered and kissing Kathy became his solace, his solitude, the secret lovely room where his wife had never lived.

The first time they made love — or rather attempted to make love — they'd discussed it ahead of time. What they wanted to do, what they would do. But when the time came, Bruce could get only so far as to lie in bed beside her with all of his clothes on and Kathy's shirt unbuttoned before he broke down. She stroked his body kindly, comforting him and refusing his apologies. The second time they made love, they actually made love, though their lovemaking was slow and sorrowful and without lust, as if they were enacting a solemn ritual on each other's bodies. The third time they made love, they made love hot and fast and then they did not stop kissing until they made love again, more slowly and tenderly this time, and laughed at the end at how they'd made her bed inch its way from one end of her loft bedroom to the other end, without their having noticed it. They slept there, on the wrong side of the room, until after dark, awakened only by the phone, which rang and stopped, rang and stopped without a message being left, two calls from her mother. The fourth time they made love, he stopped in the middle of it and asked her to marry him.

"Marry you?" She opened her eyes to see if he was serious.

"Yes," he said, almost breathless with urgency. He hadn't been legally married to Teresa all those years, but now, with Kathy, nothing short of marriage would do. *We don't need a piece of paper to prove our love*, he and Teresa used to say, but he needed it now. He wanted it written that Kathy was his and he was hers, that he would never be alone again. He knew it was childish and misguided to believe a marriage document could do that, but he didn't care. It was something. It was more than he had.

"Okay," she whispered, and touched his face, small tears of joy seeping out of her eyes.

She had one condition.

"I know you love Teresa." She rolled away from him on the bed. "And I know she will always have a place in your heart." He lay next to her, listening. She sat up and turned the lamp on and then he sat up too. "But if we're going to get married, we have to start a new life together and move forward."

"This *is* moving forward," he said, grabbing onto her bare foot.

"But I think we need to make it more . . ." She paused, as if unable to find the right word. "To close one door before we can open another. Ritualistically." Her face brightened. "We need to have a ritual."

He knew her to believe in these things. The stone at the center of the bracelet she'd made for him had a curative power, though what cure specifically he could not recall.

"We could burn a candle," he offered.

She pulled her knees to her chest and rested her chin on them, thinking.

"No. It has to be something bigger. Something more connected to —her." She looked up at him and smiled then, a light spreading over her face. "I have the perfect idea."

The following week they spent an hour at the garden store, shaking this packet of seeds, then that. In the end they decided on a wildflower mix, to cover all their bases.

"It reminds me of her," said Kathy. "Just the way she seemed. Eclectic."

"She was," said Bruce.

"Didn't she do a show on them? The wildflowers of northern Minnesota?"

"Every spring," he answered, smiling at the memory.

It was a Thursday morning. The next day they would drive to Minneapolis and get married—there they would be safe from the prying eyes and ears of all the people they knew in Coltrap County—and then they'd return home to spend their wedding night at Kathy's house. He'd asked Claire and Joshua to be home Saturday for dinner and then he'd break the news while Kathy waited at her cabin. He'd planned to tell them about it before he and Kathy married, but when he practiced what he would say to them in his head, the words became muddled and contradictory. At last, a single sentence pierced its way through, one that he could deliver only after the fact: *I married Kathy Tyson.* It was cruel, but clean, and it didn't hesitate to ask. To ask was precisely what Bruce could not afford to do. He knew it would take them by surprise, that it would be hard for them to hear, but he hoped they would understand, that eventually they would make an effort to get to know Kathy. He believed that in the end they would like her. How could they not? And if they didn't, they would have to adjust. He had his life to live.

Before they planted the wildflowers, he took Kathy on a tour of their land. He started by introducing Beau and Lady Mae, and then they wound their way through the pasture and ducked under the fence and walked deeper into the woods to the blueberry patch, the horses gazing after them into the trees, where he and Kathy disappeared from their sight. He showed her the swamp and the place where their old cabin had been, where they'd all lived while he and Teresa built the house, and then he took her the back way into the clearing and showed her the gravesite they'd made, an oval of dirt set off by stones. They stood solemnly at its base, at a gap in the stones where they would place the headstone when it arrived.

"It's lovely," she said, looking around. "Very peaceful. I bet she likes it here in this spot."

Bruce took the packet of wildflower seeds from his front pocket and held them without opening them up.

"Do you feel her?" Kathy asked. "I mean, her presence here?"

He didn't answer, unable to speak. He bent down and removed a branch that had fallen onto the grave. A few weeks before, he and Claire and Joshua had raked through the dirt and manure with their hands, mixing Teresa's ashes into it. The ashes had not been what any of them expected, not like ashes at all, but rather small jagged pebbles with pocks and pores, which looked disturbingly like shards of burnt bone. Before beginning, they had each put one of these shards into their mouths and, holding hands, swallowed.

"I feel her presence," Kathy said in a hushed voice. "It feels very spiritual to me."

"I don't feel her," he said, though he did. He felt her so much he had to cough so he wouldn't cry. She was everywhere—in the air and the grass and the trees—but he would not admit this to Kathy. In knowing Bruce, she had come to believe she knew Teresa. In loving him, Kathy had come to love her. He'd felt grateful for this until now, out here in the clearing, in what he could only describe as Teresa's presence, where it suddenly felt that to even so much as mention her name to Kathy would be a betrayal of the person she'd once been.

"Should we get started?" Kathy asked reverently.

Bruce shook the packet of seeds. They made a rattling sound against their paper container. He hesitated, realizing he should ask Claire and Joshua first about planting the flowers here, but then Kathy put her hand on his back, and he ripped the packet open.

"Wait," she said. "Before we plant I want to sanctify the space." She pulled a bundle of sage tied in string from her coat pocket, lit both ends with a lighter, and blew on them until they burned. He watched as she walked in a large circle around the clearing, holding the sage above her head, the smoke trailing white behind her. She made smaller and smaller concentric circles, until the last one encompassed the plot where Teresa's ashes lay, as well as Bruce, who stood at its edge. She knelt and crushed the burning ends of the sage out in the dirt where Teresa's stone would go.

They were silent together for several moments and then Kathy cupped her hands and Bruce shook the seeds of wildflowers into them.

Joshua and Claire were sitting on the front porch when Bruce pulled up to the house that Saturday afternoon, waiting for him, as he expected.

"We just saw a hot air balloon fly over," Joshua called to him when he got out of his truck.

Bruce looked up at the cloudless June sky. "They're having some kind of festival out of Brainerd. It's in the paper this week." He continued to gaze at the sky in order to delay having to look at either one of them.

"So we were thinking we should go up to the Lookout for dinner," said Claire from the rocking chair. "There's nothing in the fridge."

"It'll be crowded, but who cares," said Joshua. He was bouncing a tiny rubber ball and then chasing after it when it bounced away. "We can sit at the bar if we want."

Bruce continued to look at the sky, as if searching for more hot air balloons. His hands trembled and he pushed them into his pockets to still them.

"Kathy Tyson and I got married," he said without turning to either of them. He said it quietly, almost privately, as if he hadn't spoken at all.

"What?" Claire asked, standing so quickly from her chair that it rocked wildly behind her.

"Kathy Tyson and I got married," he said more slowly and kindly this time. "Yesterday. I know this is hard but—"

"Hard?" shrieked Claire. "What are you talking about? I don't even understand what you're saying." She turned to Joshua, as if he would explain.

"I'm saying that I loved your mother very much—I *still* love your mother—I will *always* love your—"

"Bullshit," said Claire savagely, and then burst into tears. "You married Kathy Tyson? You *got married?* Mom has been dead for two months and you're already married?"

"Almost three. It will be three on Monday," he said quietly. He was looking at the ground now, at a tiny beige row of anthills. He obliterated one with his foot.

"*Almost three!*" Claire howled, as if he'd physically wounded her. "Forgive me if I lost track. Forgive me if I wasn't *counting the days* until I could dump my mother—"

"I'm not dumping your mother."

Claire sat down on the step and put her face into her hands and cried without caring what she sounded like. Joshua sat down next to her and put his arm around her shoulders.

"This is what she would have wanted," Bruce said, appealing to Joshua. He felt that perhaps Joshua would have more sympathy for him, man to man. "She would have wanted for me to move on, you know? To *live my life . . .*"

"What about *our* life?" he asked, his face, his entire self, like a stone.

"Yeah," said Claire from behind her hands. She stopped crying and abruptly looked up at him with her red eyes and demanded an answer. "What about *our* lives?"

"Your lives?" he stammered. "She wanted you to have a good life too."

"I thought you didn't believe in marriage," said Joshua.

"Look, you two are not some goddamned committee that gets to approve or disapprove of what I do with my life. Let's just get that straight right this minute." *Fuck the kids,* he thought. He reached for the pack of cigarettes in his shirt pocket. When he lifted the cigarette to his mouth, he could see his hands were shaking harder than before, which made him think *Fuck the kids* even more.

"Okay, so let me understand this," Claire said after several moments, her voice even and hard. "You believe in marriage. You just didn't believe in it with our mom."

"No. I believed in it. Your mom did too. Listen, we *had* a marriage. Just because it wasn't legal it doesn't mean that it meant anything less to either one of us."

At this Claire began to sob hysterically again. Bruce knelt down in front of her and rubbed her arm. Joshua walked to the end of the porch so he wouldn't have to be near Bruce.

"Don't touch me," Claire begged weakly, after taking several heaving breaths, and when he continued to stroke her arm she cried out "Please don't" so piteously that he stopped.

"Do you love her?" asked Joshua.

"Who?"

Joshua just stared at him.

"Kathy?" Bruce asked.

Joshua made no response.

"Of course," Bruce said, more adamantly than he felt. And he did love her, though when he thought about his love for her his mind careened from one thing to the other, landing almost always not on Kathy herself but on how unbearable it was to be without her. "I don't love her the same way as I loved your mom, if that's what you're asking. It takes years to build that kind of thing, but yes, I love her. Of course I do." Joshua was looking directly into his eyes and then Claire sat up and looked at him with her wet eyes too, both of them looking out of Teresa's eyes. He looked away from them. "What I want you to know is that this has nothing to do with how I feel about your mom. It has to do with the fact that I can't live alone."

"You don't live alone," Joshua said. "You live with me and part of the time with Claire."

"I know—and that doesn't have to change. But I need a companion. I need company."

"What about us?" Joshua asked. "Where do we get company?"

"You have Lisa. And Claire has David."

"*We broke up*," Claire said bitterly. "You *know* we broke up."

"I thought you were just taking some time apart," he said, and saw that this only made her more upset. "Okay, I'm sorry. I mean, you'll *have* someone someday. Someone special. You will."

Claire huffed in disgust and shook her head.

"But they're not our mom," said Joshua. "We can't just go out and find someone to replace our mom like you."

"I'm not replacing your mom."

"You have a wife," Joshua pressed on. "We will never have a mother. Okay? *Never.*" Tears began to drip from his eyes. They made a trail down his face and fell off his chin.

"Josh," Bruce whispered, but didn't go to him. Mosquitoes landed on Bruce's neck and arms and he slapped at them until Claire reached for the bug spray on the porch ledge and handed it to him without a word.

"You're always welcome here," he said at last. "Both of you. Always."

"'Welcome?'" parroted Claire, and then let out a small sharp laugh. "*Welcome?* This is our *home*, Bruce. Did you think we thought we weren't welcome here?" She paused, and then another thought played across her face. "No. No way. Don't tell me she's *moving in*."

"Claire."

"Oh my God."

"*Claire.*"

"Don't say my name," she snapped. "Just don't even fucking speak to me."

"She has a really small house. It's not even a *house*—it's a cabin. It's one room. It wouldn't make sense for us to live there," he explained, though Claire would not look at him. "But this won't change things for you. Your room is still your room. And I think you're going to like—"

"When did this start up?" asked Joshua.

"*When?*" Bruce asked, uncomprehendingly.

"Has this been going on for a while?"

"Not until after your mother died, if that's what you're asking. If you're asking whether I cheated on your mother, the answer is no."

"That's very big of you," Joshua said.

"Fuck off," said Bruce. "I have my life, you know."

"So," Claire said. "Let us get this straight. This means we have to pack our mom's things up, right? Like *tomorrow*."

Bruce thought about it for a moment. He hadn't considered every detail. "It means—"

"Does it mean that Kathy is moving in tomorrow?" Claire demanded. "Just say yes or no."

"Not tomorrow," he said. "For the weekend we plan . . . I'll stay over there. But yes, Kathy will move in. It doesn't mean that all your mom's things . . ."

"Thank you," she said, holding her hand up.

"I'm sorry I hurt you. I didn't want to." He paused, looking at them imploringly. "Do you want me to suffer forever? Don't you want me to be happy?"

"We want you to be happy," Joshua said.

"Of course we do," said Claire, softening now. She turned away from him and looked down at her bare feet, her arms wrapped around herself, each hand holding the other shoulder. "There's one thing I ask, and I'm sure Joshua agrees." Her voice was trembling, so she paused. "I want Kathy to stay away from Mom's grave. I just want that to be our private place. There's no reason that Kathy needs to even go back there. She has nothing to do with Mom. It's our sacred ground."

"Okay," he spat. He knew he would have to tell them about the wildflower seeds he and Kathy had planted, but he couldn't do it now.

"Do you promise?" Claire asked.

"Yes," he hollered, suddenly enraged. "Yes! Yes!" he yelled louder. "I fucking promise."

Neither one of them would look at him.

"Are you happy now?" he shouted so loudly that the horses, grazing near the fence, lifted their heads. "What else do you want? Is Kathy allowed to use the bathroom? Does she have your permission to heat up a pot of water in the kitchen or is that *sacred ground* too?"

Fresh tears streamed down Claire's face. Joshua became incredibly still and quiet, standing on the opposite end of the porch.

"Huh?" he demanded. "*Huh?* I asked a question and I'd like an answer. Is there anything else you want?"

They made no response.

"*Answer me!*" he screamed.

Ever so subtly, Claire shook her head.

"Nope," Joshua said coldly.

"Good."

He walked to his truck and then turned back to them, still seething. "You know what? I'm *not* your father," he said, hating himself already but unable to stop. "And I don't owe you kids *anything. You got that? You understand?*"

He got in and started the engine with a roar. His anger was spent the moment the truck began to move, having left him as quickly as it came, but he continued on anyway, letting the truck roll slowly down the driveway. He wasn't going back to Kathy's. He wasn't going to a bar. He wasn't going to town or to the river or to the lake. He didn't know where he was going, but he was *going*. He watched Claire and Joshua in his rearview mirror as he drove off and he kept watching them for as long as he was able to, until the trees and the high grass and the glint of the sun and the curve of the land overtook them and they were gone.

13

ON MONDAY MORNING Joshua found a notebook. *Lisa Boudreaux* it said in his own handwriting on the back cover, with a fancy heart scrolled around it. A small rush of sorrow and nostalgia and anger surged through him at the sight of it, and he tossed the notebook back to where it had been, amid the scatter of junk behind the seat of his truck, among the half-full cartons of oil and empty cans of Coke and old pens without their caps, and he kept searching for what he was looking for—his proof of insurance. He could picture it in its double-sized white envelope with the little translucent pane in the front. He shoved the seat back into place and turned to Greg Price, who stood leaning against the side of Joshua's truck in his neat beige police officer's uniform. He was the Midden town cop, the only one, and he'd been the cop for almost all of Joshua's life.

"The thing is that I have insurance. I just can't find the papers." He put his hand in the pocket where his cell phone was and said a little prayer that it wouldn't ring. The idea of Vivian even so much as leaving a message while he stood there with Greg Price made his stomach turn.

"You gonna speed through town anymore?" Greg asked him.

"No," Joshua said and then added, "sir."

"You gonna speed once you're outta town on the open road?"

"No sir, I'm not." Greg stood studying him for so long that Joshua looked down. A kaleidoscope of glass shards was splayed in the dirt, white and orange and clear, someone's headlights or taillights smashed to bits. "It's that I was running late to get to my girlfriend's house," he explained.

"Who's your girlfriend?" Greg asked gruffly, his beefy arms crossed over his barrel of a chest.

"Lisa Boudreaux." He put a hand on the rim of his truck bed, warm already, though it was only ten o'clock in the morning. "Not that that's an excuse."

"No, Mr. Wood, chasing after pussy is not an excuse," Greg said, and smiled, as though everything suddenly amused him and then the smile left his face and he continued to stare at Joshua without saying anything for several moments. "Ain't you buds with R.J. Plebo?"

"Yeah."

"Haven't seen him around in a while."

"He moved up to Flame Lake." He kicked the dirt and an orange shard of glass moved a few inches. "That's where his dad lives."

"But I seen your truck over at the Plebo place a lot."

Joshua concentrated on keeping his breath even, though he felt suddenly like he was being choked. He didn't have any drugs on him aside from a small bag of marijuana in a tackle box beneath the seat, which was nothing but a lucky stroke.

"We're friends."

"You and Vivian?" Greg winked at him. "You like the older women?"

"No," said Joshua, blushing. "Me and her and Bender are friends." He looked up at Greg, his face intentionally open and tender, almost directly appealing for sympathy, and continued earnestly, "Sometimes they make me dinner." Everyone in Midden knew that Vivian and Bender were stoners and drunks, but they also knew Joshua didn't have much of a home anymore.

"Bender a good cook?" Greg said, and winked again and then began a laugh that turned into a nasty smoker's cough, so Joshua knew he was off the hook. Greg hardly ever ticketed anyone from Midden anyway, targeting instead the people from the Cities or sometimes Blue River, or, more often than not, the Indians from Flame Lake. "Consider this your warning, my friend," he said, slapping him on the back. "Watch your speed."

"Will do," he called as Greg walked back to his car and got in. The lights were still spinning, their flash muted in the sun.

When he got to Lisa's house she was standing in the doorway, giving him her look.

"Hey, beautiful," he said, and kissed her on the cheek, hoping to avoid a fight. They'd been arguing a lot for the past couple of weeks, ever since they found out that Lisa was pregnant. She'd been moody and nauseated, crying and throwing up a couple of times every day for a week.

He went to the refrigerator and poured himself a glass of juice, without bothering to explain why he was late. He practically lived here with her now, in Pam's trailer, ever since Kathy had moved in with Bruce and Lisa had graduated and Pam had said her "work was done" and had moved in almost entirely with her boyfriend, John. Occasionally, he slept in the apartment over Len's Lookout, when Lisa thought he was up in Flame Lake visiting R.J. or down visiting Bruce. He'd done neither, though he and R.J. kept meaning to get together. Bruce, he saw only around town, at Jake's Tavern, or at the Tap, and once at Len's Lookout. When they met, they'd sit and talk for a few awkward minutes about what jobs Bruce was working on and what the weather was doing or if Joshua had heard from Claire and what she was up to. Last week he'd seen him at the Coltrap County Fair, walking arm and arm with Kathy. Joshua had ducked back into the crowd before they'd seen him.

He had spent the night before in the apartment, so Lisa and her mother could have a rare night alone. It was different than it had been all through the spring, when he'd thought of the apartment as his own secret world. Now it was packed with boxes full of his mother's things and small pieces of furniture she'd refinished and paintings she'd made over the years. He and Claire had hauled it all there on one long Sunday back in June, before Kathy moved in. Most of the boxes weren't even taped shut, as they'd had none on hand and were too frantic to drive to town to get some. Claire did most of the packing, jamming together unlikely combinations of things into boxes: a pair of scissors, a camera, a half-used bottle of Vick's Vapor Rub, and a collection of Johnny Cash CDs might be in one box; a salad spinner, their mother's ancient reading glasses, an unopened jumbo packet of sugar-free gum, and a lampshade in another. Claire refused to throw anything out. If he questioned why they needed to take a half-used bottle of Vick's Vapor Rub, she explained that it was because their mother's fingers had jabbed into it; the gum was possibly the last pack of gum their mother had purchased. Sometimes, in the mornings when it was light enough to see, he'd open one of these boxes and peer inside. The sight of his mother's things alternately comforted and slaughtered him, depending on the day, depending on what his eyes landed on, and what image then leapt into his mind. Once, he came across her moccasins and immediately held one up to his nose and the familiar stink of his mother's feet—a smell he had not until that instant known he knew—shot into him like a bullet that left him gasping and stunned.

"Did you have fun with your mom last night?" he asked Lisa, after he finished his juice.

She nodded and took his empty glass from the table and went to the sink and emphatically washed it.

"I was going to do that," he said.

"We should get going," she said, turning to him.

Today was Lisa's first appointment about the baby. He'd told Vivian and Bender that he needed the day off but hadn't told them why. For now, Lisa's pregnancy was a secret, and they had decided to keep it that way as long as they could. They were driving all the way to Brainerd instead of going to the clinic in Midden or Blue River to avoid seeing anyone they knew.

"Did you have breakfast? I can make you some toast," he offered, but she shook her head. Sometimes it made her sick just when he mentioned certain foods, but until he named them, he never knew which ones they would be.

"I'll bring my stuff so I can study," he said, reaching for one of the GED books that sat in the middle of the table. He'd been neglecting them for months. "I figure then I got something to do in the waiting room."

She made a disgusted sound.

"What?"

"You can go in with me, you know."

"To the doctor?"

She nodded like he was an idiot.

"Okay," he said. "I didn't know. How would I know?"

He stood and put his arms around her. He could smell the lemon drop she was sucking on to keep from throwing up and the gel she put in her hair.

"Let's go," she said, and took her purse from the table, walking to his truck without turning to see if he was following her.

By the time they got to Brainerd, Lisa was in a better mood.

"Do you think it's a boy or a girl?" she asked, sitting next to him in the waiting room of the clinic, a magazine called *Baby* in her hands.

"I don't know."

"It's already been decided," she said, her voice mystical. "That's what I just read. That everything having to do with its genetics is already set in stone the minute the sperm met the egg."

They were fairly sure when that minute was, when the sperm met the egg, about six weeks before, in the little lake behind Lisa's house that didn't have a name as far as they knew. It had been a hot summer, and dry, so most days after Lisa came home from her job at the Red Owl—she'd gone up to full-time after graduation—and Joshua was done delivering drugs for Vivian and Bender, they followed a trail that wound its way behind the dump and over the railroad tracks to the lake. They never saw anyone else there, despite the trail and the occasional signs that other people had been there—aluminum cans in the fire ring, a candy wrapper that blew and caught in the grass—so they thought of it as their secret, private lake. They'd peel off their clothes and dive in and splash each other and then lie peacefully floating on their backs in silence together, staring at the sky. Once, a bear crashed out of the woods and approached the shore. Lisa screamed and Joshua smacked the surface of the water and the bear looked up at them and ran, most likely on his way to the dump. Sometimes Lisa wrapped her legs and arms around him while he stood on the slimy bottom, bobbing to keep both of them up, and they made love, though they tried to keep themselves from it because they didn't have any condoms out there with them. Usually he pulled out. Except for the one afternoon when he didn't. Afterward, they'd returned to the hot trailer and ate the salami and cheese and crackers and cold pasta salad that Lisa had brought home from work, and talked about the fact that there was no way she could have gotten pregnant from one mistake.

"Plus," said Joshua, "wouldn't the fact that we were in a lake make it less likely? I mean, wouldn't the water in the lake . . . dilute it?"

"Maybe," Lisa said dubiously. Her eyes were red from having cried.

And then they waited, forgetting about the whole thing, forgetting it for one week and then two and three and almost four before Lisa took a test in their bathroom and they couldn't forget it anymore.

"Mrs. Boudreaux," a woman called from a doorway.

Lisa closed her magazine and looked at Joshua, fear flashing across her face, and together they rose and walked toward the woman, following her down a hallway into a room that was so narrow it was like another hallway.

"Please take a seat." She gestured toward two plastic chairs that faced each other and then when they sat, she pulled up a chair next to them. "I'm Karen. I'm a nurse here. I need to get some basic information from you first." She opened the folder and began to read the long questionnaire that Lisa had filled out in the waiting room. "So, you're pregnant," she said, still looking at the papers in the folder, and then she looked up at them and smiled tentatively. "And is this good news?"

"Yeah," blurted Lisa. "I mean, it wasn't planned, but now that I am pregnant we're happy."

"Good," said Karen.

Lisa looked at Joshua, her eyes flaring wide for a moment.

"Yeah," he said.

"Well then, congratulations are in order," Karen said, taking out a pen.

They had discussed abortion, but Lisa decided she shouldn't because she was Catholic. *If you're so Catholic, you weren't supposed to be having sex in the first place*, Joshua had said, much to his later regret. They'd ended the argument by agreeing they'd get married after the baby was born, so they could have a real wedding to which Lisa could wear a real wedding dress. Now they were technically engaged, though they'd told no one and he hadn't given her a ring.

"So today you're seeing . . ." She turned to the folder again.

"Dr. Evans."

"Yes," Karen said. "Sarah Evans. She's not a doctor, actually. She's a certified nurse-midwife. She works with the doctors in the practice here and does everything the doctors do pretty much. You'll like her a lot. She has a very hands-on approach."

Karen spun a little cardboard wheel and told them that the baby was due to be born in mid-March. *The week his mother had died*, Joshua thought instantly. He cleared his throat and shifted in his chair. The moment they walked into the clinic, he'd begun to feel her, his mother — and in particular the day he'd gone to the hospital where he'd never seen her alive and instead saw her dead — but now that they were back in this room, full of its smells of cotton balls and rubbing alcohol and whatever they used to clean the floors, he felt her even more. He sat trying to let his mind go blank, trying to focus only on the long list of questions that Karen was asking Lisa, about her health and the health of her parents; most, it seemed, she'd already answered on the questionnaire.

"How many sexual partners have you had?"

"Three," Lisa said, without looking at him. A little dagger of heat jabbed his heart and he forgot all about the smells in the room. As far as he knew, she'd only had two: him and Trent Fisher. He could see her pale face growing pink as she stared at Karen, intentionally not looking his way.

"Ever had any sexually transmitted diseases?"

"No," she said, as if the question were absurd.

"What?" she asked when they were at last alone together in the examination room, left there by Karen to wait for Sarah Evans.

"Three?"

"Josh. It's not like you haven't slept with anyone else."

"Who?" he whispered angrily so no one in the hall would hear.

"It was this guy from Duluth," she whispered back. "It was before we were even *together.* Like, back in eleventh grade I went up there for that trip with ornithology for the science fair and we spent four days. I met this guy—Jeff—and I slept with him once, Josh. *Once.*" She was sitting on the edge of the exam table, wearing nothing but her socks and the gown they'd given her that tied in a few places down the front. He could see intimate slices of her body through the gaps in the gown as she spoke.

"So you cheated on Trent?"

"Duh. I cheated on Trent with *you.*"

"But you cheated on Trent with someone else too." It enraged him, though in some faraway place inside himself, he knew he was being irrational. For him, aside from Lisa, there had only been Tammy Horner.

"Yes," she said at last, miserably. *"Once."*

"I can see your . . ." He gestured at her.

"What?"

"Your . . . *thing.*"

"It's just my pubic hair, Josh," she said too loudly, covering it up.

They sat in a tense silence for several moments. On the wall behind her hung a diagram of the female reproductive system, and then a smaller diagram of the male. There was a tap on the door, and before they answered, Sarah Evans came into the room and introduced herself, shaking first Lisa's hand, then his. She sat down on a little stool with wheels and smiled at them.

"Congratulations!" she boomed.

"Thank you," they both said in unison.

She told them they should call her Sarah and talked to them about what Lisa could do to help with her nausea; what vitamins she needed to take and which foods she should eat and not eat, about not drinking alcohol or smoking or being around others who smoked, then she scavenged through a drawer and found several brochures, which she handed to Joshua, about cystic fibrosis and exercise, miscarriage and nutrition, and then another one entitled "Special Circumstances: Teen Pregnancy" that featured a worried-looking Latino couple on the cover. Sarah's hair was cut short like a boy's, like Joshua's, like she didn't do a thing with it aside from keeping it clean; she wore no makeup or jewelry. She reminded him remotely of the women who used to come to the school to teach their special sexual education courses or women who volunteered at the radio station with his mother, particularly the women who hosted a show called *A Woman's Place*, though she did not remind him, actually, of his mother. She was too athletic-looking and self-assured, too possibly a lesbian, like half the women who worked on *A Woman's Place*. When she was done talking to them about everything they needed to do now that Lisa was pregnant, Sarah asked if Lisa minded if a student came in to observe the exam. When Lisa said no, a man named Michael materialized immediately, as if he'd been standing outside the door listening in, or Sarah Evans had pressed a secret button indicating that it was okay for him to enter. They each shook his hand and he retreated to the corner of the room to stand near Lisa's feet.

Lisa lay back on the table and Sarah untied the gown at the top, exposing her body from the waist up. Sarah pressed the flesh around one breast and then the other, working her way in toward her nipples in concentric circles, not looking down at Lisa, but past her as if trying to rely only on what she felt rather than saw. Joshua couldn't help but blush. Why he had to be here for this, he did not know. A dizzy, almost sick, feeling rose inside of him, like he could burst into hysterical laughter at any moment, though he urgently knew he must not do so. He looked at Michael, who was looking in the direction of Sarah and Lisa, but seemed to be thinking of something else entirely, something grim or incredibly boring, going by the expression on his face.

"Think we're going to get rain anytime soon?" he asked him.

Michael shifted his eyes to Joshua, uncomprehending for a moment. "Oh—yeah—I don't know. It's been awfully dry, hasn't it?"

"It sure has," he nodded, and stared at the floor, trying to think of what else to say, hoping that Michael would pick it up from here.

"Do you see these veins?" Sarah asked when she had finished prodding Lisa's breasts.

"Yeah," Lisa said hesitantly, looking down at herself.

"Here." Sarah pulled on a mirror that was attached to the wall on the end of an expandable accordion arm that could reach halfway across the room. "You can really see them from this angle," she said, and positioned the mirror beneath Lisa's breasts. "All these blue veins."

"Check this out, Josh," Lisa said.

He stood by her head and gazed impassively at her swollen breasts. A network of blue veins crisscrossed over them like the lines on a road map. "Is that a good thing?" he asked.

"Totally normal. It's the breasts preparing for lactation," said Sarah, and pushed the mirror away. "Can I get you to slide down here?"

Lisa pulled the gown over her chest and scooted down to the end of the table and put her feet up in the stirrups. The gown over her knees formed a tent behind which Sarah worked by the light of a very bright beam that pointed directly between Lisa's legs. Joshua stood near Lisa's head, not sure where he should be, as Sarah reached for a tube of lubricant and then for a metal device. Again he had the mad urge to laugh. He had to cough in order to stop himself.

"Now I'm going in," Sarah said. "You'll just feel a little pressure." He could hear the metal device click and then it made a horrible cranking sound like a miniature car jack. He stroked Lisa's hair, trying to comfort her, but her hands fluttered up to stop him and their eyes met and he knew that their argument about how many lovers she'd had was over. He squeezed her hand, feeling protective of her, like it was the two of them against Sarah Evans and Michael.

"It all looks good," Sarah said after a few minutes, peeking over the gown. Joshua glanced at Michael, who was staring directly at Lisa's exposed parts in the beam of light. He felt like going over and smacking him in the head.

"Have you ever seen your cervix?" asked Sarah.

"No," said Lisa. In that single word Joshua could hear all of her uncertainty—over whether she ever wanted to see her cervix and also over what, exactly, a cervix was in the first place—but Sarah pressed on.

"Everyone should see their cervix at least once." She pulled the mirror toward her again, flipping it over to the side that was magnified, and positioned it a few inches away from Lisa's vagina. Lisa pushed herself up onto her elbows and then leaned awkwardly forward, her feet still in the stirrups. "Wow," she said after several moments. She lay back down and looked up at him. "You want to see it, Josh?"

He didn't, but he knew it would cause trouble if he said so. Wordlessly, he stepped forward to look into the mirror. The metal contraption held Lisa's vagina open like a tunnel and at the end of it there was a round, wet-looking bulb, slightly blue, slightly pink, covered with a glaze of whitish goop. It reminded him of the faces of a litter of mice he'd seen once; they'd been born in the barn moments before he'd come across them, blind and translucent and wet and gaping and repulsive as creatures from a science-fiction film.

"Cool," he said, and returned to his station near Lisa's head.

"Just think, Josh, that's where our baby is."

"Well, almost," corrected Sarah, removing the metal device, and switching the lamp off. "Your baby is actually in your uterus." She tapped on Lisa's knee. "You can put your legs down. We're all done."

She flicked off her gloves and came to stand in front of the diagram on the wall, tracing over its laminated surface as she walked them through the reproductive system, first female, then male, like they were two kids.

By four they were back in Midden, in the parking lot of the Red Owl. Lisa had exchanged her day shift for a night shift so she could go to her appointment. Her mother worked at Red Owl too, so she'd had to concoct an excuse: that she and Joshua were driving to Brainerd to go out to lunch to celebrate their six-month anniversary, which was not completely a lie, since indeed today was that day.

"See you at nine," Lisa said, and kissed him before getting out of the truck. They'd had a good afternoon, having not fought since they were at the clinic.

After she left, he had to get to work too. He'd promised Vivian and Bender he'd do the day's deliveries that evening, just as he had the evening before. He'd taken yesterday off too, so he could drive to Minneapolis and help Claire move out of her apartment and into a house where she'd rented a room. When he'd gotten back to Midden he needed to make only a few deliveries, Sunday being his slowest night. As he drove out of the Red Owl parking lot, he clicked his cell phone on and listened to his messages. He had fourteen. Aside from one from Mardell, inviting him and Lisa to dinner, and another from Claire, thanking him for helping her the day before, they were all from Vivian or from people who had somehow gotten his cell phone number and had taken to calling him directly to get their drugs.

He dialed Claire's number and got her recorded voice. It struck him for the first time how much she sounded like their mother, not in person, but the way she had sounded on her radio show, smooth and cheerful. He missed her more than he guessed he would, now that she stayed in Minneapolis on the weekends. Since Bruce married Kathy, she'd come up to Midden only once, for the annual Fourth of July bash at Len's Lookout. Bruce and Kathy had been there too, though he and Claire had escaped them as soon as they could. One after the other, they'd shaken Kathy's hand, as if they were meeting her for the very first time, and in some way they were—they had not seen her since she had become Bruce's wife. With Bruce, they each exchanged a stiff hug and discussed how the animals were. They sauntered apart then, Bruce and Kathy going inside the bar, and Claire and Joshua heading to the tent, where there was a band and a keg, a shadow of grief settling over them. The rest of the afternoon he and Claire sat together on the bench behind the bar where they used to sit to watch the bears when they were kids, talking in the kind of open, lucid, sentimental way that they did when they were both slightly drunk—Joshua, being underage, had snuck sips of beer from Claire's cup. Together they remembered things that no one else would remember. The way, for a time, they'd had only one bicycle between them, and how, instead of taking turns with it, they would pile on together, one of them inevitably balanced painfully on the metal bar that ran between the seat and the handlebars. Or how they used to play Madam Bettina Von So and So with their mother. Or the time when they couldn't any longer resist the urge to see what would happen if they pulled the pin on the little fire extinguisher that hung near their wood stove.

"Hey. It's me. Just calling to say hi," Joshua said, after her machine beeped, and then he clicked his phone off and drove to Vivian and Bender's and picked up what he needed for his deliveries.

He did not so much think of himself as a drug dealer as a mailman who brought only good mail. Most people were happy to see him and aside from the few who were paranoid or tweaking on meth, they were nice to him, offering him coffee and cake, or on occasion an entire meal. He came to know their houses, their gardens, their dogs and kids. And then other times, a different, darker reality would come crashing in and he hated his job and the ugliness in which he had become an active participant. He resented Vivian and Bender for sucking him in, for behaving like they owned him, for calling him night and day to order him around. Incrementally, over the months, he'd begun to put his foot down about whom he would sell to and whom he wouldn't, especially if the drug of choice was meth. It wasn't selling to the kids at the high school that bothered him. He did not think of them as kids, and even in the case of those he did—the ninth and tenth graders—he did not feel responsible for them. They were self-contained and powerless, incapable of truly ruining anyone's life but their own. It was the mothers and the fathers that disturbed him. His refusal to sell meth to certain people began with Marcy from the café. The last time he'd seen her she'd looked haggard and grossly thin. Her husband had left her by then and she didn't work at the café anymore—to everyone's astonishment, her own mother had fired her. She sat and made clove oranges at her kitchen table while her children ranged freely through the house, getting into things. He'd had to suggest that one be given a bath; he'd had to keep the youngest, a three-year-old, from eating Marcy's tube of lipstick, prying it from the tiny wet clench of her hand. In response, Marcy had laughed hysterically, cackling so hard she practically fell off her chair. From Marcy, he branched out, refusing to sell meth to anyone with kids under the age of fourteen, a decision that enraged Vivian, but about which she could do nothing. Joshua knew that his decision meant little in the end: everyone who wanted meth still got it. They came to Vivian and Bender, or Vivian and Bender went to them, or some of them stopped buying it and learned how to make it at home themselves. But it meant something to Joshua, to his idea of the world and what a mother should do and what a father should do: prevent, at the very least, their children from consuming cosmetics.

It was nearly eight when he finished his deliveries—too late to drive out to Lisa's only to turn around and be back in town by nine and too early to pick her up from work. He drove past the Midden Café and the bowling alley, past the closed-down bakery and the motel, past the Red

Owl, where he could see Lisa sitting on a high stool behind her register in the fluorescent glow of lights. She didn't see him. He considered stopping and going in. He could stand in the magazine section, reading magazines he'd never dream of buying, until she got off work. He did that sometimes in the late afternoons, after he'd finished his deliveries, waiting for Lisa to finish her shift.

He drove to the Dairy Queen and parked. He'd started coming here lately on the nights that Lisa was so tired that she fell asleep immediately after dinner. He would have a slush and talk to the girls who worked there. He knew them all from school: Emily and Heidi and Caitlyn and Tara, any two of them, depending on the night.

He watched Heidi sweeping the floor, and then she walked into the back and the big red and white DQ sign outside went dark. She appeared again to lock the glass door, a thick ring of keys in her hand. When she saw Joshua sitting in his truck, she waved and he got out.

"Hey," she called. She held the door open for him and then locked it behind him.

He looked toward the back to see who would be there, making Dilly bars or stocking the flavorings.

"It's just me," Heidi explained. "Caitlyn went home early because we were so slow."

He sat on the counter and pushed a button on the cash register so it sprang open with a ring.

"Don't!" yelled Heidi, though she was smiling. She slammed the money drawer shut and punched his arm.

"Where's your girlfriend?" she asked.

"I don't got one," he said. It had become a familiar refrain between him and the girls at the Dairy Queen. They teased him about Lisa, and he would deny his love for her so adamantly that, at least in those moments, it felt true. He became giddy and uncharacteristically boisterous while at the DQ, flirting and joking with these girls he only half knew. It was as if he'd been cut loose entirely and set free from the people and things that composed his actual life.

"Make me a slush," he ordered, tapping the top of Heidi's head. She was a year younger than him, just out of eleventh grade, short and blond.

"Go make yourself a slush," she said, but then she got a cup and asked what kind.

"Suicide," he said, and watched her as she put a bit of each flavor into the cup. She gave it to him without making him pay. Seldom did they ask him to pay. A rich guy from Duluth owned the Dairy Queen. He owned several, all across the state.

"So, how's Brad?" he asked in a mockingly sweet tone, as she mopped the floor. Brad was Heidi's boyfriend who lived in Montana. Joshua poked fun of the two of them the same way Heidi teased him about Lisa.

"We broke up," she answered. She stopped mopping and looked at him earnestly, hurt flashing across her face. Her eyes were brown and lined with black eyeliner that had melted and smudged.

"You'll get back together," said Joshua dismissively, not wanting to encourage her to confide in him. He leapt from the counter and walked into the back, where he'd never been before. There was an enormous freezer and a walk-in cooler and an industrial-sized sink and shelves piled high with boxes of DQ cones and napkins and toppings and giant unopened cans of liquid fudge.

"What are you doing?" Heidi asked, dragging the mop and bucket behind her.

"Checking things out."

She took off her brown DQ shirt and tossed it on top of the freezer. Underneath, she wore a white tank top, through which Joshua could see the whiter outline of her bra.

He leaned toward her urgently and kissed her with an open mouth. She pressed her tongue against his in an unpleasant, pulsing pattern.

"Do you have to work tomorrow?" Heidi whispered, pulling back from him.

"Yeah." For the benefit of Claire and Bruce and whoever else bothered to inquire, Joshua had concocted a part-time job logging with Jim Swanson—which in truth he'd done for three days last spring.

"Well, I have the day off, in case you want to hang out."

He didn't want to hang out. The idea that he would see Heidi tomorrow was preposterous to him, but he didn't have to pretend otherwise because his phone rang. He pulled it out of his pocket and saw that it was Vivian and pressed a button so it went silent.

"Was that your girlfriend?" Heidi asked, and laughed. She hopped up to sit on the freezer and swung her feet out to him and hooked his thigh between her sneakers. Desire rippled instantly through him and he allowed himself to be dragged in between her legs. He rested his hands on top of her thighs noncommittally, then moved them to her hips and held on. He could feel the points of her hipbones jutting through the brown pants of her uniform under his thumbs. She smelled like the DQ, like grease and slightly sour, slightly inviting milk.

"What are you doing?" he asked, though now he was the one doing the doing, running his hands up under her little shirt.

"What are *you* doing?" She smiled.

"What I'm not supposed to be doing," he replied, kissing her throat.

"I thought you didn't have a girlfriend." She giggled.

He took her face and brought it to his, brought her mouth to his mouth without a moment's hesitation, plunging in.

"Did you eat?" Lisa asked when she got into his truck. She'd been standing outside the Red Owl near the pop machines when he pulled up.

"What time is it?" he asked. "Were you waiting long?"

"Only a few minutes," she said agreeably. "Actually Deb just pulled away when you came up." She seemed more relaxed, more stable than she'd been in weeks. "It smells like weed in here," she said, waving her hands in front of her face, though the windows were already rolled down.

He'd gotten high after he said goodbye to Heidi at the DQ, sitting in his parked truck, gathering himself to face Lisa. He kept a personal stash of marijuana in a little tackle box under the seat, pinching a good bit for himself each day from Vivian and Bender.

"How do you feel?" he asked.

"Okay," she said, sliding in close to him, her legs straddling the clutch. "I did what Sarah said and ate every couple of hours so my stomach never got empty."

He set his hand on her thigh and she reached over and did the same. His leg trembled slightly, and he tried to will it to go still, his heart racing. He took a deep breath and let it out. Only minutes before he'd been fucking Heidi, her legs wrapped around him, her rump pressed up against the freezer, and then he'd pulled away from her for a moment and turned her around. A bolt of lust and disgust quaked through him remembering it, and then a thought: *he would never do it again.*

"Were you busy tonight?" she asked. She put a hand in his sweaty hair.

233

"I had to drive all the way up to Norway and back and then I had to go all the way down to Sylvia Thorne's place."

"Sylvia Thorne?"

"Don't you know her? She lives in Gunn." He turned to her, loving her desperately, more than he'd ever loved her before, feeling crushed, almost panicked by the weight of his love. He wanted to take her home and make love to her without taking any pleasure for himself, to touch her with his fingers and mouth, to make her come the way he could from time to time, when he put all of his attention to the task and she was in the right state of mind.

"I know her," she said. "I just don't think of her as someone who'd be into drugs." She sighed. "It seems like meth is taking over the whole town."

"I wouldn't say the *whole* town," he said as evenly as he could. He squeezed her thigh. Sometimes they argued about what he did and why. They'd agreed that once the baby was born he would get what they called a "real job."

"I can think of, like, ten people right now who are totally becoming tweakers."

"Well, ten people isn't the whole town," he countered, though in truth he could think of dozens more. At times, he wished he'd never told Lisa about what he did for a living.

"What's Claire's middle name?" Lisa asked.

He had to think for a moment. "Rae. Why?"

"I'm thinking of names for the baby."

Rae was his mother's middle name too, he almost added. An image of her face came into his mind then, bony and stark and startled and lonely, the way it had been when he'd walked into her hospital room and seen her dead.

"What names do you like?" Lisa asked, turning to him, and then, abruptly, she turned all the way around, to see the lights of a police car blazing behind them.

Joshua saw it in the rearview mirror in the same instant and banged on the steering wheel.

"Do you have anything on you?" Lisa whispered as he slowed the truck.

"Quiet," he said.

"Josh!"

"I said shut the fuck up," he snapped. They stopped on the side of the road and waited for Greg Price to get out of his car and come to them.

"We meet again, Mr. Wood," Greg said a few moments later. The beam of his flashlight hit their faces through the open window, a dagger of light, slicing them in two.

14

TWO NIGHTS AFTER Claire moved out, she drove past the apartment where she used to live with David. She'd left a candle there, propped in the window of what was once their bedroom, and as she passed by she could see it sat there still, precisely as she'd left it, a beeswax taper in a bottle, unlit and unmoved.

Her new house was a dilapidated mansion that was owned by a punk rocker and trust-fund baby named Andre Tisdale. He'd inherited the house from his grandmother. All the houses on the street were the same as Andre's: grand old wrecked beauties that used to belong to the Minneapolis aristocracy back when the rich still wanted to live in this section of town. A few of the houses were in worse shape than Andre's, their windows and doors boarded up with warning signs plastered over them; a few were in better shape, painted in surprising period colors to show off the intricacies of their architecture. One was hardly even a house anymore at all, since it had caught fire a few months before, though its charred remains hulked like a ship caught on a sand bar, presiding over the street.

From the outside, Claire's room hung like an ear that had been attached to the third story of the house as an afterthought. Inside, it was cut off from the rest of the rooms that made up the third floor. Eons ago, it had been occupied by the maid, Andre had explained when he had shown her the place. *To a series of maids*, Claire thought at the time, but didn't correct him. Even to her, from the distance of time, they all seemed to be one person: maid after maid after maid. The floor was warped and there was no door on the closet, but the room had its own bathroom and its own stairway that snaked through the hidden interior of the house like a laundry chute, leading to all the places that the maid would most often have needed to go: to the kitchen and the basement; to the back door, where the garbage bin was kept. The stairway served now as something of a secret passageway and Claire was at a time in her life when a secret passageway was what she believed she needed more than anything. A place private and anonymous that made it possible for her to live the transient, borderless, wild animal life she believed she had to live now that her mother was dead and David was no longer her boyfriend and Bruce made only feeble attempts at being her father. She still had Joshua, and to him she clung even though she seldom saw him.

He came to Minneapolis to help her move. He'd never been to see her in Minneapolis before and she prepared for his visit the way she would an honored guest, though he would be there only for the afternoon and only to haul boxes from an empty apartment to an empty room. She bought Mountain Dew and pretzel rods and a tin of chocolate-covered caramels to send home with him as a thank you.

"Hello," she called when he pulled up and parked on the street. She'd been waiting for him on the porch. It was the middle of August and they hadn't seen each other since the Fourth of July, since before she bleached her hair the whitest possible shade of blond. As he approached, she watched the mild shock register on his face.

"What do you think?" she asked, reaching for her hair as he ascended the porch stairs.

"It kind of makes you look like a hooker," Joshua said.

She punched his arm and a look of indignation spread over her face.

"And the rest of the getup doesn't help." He gestured to what she was wearing: a little beige top and a tiny pair of cut-off jean shorts slung low and wooden thongs that had a fake daisy between each toe. She'd kept out a T-shirt and sneakers that she would change into once they started to load the truck.

"I think it looks good," she said archly.

"To go around in just a bra?" asked Joshua.

Claire glanced down at her chest. "It's not a bra, so fuck off. It's a shirt, for your information."

"Well, it looks like a bra to me."

"Well, it's not." She gave him a threatening look. "My God, Josh. It's almost a hundred degrees outside. Do you expect me to wear a turtleneck?"

"Are you on crack?" he asked suddenly, humorlessly. "Or meth or coke or something?"

"What's your problem today?" she asked, wounded. Their eyes met for the first time and she saw his expression shift as he realized he was wrong. She looked away. "I thought you'd be happy to see me."

"I am," he said, softening. "It's that you seem different. Kind of city."

Claire smiled and stretched her arms wide. "Here we are in the city, Josh. This is what people dress like here." She turned abruptly toward the house and tugged on his arm, guiding him inside. "Can we please stop talking about what I look like?"

She led him past the boxes she'd packed and stacked up in the living room and into the kitchen, where she gave him a cold Mountain Dew.

"So what do you think?" she asked, looking around at the bare counters and cupboards. "I mean, I wish you'd have seen it before I had it all packed up, but—"

"It's nice," said Joshua. He cracked his can of pop open and stood holding it uncertainly.

Before he arrived, Claire had walked through each room, attempting to see it all through Joshua's eyes, hoping he would think it was cool. She gestured toward his Mountain Dew. "I'd give you ice and a glass, but I already packed them up."

"That's okay." He took a long sip as she watched him and then he held it out to her. "You want some?"

"No thanks," she replied politely. In all of their lives they'd never met up intentionally or made plans with only each other. It felt strange and formal and grownup.

"So I suppose you're wondering what happened." Her voice echoed against the emptiness of the kitchen.

"With what?" he asked, and burped.

"With David." She leaned against the counter and then hoisted herself up to sit on it. "I never told you why we broke up."

"I thought you were just taking time apart," he said, without sympathy.

"No. It's over."

He nodded.

"But I'm coping." She took a deep breath. "Of course, I miss him sometimes, but I think it's probably for the best."

He nodded again.

"I was unfaithful," she blurted. She hadn't planned to tell him this, but now she offered it up, wanting to force him to respond. "I had this—" she folded her hands on her lap and then released them "—*thing* with a guy in Duluth."

Joshua kept his expression still and unreadable, as if he already knew everything she could possibly say, but then she saw his face flush pink. She wondered if he'd ever cheated on anyone and immediately decided he hadn't.

"He's older. He's, like, almost forty." She paused, to give Joshua time to react, but he didn't. He only took another swig of his Mountain Dew. "And—I mean—it's completely over now," she said, though in truth she'd gone up to see Bill in Duluth three times over the summer, sailing past the exit to Midden on her way. "He's not the reason that David and I broke up. Well, I suppose he's *part* of the reason ultimately. Let's put it this way: he didn't *help* the cause. But I don't know. It's a lot of things. It's complicated." She was talking fast, wired from having consumed so much coffee in the past few days as she'd packed her apartment, leaving too much to the last minute. "Anyway, I haven't seen him for a month—this guy, the old guy, Bill. It's not like we're in a relationship or anything."

She stopped talking and looked at Joshua, regretting having asked him to come, regretting having involved him in her Minneapolis life—the life she considered her real, private life. It wasn't until this instant, as he stood silently in her kitchen, that she realized she had concocted a fantasy of what it would be like to have her brother here. In it, he would talk and want to know everything; he would tell her things and make sounds of approval or curiosity as he listened. Instead, he was like always, secret and unattainable. Just as a part of her was to him, she thought now. Without their mother and Bruce to hold them together, they were not a family anymore, but siblings—a leaner, sparser thing. Just Claire and Joshua: two people wandering in the wilderness, each of them holding one end of a string.

"So how are you and Lisa doing?" she asked, pushing off of the counter, stumbling off of one of her shoes as she landed.

He shrugged.

"You're getting rather serious, it seems."

"Why do you say that?" He set his empty can on the counter, and Claire picked it up and put it in the recycling bin by the back door.

"Because you've been together for a while."

"Not even six months."

"Okay, Josh. No reason to get defensive. I was only saying—"

"It'll be six months tomorrow," he said, as if he felt guilty about having downplayed it a moment ago.

"Are you going to celebrate?" Claire asked.

"We're going to Brainerd," he said, and opened the refrigerator. Inside there were two more cans of Mountain Dew and the box of caramels she was going to give him. He closed it and turned to her. "But I'm too young to settle down."

"No one said you were settling down," said Claire. She looked at him quizzically, as if just now she was seeing him. His arms were manlier than she'd remembered them, and tan; the hair that grew on them thicker, and golden.

"Lisa's great, but she's not the only woman in the world."

"*Woman?*" Claire said in a teasing, ecstatic voice. The possibility that her brother could be dating anyone that could be described as a woman seemed absurd to her.

"Shut up."

"Wo-man!" she warbled.

"Don't we have work to do?" he asked, and she followed him out of the kitchen and into the living room, where they stood looking at all of her things.

"I'm thinking we should load the bed first and then pack all the smaller stuff around it," he said.

She looked out the window at his truck. It was dustier, more worn than all the others parked on the street. She recognized the dust as Midden dust, the mud that rimmed the wheel wells, Midden mud. It wasn't just dust and mud, it was Bruce and it was her mother, it was Joshua and home. Seeing it made her feel happy and sad at once.

"You forgot something," Joshua hollered. He had wandered away into her old bedroom.

"What is it?" she asked.

"A candle."

"Oh that," Claire said, going to him. "That stays."

Joshua left as soon as his truck was unloaded, though Claire tried to convince him to spend the night. Once she was alone she paced the room, thinking about how she should arrange the few pieces of furniture she had. From the windows she could see both the front and back of the house, east and west, from street to alley, from hulking ship to garbage bin. She stopped pacing and stared out the window to the street, as if she were waiting for Joshua to return, watching for his truck, though she wasn't waiting. She only seemed to be.

"Boo," Andre whispered, standing in the doorway.

She turned to him, startled. He had a smile on his face that made her feel that he'd been watching her for some time.

"Hey."

"So now that you're in, do you want the grand tour?"

She followed him down the stairs and through the kitchen and living room and up the curving stairway at the front of the house that led to most of the housemates' rooms. Some were cavelike, cloaked with dark curtains; some were scattered with clothes and books and bits of uneaten food and a garble of things that couldn't be instantly identified; some were bright with sunlight or painted in wild colors; and all of them were scented with the smoke of cigarettes or marijuana or heroin or incense, depending on the habits of their occupants. None of the housemates were home, but Andre named each one as they passed. There was Ruthie and Jason and Victor—all members of Andre's band, Binge—and Sean, who preferred to go by the name Elk, and Patrick, who was almost always at his girlfriend's place, and a woman named Melody who technically still lived in the house but wouldn't be home until December, after she was done traveling in Southeast Asia.

When they returned to the kitchen Claire wandered around it appraisingly, as if pondering whether it was going to be sufficient for her cooking needs, though she'd seen it a couple of weeks before when she'd come to see the room. "Is that a breadmaker?" she asked, pointing to a bright yellow piece of equipment shaped like a giant marshmallow that sat on the counter.

"A microwave." Andre went to it and pressed a button so the door popped open. "Everyone thinks it's a breadmaker. I suppose 'cause it looks like one."

"I know how to bake bread," she blurted, feeling instantly like an idiot, but then she went on, hoping to seem valuable as a housemate. "I mean, from scratch. Not with a breadmaker."

"Awesome," he said. He wore a cowboy shirt that he'd cut the sleeves off of and a pair of jeans that were ripped at the knees. On the inside of his forearm, from wrist to elbow, there was a tattoo of a cucumber on fire. The cucumber was actually a person with dots for eyes and a chef's hat on his head and little green arms that extended out from his sides. In one hand the cucumber held a spatula, in the other a butcher knife. The cucumber man also had a mouth, which smiled, though flames were bursting up from the bottom of his cucumber body and would soon, it seemed, overtake him. Claire thought this tattoo was preposterous. Not that she was against tattoos. Rather, she thought that they should not be comical.

"I like your tattoo," she said.

"Thanks."

"It's got a sense of humor."

"Yeah." He smiled at her appreciatively, nodding his head slowly, as if she'd said something profound. "That's so true. You know, you're one of the only people who have gotten that."

Pride and inane joy surged through her, and in her mind she cast about for more brilliant observations about the tattoo but came up with none.

"You want some toast?" he asked, beginning to make some for himself.

"No thanks." She leaned against a counter, trying to seem comfortable, trying to seem like a housemate, though she didn't feel like one at all, as she watched Andre smear first peanut butter, then maple syrup onto his toast and then press it together, sandwich style. She turned away and stared numbly into the living room, where there was a glass terrarium against the wall.

"Oh. I forgot to show you. Ruthie's pet," said Andre, gesturing in the direction of the terrarium.

She walked toward it and saw, as she got closer, that there was a tarantula half the size of her hand inside. When she stooped near the glass, it rose up on its hairy tiptoes, as if about to lunge at her. She stepped back.

"It'll bite," Andre yelled from behind her, and then laughed with exaggerated wickedness, so she didn't know whether to believe him or not. He was a few years older than her, though he seemed younger. He had a boyish quality about him that she'd picked up on immediately. It wasn't innocent, the way an actual boy would be, but a grownup version of a boy: menacing and pranksterish, like any moment he would do anything he wanted. "Sometimes, when Ruthie feeds it, it tries to bite."

"What does it eat?" Claire asked, and the bears came into her mind then, the bears that ate from the canoe in the summertime behind Len's Lookout.

He sat down on the couch without answering her and set his plate on the coffee table. His forehead was rimmed neon green along his scalp, the remnants of a recent dye job. He wore a necklace of silver beads that looked like it came from somewhere far off—India or Guatemala. The hair and the necklace and the extravagant tattoo didn't seem to belong to him, Claire thought, as if the moment they were detached from him, he would look entirely like someone else, like the person who he actually was.

"So did you say you work at Giselle's?"

"Yeah. Have you been there?"

He nodded and took a bite of his sandwich.

"I'm a waitress—or I guess I should say 'server.'"

He nodded again and continued to look at her, which made her wary that he would press harder, ask more, ask the question that so many of her customers asked every day—what it was she "really did." This, despite the fact that they'd been watching her doing what she did all the time they were there—racing around with trays of food and drinks in her hands, clearing and scrubbing the surfaces of tables and chairs. Still, she knew they meant no harm. Giselle's was the kind of restaurant where all the employees except for Giselle herself at least *claimed* to be some-thing else—artists of one sort or another mostly—and some in fact were. Claire had gone to gallery openings, dance performances, and con-certs that featured her coworkers. "I'm a student," she'd murmur to the customers who asked, pushing a strand of hair from her damp forehead, even though that was no longer technically true. She hadn't gone back to school since her mother died, though she intended to. To graduate she needed only two more classes, but the customers didn't need to hear the details. They would smile sweetly at the news of her student status, and she would walk away with their dirty plates in her hands and escape to the humid privacy of the kitchen.

"So, the spider can't escape or anything," Andre said, speaking more gently than he had before. "There's no reason to be afraid."

"I'm not," Claire said, and then to prove it she almost told him about how she'd grown up, how there were bears and moose and wolves. How she hadn't been afraid of them, even when her family lived in the apartment above Len's Lookout and she'd had to trek out to the bath-house—though in fact she'd been terrified. But something kept her from telling him this, something quiet and protective that she could feel rise up like a veil inside of her from time to time. "So what do you do?" she asked. "I mean, for a job." The room was large, but void of furniture other than the coffee table and the couch and a giant poster of Kurt Cobain on the wall. She considered going to sit next to Andre but remained where she was, her arms wrapped around herself.

"The law," he said after having seemed to carefully consider her question, and then he snorted and laughed again in the way that made it impossible for her to tell whether he was serious or not. She gave him a kind of bemused smile so as to communicate that she neither believed him nor disbelieved him, that she was the kind of person who was wise enough to know that anything could be true or not true, but he didn't explain himself any further and so she went to the window, pretending that something had caught her interest.

There was a cat sleeping on a splintered wicker chair on the front porch. Earlier in the day, while she and Joshua were unloading the truck, this same cat had skittered away from her in the backyard.

"Kitty," she called, and tapped gently on the glass.

He opened his eyes and turned majestically to meet her gaze, fearless now that she couldn't touch him.

Her heart shrank when she got to her room, seeing everything she owned in a pile, her bare mattress on the floor. She ripped a plastic trash bag open, too impatient to untie the knot she'd made of the handle, and extracted a blanket, which she spread over the mattress to cover the stains. A painting of her mother's she'd taken from home leaned against the wall and she picked it up and went from wall to wall with it, deciding where it should go. It had hung in her mother and Bruce's bedroom up until a couple of months before, when Claire had packed it up with everything else before Kathy Tyson moved in. She'd put most of her mother's possessions in the apartment above Len's Lookout, but the painting she kept with her, believing that Bruce would call and protest, demand that she bring it back since it belonged to him, a gift from her mother. But he hadn't called — hadn't, Claire assumed, even missed it — which made her insides go bitter and hard, made her feel that their entire life with Bruce had been nothing but a sham. There was a nail in the wall between the two windows that looked out onto the street and she hung the painting on it temporarily, though it was off-center and too high.

She went back to her things, not really unpacking but searching and taking out whatever moved her. She extracted a rhinestone necklace from a tangled lump of jewelry and went into the bathroom and put it on and stood in front of the mirror. The necklace looked ridiculous with the T-shirt and jean shorts she wore, but she left it on, like a little girl playing dress up. She got a lipstick from her purse and applied it and then blotted it on the back of her hand and stood staring at herself in the mirror. A dark stripe ran the length of her part on the top of her head, the blond growing out. She pushed her hair away from her face and then secured it with a clip and then took it out and did it again, better this time. She turned away and went back to her work in a more orderly fashion now, emptying a box of books and then a bag of clothes, which she hung in the closet. She found her phone and plugged it in and dialed Bill's number.

"It's me," she said when his machine picked up. "Just wanted to call and say hi." She hung up the phone and stared at it, waiting for it to ring. Often, Bill screened his calls and then called her right back. She hadn't seen him for a month, but they talked about once a week. They had settled into an easy friendship on the phone, sharing the banal details of their days. In these conversations, Bill felt to her like one of the regular customers who came into Giselle's, familiar and yet vague, intimate yet harmless, giving her advice about her car, listening to her stories about what she did on Friday night, about what movies she saw and whether they were any good or not. In person—on the occasions that she'd gone to visit him over the summer—Claire felt differently about him entirely, as if he wasn't the Bill she'd been talking to on the phone all these weeks but a sexier, more robust brother. In his presence she became provocative and petty, falsely jealous and insecure. She believed it wasn't so much Bill that brought this out in her but his house. While there, she often had the feeling that she was being watched—and in some ways she was. Since Nancy's death, Bill had displayed framed photographs of her all around, on every shelf and nook, on every counter and table. Nancy as a baby, Nancy as a bride, Nancy with her students on the last day of school, Nancy standing in the front yard, a rake in her hands. She was everywhere, in every room, her same sardonic smile watching them and all they did together in her house. Watching them have sex and shower and grill dinner on the back deck and listen to music and read books on the couch. Books—some of them—that

Nancy herself had bought, had read or had hoped to read, had loved or hated or been bored or riveted by.

"Who was her favorite author?" Claire had asked Bill.

"Author?" he'd asked back, as if he were unsure of the definition of the word.

She couldn't help herself; her mind went in these directions. On her visits to Duluth, she wanted to know both everything and nothing about Nancy. But wanting to know everything won out and so she pumped Bill for information every chance she got. What Nancy was like in bed, why Nancy had decided to become a teacher, who Nancy's best friends were, and what she had loved and hated about them.

When Bill spoke to her of Nancy he had the demeanor of a talk-show guest, not wanting to go on too long, always ready to be interrupted. He said he couldn't remember certain things, or if he could, he didn't know how to explain them. He'd take Claire in his arms then and pull her close. He'd say, "But that was the past and this is now," or "That's ancient history anyway, kiddo," and kiss her throat and Claire's jealousy or uncertainty or curiosity—it was all three—would be sated and they would go forward, forgetting about Nancy.

Bill didn't ask about David, didn't even seem to recognize his importance when Claire spoke of him. He listened as if all along David had been nothing more than a friend.

She picked up the phone again and pressed the redial button. "Hey," she said to Bill's machine, making her voice sound lax and light. "I forgot to tell you—I'm all moved in to my new place! It's great so far. But anyway, you can call me at my old number. I had it transferred. Anyway. I should be here unpacking all night, so you can call me late—whenever. Because I'll just be here. Bye."

She hung up the phone and sat staring at it again, not because she believed anymore that it would ring in a moment, but because she wished she could take it back: the second message, the first. And also because she had to fight the impulse to pick up the phone and call him again, to say something that would obliterate everything she'd said before. Something that would make her sound stronger, better, less lonely than she was. She dialed his number again and then hung up before it rang. In a flash she hated Bill, his pathetic little paunch, the way he had to clear his throat violently upon waking and then again after sex, how he cut the meat on his plate entirely before taking a single bite.

She went to a box of things she had kept under the bed when she lived with David and picked up a doll that she had been given for Christmas more than a decade ago. It was pristine, barely used: as a child she hadn't been interested in playing with dolls. "Claire was always my reader," her mother would exclaim on her radio show every chance she got. "But now Josh," she would continue on, "he's the artist." The doll was made of a malleable plastic and topped with a crown of impossibly shiny hair. When Claire squeezed its fat center it said "mama" and "papa" and "baba" in alternating turns. She squeezed it until it said each thing four times and then she tossed it back into the box with enough force that it said "mama" again.

"Knock knock," said Andre from the door, stepping into her room. Behind him there was a man and a woman. "This is Claire," he said to them. "Claire, this is Ruthie and Victor."

"Oh, hi," she said. "Nice to meet you."

"So we had an idea," said Andre.

"What?" she asked, but he ignored her and looked at Ruthie and Victor instead and asked them what they thought.

"Oh, totally," said Ruthie. She turned to Victor, "Don't you think?"

"I do," said Victor, nodding. His flaxen hair was matted into five enormous dreadlocks, a pair of bright barrettes meant for little girls embedded into the ends of one.

"Do what?" asked Claire, feeling daffy and self-conscious and elated to be included in whatever plan they had.

"Okay, Claire, just say yes. You *must* say yes," said Ruthie. She had the air of a cartoon witch about her, big leather boots and long hair, dyed jet black, a tattoo of a spider's web splayed across the top of one hand.

"Yes, *what?*" Claire asked, doing an excited little hop.

Their band, Binge, was making a music video the next day, Ruthie explained finally, and the woman they had cast in the lead role had backed out an hour ago.

"What's it involve?" asked Claire, though she already knew she would do it.

"Just some rolling around on a bed," Ruthie answered. "It's our one love song."

"I wouldn't say that," Victor disputed her contemplatively, fingering one of his barrettes. "I would call 'Avenue Nine' a love song too. Granted, a highly, highly demented love song."

"I'll be in it too," Andre added. "You and me on a bed, but it's very G-rated."

"Oh, totally," Ruthie agreed. "We're trying to get this on *Soundquake*—do you ever see that show? It's this late-night thing. Anyway, it can't be porno or anything."

"Okay," said Claire with tentative glee, and then they each hugged her, one by one.

They all drove downtown together in Victor's van the next day to the warehouse where they would do the shoot. The music video, Claire quickly realized, was more a home-based arts and crafts project than a film production, paid for by Andre, and shot by an undergraduate film major who wore thick leather bands that attached with silver snaps around each wrist. It took them nearly three hours to get the set in place, first hauling a bed up the roasting stairway, and then meticulously arranging it the way the film major thought it should be.

"Where the fuck is Jason?" Ruthie kept bellowing as she stomped around in her boots, but no one ever answered her. Jason was the drummer and her former boyfriend and a heroin addict, she confided to Claire as they stood together in the little area they had made for her to get dressed, a room formed by bed sheets that served as walls.

"How's it look?" Claire asked Ruthie when she put her outfit on. It was less revealing than a one-piece bathing suit, a white lace teddy with a tiny pink bow at the front.

Ruthie only nodded and tugged at the top. She was grumpier than she had been the evening before, when she was so intent on getting Claire to say yes. "Now how about your hair? Let's try it up," she demanded.

Claire lifted it into a pile on top of her head, and they both stood staring into the mirror that was propped up against the concrete wall.

"Now how about with it down again."

Claire dropped her hair and Ruthie reached over and pulled it up again, a skeptical expression on her face. Her eyebrows were hairless black swathes, painted into a lurid arch above each eye. Claire wondered if they smeared when her face got wet, though she didn't dare ask.

"We're going for post-punk, post-feminist baby whore," Ruthie said almost angrily, as if Claire were wrecking her video.

"Post-feminist?" asked Claire, but Ruthie didn't explain. Instead, she turned and pushed her way out of the sheets and howled Jason's name.

Methodically, Claire removed her own bracelets, the ones she wore every day, two from one wrist, three from the other; each was different but also essentially the same, composed, alternately, of silver or colorful yarn. When she was done she tucked them into the pocket of her jeans, which sat folded up on a chair. Beyond the sheets, Andre and Ruthie were arguing about whether there should be a bottle of beer in the shot or not. They had gone to high school together, some exclusive private school in Edina, and the way they talked was like husband and wife, in equal parts worn down and enraged by the other's opinions.

Claire played with the bow on the front of her outfit, trying to get it to sit straight, and then gave up and began toying with her hair again, glumly attempting to make it stay in a formation fitting of a music-video babe. When she had bleached her hair the month before, she had intended it to seem ironic, though standing here now she realized she was not the kind of woman who could pull off ironic hair. Ruthie was that kind of woman. And what kind of woman was Claire? *A big farm girl*, she thought immediately, remembering what David had once said.

"Okay," Ruthie said, pushing through the sheets, invigorated from having won her argument with Andre. She studied Claire. "I'm thinking your hair is good that way, but now mess it all up. Make it look like you just got fucked and fucked." Together, with bobby pins and hair spray, they set themselves to the task, until it became too complicated for Claire to help and she stood watching Ruthie work in the mirror.

"Perfect," she said at last, and parted the wall of sheets so Claire could pass through without disturbing her exquisitely disheveled hair.

"Over here," Andre ordered from behind a very bright light. His hand appeared, directing her to the bed.

Afterward, she didn't ride home in the van with them, deciding to walk back to Andre's house instead, relieved to be alone after a long day of writhing on the hot bed. It was nearly seven by the time she left, the sun slanting against the industrial brick buildings she passed. They seemed impenetrable from the street, aside from one in which a garage door gaped open, revealing a loud generator humming inside. She passed a shoe store and a dry cleaner and then came to a series of blocks that she drove past each day on her way to work. Most were lit with white Christmas lights and filled with pretty silk pillows and wineglasses arranged into pyramids and cutlery set up on gorgeous tables, as if someone were about to sit down to dinner. In between these stores, she noticed the darker, quieter places that she hadn't been able to identify driving past, tiny used bookstores and antique stores and a wig shop that had a window display in which half of the dusty mannequins were bald.

She walked slowly, lulled by the warm evening. She used to wander in this aimless way a few years before, when she'd first moved to Minneapolis and started college, before she met David. She liked to look into the houses as she passed, seeing whatever she could see—people eating dinner, talking on the phone, watching TV. Sometimes she struck up conversations with people she met along the way, innocent and curious, stupid and at ease. Once she met a man who asked her if she was working and she took it to mean did she have a job, though it soon became apparent that what he really wanted to know was whether she was a prostitute. "No," she'd said and run away, instantly terrified. She thought of that from time to time, about what if she'd said yes. About how a single word could change everything and how other words could change nothing at all.

She entered a café a couple of blocks from Andre's house, not yet wanting to return to see either her housemates or her unpacked room. The café was filled with worn-down but comfortable chairs and low tables smattered with magazines. She ordered a cup of chamomile tea and sat down with it, setting it on a table nearby. After a few minutes, she took a sip of the tea, though it was still too hot, and then set it loudly back on its plate. There was a man sitting across the room from her, gazing into the screen of his laptop. It took her a moment to realize who it was.

"Andre," she called.

"Hey." He closed his computer, thin as ice, and carried it with him to her table. "Did you have fun today?"

"Yeah. It was a new experience." She gestured to the chair beside her.

"I'm glad you found this place," Andre said, sitting down. "It's kind of our second home—the housemates." Even when he said the most ordinary things, he spoke in a way that seemed to contain both mockery and a flirty sweetness that Claire found insulting and appealing in equal, oscillating measure.

She took a careful sip from her cup. "I like the song."

"The song?"

"In the video. It's good."

He gave a private, disparaging snort. "It's our biggest hit to date." He paused, like he might tell her something about it, but then he shifted in his chair. "You know, I realized I think I know the town where you're from. I think my cousin has a cabin there."

"Probably. Lots of people have cabins on the lakes."

"His name is Doug Reed."

"I don't think I've ever heard of him. I don't know too many of the city people, except for their faces." Talking with Andre about it, she had the feeling that Midden was suddenly like her old apartment with David —so far off, so far in her past that it seemed preposterous that she'd had any relationship to it at all.

"Do you go up there often—to see your parents?"

She nodded and then contradicted herself. "Not too often. Not anymore." She reached up and twiddled the sharp points of her rhinestone necklace. Ruthie had seen it on her the night before and insisted she wear it in the video. "My mom died last spring, actually."

"Oh my God," he said in an exaggerated voice, as if she'd told him something more scandalous than sad. "I can't even imagine."

"I can't either," she said, and then smiled to lighten the tone.

"What about your dad?" Andre asked.

"He's—gone," she answered, rolling Bruce and her real father into one for the sake of simplicity.

"I'm so sorry," he said, hushed, reverent now.

"Thanks," said Claire, realizing that Andre thought her father was dead. Though she hadn't meant that, she didn't bother to correct him. As a child she'd often wished that Karl had been dead. Not out of any kind of rancor, but instead so that she could have a place for him, a story that explained why things had gone the way they had. In her fantasy he had been a fireman, killed on the job.

"You're so strong," Andre said, staring at her with awe.

"I don't know if that's true. I just—"

"You are," he insisted, more fervently now.

A brittle, sealed-off joy rattled through her, as if, in truth, she was perfectly fine with the death of her mother and the alleged death of her father, as if she really were incredibly strong, but only shy about admitting it. She looked down at the table, at her hands, which had gone completely numb. This same thing happened to her whenever she was extremely nervous or excited, whenever, in the past, she'd been about to mount a stage to collect an award or give a speech. She willed herself to stop feeling this now, but the more she tried, the more nervous or excited and numb she became. She'd never done this before—basked in the glory of her mother's death, of her own orphan story. It felt dirty and cruel and yet also like a complete relief, as if her grief really had passed away from her entirely now, as if her life was only a story that she could hold up for display.

With great concentration, she picked up her cup with both her hands and finished the last of her tea and set it carefully back on its plate. "Are you going home now?"

Together they left the café. The streets seemed different now that she was on them with Andre. It was nearly nine and the air had cooled. After they'd gone a block, Andre took her hand and they continued on as if nothing was different, though everything between them, in that gesture, had changed. By the time they approached their house, Claire had laced her fingers into the waistline of his shorts, her knuckles brushing against a tiny patch of his skin as he walked. She led him into the backyard so they could enter through the back door and ascend the dark stairway to her room undetected. When they were there, she turned and kissed him without switching the lights on.

"I'm breaking my rule," he said, stepping away from her.

"What rule?"

He reached out and undid the zipper of her jeans. "The rule about not sleeping with my tenants."

"I thought we were housemates," she said coquettishly, and pulled her shirt over her head and stepped out of her jeans and stood before him in her bra and underwear. He looked at her earnestly, as if he were truly pained by the sight of her, as if he hadn't been rolling around with her in a bed simulating sex only a few hours before. They grabbed onto each other and kissed while she removed his clothes.

"I have a condom," he whispered after several minutes. They were lying on the mattress by then, which still sat on the floor near the boxes she hadn't had time to unpack. She watched Andre as he found his shorts on the floor and took his wallet from them and extricated the condom. When he ripped it open, she laughed raucously, as if she were drunk.

"What's so funny?" he asked, rolling the condom on.

"Nothing," she said, and laughed again. The feeling she had for him now was the same as the feeling she'd had all day. It was not so much sexual as it was good-natured, and not so much good-natured as it was unavoidable, as if their connection was nothing more than that of two children who'd been introduced and then forced into the backyard to play.

"I don't usually do this," he said, hovering over her. She kissed him again and then rolled over onto her stomach and he pushed into her. She felt a searing half happiness while her chin rubbed rhythmically against the blanket, though another part of her traveled ahead to the next day. How she would hide in her room until she was sure Andre had left the house, empty and depressed and remorseful as she tried to make sense of her boxes of things.

Andre came with a moan and then momentarily collapsed on top of her.

"Do you want me to make you come?" he asked, his breath so close to her ear that she shuddered. She twisted around and saw the edge of his face, phantomlike and girlish in the pale streetlights that streamed in through the windows.

"I came," she lied, and squirmed out from beneath him. She wandered around the room finding her clothes, putting them on piece by piece while he lay on the mattress. She tried to seem carefree and dignified, sexy and bright as she dressed, in case he was watching her, but then she saw that he'd fallen asleep.

"Andre," she whispered. "Andre," she said more loudly, so he stirred, but made no reply. "You have to go." She went to a desk lamp that sat on the floor in the corner and switched it on.

"Huh?" He sat up, disoriented by the light, as if he'd only now realized they were together in her room.

"I can't sleep if you're here," she explained, though she didn't know what she was talking about. Aside from her dalliance with Bill, she'd never done this before either, gone to bed with someone she'd only just met. For all she knew, she could sleep next to him as well as if she were alone.

He laughed and looked at her like she would take back what she said just because he wanted her to.

"But—that was fun," she said, so his feelings wouldn't be hurt.

"Whatever," he said, and sat up.

The phone rang. She went toward it, to turn down the volume on her machine so whoever it was could leave a message without Andre hearing it, but he picked it up before she could get there.

"Hello?" he trilled in a falsely high female voice. He paused, listening. "Claire? Claire who?"

"*Don't,*" she whispered fiercely, trying to wrest the phone from him.

"Oh. *Claire.* Well, okay then. Here's Claire." He held the phone out to her, a smirk on his face.

"Hello," she said, turning away from Andre. "What?" she asked. It took her some time to comprehend that it was Lisa, Joshua's Lisa. She was crying and speaking in nonsensical fragments about Greg Price and Joshua. "Greg!" Claire cried out in her confusion, and then Lisa gathered herself and got it out: Joshua had been arrested and was being held at the jail in Blue River. As she listened, she grabbed her purse and her coat and shoved her feet into her clogs.

"Lisa, hold on. Listen—" she interrupted, "I'm coming. I'll be there as soon as I can. Tell Josh, okay?" She clicked the phone off and tossed it onto the mattress.

Andre picked it up and placed it back on its receiver. "What's wrong?" he asked conciliatorily.

"I have to go," she said, almost panting with panic, leaving the room. She had the feeling he was following her, but she didn't look back as she descended the dark stairs, her legs shaking from sex and fear.

Once outside, she ran to her car parked on the street. Her hands shook as she jammed the key into the lock and then into the ignition. She gripped the steering wheel firmly to still them as she drove through the streets of Minneapolis, past the apartment where she used to live with David, and then out onto the interstate. On the seat beside her there was a plant she'd forgotten to unload the day before. The edges of its withered leaves tickled her bare arm. She tried to picture Joshua in jail, for what she did not know. In her shock, she had forgotten to ask. *For driving drunk,* she decided, to keep herself from going mad. She wished that she could see his face this instant. The longing for it made her nose tingle and ache.

After a while, it occurred to her that she didn't know where she was going. As a child, she had taken a field trip to the jail in Blue River, but she didn't know where, precisely, she should go at this hour in order to get in to see Joshua—by the time she arrived, it would be the middle of the night. Most likely they would tell her to come back in the morning, and then what would she do? She imagined driving up her old driveway, knocking on the door and waking Bruce up—she supposed, now that it was Kathy's home, it would be only right to knock—and then she crossed the thought out of her mind as absurd, the notion of going to Bruce at all, even with the news about Joshua. She could go to Lisa, but she didn't know where Lisa lived—somewhere on the road to the dump is all she knew.

Halfway home, she pulled off the interstate, needing desperately to pee. She parked at a truck stop that was painted to look like a red barn. She had never stopped here in all the times she'd driven by. It was a tourist trap famous, she knew without having ever set foot in the place, for its frosted cinnamon rolls that were as big as your head. She got out of her car and went inside. There was a bin of self-service popcorn by the door and another with stuffed animals of varying shapes and colors and species that you could attempt, one quarter at a time, to capture with a mechanical claw. There were kiosks selling postcards that said "Gateway to the Northland" and "Minnesota Is for Lovers" and rows of shelves selling statuettes of loons and ponies and beavers. There was a counter where you could buy giant soft pretzels and caramel-covered apples and the famous monstrous cinnamon rolls.

Claire ignored these things and made her way toward the women's room. Inside, she was the only woman in sight, walking along a bright bank of sinks. Several faucets came on without her having touched them, riled by her passing, and then, when she entered a stall, several toilets flushed of their own will. Afterward, standing at the sink washing her hands, she saw herself in the mirror, thin and bluish and exhausted-looking in the fluorescent light, still wearing the rhinestone necklace. She took it off and put it in her purse. She remembered Andre saying *whatever* to her when she had asked him to leave. She didn't know when she would go back to that house, didn't know what she would be dealing with once she got to Joshua. It seemed entirely possible to her that Andre was in her room that very minute, rifling through her things. She remembered a little clay gargoyle that David had given her after she'd told him about having been called a gargoyle by a mean boy in the seventh grade. She imagined Andre finding it and holding it up to the light, wondering what it was.

On the way out, she bought a cinnamon roll and carried it out to her car on a piece of wax paper and set it on her lap, reaching down to tear chunks of it off as she drove north. She'd scarcely eaten anything for days, and now she ate the entire cinnamon roll and could have eaten another. Her mind was a metronome, moving back and forth, but always between the same two things, to Joshua and Joshua. She prayed that he would be okay, that whatever he did would come to nothing, that in the morning they would laugh or argue the way they did with each other about the ridiculous events of the night before.

She took the exit to Midden and her mind emptied out and she drove without thinking, drove like the car was driving itself, racing in the night. She was far enough north now that the trees pressed up close to the sides of the road. Pine trees and birches, poplars and spruce, their silhouettes as familiar to her as people she'd known for years. She could see them in the dark, their shadows looming and kind, watching her the way they had seemed to be watching her all of her life. Their knowing branches reached out to her, knowing, but not telling, knowing but not telling who on this earth she was.

PART V

Torch

And did you get what
you wanted from this life, even so?
I did.
And what did you want?
To call myself beloved, to feel myself
beloved on the earth.

—Raymond Carver, *Late Fragment*

15

THE RAIN WAS STILL COMING DOWN when Bruce left Doug Reed's place, freezing to slush on the windshield before the blade could clear it away. It was the second week of December and ten inches of snow was on the ground, coated with a thick layer of ice now, shining like glazed porcelain in Bruce's headlights at five P.M.

"Whattya know about them roads?" Leonard asked when Bruce walked into the Lookout. He tossed a cardboard coaster onto the bar in front of him. "You want your regular?"

"Nah, I'll take a Coke," he said, though in fact he did want a beer. He'd promised Kathy he wouldn't until after she'd ovulated and they were in the clear. They had been trying to conceive a baby for six months. Kathy had brought it up the first night they were married, how badly she wanted to have kids, asking him whether he wanted them too. He had answered that he had them already, but Kathy just looked at him with a funny expression.

"*What?*" he asked.

"I'm talking about your own kids," she persisted.

"They *are* my kids, Kath," he had said.

"You know what I mean," she replied.

And he did. An infinitesimal hairline crack of him did. Besides, who was he to stand in the way of Kathy's dream? They began immediately. Kathy had been keeping records of her cycles for months, tracking her ovulation and menstruation, monitoring her cervical mucus and her luteal surge. Initially, Bruce took this as a sign not so much of her determination as it was a reflection of her profession as a cow inseminator, though he quickly learned that he was wrong. She wept each time she got her period, bitterly remorseful for having waited until she was two weeks shy of her thirty-fifth birthday to even begin to try.

Bruce did what he could. He held her and stroked her hair and reassured her when she cried. He drank tea with her in the evenings called "Fertile Blend." He took vitamins with zinc and avoided hot baths and had sex with her only missionary style and only on certain days, according to the demands of the chart she kept on the last page of her journal. And at last he even agreed to call her psychic, Gerry, and submit to a reading over the phone. "I sense a presence," Gerry declared the moment Bruce finished giving him the numbers of his credit card.

"Could it be the baby?" Bruce asked.

"No!" Gerry shouted, changing his mind already. He had a Brooklyn accent, though he lived now in upstate New York. Kathy had met him years before, improbably, at a conference for people who raised and worked with cows. They had been drawn to each other immediately, she had told Bruce, seeing that they were of the same ilk, recognizing each other by their numinous jewelry. He was a small-time guru, holding workshops on occasion in a converted barn on his farm. Kathy had gone there once and camped out in his yard for a week, learning how to read rune stones and tarot cards. She showed Bruce a picture of Gerry she had glued inside her journal. He was a chubby, graying man who looked more like a college professor to Bruce than either a farmer or a psychic, his pink face pocked with old acne scars. "It's not a presence. Not a person," he continued with Bruce on the phone. He spoke with agonizing precision, making every few words its own sentence. "It's an idea. A thought you're having. It's getting in the way. It's blocking the road. There's a logjam in the river. A mud slide on the path, so to speak."

"A thought?" asked Bruce, trying to empty his head of everything he knew and believed, not wanting Gerry to divine what was inside, just in case he actually could.

He didn't believe in psychics or crystals or any of this New Age business, but when they got off the phone, Bruce knew that, in a sense, Gerry had been right. He did have a thought. He had it each time he and Kathy made love during her fertile week, each time she got her period again. It was the thought that when he'd had the idea to marry Kathy, this was not what he expected. He realized now how ignorant and self-absorbed he had been, but Kathy's desire to have children had taken him completely by surprise, so much was their courtship focused on his grief, his life, his wife and his kids and their loss. Kathy had been his counselor and confidante, his shoulder to cry on. She had been warm and female and sexually available, expert at drawing him out of his shell, back when the shell he needed to be drawn out of was composed entirely of his eternal love for Teresa Rae Wood.

When they married, all of that changed in a day. Teresa was no longer his wife, Kathy was. "Kathy Tyson-Gunther," she decided to be called. And even Claire and Joshua seemed to belong to him less than they had the day before. Kathy referred to them as his "late wife's kids," a shadowy dejection coming over her each time Claire or Joshua came up in their conversations, though she would not admit her mood had anything to do with them. All through the summer and early autumn, they had talked in an abstract way about having Joshua and Claire over for dinner, though nothing ever came of it. Finally, in November, he and Kathy extended a tentative invitation to them for Thanksgiving dinner, but then they learned that Joshua was going to be a father and their plans dissolved.

"It isn't that I'm not happy for them. I *am*," Kathy said to him sincerely, after having wept over the news. "It's . . ." she struggled to think of what, exactly, it was. "It's that seeing Lisa's belly will bring it all to the forefront. How we've failed."

"We haven't failed," he told her.

"How about they all come over for Christmas?" she suggested.

"Josh could be in jail by then," Bruce said, and he could. His court date had been scheduled at last. Joshua had been arrested in August and charged with possession of marijuana, though Bruce had sighed a breath of relief when he heard the charge. All summer long, he had been hearing things around town, rumors that Joshua was dealing for Rich Bender and Vivian Plebo, and not just marijuana, though he had allowed himself to ignore the talk until he got the call from Claire. She had been distraught when she called, almost begging him to come to Blue River, where she was. She had driven up from Minneapolis the night before and spent half the day going from the bank to the courthouse and back to the bank again, getting money and notarized statements and filling out forms so she could bail Joshua out of jail. But Bruce hadn't gone to Blue River. He couldn't, he explained to Claire, especially since she already had it covered. He had a job to finish and then, that evening, a softball game to play. It was the regional semifinals and the Jake's Tavern team had made it all that way.

A few weeks later, he and Joshua were going in opposite directions on Big Pile Road. They stopped and talked to each other through the open windows of their trucks with their engines idling, the way they had taken to doing since Bruce had married Kathy and Joshua stopped coming home.

"What you doing with yourself these days?" asked Bruce, not wanting to mention his arrest directly.

"Pulling out docks for Jack Haines," Joshua answered.

"That's good work."

"It's just till the lakes freeze up," said Joshua, and then they looked away, out their windshields, both of them thinking that by the time the lakes froze up Joshua might not need a job anyway, because very likely he would be in jail. He had been busted with a fair amount of marijuana, Claire had told Bruce. She kept him up to date on the tug of war between Joshua's court-appointed attorney and the county prosecutor. He saw her about once a week, when he stopped in at Len's Lookout. She worked there now, picking up her mother's old shifts, living in the apartment above the bar, the way she had when Bruce had met her as a child. She had moved to Midden when Joshua got arrested, wanting to be nearby to assist in his defense. There was some debate as to whether the marijuana that Joshua had in his possession was for his personal use or for sale. On the eleventh of December, the judge would decide and sentence him accordingly.

"Bruce!" Claire called to him now on the evening of the ice storm, a moment after Leonard handed him the Coke that Bruce wished were a beer, though she didn't stop to talk. Instead, she glided past him with several plates in her hands and went to a table of customers he didn't recognize. Bruce followed her with his eyes, nodding to the few people he knew and glancing briefly at the people he didn't—city people up to hunt. He took his wool hat off and set it on the bar. "You're busy, for the roads being what they are," he told Leonard.

"It's these dumb Finlanders," Leonard said, and laughed because he was a Finn himself. "They think they know how to drive. Them and the city apes. The Finlanders got the balls and the apes got their big fancy trucks."

Claire approached and thumped Bruce on the shoulder. Something caught inside of him and kept him from hugging her. It caught every time he saw her. "What's new?" she asked.

"Not much." He took a sip of his Coke. "How about yourself?"

To his surprise, she sat down on the stool beside him. "Did you get your hair cut?"

He shook his head truthfully. He hadn't cut it recently, though months before, he had cut his ponytail off.

"It looks like you did," she said. "Or that you're doing something different to it."

He combed his hair with his fingers, feeling self-conscious. Kathy had bought him a special conditioner and, after being repeatedly encouraged by her to try it, he'd started using it the week before. It made his hair softer, fuller than it had ever been. He wasn't going to admit this to Claire. He took his hat from the bar and put it on, remotely regretting that he had stopped by. Since he married Kathy, whenever he saw Claire he got a little nervous, like she was watching his every move, analyzing his every word, like nothing he could do or say would be right. He felt the same way around Joshua. They were a committee, a club, an injured gang of two. He knew without needing to be told that they reported back to each other about him. That they'd look at each other with skeptical smiles and say, *So guess who I saw.*

"Are you ready for tomorrow?" she asked, referring to Joshua's court date.

"I thought we couldn't go in with him."

"I *told* you!" she said vehemently. "We can't go in to the judge's chambers, but we can go to the courthouse and sit outside in the hall." She looked at him fervently. "Don't tell me you're not going to be there."

"I *hope* to," he said. "But I got to finish up at Doug Reed's place and if we can't go in anyway, I don't see why—"

"For moral support, Bruce," she interrupted, and then a bell rang back in the kitchen, Mardell signaling that an order was ready. Without another word, Claire bolted away from him, through the swinging doors.

Bruce was relieved when she left. He was almost always relieved when she left, though it was her he came into the Lookout to see. He preferred to talk to her in fits and starts, in the pleasant exchanges they could manage as she strode past him bearing food or dirty dishes or stood waiting for Leonard to make her drinks at the bar. In this manner, he talked to Claire about once a week, though seldom did they actually talk. Kathy didn't know that he saw Claire as often as he did, didn't know that when he stopped off after work, he was stopping off at the Lookout. Sometimes, without directly lying, he let her believe that he had gone to Jake's Tavern. It was their place.

"I told Lisa we'd meet her and Josh at the courthouse at noon," Claire said a few minutes later, returning to stand next to him with an empty tray, as if his presence the next day had been agreed on. "Can I get three bourbons on the rocks?" she asked Leonard. Together they watched as he lined up the glasses and poured the drinks. Bruce had the feeling that Claire was waiting for him to speak, silently daring him to dispute her or praying he would agree to go, one or the other, so she could respond.

"I'll see what I can do," he said as she placed the drinks on her tray.

"Did she tell you what came in the mail today?" Leonard asked Bruce before she left again, and then turned to Claire, "Why don't you tell your dad?"

"Oh," she waved her hand in front of her face, as if she were embarrassed to even think about it. She looked tired and pretty, like her mother, only darker, now that she'd dyed her hair brown to cover the bleach blond she'd done last summer. "I finished those classes I had to take. I did them online. So now I have my degree."

"It came in the mail today," repeated Leonard. "A fancy piece of paper with calligraphy and a big golden seal."

Claire stared at the bourbons on her tray. "It's a little behind schedule, but at least I can say I finished up." She looked at Bruce with the eyes she looked at him with lately, private and tentative, as if she were peering out at him from behind a curtain.

"That's right," he said. "Better late then never."

Her eyes flickered away. "True."

"Your mom would be proud," said Leonard, more to Bruce, it seemed, than to Claire. She took her tray and walked away from them and he was glad again, in a remorseful way. "I'm proud too," he said to nobody, though Leonard heard him and nodded. He went to the till and began to count the day's money, stacking the bills into neat piles and binding them in rubber bands.

"How's Mardell doing?" Bruce asked.

Leonard paused in his counting and glanced up. "Her sister's coming for Christmas. The one from Butte. How's Kathy?"

"She's good." He took the last sip of his Coke and shook the ice in the glass. Since he'd married Kathy, he detected the slightest disapproval from Leonard and Mardell, the slightest lowering in their esteem. "Well, what about the kids?" Mardell had huffed back in June, when Bruce had told her the news, as if they were still in diapers. And then, before he could reply she said, "I can take them, if need be."

"Take them *where?*" he'd asked sharply, not caring whether he hurt her feelings, though she'd always been something of an aunt to him and Teresa.

"Take them *in*," she exclaimed, and then looked at him with undisguised shock and disdain. Her hair was sheer white and styled into a dense yet airy bush, like cotton candy spun around a cone. "They need a mother, you know. Or at least a mother figure."

"Well, I'm not going anywhere," he said, softening. "I got married, that's all."

"Oh, Bruce, I know," she said apologetically, and began to cry. She took her glasses off so she could wipe her eyes. He put his hand on her arm. "I didn't mean anything. It's just that . . ."

"It's that you miss Teresa," he said.

"I guess that's it," she said, with a tone that told Bruce that that wasn't it at all—or rather, that was only part of it. That behind her longing for Teresa, there was judgment for what he had done so soon. He'd heard it already, all around town, without actually having to hear the words. *So soon, so soon,* like an inane bird swooping over his head, calling to him everywhere he went. It made him love Kathy more, or at least to feel more protective of her, like it was the two of them against the world.

Leonard hadn't been there when he'd told Mardell about marrying Kathy and he made no mention of it the next several times Bruce came into the bar, until one day he asked Bruce how Kathy was in a voice as plain as day, as if he'd asked that same question for a thousand years.

"Hey, Len," Bruce said now, standing and pulling his coat on. He opened his wallet and set two dollars on the bar. "I better get home before the roads get worse."

"You'd better," he agreed.

"Tell Claire I said bye," he called as he walked to the door.

Leonard waved him off, signaling he would. It's what he did all the time.

· · ·

"There you are," said Kathy when he got home. "I hope you're not too hungry," she said and smiled, sly and flirtatious. "Or I should say, not hungry for *food*." She pulled him to her and kissed his ear. "I got a positive on my ovulation stick, which means we have to do it *now*."

"Now?" he asked, running his hands up her sides. She laughed and pulled him into their room. Despite their troubles with conceiving, they always had fun in bed.

"What do you think?" he asked, when they were finished.

"About what?" She was lying the wrong way on the bed, her feet propped up on the headboard in an attempt to assist his sperm in their mad journey to her egg.

"About being pregnant. Do you think this was the one?"

She inhaled deeply and closed her eyes, pondering the question. A few months before, Gerry had told her that she would know when it happened. That she would feel a bolt of energy or a shot of light: the spirit of their future child, taking root.

"I feel *something*," she said, and opened her eyes. "A kind of intensity in my womb, but I don't know if I can say for sure." She turned her head to face him, keeping the rest of her body perfectly still. "What about you? What do you feel?"

He felt sleepy and hungry and he yearned for a cigarette, but he thought it unwise to mention any of those things.

"I feel like maybe this was it," he said, and she smiled and big tears blossomed in her eyes. He hovered close but didn't touch her, afraid that to jostle her would ruin their chances of conception, but then she began to cry harder and he placed his hand on her arm ever so delicately, as if her flesh were wet paint, waiting to dry.

"I'm sorry," she said, wiping her face with her hands. "It's that sometimes I just . . . I mean, how ironic can it be that I inseminate cows for a living and I can't even get myself knocked up?" She looked suddenly at him, her eyes bright with offense, as if he'd contradicted what she said. "It's my *job*, Bruce. And I can't manage to get it right when it comes to myself."

"It'll happen," he soothed.

"*It will*," she said emphatically, her mood shifting suddenly. "It's that I've gotten all off-kilter. That's why it's not happening." She sat up even though thirty minutes hadn't passed since they had finished making love. "I need to find my center. I need to do a reading. Would you mind, honey, if I went over and spent the night at my cabin?"

"Your cabin?"

"Just for the night." She stood and began to dress. "Kind of like a retreat, so I can get centered."

"You could do it here," he offered. "I could sleep out on the couch." He went to her and tried to hug her so as to prevent her from putting her pants on, but she only patted his arms and continued on with what she was doing.

"I need to get centered, Bruce. This baby stuff has put me off balance. It's taken over my entire psyche with negativity." She pulled a sweatshirt over her head.

"But it's cold there. It'll be freezing, Kath." He had the feeling that someone was pressing a boot against his chest.

"I can start a fire. I did it for years." She came and put her arms around him. "This will be good for both of us. It will give us perspective on this whole journey."

"What about the roads?" he pressed, though she only chuckled at him and walked from the room. He followed her into the kitchen, where she was loading her backpack, taking a container of yogurt and a banana, some rye crackers, and a few bags of Fertile Blend.

"Now, don't forget to drink your tea tonight. And there's a casserole in the oven. I set the timer for you." She looked at him and laughed at the hurt expression on his face. "You're being silly, hon," she said, pushing her hand into his hair.

"It's that I'll miss you," he said. This was the second time she had left him. She had done it back in September on the night of the equinox, and he had hated it then too.

"Love you." She kissed him and began to walk out the door.

"And I wanted to talk to you about something too," he said, to keep her home.

She turned abruptly with her backpack slung over her shoulder. "What?"

"Josh's hearing is tomorrow."

"*Tomorrow?*" she said with some surprise, though he had told her about it weeks before. She set her backpack on the kitchen table, still holding onto the straps. "What do you want to talk about?"

He shrugged. "Whether we should do anything."

"Like what?"

He shrugged again, not wanting to mention that he could go and sit on the bench outside the judge's chambers with Lisa and Claire, not wanting Kathy to either encourage him to go or get moody and defensive because he had suggested it. He didn't know which she would do and he didn't want to know.

"I'll hold him in my thoughts," said Kathy, lifting her bag again. "I'll burn some sage."

After she left, he put his boots and coat on and sat out on the porch with the dogs. The rain had stopped by now. For several minutes he listened to the ice clattering and tinkling in the branches of the frozen trees and then he lit a cigarette. He smoked out here again, the way he used to do when Teresa was alive, though Kathy hadn't asked him to. It seemed like the right thing to do, the civilized way to live, and it gave him an excuse to be off by himself, which he liked to do most nights. He didn't like it this night, however, with Kathy off at her old house. His enjoyment of his solitude depended entirely on Kathy being thirty feet away, dozing in their bed, he realized now, feeling a swell of anger toward her rise inside of him, though he knew he didn't have the right to be mad. Before they had married she'd warned him that this might happen, that from time to time she would need her space and he'd told her that he would need his too. It felt true then, but it was a lie. He didn't need his space. His space was a box of grief, the place where Teresa lived now, and he wanted more than anything to keep it closed. When he was alone without Kathy he had too much time to think, too much silence to fill the void, and Teresa would come at him in the smallest, most penetrating ways.

Without wanting to, he remembered her now, remembered a particular meaningless day the autumn before when she had made batches and batches of zucchini bread and how, later, they'd driven around together, bringing a loaf to everyone they knew, bringing a loaf, even, to Kathy, who hadn't been home. They'd left it on her porch, on top of a pile of neatly stacked wood. He could see it there now, feel the damp heft of it in his hands, which he shook to break the memory loose. He was grateful he had only his memory to keep Teresa around. Grateful that Claire and Joshua had packed up everything that had belonged to their mother and taken it away. When he'd walked into the house after they'd gone his body filled with a daffy joy. He was free, or so it seemed. He could start anew now, with Kathy and Kathy only.

But he hadn't been freed entirely. On occasion something that had been Teresa's would emerge from the depths of the house: a dried-up pen that said REST-A-WHILE VILLA on its side, a leather bookmark embossed with her initials that Joshua had made in school, a tube of pink lipstick that she'd worn when she went to work or town. The sight of each of these things stopped him short, though he had to pretend otherwise if Kathy was in the room. It was like coming across a bear in the woods: you were supposed to stand still and remain calm, against every impulse. He couldn't bring himself to throw Teresa's things out. When he had the chance he secreted the things he'd found out to his truck, where he put them in the glove compartment and never looked at them again.

He went back inside the house after smoking two cigarettes and stood in the fluorescent light of the kitchen. The timer Kathy had set had gone off already. He turned the oven off and opened the door, the heat hitting his cold face like a fist, and removed the casserole. The top had baked to almost black, but he could see it hadn't been ruined entirely. He set it on top of the stove to let it cool and got a beer from the refrigerator, not caring whether it would impede his sperm. He pulled his wallet from his pocket and began removing all of its contents. He and Teresa used to call it his office—his wallet—because Bruce kept it so packed full of important things. Bids and business receipts, notes about his customers. Months ago, he had put a tiny blue scrap of paper there that had Joshua's cell phone number written on it. At last he found it and picked up the phone.

Joshua's voice sounded alarmed, once he recognized who it was. Bruce had never called him before, though he'd meant to whenever, in his passes through his wallet, he'd seen the number.

"How you doing?" he asked Joshua.

"Not too bad."

Bruce removed a tack from the corkboard near the phone, trying to think of what to say. This was possibly Joshua's last night of freedom for a while, though Bruce could not convince himself to believe that was true. The judge would see how young he was and take pity, despite his crime. It's what Bruce had thought all along, since the phone call from Claire back in August.

"Is everything all right with you?" Joshua asked tentatively.

"Yep." He jabbed the sharp end of the tack into a callus on his thumb and didn't feel a thing. "So I guess tomorrow's the big day," he said, though Joshua knew that Bruce knew this for a fact. "It sure came up quick."

"Yep," said Joshua. There was a rustling sound, as if he were going from one room to another.

"I was thinking I'd come over with Claire, you know, but I got this job out at Doug Reed's place, back by the Paradise Town Hall. They're weekenders," Bruce explained. He pulled his pack of cigarettes out and lit one up. "They got a big house that they just redid and I'm finishing up with the small stuff, some shelves and cabinets. I was going to say you could stop out there tomorrow morning on your way, in case I can't make it to the courthouse after all. I'm going to have to play it by ear, to see how much I can get done."

"I got plans in the morning," said Joshua without any emotion in his voice and then he added, more gently, "with Lisa."

"Of course you do, bud. I was just saying, if you had the time. I know your hearing's not till the afternoon."

"Twelve thirty," said Joshua.

"Right," Bruce said. He took another drag from his cigarette. "I told Claire you should bring some of your drawings to show the judge. The ones of cars and things," he suggested. "It would help the judge see you're a good guy. To sort of build your case."

"Maybe," said Joshua, though Bruce could tell he wasn't even considering it.

"Well, good luck if I don't end up seeing you."

"Thanks," Joshua said.

Bruce sat there long after Joshua had hung up, the silent phone pressed to his ear. He sat so long the telephone became a part of him, an extended plastic ear — warm and vacant, expressive and familiar. At first he had the sensation that he was on hold and simply waiting, that someone would come to him eventually on the other end of the line. And then, after several minutes, the notion that he was on hold left him and another feeling took its place, that he was about to either cry or punch the wall, or that he would do both in quick succession, but his fear of doing either roused him from his trance and he put the phone back on the receiver.

He went to the refrigerator and got another beer and then went to the stove and stared at the casserole and poked a finger into its center. It had cooled entirely now, but he wasn't hungry anymore.

"Tanner," he called. "Spy."

They came clattering into the kitchen, running and then sliding on their nails when they reached him, loving him the way nobody else did, the way they always had.

"Dinner," he said, and set the casserole down before them on the floor.

The road was a frozen river the next morning as Bruce drove down it, slow and steady, in the first gray light of day. When he turned into Doug Reed's driveway he lost his concentration and his truck fishtailed and skidded into the mailbox mounted on a metal pole that didn't budge. He shifted into reverse and backed away from it and crept up the driveway. His glove box had sprung open with the impact and he reached over to push it closed, though it wouldn't go because something was jammed in its hinge. Teresa's lipstick, he saw, and let it be.

Doug Reed's house smelled like new carpet and glue, fresh paint and sawdust. There were slate floors and ten-foot windows that faced out over Lake Nakota, and a hot tub sunk into the floor. The kitchen was especially state of the art, with a special machine that could chill a bottle of wine in five minutes and a garbage disposal that could grind even the thickest bones. George Hanson had put in the garbage disposal the day before and, afterward, he and Bruce had stood around testing it out, pushing in kindling from the bucket near the fireplace and listening as it ground the wood to nothing in the depths of the sink. Bruce was the last man in, the one to finish up, installing the kitchen cabinets he'd made and building in bookshelves.

He walked through the house to the living room along the sheets of plastic that had been set down to protect the carpet and turned up the thermostat and then went into the kitchen. He poured coffee from his Thermos into the little cup that served as its cap. Through the huge windows, Lake Nakota was spread out before him, covered with a layer of gray ice. He could see the cross atop the church on the opposite shore, almost a mile away. He wondered what Kathy was doing now, if she was even awake yet. He hadn't slept well without her. Their bed was like a ship that had become unmoored. He kept waking and remembering that he was alone and then it would take him some time to fall back asleep. He dreamed of Teresa, but he didn't recall the dream and didn't try to. Kathy always remembered her dreams and then wrote them down in a

271

little notebook she kept in the drawer in the bedside table. She would tell him about them each morning, while he showered and dressed and made his coffee, following him from room to room.

He poured another capful of coffee and drank it down like a shot, then opened the cabinet where he'd stashed his tools.

It was eight and then it was nine thirty. Bruce told the time by the radio as he worked, moving through his day the way he always did, listening to one show after another, to the national news and *Northland Beat*, to *Native Rhythms* and *A Woman's Place*. At ten thirty he stood up and stretched his back, still holding his hammer. If he wanted to make it to Blue River by noon, he should leave now. The thought played in his mind lightly, like something skittering across the ice before falling out of sight. He would work another hour or two and meet them afterward, he decided. He'd take them all out for a big late lunch, Claire and Lisa and Joshua too, he allowed himself to assume.

But he didn't do that. He worked past noon, when he normally stopped to eat his sandwich, and past twelve thirty, when Joshua would be meeting with the judge. When it was nearly two, he heard Teresa's voice and he turned the radio up, though by then she wasn't speaking anymore. She had said only a single sentence, the introduction to her old show, fading out as the broadcaster spoke over it. Bruce had heard the same thing twice yesterday. It was a teaser, an advertisement for a marathon of *Modern Pioneers* that the station had in the works. Bruce had received a letter from the station manager, Marilyn, the week before, explaining that they would be broadcasting the top ten listener favorites of Teresa's show in January. There was a poll on the station's Web site, Marilyn had written. She encouraged Bruce to visit it and cast a vote for his own favorite show. He didn't have a favorite show. He loved them all. Loved the sound of his wife's voice as it had come to him every Tuesday at three. He had listened to it again on Thursday evenings, if he happened to be working late, not caring that he had heard the show already. Sometimes on Tuesdays, after she asked the question at the end of the show, he would call in and tell her the answer, though she would never allow him to say it on the air, reserving that privilege for her less intimate fans. She would put him on hold and he would listen as she signed off— "Work hard. Do good. Be incredible. And come back next week for more of *Modern Pioneers!*"—and then she would come back on the line and ask him what he was doing. "Working hard," he would tell her every time.

"Doing good. Being incredible." Teresa had borrowed the lines from his mother, after having come across the card she had given him for his high school graduation in a box of his old things.

He turned the radio off and went out to his truck and took the two sandwiches he'd packed that morning from his insulated lunch bag. Usually, he ate inside, but today he sat in his truck, idling the engine and running the heat. When he had started it up, he thought he would start driving to Blue River, eating along the way, but then he realized it was too late for that. They'd be on their way back to Midden by now, knowing whatever they knew about Joshua's fate.

He saw his open glove box and reached over to slam it shut with more force than he'd been able to that morning as he drove, hoping the tube of lipstick would be knocked out of the way, but it wasn't. He picked it up and examined it for several moments. There was a crack along the plastic cap. He didn't know whether it had always been there, or whether it had happened when he'd tried to close the glove compartment on it. He pulled the cap off and rotated the tube, and a pink triangular nub appeared. It struck him as deeply familiar, like a face he had known and studied without being aware of it. Its angular silhouette suggested to him not only Teresa's mouth, but other, deeper, more intimate things about her that he couldn't bring solidly to his mind, but rather that resided somewhere else inside him, present but unreachable.

He held the lipstick to his nose and inhaled. It smelled chemical and slightly fruity, like Teresa used to smell in the last moment before she stepped out the door when she was going somewhere. He'd hated to kiss her when she'd had it on. He'd hated the taste and the fact that it would leave pink marks on his face. He traced a faint line of it on his hand now, as if testing the color, and then he drew another line and another, making each one darker, until he'd colored in half of his hand. The pink was softer there than it appeared in its solid form. It was the way it had been on Teresa's lips—translucent and shimmering, the palest rose. He almost kissed it, like a teenager practicing how to make out, but then he looked away from his hand, to get ahold of himself, feeling ridiculous and driven, stupid and compelled. He didn't cry, though he felt his sorrow roiling up from his gut. He didn't cry at all anymore, or listen to Kenny G, or allow himself all the kinds of things he'd wallowed in during the spring before when he could scarcely get out of bed.

He got out of his truck and threw the lipstick as hard as he could into the trees at the side of the house. It skated along the icy surface of the snow and then came to a stop and rolled back down the slope of the land, almost all the way back to him. He picked it up again, meaning to throw it farther away, but instead he turned back to his truck and reached into the glove box and pulled everything out—his insurance papers and owner's manual, old napkins and receipts—until he found the other things that had belonged to Teresa, the leather bookmark and the Rest-A-While Villa pen. He carried them into Doug Reed's house and went to the kitchen and pushed them down the sink and turned the garbage disposal on. Its grinding sound was not as loud as it had been yesterday, when he and George Hanson had shoved the sticks of wood down, and it did not go on as long.

He listened to it until it finished its job, and then he turned it off and stared at his hand, smeared with pink. He ran the water as hot as he could bear, attempting to scrub it off, but it had little effect. He went into the bathroom and pumped out soap that Doug Reed kept in a pretty blue bottle, lathering his hand with it, scraping the lipstick off with the blunt edges of his fingernails. He caught glimpses of himself in the mirror as he worked and then he stopped and looked closely. Without a thought, he punched his image. The mirror didn't break, so he punched it again harder. It occurred to him that the mirror wasn't glass, but rather some high-tech material that would never shatter, which made him want to wrench it from its screws and break it all the more. He grabbed one of Doug Reed's towels and scoured his hand dry with it, until there was only the faintest pink shadow.

He heard the sound of a car engine outside and he went to the door and out onto the front porch, watching Claire park her Cutlass. He could see, even from this distance, she'd been crying. She got out without a coat on, her arms crossed in front of her chest to keep warm.

"Where were you?" she yelled, coming toward him, slipping a bit on the ice.

"How'd it go?" he asked, stepping off the porch.

"Where were you?" she screamed more loudly.

"Claire. I told you—"

"*No!*" she boomed, and came at him with an intensity that made him believe she might tackle him when she reached him, but instead she only clutched onto his arm, as if she needed help standing up. "Why weren't you there?" she stammered. "Why weren't you . . ." Her teeth began to chatter so hard she couldn't go on. This had happened once before, when she was twelve and she'd fallen through the ice of their pond, thigh deep in the water, though he knew this time it wasn't from the cold. He almost laughed with the strangeness of it, the clownish clank of her jaw, but then she began to gasp for air. He grabbed the points of her elbows, but she pulled away and huddled into herself, trying to talk again, despite it all. "You . . . you . . . you," she panted.

"Claire," he said, pounding on her back, as if she were choking on something.

"You," she panted again, and then made a terrible noise, an injured howl that dissolved into several more gasps in which it seemed she could not get a single bit of air.

"Breathe," he said to her, and then he gently shook her. "Listen to me. Take a breath in." Her eyes went to his, wary and feral, like those of an animal whose trust he would never win, but he could see that she was listening to him, so he went on. "Breathe out. Now in . . . and out." He waited and watched her breathe. "In. Take another one in. And out."

She stood up and turned away from him, calmed now, and put her hands over her face, her teeth still chattering lightly, her hands trembling.

"You lost your breath," he said, not wanting her to be embarrassed. "Just don't think about it. If you think about it, you'll get all worked up again. That's probably how you got started in the first place."

She took her hands from her face. "Why weren't you there?"

"I never said—"

"*Why weren't you there?*" she demanded.

"I had to work, Claire. I—"

"Oh no, don't say that. Don't give me that crap, Bruce. Please, just don't even . . ." A sob escaped her and she took another breath to gather herself and she spoke again, stronger now. "You don't want to be our dad anymore."

"I don't know what you're talking about. I don't know why—"

"You can't even do the bare minimum, can you? You can't even do that." She looked at him, tears rising into her eyes.

"Yes, I can," he said softly.

"*What?*"

"The bare minimum. That's what I can do, Claire." Once he spoke the words they exploded in his chest, so true he almost wept.

He pulled her to him and held her and stroked her cold hair, aching to make her happy. He wanted to promise her something, to say that things would go back to the way they were, or that they would be different than they had become, but he loved her too much to lie and needed her too little to make it true.

"Where's Josh?" he whispered, after several minutes.

She pulled away, stumbling back a step, and looked up at him. Her eyes were blue and endless and scared. "In jail," she said at last, her voice wavering. "He was sentenced to eighty-five days."

The words entered Bruce like dull bullets, though nothing in his posture changed. He took Claire's hand and held it, as if he were shaking it to say hello or goodbye. "You did what you could," he said.

She nodded, still holding his hand.

"You did, Claire. You played every card. You did the same thing when your mom was sick. You were always there. You never let us down."

He squeezed her hand and she squeezed his back and they repeated it a couple more times, as if they were speaking a secret silent language, a long-known code, and then they both let go. She was breathing normally now. He could see it like smoke in the cold air. Her breath, his. Thin ghosts that appeared then vanished, as if they were never there.

16

ON SUNDAYS CLAIRE DROVE to Blue River to visit him. She was not allowed to wear black, or at least not black *entirely*. Nor could she wear clothing that had writing on it, or was made of an even remotely translucent fabric, and most of all she could not wear clothing that failed to cover what the powers that be at the Coltrap County Correctional and Rehabilitation Center considered an adequate amount of skin. To illustrate the rule about the concealment of skin, a six-foot-tall drawing of the human form on a piece of white butcher paper was taped to the wall of what was called the "processing room," its body inked in with black marker where the clothes of the visitors should be: from toes to collar bone, with a sleeve that extended down midway to the elbow, no matter what month of the year.

"*He* gets to wear all black," joked Claire, referring to the butcher-paper person. She was not normally a jokester, but jail, Joshua realized, brought out the jokester in his sister. "He finds black very slimming," she said in a mock snooty tone, and Joshua smiled without her seeing it, her voice echoing across the distance between them, out the long barred windows of the processing room, down the concrete tunnel of a hallway, and into the room where he sat waiting for her, his heart—he couldn't help it—pounding with joy. She laughed alone at her own silliness and her laughter traveled to him as well. It seemed to reach him and then ricochet back to her and again return to him, like when they were kids and would stand on opposite ends of Midden's ancient indoor swimming pool with the place all to themselves, yelling and laughing and hooting, daring each other to dive in.

When her laughter died down, he waited to hear the terrible buzz that meant the locks on the two heavy metal doors that separated him from her and from the rest of the world had been released. The silence, he supposed, meant that she was busy carrying out some command: raising her arms in order to be frisked or removing all the items from her pockets and placing them into a plastic basket that would be taken away and later returned, or filling out the form that asked the five questions about her reason for visiting and her relationship to him, though every single person who had anything to do with the Coltrap County Correctional and Rehabilitation Center already knew that she was his sister, as did half the people in Coltrap County itself.

At last he heard the mechanical buzz and the scuffle of her shoes as she stepped into the hallway, and then her voice saying hello to Tommy Johnson, who had been waiting for her all this time, as he did every Sunday, on the other side of the locked doors. Tommy had first escorted Joshua from his cell to the visiting room, where he left him handcuffed to the table that was bolted in six places to the floor while he went to fetch Claire.

"How was your week?" she asked Tommy melodically.

"Pretty good," he said. "How about yours?"

"*Good.*"

Claire and Tommy had been in the same grade, graduated high school together nearly five years before, and Joshua knew without seeing his sister's face that it was flushed at the moment—flushed every Sunday at this very moment—in shame. Over being here. Over her *brother* being here, an inmate, and to at least some extent, under Tommy's charge. "How *could* you?" she'd asked Joshua bitterly, time and time again, when he'd first been arrested, and then, after he'd half-attempted to explain, she'd interrupted him to hiss, "Thank God that Mom is dead."

He knew, without seeing her, the way she would walk down the hall: straight-backed with a polite smile on her face, her arms crossed in front of her as if she were chilled, doing everything in her power to conceal her humiliation, to resist without seeming to resist the knowledge that for the duration of the visit she too was under Tommy's charge.

"It's been so cold," she said. Their footsteps grew closer now, walking up the incline of the hall, where it became a long ramp that spilled out into what was officially considered the jail.

"It's February," said Tommy. "What do you expect?"

"Yes," she agreed, laughing falsely. "You're right—not much."

Joshua sat staring at his hands and wrists, cuffed to the table, hearing her steps grow louder. Aside from the four barred windows that sat high up near the ceiling at ground level, the room was subterranean, lit by fluorescent lights that gave his flesh a remotely green cast.

"Josh," she gasped the moment she saw him, a little breathless but not crying—he was grateful—this time. It had taken her three Sundays to harden up. This was his seventh Sunday in jail; he had five more to go. She came toward him, her footsteps now muffled on the vast gray carpet of the room, and then waited as Tommy unlocked and removed his handcuffs.

Freed, he stood and hugged her and they held on to each other longer than he'd ever imagined he would hang on to his sister in all of his life. Each visit they were granted two hugs—one for hello, the other for goodbye—and there could not for any reason be an additional hug in between. Because of this, they both knew to drag out each hug for as long as they possibly could. Claire smelled to him like she always did, like her hair, or rather her shampoo and conditioner. He had not, in his life previous to jail, thought to note her scent, but now he registered it as if he'd gone years without the ability to smell. He let himself take it in, her familiar aroma of rosemary and mint with an undercurrent of cherry.

"So . . . hello!" she said once they'd sat down across the table from each other. She took his hand and held it in both of her own. Though they'd often gone far more than a week without seeing each other, now that he was in jail, a week seemed like ages.

"Hi," he said, and their conversation spilled forth in the most ordinary way—how was work, how are you, and what else is new? But for those first several minutes of her arrival his heart continued to race as if she had come with the most important news. Each week he was allowed four half-hour visits. Lisa came twice—no one person could come more than twice in any given week—Claire once, and the last slot was available for whoever cared to come. Usually it was R.J. or Mardell or Leonard, though Bruce had come once. On occasion, it would be someone new entirely, someone who'd thought to come and see him, old friends from school. Each Monday a new week began and he would be granted four more visits, and only four, even if the week before one visit had gone unused. He carried the knowledge of his four visits with him, as if they existed not in the records kept on the computer system of the jail, but in his chest, on an imaginary card that felt as if it had been embedded there into which a hole would be punched each time someone who wanted to see him walked through the two locked doors.

Claire smiled. "So Lisa and I—we're starting our class this afternoon."

"I know," he said. "She's coming to see me afterward, so I'll hear all about it."

He noticed that Claire was wearing their mother's mood ring, which they'd played with together for hours as kids, believing that it would tell them what the future held.

"She's huge," she said. "I mean, all of a sudden. It's like she went from hardly looking pregnant to looking like she could pop."

He and Lisa had delivered the news that they were going to have a baby at the last possible moment, in the middle of November, when Lisa could no longer conceal the fact. Upon hearing the news, Claire had raged and wept. She'd warned Joshua that the baby would ruin his life and spouted out statistics to prove it. It astonished him, the things she carried around in her head. She knew what percentage of teen parents spent their entire lives living below the poverty line, how few of their children earned college degrees, the outrageously large unlikelihood that he and Lisa would still be together in two years.

"*Our mom* was a teen mom," he'd said to Claire when she was done with her statistics, believing he had an unassailable defense.

But she just shook her head, smiled at him incisively, and whispered, "Precisely my point."

Despite everything, Claire had quickly warmed to the idea of being an aunt, and not only an aunt but also something of a stand-in for Joshua while he was in jail. She was the one who accompanied Lisa to her prenatal appointments, who gave her books to read about pregnancy and what to do when the baby arrived. She'd even volunteered to be a replacement for Joshua at Lisa's labor and birth class and, as a gift to them, paid the tuition in full. Joshua would be released on March 5—two weeks before the baby was due—and Claire would tell him all the things she'd learned at the class that he'd need to know, so during the birth he could be of use.

"It's over at the hospital—the birth class," Claire said to him now. They both glanced toward the windows near the ceiling, from which they could see the sidewalk above them and the shoes of a rare passerby, and beyond that, but only if they got a chair and climbed on top of it to look out, the Blue River Hospital directly across the street, where Joshua and Lisa's baby would be born. They'd not learned the gender, wanting it to be a surprise.

"We'll wave at you," she said. "It gets over at four o'clock."

"How will I see you?" he asked, sharp irritation in his voice. It angered him when she pretended that things were not as they were.

"I meant, if you're in here and you look out the window." She pressed her hands against the edge of the table as if she were attempting to slide her chair back, but it stayed anchored in its place, drilled into the floor.

"Well, I won't be."

"I meant if you *were*, Josh."

"But the point is I won't be."

"Okay. You won't." She crossed her legs, her knees bumping against the bottom of the table. When she was settled she asked, "What's your problem today?"

"Nothing."

"Okay," she said tentatively. "Then don't wave at us. I was just trying to be nice. I was trying to *include you*, for your information."

Their eyes locked for a moment, then they each looked away, disgusted with each other. The room was large and open, the carpet like a field across its center. Despite the long table at which they sat with its bolts and metal loops for handcuffs, it had the feel of a kindergarten classroom. There was a sink and a cupboard, a terrarium filled with stones and small desert plants, and off in the corner a big chair with a floral-patterned fabric and a couch covered in dark green plaid that surrounded a coffee table scattered with magazines and plants and a box of Kleenex. It was called the "community room," the room where most things in Joshua's new jail life happened. It was where on Tuesday afternoons he, along with his fellow inmates, met with Pat McCredy for what she called "group," and where, every Thursday afternoon, he met with Pat McCredy for what she called "individual." And also where twice a week he took his exercise class, which was, to Joshua's great relief, not conducted by Pat McCredy, but by a shifting series of people who volunteered for a program whose sole concern was the physical fitness of inmates. Sometimes it was yoga, other times step aerobics or a thing that all of the inmates dreaded called "NIA," a new aerobics crossbreed that required of its participants periodic interludes of free-form dance improvisation. Joshua refused to improvise and instead kept his eyes on the instructor during these parts, attempting reluctantly to mimic her frenzy and pass it off as his own. On occasion no instructor showed up and whatever guard was on duty would wheel out the TV and VCR and put the exercise tape in—they had only one, *Hips, Abs, and Buns*—and then stand by to make sure everyone participated. By state law, they had to exercise two hours each week.

"I always feel like I should bring something," Claire said, breaking their silence, making the kind of unspoken truce they made over and over and over again all of their lives, to have their arguments and then to move on. "A cake or something." A mischievous smile came over her face. "Somewhere to hide the file or the razor blades or whatever." She spoke louder than necessary, so as to include Tommy Johnson, who stood guard just inside the locked door, listening to every word they said, and also to indicate that she was only joking. Tommy didn't move, didn't smile, didn't appear to have even heard Claire, though they knew he had. She turned back to Joshua and more quietly asked, "So, have you seen Bruce?"

"Not since he came that one time."

"He came into Len's on Wednesday. He said he'd visit you soon." In her voice he detected a slight tilt, a microscopic embarrassment over the facts of her life now: not only that she worked as a waitress, but also that she lived in Midden, working at the very bar that their mother had. *Claire Wood*—teachers, the people at the bank, the people he used to sell drugs to, everyone in the town, they all said to him in that same voice, the voice that contained their pride and contempt, their scorn and unmasked joy, they said it like a chant—*Your sister is Claire Wood? Now there's a girl who will go far.* When people asked what she was doing these days, she told them she was in transition, waiting to see what she really wanted to do, saving her money in the meanwhile.

"How's he doing?"

"Fine, I guess." She looked up at him, the veil he had come to recognize whenever they spoke of Bruce falling over her eyes. "He's starting to look . . . weird."

"How so?"

"I don't know. Just different. Hipper maybe. Not actually hip, but more *updated*. Like suddenly he cares what he looks like."

Joshua put his fingers into the metal loop on the table through which the chain of the handcuffs had been strung while he'd been handcuffed. He ached for a cigarette. "I think it's very funny," he said.

"What?" Her eyes cut sharply to him.

"Everything." Then added, "Bruce." They sat in silence together for several minutes, neither of them wanting to get into what they'd come to refer to as "the whole Bruce thing," but also not able to think of anything else to talk about at the moment.

"You'll never guess what," Claire said at last.

"What?"

"I saw a moose. Driving here. On the road. I took the shortcut across and there it was right in the middle of the road." She shrugged and looked away, as if she realized that seeing a moose was something that in fact he could have guessed.

"That's good luck," he said.

"It is?"

"Yeah."

She pushed her hair back behind her ears. It was shorter than it had ever been, cut into a bob above her chin and colored with a remotely maroon henna dye that would allegedly fade out naturally over time.

"I always thought it was a white horse. If you saw a white horse it's good luck."

"A moose too," he blurted. "Any wild animal. And also white horses." He realized that he could not be sure if indeed it was good luck to see a moose, but he wasn't going to admit that now.

"Well, good. We could use some luck." She reached out again and squeezed his hand. Her hands were cold, all of her life she'd had cold hands and cold feet. Her sock had started to burn once, smoke coiling out of a black hole while it was still on her foot after she'd held it too long and too close to the wood stove.

"Did you make a wish when you saw it?" he asked, immediately regretting he had. His mouth had grown dry. She'd been there for twenty-five minutes. In five more minutes Tommy would tell her it was time to leave. At this point in the visit he found himself almost always wishing that whoever had come to visit him was already gone so he wouldn't have to spend five minutes with the knowledge that soon they would be.

"Of course I didn't," she said. "How was I supposed to know to make a wish if I didn't know it was good luck to begin with?"

"You should have known. Now it isn't good luck," he said, without sympathy.

"Fuck you," she whispered somewhat sweetly, somewhat honestly angry. She drew an invisible spiral on the surface of the table with her index finger. "You always do that, Josh," she said, her face going serious, her hand going still.

"Do what?"

She looked away, toward one of the windows, where a dry yellow leaf that had somehow managed to survive the winter scuttled against its surface, trapped between the glass and the bars, then she turned her eyes back onto him, so bright, so large.

"Ruin everything."

Nine was the number of inmates at the jail during the months of Joshua's imprisonment, though only eight actually lived there. The ninth was a woman named Tiffany—the lone woman among them—who was housed, like all the rare female inmates, in a locked room in the basement of the hospital. For meals and visitors and for all the mandatory activities except exercise the guards brought her from the hospital to the jail in handcuffs, following an underground passageway that ran below the street. A different section of this same passageway was the one that Claire had walked down to visit Joshua, and it continued on to connect a series of buildings: the courthouse to the jail, the jail to the hospital, the hospital to the nursing home, and the nursing home back to the courthouse. At lunchtime on days when the weather was too hot or too cold, too rainy or icy or windy, the women who worked in the buildings through which the underground hallway passed did loops, walking fast together or alone, wearing sneakers and leggings with giant T-shirts that covered their behinds. If Joshua was in his cell, he could not see them pass by, but he could hear their footsteps and voices, echoing in the tunnel.

His cell was not as bad as he had expected. It was not dank and chilly and dark; sludge-filled cracks did not line the floors. Instead the floor was seamless and shiny, painted periwinkle. The periwinkle extended from the floor to midway up the wall and ended in an undulating border meant to suggest the ocean. From the edge of this sea, the wall was painted sky blue, as was the ceiling, which featured, in the far corner, a bright yellow sun with eyes and a mouth that smiled endlessly down upon him. The feel was not so much of a jail cell but of a neatly arranged cabin on a ship. Two cots sat on opposite walls, with a toilet behind a small panel in between them at the far end. At the head of the cots, both Joshua and his cellmate had a two-by-three-foot table that was bolted to the wall and a bench bolted to the floor before it. Above the table there was a small cabinet where they could store their belongings—they were each allowed a few small things. Joshua had his sketchbook and a sweater that his mother had knit that itched him, and a photo of Lisa holding her cat, Jasmine, in a vinyl frame that folded up and snapped closed.

His cellmate, to Joshua's great surprise, turned out to be Vern Milkkinen—the Chicken Man—his old coworker at the Midden Café. It hadn't occurred to Joshua that he'd been absent from his regular post in the Midden Dairy Queen parking lot the entire summer before. The Vern whom Joshua knew in jail was not the Vern he'd known at the café. At sixty-six, he had found religion. He was a new man, a reformed man, Pat McCredy's model inmate. Vern had been busted for driving drunk so many times, he'd been sentenced to a year. He'd be released a couple of months after Joshua. In the time that Vern had served before Joshua's arrival he had found God, vowed to never drink a drop of alcohol again, and written long letters addressed to everyone he loved, trying to make amends. To his son, Andrew, to his sister, Geraldine, and to his wife, even though by now she was dead.

In jail Joshua's mornings had a rhythm: at seven he would be awakened and escorted along with his fellow inmates to the shower; after showering and dressing they were led to the small dining room off the kitchen to eat. Tiffany would be there already, her wet hair falling forward, making a shield across her face as she bent over her bowl of oatmeal. After breakfast his job was to clean his half of the cell from top to bottom, including the walls and floor and ceiling on his side. Vern cleaned the other half. It kept them both occupied for a good thirty minutes each day and gave their cell—the hallway of four cells in a row—the persistent aroma of ammonia, a scent that Joshua associated always with his mother during the years when she had worked at the Rest-A-While Villa and come home smelling of it. When the cleaning was done, they had two hours in their cells for what was called "self-reflection." In the schedule that was taped to the wall in the community room there was a note of explanation written in this time slot, most likely, Joshua believed, composed by Pat McCredy: "Two hours in which you may reflect upon what it is that brought you here and where it is you may go after you leave."

Seldom did Joshua reflect upon what brought him here, though often he thought about where he would go after he left and that was straight to Lisa's bed, though he could not think of this too long or in too detailed a manner since Vern lay self-reflecting in his cot only a few feet away. What brought him to the jail was hardly worth a thought. Greg Price had found the bag of marijuana he kept in a tackle box in his truck. It could have been worse; he didn't have to be told. Greg Price could have found the Baggie full of the crystal meth that he had in an empty thermal mug in his glove compartment when he was stopped — a discovery that would have made it impossible for anyone to deny intent to sell, which would have put him in a different, more serious, criminal category and would have landed him not in the Coltrap County jail, but a state or federal prison most likely in St. Paul. He'd held his breath as Greg lifted the Thermos and shook it, listening to hear if anything moved inside, and then he tossed it back where it had been. Later, after he'd been arrested and Claire had come and paid his bail, he'd thrown the crystal meth into the Mississippi River, out behind Len's Lookout, wanting to make Vivian and Bender pay in at least this small way.

In the end he had not been charged with dealing marijuana because his attorney had convinced everyone involved of what, in fact, was true: that bag of marijuana in the tackle box had been only for Joshua's personal use. It had helped that the judge was a regular customer at Len's Lookout and had known his mother; it had helped that Bruce had built the cabinets that sat in the judge's kitchen. At his hearing it was agreed that Joshua would go to jail for eighty-five days and be on probation for a year afterward, waiving a trial or a right to appeal. He signed the papers in the judge's chambers of the Coltrap County Courthouse with his attorney standing next to him — Lisa and Claire were waiting out in the hall. Immediately afterward, he was led away in handcuffs, past Lisa and Claire, who both gasped and wept upon seeing him, down a staircase to the basement, to the underground hallway that took him to the processing room where the little paper man dressed in black marker held vigil, and then past him, to the locked world beyond, to jail.

The afternoons in the jail were great fields of time, punctuated by group or individual, exercise or visitors, or nothing at all, in which case Joshua would convince one of the guards to give him a pen or pencil so he could sit at the tiny table in his cell and draw. Vern would be next to him, reading his Bible, which he read so often that it was no longer a book but a stack of pages that he had to keep in a shoebox that Pat McCredy had brought in for him, which had once contained a pair of her many Birkenstocks.

Joshua now knew a great deal about Vern from the two hours they spent together each week in group. Hour one was called "sharing," hour two was "moving beyond." Often moving beyond got cut short because sharing ran so long. Sharing did not run long because the inmates sat down with much desire to share, but because Pat McCredy was so insistent about—and, Joshua had to admit, good at—forcing things out of each of them. With Vern, at least by the time Joshua came along, she didn't have to work too hard. He told them about how he used to hit his wife and son, about his own childhood growing up on a dairy farm that his family no longer owned, about the death of his father by tractor, about his mother who drank herself into a stupor all through his childhood and then killed herself accidentally by lighting her bed on fire with a fallen cigarette when he was sixteen. He told them about his twin brother who was mentally retarded, and who still lived, as it turned out, in the very nursing home across the street—he'd lived there for almost fifty years, ever since their mother died. Joshua listened to this without looking at Vern, seeing him only peripherally in his assigned seat immediately to the left, though sometimes he had to turn and face him whenever Pat McCredy demanded that it be so, when she had an exercise for them to do, as she often did, between sharing and moving beyond.

"I want you to go back," she said to them one day, "to what you dreamed for yourself when you were a kid." She inhaled a big breath and closed her eyes and slowly exhaled her breath as if she were meditating all alone in a room.

In the silence, Joshua gazed at Tiffany, who sat directly across the circle from him, studying the ends of her hair in one section and then another, delicately tugging strands of it from time to time to snap off a split end. She was somewhat bitchy and just okay-looking, but she moved him anyway, the pure sight of her: the feast of her face, her mannish hands and flat chest, her plush hips and butt that seemed to have absorbed all the fat that refused to settle anywhere else. She was older than him, twenty-eight, and he felt more sorry for her than he did all the men combined—not only did she have to reveal her innermost feelings, but she also had to reveal them to a bunch of men in jail. All she'd done was write bad checks.

"Let's do this together, folks," Pat McCredy said without opening her eyes. "Let us all remember together when we were kids. Let's go back there. What did we want for ourselves?" She opened her eyes and stood and made her way slowly around their circle of nine chairs. She was at least six feet tall, her brown hair dim with gray and pulled back in a thin braid. Her shoulders were wide and hard-looking; her hips squarish and flabby, hoisted a few inches too high, it seemed, by her impossibly long legs. The overall effect was that she was part woman, part something else, part horse or buffalo. She wore a green turtleneck and green tights beneath an enormous beige smock that went down past her knees, her feet in purple Birkenstocks. From the loose pocket at the front of the smock she took a stack of tiny squares of construction paper and made her way around the circle, handing them each one piece, instructing them to write one of their childhood dreams. They had pens already, and journals she'd given them and forced them to decorate with finger paint and glitter, colored markers and crayons. Pat McCredy was big on writing things down. The journals, they could keep to themselves; with the pieces of paper anything could happen, but most often what happened is that they were collected by Pat McCredy, who used them as what she called "starting points" in individual.

Joshua balanced his journal on his knee and placed the square of paper on top of that. He'd painted the entire cover of his journal midnight blue and then, with glitter and glue, added tiny white stars.

"Your childhood dreams—or dream—one is fine," said Pat Mc-Credy, prompting them, as if they were on a TV quiz show and needed to have the question rephrased.

He wrote: *To move to California.* It was true enough. It was personal enough. In individual he could work up the energy to discuss this dream with Pat McCredy, if called upon to do so.

"Is everyone done?" she asked, looking around.

"Hold on," said Tiffany. Her hazel eyes flashed onto Joshua for an instant and in that instant he ached for her, felt that she ached for him, as if she'd placed her hand on his bare stomach or crossed the room and whispered something secret in his ear, but then he tamped it down. He was going to be good now, from here on out, nothing but strictly Lisa's fiancé.

"Okay," Pat McCredy said when Tiffany was done. "Now I want you to pass your paper to the left." A mumble of protest rippled across the room, but there was nothing to be done, they were powerless to her, and so they made their way around the circle, reading from the nine paper squares. *To be a singer,* said Tiffany's. *To work as a clown at Disneyland,* said Frank Unger's. *To be rich,* said Dan Bell's. And so it went until they reached Vern. "To move to California," he said while Joshua sat blank-faced and still as a doll listening to his own inane words.

He talked about it with R.J. the next time he came to visit — how they would move to California and be mechanics together someday — though they spoke of it differently now, as if it had been a joke all along.

"We should go just to prove my old lady wrong. She always said we wouldn't go," R.J. said, a flash of anger moving across his face, and then he laughed, like he always did when he spoke of his mother.

"How is she, anyway?" asked Joshua.

"The same." He stared at Joshua for several moments with his dark eyes, as if he wanted to say more, though they both knew they couldn't say much about Vivian and Bender with Tommy Johnson standing by, listening to every word. "Still fucked up," he said at last, and cleared his throat. He'd slimmed down since he'd moved to Flame Lake. Without his baby fat he looked taller and older, and, even Joshua would admit it, more handsome. "Oh, and you know my dad went back to drinking."

Joshua nodded, expecting as much.

"He's an old drunk." R.J. laughed, and reached up to adjust the pendant he wore, an oval cracked in half along a jagged line. His new girlfriend, who lived in South Dakota, wore the other half. "I knew it for a while, but I kept thinking he'd go back to not doing it. He started out with just kind of sneaking around. Having a beer now and then and acting like he didn't, but now he don't even deny it." R.J. turned and looked at Tommy, then back to Joshua. "That's the thing I learned, eh. People don't change."

"Every once in a while they do," said Joshua, feeling, without wanting to feel, affronted.

"Like who?" asked R.J., and then Joshua told him all about Vern, going on, with a kind of glee, about the details he thought R.J. would be interested to know — about Vern's retarded twin brother who lived in the nursing home, about how he beat his wife. It felt good to be talking about someone else's problems, though when he was in group listening to it firsthand it made him want to throw up. At times Joshua became almost dizzy, witnessing the mastery with which Pat McCredy would get the inmates to divulge. Her voice was like the softest stroke on a piano key, so strong and sure and hushed. She had an entire orchestra of sounds and modulations. A single word from her mouth could be pitched in a manner to mean hundreds of things, to elicit the most revealing and incriminating responses. When she was done with one person, she would move on seamlessly to the next, fixing her gaze so intently it was impossible not to gaze back. "So," she began each time, knowing, as she did with most of her questions, precisely what the answer was, "whose turn?"

There were things that nobody knew, that he would never tell anyone, no matter how hard Pat McCredy pushed. The deep jelly core of him that only he knew. It could not be spoken of. He had no words for it, what made him, what pained him, what rocked him and fucked him. This thing for which he had no words was his life, and his job in jail was to protect it from Pat McCredy. And so he did, speaking to her of arguments he'd had with Lisa or Claire, of career paths he might take, or what had kept him from once and for all getting his GED. For Pat Mc-Credy he created the story of his mother and the story of his father — sad, heartbreaking really, but he'd survived, he was forging on (he left the story of Bruce out of it entirely, by maintaining that all was well on that front) — and Pat McCredy gave him the words. She gave him *closure* and *forgiveness*, *adult child* and the *five stages of grief*. She was good, she pried, she challenged him and applied her techniques, made him pour what she thought was his soul out onto paper, but he was better, fiercer, more who he was than she believed he had the strength to be, and so he held on, safe against her.

On one front she had made progress, he would grant her that. He'd made the mistake, in his first week in group, of writing the words *drugs and alcohol* on one of Pat McCredy's squares of construction paper in response to her question, "What techniques do you use to ease your pain or sorrow?" He'd meant it as something of a joke, though in fact it was true. Over the past year he had become one stop short of what his mother would call a "big drinker"—not exactly an alcoholic, but someone who probably drank too much, too often. When he wasn't drinking, pot kept him on balance throughout the day as he drove from place to place, delivering drugs. Meth he did not touch, a point that he, in his own defense, returned to over and over again in his individuals with Pat McCredy, though she was unmoved by this.

"It's not what others do, Joshua. It's what *you* do. Marijuana can be an addiction as serious as any other. As can beer."

"But don't tell me it's like meth," he insisted. "Are you aware of what's happening with meth? It's everywhere around here. It's a serious, serious thing."

"I *am* aware," she said sternly. She loved to talk drugs and alcohol; they were her professional forte. "We're not talking about this as a societal problem, however. We're talking about *you*."

"What *about* me?"

"Well, why don't you tell me?" She smiled at him, waiting, and then she couldn't help but say more, "I'm not the one who wrote that I use drugs and alcohol to ease my sorrow, am I?" She waited again. "Who was it that wrote that down, Joshua?"

"Me," he almost yelled.

"Okay," Pat McCredy said, more calmly than ever. "Then let us begin from there."

In the end, much to Joshua's relief, she did not pull out a yellow "permission to depart" sheet to request that he be allowed to attend the AA meetings in the basement of the hospital, as Vern and five of the other inmates, including Tiffany, had to do three times a week, all of them sitting there shackled in chains, one to the other, among the free-roaming alcoholics of Blue River. She warned him that this decision could change, as they "continued on this journey of self-discovery together." For now, he was not an alcoholic or a drug addict and for that he was thankful. Instead he had what Pat McCredy called "issues with chemical dependency." His use was situational, in her assessment, perhaps tied directly to his grief.

And it was, he realized one afternoon after his session with Pat McCredy, having not realized it before. She was right — *he* had been right when he wrote those words on the square of paper in the first place. In jail, he missed his nightly drinks, his daily joints more dearly than perhaps he missed any person. Drink did not open him up, it did not allow him to think and weep freely. Instead it bolstered him against his thoughts, against *her*, his mother. It was the thing that had helped him, all those nights in his apartment, or lying next to Lisa, go into his torpor. Three beers or shots were all he needed, though often he had more, each one a seal, a lid, a cure.

The nights in jail were the worst, as he lay on his cot stone-cold sober next to Vern, staring at the dark ceiling, the yellow of the painted sun the only thing he could see. Early on, he'd had to strike a deal with himself: each night he would allow himself to cry, but only for thirty seconds. If he could not keep himself from crying, at least he could contain it with the voice in his head counting *one, two, three* as the tears streamed silently down his face, into his ears and hair. It wasn't that he willed himself to cry, or that he was thinking particularly of his mother, or remembering things she'd said or done. It wasn't even precisely *his mother*, though what he felt was directly tied to her—her life and her death. It was that he felt all of his sorrow, lodged in a furrow in his chest, palpable and real as an apple. It was there and it could not be avoided, would not be denied, and each night, for thirty seconds, he bowed to it. He was aware, as he wept, that his tears would gratify Pat McCredy, but he would never tell her about them. She would name them, define them, turn them into something other than what they were, something other than his own.

When he finished crying, he got up and went to the little bathroom cubby and wiped his face and blew his nose into a wad of toilet paper. Vern sometimes turned then, though his breath never broke its long, deep sleeping rhythm. Joshua would lie back down on his cot and stare at the ceiling for a while longer. The jail always seemed, at this moment, quieter than it had been before, and also more open, as if there weren't a series of barricades and bars and locked doors between him and the rest of the world, as if he could have stepped outside to take a look at the cold night sky if he'd cared to. From his cot he felt that he could feel the gentle presence of the entire town of Blue River that surrounded him: its every dim streetlight, its old brick school, its Burger King lit up like a circus on the town's one low hill, and, more than anything, he could feel the river, the Mississippi. He could feel Midden, far off, to the north, and Flame Lake a paler star north farther still.

Often, as he lay there after crying and before sleep, he had the sensation that his mother was in his cell with him. In the weeks immediately after she'd died he had invented various tests for her to see if she was watching him. He had commanded her to turn on or off a light or make a chair move or the wind come through the curtain at a certain time. She had failed every one, but now he didn't need her to pass any tests. Sometimes he simply allowed himself to believe that she was there, above him in the painted sun, watching him. Other times he closed his eyes and let the breathing, sleeping person in the cot beside him be his mother, not Vern Milkkinen. To his surprise this was not so hard to do. The moment he allowed himself to hear the rhythm of his mother's breath in that of Vern's, she was there, in his every sigh and twitch. Twice he'd gone so far as to extend his arm midair into the center of the room. He imagined his mother reaching out from the opposite cot and taking his hand. He imagined all the things she would do and did, the things he hadn't been grateful for when she was alive, the things he would say sorry for if he had one last chance and he could. But then Vern would move and an unmistakably masculine grunt would issue forth from his dry mouth, and as fast as she had appeared, Joshua's mother would be gone.

"They did a marathon on the radio of your mom's old shows," Bruce told him the next time he came to visit—it was only the second time he'd come.

"They did?" asked Joshua, his voicing squeaking embarrassingly.

He nodded. "I caught some of it. They did a segment at the end where they interviewed various people at the station who knew your mom. Who she was, what she did, what she was like, and so forth." He reached up and twirled the diamond stud in his ear. "A tribute, I suppose."

A heat, a pressure, a vapor, rose like a hot hand behind Joshua's face, making his eyes water, his cheeks grow warm, as if he'd had a glass of whiskey in one straight shot. "What did they say?"

Bruce sat thinking about it for a moment, the expression on his face quizzical, as if he were pondering something philosophical, utterly unrelated to him. "That she was a nice lady," he said, scratching his arm. "That everyone enjoyed listening to her show."

Joshua forced himself to cough, feeling the hand, the vapor that felt like whiskey but wasn't rise again and press behind his face, wanting, with the cough, to force it down, for fear that he would burst into tears. *Fuck*, he thought over and over again, *motherfuck*, to get himself back in line. He shifted in his chair, wanting to be two people: to be the person who demanded, *Tell me what my mother was like*—he knew, of course, but still he *wanted to know*, to hear, and in particular to hear it from Bruce— and also to be the person who sat still and hard and calm as a statue in his chair, as if no part of him could be moved or reached or known.

He opted, on instinct, to be the latter. It was the easier person to be.

He willed himself to think of whatever he could that was not his mother, which, instantly, was Tiffany, and the way in group that afternoon she'd picked indifferently through the ends of her hair and then, suddenly, erotically, it seemed, looked up at him.

"I wonder how much time we got left," asked Bruce after a while, patting his hands on the metal table.

"Twelve minutes," Joshua said, staring at the clock behind Bruce's head, in a voice as leaden as he could muster.

"Feel this," said Lisa the following week, pulling Joshua's hand toward her, pressing his palm onto the side of her round belly. He had to lean forward hard, trying not to actually rise from his chair. Anything that could be construed as standing during the visit—other than the hello and the goodbye—was strictly against the rules. She pressed her palm more firmly on top of his and together they waited until he felt a tap and then another one in quick succession.

"Cool," said Joshua. It surprised him every time. Even with less than a month to go before the baby was due, he found it hard to honestly believe that inside of Lisa there was a baby.

"It's been like that night and day lately," she said, letting go of his hand. "I can hardly sleep anymore."

"No?"

"Oh, I try. I lay there. When you're home I'll sleep better."

"I don't sleep well neither. But we only have a week to go." He squeezed her hands. They were slightly puffy, like the rest of her except for her legs, which were as long and bony as they'd always been.

"So, Claire and I are making progress. This class is really good, Josh. I wish you could go. Today they taught us how to breathe." She took a deep breath in and then exhaled it.

"To breathe deep?"

"Yeah—but it's a special deep breath. Like this." She demonstrated it again. "In through the nose, out through the mouth. You'll have to remind me to do that when I'm in labor."

"Okay."

"Oh—and guess what? Next week we're going to see a video of an actual birth."

"That should be interesting." He felt what he always felt when they were talking about the baby: that he had to smile and nod and say yes in all the right places, the way he did when he was listening to charming stories of someone else's child. Lisa was the opposite, in love with the baby already. She'd put her hands on her belly and talk to it, telling it how they were going to spoil it, and how cute it would be and that they were going to get it special things to wear, like a pair of red baby cowboy boots.

"Some people, when they see the video, get kind of afraid—that's what the lady who does the class said—but other people get more excited." She looked at him, her eyes fervent like they were whenever they spoke of the birth. "Are you afraid?"

"Of what?"

"Of the birth. Of everything going okay."

"It'll go okay."

"It's a big deal, you know."

"I know." He rubbed the tops of her forearms.

"Sometimes I don't know if you know how big of a deal it is."

"I do," he said, tracing around several of the freckles on her arm with his finger. "It's a very big deal. But we have to think positive."

She stared at him for several moments, her brown eyes getting watery. "I could die, for your information," she said, her voice wavering with tears. "I mean, people have. Lots of people."

"But not anymore, Lees. That was back in the olden days."

"That isn't true," she said passionately, her eyes cutting back to him. She wiped her face with her hands. "Okay, it isn't *common*, but it happens. You never know, Josh. Childbirth is a very serious matter."

"I know. But it doesn't mean you're going to die. Think of all the women who *don't* die." They sat in silence for several moments, until he asked, "Do you want me to rub your feet?"

She shook her head. Last time he saw her, she'd taken her shoes off and propped her feet up on the table so he could massage them.

"Try not to be afraid," he said, wishing he could hug her.

The door opened and the other guard—Fred—popped his head in and, seeing Tommy was there, stepped aside to let Tiffany through the door. Lisa turned to see what was the commotion.

"Hi," Tiffany called to Joshua meekly, the first time she'd ever addressed him directly.

"Hi."

"Hi," Lisa said, turning back to look curiously at Joshua. Sometimes people had visitors at the same time and they had to share the community room, but he felt too self-conscious to explain that now that Tiffany was in the room. He considered, for an instant, introducing them, but immediately cast the idea aside.

She followed Tommy hesitantly across the room and sat at the far end of the table and waited while he chained her to it.

"So," Joshua said quietly to Lisa, trying to act as if Tiffany's presence had no effect on the two of them and their conversation. "What else?"

Tommy got the cardboard divider that sat in the corner of the room and propped it on the table, blocking Tiffany from their view. Paintings that Pat McCredy had forced them to do were tacked onto the divider. "Paint for me your inner child," she'd commanded.

"What else?" asked Lisa, feeling self-conscious too, Joshua knew. Silently, he tried to purge all the lustful thoughts he'd had for Tiffany, as if Lisa might be able to read his mind. "Oh. My mom's throwing me a baby shower next Sunday. It was supposed to be a surprise, but then I found out because Deb said something in front of me at work and then they just went ahead and told me. It's going to be at Deb's house."

"I knew about it. Claire told me." In his peripheral vision, he could see his inner child hanging from its tack—a page painted entirely black with an explosion of orange and red and yellow at its center. A fire in the back of a cave is what it was, though Pat McCredy insisted it was something else entirely: something vaginal, signifying his desire to go back to the womb.

"They're doing a money tree, where everyone brings a card with money inside and hangs it on a tree and then we can buy what we want."

"That'll help," he said, stroking her beautiful arms, all the way up to her elbows. Her skin was like nothing else on this earth to him. "I sure wish I could be there."

She smiled at him, a light flickering in her eyes. "You couldn't anyway, honey. No men are allowed." She glanced at the divider, her eyes scanning the paintings without seeming to take them in—the blobs of color, the mad spirals and lopsided hearts, and the one that was blank almost entirely, aside from a nearly transparent daisy at its center. Tiffany's, of course.

"Lisa," he said, wanting to distract her so she wouldn't focus in and ask which was his. Abruptly, she turned back to him. He sat silently for a moment, trying to think of what to say. "I hate it in here so much. I want to come home."

"I know you do. I hate it too. But we only got one more week of this."

"I was thinking I could put my name on the list at the oven factory," he said, though the idea of working among the heat and toxic fumes filled him with dread. "It's a good job. Good money."

"It *is*, Josh. I think you should."

"It might take a while before I can get in, but at least I can get my name on the list. It would be a positive step that I could take for our future," he said, hearing, to his remorse, a glimmer of Pat McCredy in his voice, hoping that Tiffany was not hearing the same thing.

"A couple more minutes," Tommy said to them, and Lisa shut her eyes, then opened them and smiled sadly at Joshua.

"What about me?" asked Tiffany from behind the cardboard divider.

Joshua picked up Lisa's hand and pressed it to his lips, kissed it, then held it there. It was easier, at the end, if neither one of them said anything. They simply looked deeply into each other's eyes, silently telling each other things. He told her the same things that he'd told her each visit, but now he felt that he meant it more than he ever had, compelled, he sadly realized, by the proximity of Tiffany, who now, suddenly, repulsed him.

"I'll bring them to you when they come," Tommy said sternly. "There ain't nothing I can do."

"I know it," Tiffany said. "I just hope they didn't have car trouble. My mom's been having trouble with her car," she said to no one, the chains clanking lightly against the table, unable to keep herself from gesturing with her hands as she spoke.

"Who's coming?" asked Lisa, without taking her eyes off of Joshua, then she turned her head and stared at the divider.

It took Tiffany several moments to realize she was being spoken to.

"My kids," she said at last. "And my mom."

"How many do you have?" asked Lisa, still holding on to Joshua's hand.

"Two. Two boys. They're four and five."

"How sweet. It's nice they're so close in age. They'll always be friends." She gave his hand a squeeze, then released it and stood. She liked to stand before Tommy came and told her it was time. Joshua stood too and went around the table for their goodbye hug.

They could see Tiffany now, over the divider. The sheet of her glorious hair, the sharp jag of her nose, her tiny fierce eyes looking up at them, an expression on her face as if she were seeing Joshua for the first time.

"Lisa, this is Tiffany, by the way. Tiffany, this is Lisa," said Joshua, putting his arm around her shoulders. "My fiancée."

That night, even after his nightly cry, even after he'd stood and blown his nose, Joshua could not fall asleep. He lay listening to the silence of the jail and the underground hallway that wrapped around it for so long that he began to hear the sounds he'd never detected before: an unidentifiable ticking from the direction of the guard's room, the hum of the soda machine that sat in the hallway beyond the reach of the inmates, and, most annoyingly of all, the in and out of Vern's breath as he lay sleeping a few feet away.

The ticking from the guards' room brought to mind a particular bird that appeared in Coltrap County every spring. Joshua could remember the precise call of the bird—*tick-tick-tick, click-click-click*—but he could not for the life of him remember what the bird was called. It was a special bird, rare. People from the Cities came up to see it, parking their cars on the side of the highway where it bordered the Midden bog, spending hours looking through their binoculars. His mother had done a radio show on the bird a few years back.

He thought about Lisa. About her visit and what they'd said to each other and the way they'd kissed goodbye for so long that Tommy had had to intervene. He thought, *What if she did die? What if something went wrong during the birth and then he was left with a baby to take care of?* Claire would help him, he reasoned. And then his mind leapt again—*what if Claire died? Or Bruce?* Ever since his mother died, this was what he feared. That everyone would die—*and they would*—he knew they would, but he feared that they were going to die soon, which was different from knowing they would someday. At night, alone in the apartment, stoned, all those months, or lying next to Lisa, buzzed on a few beers, he'd been able to make up a place in his brain so when everyone died he'd be ready for it, but now, here in his jail cell, there was no place. The only place was him, alone in his body, alone in his life, having to make it all okay by himself, from scratch.

He let himself think it. He forced himself to think it: if Lisa died and Claire died and Bruce died and the whole world died but him and the baby, he would be okay. He would find a way. He lay there thinking honestly for the very first time of the baby. The baby itself. His son or daughter, whom he did not yet love. *I do not love my baby,* he thought, like a mantra, remorsefully, to himself. And then tiny tendrils of something began to creep into his mind—questions like, *Will it be smart or dumb? Nice-looking or ugly? Cry night and day or sit around all silent and dazed from staring at the lamps?* His tears welled up again and he sniffed.

From the darkness, came Vern's voice. "You doing okay over there, bud?"

Joshua instantly went silent, as if suddenly frozen solid, refusing even to take a breath for several seconds.

"Yep," he said when he was able to. He went to the toilet and unwound some paper from the roll. "I think I have a cold," he explained and cleared his throat hard and blew his nose.

"It's the damnedest thing," said Vern.

Joshua did not reply. He had no idea what the damnedest thing was. He went to his cot and lay back down again and stared at the faint light of the yellow-painted sun.

"I can't sleep here for nothing," said Vern after Joshua thought he'd fallen back to sleep already. "I lay here every night and oh, sure, I *try* to sleep. My dad used to say just close your eyes and act like you're sleeping and pretty soon you will be sleeping, but that never worked for me."

They lay in silence together for another several minutes. Joshua would not allow himself to believe that Vern had heard him crying every night, that all the while he'd thought he'd been asleep, Vern had been lying next to him, hearing it all.

"I suppose it's that I got so much on my mind," said Vern.

"Yep," Joshua said noncommittally. He did not want to encourage Vern to tell him what was on his mind.

"I suppose you do too."

"Yep," Joshua said again.

"What with the baby coming and all. You picked out any names for it yet?"

They had, but they'd vowed to not tell anyone what they were. "Luke if it's a boy and Iris if it's a girl," he said into the darkness.

"Them are nice," said Vern. "Or it could be both—you never know if you could have twins, a boy and a girl, and then you could use both Iris *and* Luke."

"It's only one. They have the tests, where they know." He turned to Vern, but couldn't see him. "The ultrasound."

"Oh, sure they do. Now back when I was born, there was no way telling. So first I come out and then lo and behold there's another one in there, and out comes Val. He was born seventeen minutes later, so I've always been the oldest."

Joshua closed his eyes. He hoped they would sleep now, or pretend to sleep, silent and private together like they always had been, but then Vern said, "There's been something I always wanted to say to you—or I suppose, in truth not always—but since I been in here, since I found my new path." Joshua could feel the tension in Vern's voice, the tension in their little cell. He opened his eyes and folded his hands on his chest and stared at the painted sun. A rustling sound came from Vern's direction, as he sat up and then turned to face Joshua. "In the past, with you, at the café, I didn't always behave like I should've. Like the good Lord put me on the earth to do."

"That's okay," said Joshua, wanting to stop him as soon as he could.

"No, it ain't okay, so don't just go saying it is," insisted Vern so loudly that Joshua feared he'd wake the other inmates up, and then he continued on in a reverent hush: "I'm gonna have to beg your forgiveness."

"You're forgiven," whispered Joshua instantly, and then, "There's nothing to be forgiven for."

"Please don't say that," Vern said mournfully. "Please let me take responsibility for the harm I've done. It's part of my path. This is a road I must walk—the road of taking full responsibility for the consequences of my actions—or I can't get any further down the path."

"Okay," said Joshua timidly, hoping to simply end this.

"Okay then, bud. For that I'm deeply grateful." He was silent for several moments, to Joshua's relief, but then he went on: "For the good and the bad. For everything that has come my way. Them are the things made me who I am today. Them things made it so it's with this face that I may greet the Lord."

"Yep," said Joshua, not wanting to seem rude, nor interested.

"Another thing I wanted to say is something I've never said and that's how sorry I was to hear about your ma."

"Thank you."

"Do you believe in angels?" asked Vern.

Joshua thought for a few moments, and then told him the truth. "I don't know. It's still something I have to figure out."

"I got this feeling that they're real," said Vern. "Sometimes I get the

300

feeling that your ma's in here, watching over you. Right here in this very room—her spirit."

"I wonder sometimes," said Joshua, staring at the sun.

"She's following you around," Vern pressed on. "Hoping you'll be happy."

"I *am* happy," he lied. The same pressure he'd felt when he'd last seen Bruce rose again. A heat like whiskey, pushing against the back of his face, misting his eyes.

"That's all a parent wants. That's all I ever wanted for my Andrew."

"You did?"

"Oh, sure—even though I failed him, even though I wasn't the way I should have been. I hoped he'd be happy with his life. You always love your kids. You'll see. That's how you'll be."

"I want to be a good dad," said Joshua, speaking words he'd never spoken to Lisa.

"You will, bud. There's no doubt in my mind, that's for sure."

"I suppose we should try and get some sleep," he said after a while, and then he heard Vern shifting on his cot to lie down.

"Good night," said Vern.

"'Night," said Joshua.

The pressure rose behind his face again and he lay there feeling it without trying to push it back. The heat and the vapor, the whiskey and the hand, the hot sting of what he was just beginning to imagine was love.

17

IT HAD BEEN CLAIRE'S IDEA to look after the house, much to her almost immediate regret. She'd made the offer in a burst of the kind of misplaced nostalgia and unvarnished optimism she was given to from time to time—brought about, on occasion, by a glass of wine, or a particular song, or the way the light was hitting a stand of trees. In this case, it was Iris. The way it felt to hold her—*her brother's daughter!* she couldn't help but exclaim—in her arms. Iris brought out things in Claire that she thought were dead or lost forever, and also things she'd never known were there to begin with. Tender, essential, happy-sad emotions that made it seem a terrible shame that things had gone the way they had with Bruce—and Kathy, Claire was reluctant to add even silently to herself, even in her most magnanimous mood, but she added it anyway, and then she picked up the phone.

"Hello," she said, trying to sound calm and pleasant and not even remotely drunk when Kathy answered—she wasn't drunk, but she'd had a drink and it came flooding into her brain the moment she heard Kathy's voice. "This is Claire," she said overly concisely, as if she were teaching diction.

"Claire! Hello!" Kathy boomed, almost hysterically. They had not, since Kathy had became Bruce's wife, actually spoken before, or rather, not so directly and only to each other. They had chatted every now and then crossing paths at the Lookout or in town. They had sat several feet away from each other at Lisa and Joshua's place, marveling over the baby.

"Bruce told me that you were going out of town in a couple of weeks and I wondered if you needed anyone to look after the animals."

"Oh!" said Kathy. "That's sweet. But you know, we're going to be camping, so we're taking the dogs and—well, actually the horses will need looking after and the chickens."

"And Shadow," Claire said, more collected now that she'd gotten the gist of it out. "I mean, I wouldn't *stay* there, the nights or anything. I just thought . . . if you needed someone to come out."

"That's very nice," said Kathy. "But only if you've got the time. I could ask my folks."

"I can do it. I'll get Josh to help me."

"Great." There was a beat of silence and then Kathy said, "Well, Bruce isn't home or else I know he'd want to talk to you."

"Okay."

"He can talk to you about where the key is now and everything. We moved it from its old hiding place."

"I have one on my ring," said Claire, and then wished she hadn't.

"Good." She paused. "I'll let Bruce talk to you about the details later."

When they hung up she called Joshua immediately, even though he was at work. He had a job at the oven factory now, thanks in part to Lisa's mom's boyfriend, John Rileen, who was a manager there and had pulled some strings. When the secretary answered, Claire insisted that she go out onto the floor and bring Joshua back to the phone, a thing she was supposed to do only in emergencies.

"We're housesitting for Bruce and Kathy," she burst the moment he said hello.

"What?"

"They're going camping in Arkansas, on some honeymoon they never had, and I said we'd take care of the place." She attempted to modulate her voice so it sounded both casual and authoritative at once, so he would not dispute anything she said, but it didn't work.

"I don't know what you're talking about, Claire. I have my job and Iris. I never said I'd stay out at the house."

"We don't have to stay there!" she said, as if that would change everything, but he didn't reply. "Okay. I know you've got to get back to work. We can talk about it more later."

She hung up the phone and shot out of her chair and paced around her apartment, galvanized by what she had done, what she'd said she would do, with Joshua or without. She tried to imagine the house now, with Kathy's things inside. She had been to Kathy's little cabin once years ago, but she'd only stepped inside the door, dropping something off. In honor of her profession, Kathy had on display a collection of black and white mugs shaped like cows, their tails the handles, their comical faces jutting out near the curvy rim. Claire imagined them in her mother's kitchen now, sitting on the shelf above the sink. But then she couldn't imagine anything else, or at least not anything else about the house. Her mind jangled and jumped from one thing to another, to a series of disconnected memories of home. Of her mother standing on a chair pounding a nail into the wall to hang one of her paintings, the tiny, secret veins that flowered at the backs of her knees. Of the way Bruce's hair would look, knotted and flattened, in the winter when he removed his hat after wearing it all day. After a while, she was able to see it, but only from a distance, as if she were standing at the end of the driveway. The house, the chicken coop, the barn, and Bruce's shop: the tribe of buildings that used to be home.

On the morning she was meant to go there she woke early and made herself a cup of tea. "It's going to be fine," she said to the aloe vera plants and the chairs, the cuckoo clock that hung against the wall, its silver pendulum making a clicking sound each time it reached the end of its range. She did this often, spoke to herself and the objects in her apartment, telepathically or out loud, though she felt in some faraway place inside of herself that she was actually speaking to her mother. It was easy to do, surrounded as she was by her mother's things. In September, when she'd moved in, she'd had to unpack not only all the boxes she'd left at Andre's and then retrieved, but also all the boxes of her mother's things that she'd packed up frantically and stored in the apartment back in June. She'd given Joshua a good portion of it. He had filled Lisa's trailer with their old furniture, playing house, it seemed at first, and then making it a home for real. What remained in Claire's apartment was an eclectic mix of the things she either needed or could not bear to let go of: a set of china and a plastic colander, the quilts Teresa had made for each of their beds and a rickety shelf that held Claire's books.

After breakfast she went down to the Lookout. It was her day to clean the bar. She did it each Sunday morning in exchange for rent. Inside, empty of the people and the sounds of the dishwasher or the jukebox or the deep fryer, the bar felt almost holy to her in its hush. It was her favorite time to be there, all alone each week, the first of her three days off. She took her supplies from the utility closet and got to work.

When she was finished with the bathrooms she went behind the bar, poured a glass of orange juice, and switched the radio on. Ken Johnson was going on about something that the school board had done. It was the *Ken Johnson Hour*, a show, like most of the shows produced by locals, about anything Ken Johnson wanted it to be. Some weeks he played music—it could be the Grateful Dead or Maria Callas—other weeks he discussed whatever was on his mind, rambling and occasionally incisive, self-deprecating and self-aggrandizing in equal turn. Shows like Ken Johnson's were punctuated by the national broadcasts that the station could afford to buy. Claire listened to them all, the local shows and the nationals, each Sunday morning as she cleaned and also upstairs in her apartment when she wasn't at work. She didn't own a TV, and the radio had become again the way it had been to her as a child, when she and her mother and Joshua had first moved in with Bruce and they didn't have electricity yet, when a windmill had powered their radio. It was her friend and constant companion, shaping the rhythm of her days.

One Sunday morning back in January, before Claire had gone downstairs to clean she turned on the radio and heard her mother's voice. "Welcome friends and neighbors!" Teresa said, the way she always had. "This is *Modern Pioneers!*"

Claire had the feeling someone had walked up and slapped her across the face. She switched the radio off immediately, as though dousing a flame. In the silence that followed she sat staring at the radio, as if it might combust, knowing that she would have to turn it back on. Of course she would. Her mother was there. Before doing so, she adjusted the volume down so low she couldn't hear it when she turned it on. In slow increments, she turned the dial. Eventually, she heard the murmur not of her mother's voice, but that of Marilyn Foster-Timmons, identifying, one after the other, the station affiliates, their lyrical numbers and letters and towns. When Marilyn was done she explained that nearly a year ago a woman named Teresa Wood had died of cancer—"Many of you will have known her," Marilyn said in her voice that was at once gravelly and warm—and that she had hosted a show called *Modern Pioneers*. In a moment they would commence a broadcast of listeners' top ten favorite editions of the show, a mini-marathon that would last all day long.

Claire did not have to listen. Marilyn Foster-Timmons had sent her a box that contained CDs of every one of her mother's two hundred and thirty-six shows. But she listened anyway. Reluctantly at first, rapturously by the end. She listened all through that Sunday, not bothering to go downstairs to clean. During a station break she scribbled a note to Leonard and Mardell, explaining that she had a fever, ran downstairs and left it on the bar, and then dashed back to her apartment before her mother came on again. Claire listened for hours, unmoving on her bed. To move, even in the meditative silence with which she cleaned the bar while listening to the radio on other Sunday mornings, would break her concentration and obliterate her mother. It would keep Claire from being able to believe things that weren't true. Or rather, from believing one thing over and over again: that her mother was in a small dark studio in Grand Rapids, Minnesota, alive and well, her gigantic earphones clamped on her head. Believing she was there, talking to Mimi Simons about heirloom seeds, or Patty Peterson about dowsing, or John Ornfeld about building your own indoor compost toilet, or holding forth for two of the hours herself, telling all the listeners within a hundred-mile radius about the things they'd done, the life they'd had — Bruce and Teresa and Claire and Joshua, when there had been such a thing — about the garden she'd planted, the wool she'd carded and dyed, the loom Bruce had made, her recipe for dill pickles.

Claire didn't have to listen, but she listened like she'd never listened before, like her ears had been made for this one thing. Her mother's voice was utterly unchanged and yet, to Claire, it was an entire revelation. In it, she heard every nuance and breath, every lilt and tilt and inflection that she used to know. Every hint of regret or braggadocio, satisfaction or scorn. "I'm moving into a time of my life when I can sit back and enjoy the full fruits of my labor," she said, in the course of a soliloquy about Claire and Joshua becoming young adults. "Now, what you want to do is *pulverize* the eggshells first," she advised her listeners, in a discussion of nontoxic methods of pest prevention.

An hour after sunset, Teresa wound up the final show by asking a trivia question as she always did at show's end, encouraging her listeners to call in with the answers. This one was: *What is the traditional use of pipestone?* Claire turned the radio off, knowing the answer already, not wanting to hear her mother say, "And this, folks, brings us to the end of another hour. Work hard. Do good. Be incredible. And come back next week for more of *Modern Pioneers!*" In the silence of the evening, Claire made her way around the apartment, turning on lights, the words *work hard, do good, be incredible* ringing in her ears. Those three phrases contained everything Claire had most loved and most despised about her mother, what she could not now shake herself loose from—all of her mother's optimism and cheer, her munificence and grace, her indestructible belief that to be incredible was the most ordinary thing in the entire world, that most people, when you looked closely enough, *were* incredible. "Is Hitler incredible?" Claire had asked her mother once, trying to rattle her. "I said *most*, smarty-pants," her mother had answered, jabbing her affectionately in the side. "How about Pol Pot?" Claire pushed on.

After listening to the radio-show marathon that Sunday in January, Claire toasted a bagel and ate it slowly, feeling as if she were balancing a book on her head. Feeling that if she moved too quickly the false sense of restoration listening to her mother's shows had given her would come crashing down and her mother would be dead again. Which happened, of course. It had happened also on the day she went to Duluth and held her mother's ashes in her hands, and she feared it would happen again once she set foot in their old house. A small piece of what she was able to believe was still intact about her mother would reveal itself to her and show itself to be gone for good.

She hadn't been thinking of this when she'd called Kathy and offered to look after the place. But she thought of it now, on the Sunday in April that she was meant to go out to the house, as she scrubbed every surface of the Lookout, getting down on her hands and knees to scour the floor, polishing the wooden corners of the pool table to a glossy sheen.

When she was nearly done with her work she saw Leonard and Mardell's truck pull into the parking lot. She went to the door and held it open for them.

"Did you miss me too much to stay away?" she asked when they approached. On Sundays, the bar didn't open until two, and usually Leonard and Mardell waited until well past noon to come in. After cleaning up, Claire had the rest of the day off.

"Len forgot his thingamajig," Mardell explained as they came up the steps.

"My computer!" he bellowed. "For Christ's sake, Mardy. Call it what it is." He kissed Claire's cheek as he passed by.

"A year ago he didn't know what e-mail was and now he can't go twenty minutes without being on it," said Mardell. She untied the strings of her transparent rain bonnet and put it on the bar to dry. "I said to Ruth and Jay if I didn't know any better, I'd think their dad was having an affair."

"Oh, for God's sakes, Mardy!"

"Well, I didn't say you *were*, Len. I said that's what I'd think if I didn't know any better." She looked at Claire and winked.

"Why don't we all sit down and have a soda pop," suggested Leonard from behind the bar. He reached into the locked cabinet beneath the till and pulled out his tangerine-colored laptop.

"So you're going out home today, isn't that right?" Mardell asked, sitting down on a stool next to Claire.

She nodded and took a sip of the root beer Leonard handed to her.

"It'll be nice to see it after all this time, I suppose," said Mardell. She put a hand to her wrinkled throat, pulling back the sagging flesh there momentarily. "But emotional. What with all that's gone on. You know, Claire, I don't know if I ever told you how I cried when I found out Bruce married Kathy. It broke my heart, the way it came so fast. The way you and Joshie were just . . ." She made a whisking motion with her hand.

"Mardy!" bellowed Leonard.

She continued on, ignoring him. "If you want to know the truth, I had to ask the Lord to help me find forgiveness in my heart, Claire. I honestly did."

"There ain't no need—" Leonard began.

"I did!" crowed Mardell, looking at him now, instead of Claire. "And there isn't a thing in the world wrong with saying it, Len. You tell me what's wrong with saying it if it's the God's honest truth."

"You're fanning the fires," grumped Leonard.

"I'm not fanning any fire." She looked at Claire. "Am I fanning the fire?"

Ever so slightly, Claire shook her head, hoping to seem neither entirely on Leonard's side nor on Mardell's, a pose she'd become expert at in the past months to keep herself from being drawn into their quarrels.

"Claire don't think I'm fanning the fire," Mardell stated in a tone that conveyed that there was nothing more to say about it.

"It's okay," Claire said to both of them, wanting to reassure them, without at all being reassured herself. "I mean, everything will be fine, with Kathy and all. With going out to the house."

"Of course it will!" Mardell yelled, and reached over to pat Claire's arm with her soft hand, blue with veins.

"It's a long life, sweetheart, and time heals all wounds," said Leonard.

Claire's eyes misted with tears. She swirled the ice in her root beer with her straw. She didn't know whether she believed that time healed all wounds, but she believed it healed some. In regard to Bruce and Kathy, time had begun to do its work. She could feel it inside of her—softening, safening, making ordinary what was once appalling. She didn't know whether she liked it or not, this healing. It made her feel like she was betraying her mother in some small way.

"Here they come already," said Leonard.

They all turned to the front window, watching a car pull up and pause long enough for its passengers to absorb the CLOSED sign on the door and drive away.

"So we've got a little announcement to make," Mardell said.

"We don't have to go into it now," Leonard protested.

"Tell me one reason why not, Len?"

"Because she's got to go. She's got to get out to the house."

"No. I'm fine," Claire said, curious about the news. "Actually, I haven't even finished up here. I've still got to mop the bathrooms."

"It has to do with the fact that we're getting old, Claire—and tired." Mardell looked at Leonard and winked. "Hon, why don't you go ahead and tell her what we thought to do?"

Claire dressed carefully, as if going on a date, fussing with the zipper on the sweater she wore, raising it and lowering it to various heights on her chest, trying to find just the right place, though she'd be arriving to an empty house. Bruce and Kathy had left early that morning. It would only be her and Shadow and the chickens and the horses.

It was raining as she drove. The side windows of her car fogged up with the humidity, turning the woods and farms she passed into a blur of gray and green. She recognized them anyway, even at this level of abstraction. She'd covered this ground so many times before, in so many states of mind. The trees and weeds that grew along the sides of the road, the driveways that led to cabins owned by city people—so rarely used in the winters that by this time of year they had turned to phantoms. She thought about what Leonard and Mardell had told her that morning, thought about what she'd say to Joshua when she saw him. She pushed the thoughts from her mind as the miles ticked off, one by one. She slowed before she needed to, letting her foot off the brake so the Cutlass coasted down the highway, the only car in sight. And then she turned tentatively onto the gravel road—"our road," she used to call it, as did Joshua and her mother, as did Bruce and, she supposed, Kathy. The road that led home.

In the driveway she turned the ignition off and sat for several minutes looking at the house and the barn, the chicken coop and the old broken-down tractor that hadn't moved an inch since she'd last seen it. It was the middle of April and blades of grass and the shoots of flowers her mother had planted years before were making their way up out of the mud in the yard. When she got out of her car she realized how strange it was, the silence, without the dogs. "Kitty," she called when she saw Shadow. It was still raining, and the cat looked at Claire without moving from the dry haven of the porch.

"How about we go inside?" asked Claire, finding the key on her ring, trembling as she pushed it into the lock. She was suddenly giddy with the foreignness of being here, which collided with an almost surreal familiarity. Her eyes landed on things she'd seen a million times, conscious of them only now that she was seeing them again: the grain of the wooden porch rails, the slant of the trim around the door. She stepped inside and comprehended the entire contents of the house in a single glance, felt instantly able to discern all that had changed and all that hadn't. There were Kathy's curtains, Kathy's chairs, Kathy's serving spoons hanging from hooks over the stove. And yet, despite this, the house felt to Claire profoundly, sickeningly, still *theirs*—still Claire and Bruce and Teresa and Joshua's. The most banal objects of their life together remained, things that Claire had not opted to take because they seemed to belong more to the house than to any one of them: the pair of red oven mitts with the black burn across one fat thumb, the metal yardstick they used to measure the depth of the snow, the yellow book that said *Birds* in block letters along the spine. Even the least personal objects—the stereo, the refrigerator, the kitchen sink—seemed to speak to her, to know her, to reach out and grab hold of her throat.

"Hello," she called, not expecting anyone to answer. Shadow jumped up onto the kitchen table and Claire stood petting her, looking into her green eyes, feeling both wary and elated about being home—*here*, she corrected herself. She didn't know what to call this place anymore.

"So, I'm here," she said to Joshua a while later on the phone. She took a tack from the corkboard and then dropped it and got down on her knees to see where it went.

"How is it?" he asked. He had been out to the house once already, to return a pan that Kathy had baked lasagna in after Iris was born, though he hadn't come inside.

"It's . . ." She paused, searching the floor. "It's weird and okay and interesting and bizarre." She stood up, giving up on the tack. "It's fine though."

"I'll be down first thing in the morning. Probably about eight thirty."

"I was hoping you'd come this afternoon." She pinched the hem of the new curtain, yellow cotton with white dots, store-bought.

"I told you I couldn't get there until about six and then it'll start getting dark. Plus, it's raining. It's supposed to be nice tomorrow."

"Okay." She sighed, and said goodbye to him.

Tomorrow she and Joshua would do what they'd planned to do with Bruce the summer before—plant flowers on Teresa's grave, in the dirt where they'd spread her ashes. Claire had gone to the nursery in Blue River the day before, wandering around for an hour, trying to figure out what to buy. In the end she'd purchased two packets of seeds, each one a wildflower mix that would start blooming in a month and bloom all summer long, one flower after another taking its turn in the sun—bloodroot and daisies, yarrow and Indian paintbrush. She and Joshua hadn't been out to their mother's grave since the day they'd mixed her ashes into the dirt. She thought about walking out there now by herself, to have a conversation with her mother. *I'm sorry*, she'd say, *I'm sorry we never got around to planting your flowers until now.* Over the months, it had weighed heavily on her, the neglect, the disrespect, but she hadn't found a way to come out before now, hadn't been able to muster up the composure to mention to Bruce how badly she wanted to come over—not to the house, but to her mother's grave. She wondered if Bruce ever went out there and if he did, what he said.

She turned back to the house, studying it more carefully now, picking things up to examine them and setting them back down precisely as they had been so that Kathy wouldn't think she had been snooping. She walked upstairs, giving herself a tour. Her bedroom had been turned into an office and Joshua's something of a storage space. There was a stationary bicycle and a tiny wooden rocking chair meant for a toddler and a dartboard hanging lopsided on the wall. Claire removed all the darts and then threw them one by one, never hitting a bull's-eye. She went back downstairs and pushed the door to Bruce and Kathy's room open and peered inside from the doorway. A white dresser sat where her mother's vanity had been and a cedar chest where there had once been a bench. She closed the door, feeling light and happy with herself, pleased with her capacity to see it plainly at last, to stare it frankly in the face without feeling much of anything.

At four it was late enough to feed the animals and she went outside.

"Hello, girls," she cooed, the way her mother used to, herding the hens into their coop for the night, reaching into the straw to check for eggs, filling their troughs with fresh water and cracked corn. After she fed the horses, she got a brush and groomed them while they ate, and then followed them out to the pasture when they were done, brushing them for close to an hour, despite the light rain. Every few minutes she switched from Beau to Lady Mae so neither of them got jealous, moving with them as they searched out the new grass, pressing their mouths into the dirt to retrieve the tiniest blades. She'd spent a lot of time out here in the pasture during an era of her childhood—in the years after they'd moved in with Bruce and before she and Joshua became teenagers, resistant to everything their mother suggested. In the summer they would camp out without pitching a tent. They would make a fire and lay a tarp down and set their sleeping bags on top of it, the four of them sleeping lined up in a row, like logs. The horses would be with them all night, approaching at various hours to smell their hair or to push their noses into their sleeping hands. In the winter they would build snowmen and make snow angels in the deep places the horses didn't walk. Or Bruce and Teresa would bury her and Joshua, covering them entirely, aside from the small domes of their faces, and then walk away, calling their names. Calling "Claire! Joshua!" Asking "Where have our children gone?" Saying "We've lost our babies!" And no matter that Claire knew that they were only joking, that it was all a game, something enormous would mount inside of her, an unbearable mix of anticipation and unease, delight and distress, and she would crash up out of her snow grave, with Joshua a moment behind her, crashing up too, and they would run after their mother and Bruce screaming and laughing, "We're here! We're here!"

She remembered this now, out with the horses, allowing every detail she could conjure into her mind, and yet also holding them at a distance. She'd become adept at this over the past months, learning how to keep things at the same time as letting them go. She stopped brushing Beau and looked back at the house. It was getting toward evening now and her eyes caught on her car. She had left her headlights on, she saw now, having turned them on as she drove here in the rain. *She was not going to spend the night here*, she almost screamed as she sprinted to her car, bending to wend her way through the fence, as if the few seconds longer it would take to go through the gate would make a difference.

There was only a clicking sound when she turned the ignition. She pounded on the steering wheel and got out and slammed the door as hard as she could and stormed into the house.

She called Joshua, leaving him a message, and then stood near the phone for several moments, waiting for it to ring, though she knew that it was futile. It was too late for Joshua to agree to come down to jump her car, not when he was coming the very next morning anyway. She considered walking to Kathy's parents' house a couple of miles away, but she knew she wouldn't do it. She could call Leonard and Mardell, but they'd be at the Lookout until at least ten.

She took her coat off and sat down at the kitchen table and almost burst into tears of rage over her own stupidity. She picked up *The Nickel Shopper* and distracted herself by reading the ads, all the while vowing that she would not spend the night here, despite the fact that another voice inside of her knew she would. After several minutes, she went to the refrigerator and opened it up. In the freezer there was a stack of frozen dinners in slender white boxes: chicken cacciatore and fettuccine Alfredo and a thing called "Southwest Fiesta." She chose the chicken and removed it from its box and stabbed the sheet of plastic that covered it with a fork.

As she waited for it to cook in Kathy's microwave, she thought of Bill Ristow. He used to eat food like this at the hospital for breakfast, lunch, and dinner. Its very odor, as it cooked, reminded her of him. He would eat it standing up in the Family Room while his wife was dying down the hall, eating whatever she could manage. Eating canned peaches, Claire supposed, like her mother had on her good days, or one unbearable grape at a time. Eating Jell-O and hard candy just so she could claim to have eaten at all. She hadn't seen Bill since August, and shortly after she'd moved back to Midden, their phone calls had tapered off and then ceased altogether. At Christmas he'd sent her a card. *Thinking of you, kiddo*, it said. She'd held it for a long time, reading those words

313

over and over again. How sweet they were to her, and simple and plain and true. How they seemed to contain both what they said and what they didn't: how unlikely it was they'd ever speak again. She didn't feel sad about it, didn't any longer feel the blend of sorrow and inevitability she used to feel when she thought of Bill.

Her feelings for David were more complicated, though no longer fraught. They'd spoken on the phone a few times over the autumn and winter, talking like old friends, laughing about the things they used to laugh about, critiquing the things they used to critique together, in almost perfect agreement. He had a new girlfriend, a woman who lived in his apartment building. He told Claire tentative, considered facts about her. That her name was Elise. That she worked at a legal firm and liked to run. That he had taken up running too. Claire's heart seemed to simultaneously speed up and slow down when he spoke of her, but later, thinking about it, she wished him well.

"What about you?" he'd asked her the last time they spoke.

"I'm on a sexual hiatus," she said in a funny voice, to make a joke of it, though it was true. She was getting her mind and body clear of men, though from time to time she wavered. She allowed herself to flirt with a few of the guys she'd gone to high school with, when they came into the Lookout. She pondered pairings that, upon reflection, were patently absurd.

"Do you think R.J. would go out with me?" she'd asked Joshua one day when she visited him in jail. R.J. had always been around, all the years that Claire was growing up, spending the night at their house on the weekends, but she hadn't truly noticed him until she moved back home and he'd stopped into the Lookout one day.

"Go out?" Joshua asked, aghast.

"Yeah."

"Like on a *date?*"

She nodded.

"No fucking way, Claire. He's my *friend.*"

"Well, I'm not proposing to *kill* him." She laughed and held her hands up in surrender. "Okay, okay. Forget I said anything."

"I will," he said, disgusted. "He's got a girlfriend who he's whipped over anyway. You wouldn't have a chance."

After dinner, after Joshua called and they argued and finally agreed that it was silly for him to come out only to return again in the morning, she

314

made a bed for herself on one of Kathy's loveseats. There were two facing each other. When she couldn't get comfortable on the first one, she moved over to the second, but they were equally uncomfortable and neither of them was long enough for her legs. She pulled the blankets onto the floor and lay wide-awake, growing more despairing and miserable and exhausted and agitated with each passing hour. Somewhere in the depths of the night, she stood up and went to the window and looked out. It had stopped raining and the sky was clear and she could see the horses standing outside of their stalls in the light of the moon. She considered going out to sleep near them, bundled in a sleeping bag, but then she turned away and walked through the dark house.

She went to Bruce and Kathy's room and switched the light on and stood staring at the bed. It was the same bed, the one that had been her mother's too. It was the only bed in the house, the only place she could expect to get any actual sleep. She sat down on the edge and ran her hand along the unfamiliar quilt that covered it. On the nightstand beside her there was a statuette of a cow. She picked it up and examined it and put it down and opened the nightstand drawer. When she'd lived here, this had been Bruce's side of the bed, and she could tell by the contents of the drawer that it still was. There was a jackknife his father had given him and a wallet in a transparent box that he had yet to use, his old high school class ring and three rolls of pennies. Way back in the depths of the drawer there was a cassette tape. She reached inside and pulled it out: Kenny G. She recognized it immediately as the cassette she'd stolen from Bill the first time she'd gone to his house, though she didn't recall what she'd done with it afterward and didn't have any idea how it had ended up here. She had assumed it was still with her, lost in the boxes out in the storage shed behind the Lookout that she hadn't yet unpacked. She put the cassette into the stereo near the bed and reclined on top of the covers listening to it. The music struck her as corny and cloying and monotonous and after a few minutes she turned it off.

She remembered how she used to search the house on the weekends when she came home after her mother died. Remembered that hungry, insatiable urge she'd had to find what was missing without having any idea what it was she was looking for. She could let it be this, she thought. She could let it be this cassette and then she wouldn't have to search anymore. Slowly, methodically, without sorrow or anger or fear, she took the cassette out and began to pull the tape from its spool inside the cartridge, unfurling the metallic ribbon onto her lap. As it gathered into a pile she felt a kind of curiosity, a kind of childlike scrutiny that she'd had when she was picking a flower apart one petal at a time, waiting to know her fate, chanting *he loves me, he loves me not*. Only now she didn't chant anything to herself. She just let it be what it was: benign destruction, a thing that was no more. When she was done she balled it into her hands and put it in the garbage and closed the lid.

"Rise and shine," said Joshua in the morning, standing over her near the bed.

She startled awake and rubbed her face. "What time is it?"

"A little after nine," he said, and left the room.

"I didn't hear you," she called to him.

"I know. It's weird, isn't it? No barking dogs."

She could hear him opening the refrigerator and then closing it. She sat up and looked around. She'd fallen asleep finally, after crawling into Bruce and Kathy's bed with her clothes still on. "Did you bring Iris?"

"Nah," he said from the living room. "Lisa wanted to take her over to her mom's."

"I was hoping you'd bring her." She got out of bed and pulled her sweater on and ran her fingers through her hair. She had let it fade back to its original color over the past few months. From the top of Kathy's dresser she took an elastic band and used it to tie her hair back into a ponytail.

"You can see her tomorrow morning, if you want. We need someone to take her for about an hour."

"Sure," said Claire. She looked after Iris whenever she could—whenever Lisa and Joshua had to work at the same time. She loved Iris in a way that she'd loved only her brother, she came to realize, in the hours that she held her, gazing at her beautiful face, exploring her every toe and curve, her every wrinkle and bend, marveling over the excruciating softness of her skin, the exquisite bounty of her head as it reclined in the palm of her hand. She'd been there when Iris was born, though that hadn't been the plan, and had watched her emerge from Lisa, wet and gray, two weeks and three days before her due date, four days before Joshua was released from jail. The powers that be at the jail had refused to let him out to see his child born, despite Claire's pleadings, despite the pleadings of the counselor in jail, despite, even, the wishes of the guards, Tommy and Fred. An order from the judge or the warden was needed, and they were both unavailable on the day Iris was born. As a consolation, Joshua had been allowed to wait in the room where he received his visitors, shackled to the table. Minutes after Iris was born, Claire ran down the stairs and into the hallway that became the tunnel that led to the jail. "It's a girl!" she shouted from the processing room, knowing that Joshua could hear her. "It's a girl?" he hollered back to her, exuberant and stunned.

She came into the kitchen and got herself a glass of water.

"So, what's on the agenda?" said Joshua, solemn now.

"I bought seeds. But let's just walk out there first. To see her."

Shadow followed them out the door and off the porch and onto the little path that led to their mother's grave, trailing them like a dog. They slowed as the woods gave way to the clearing, as the oval of dirt they'd made the year before came into sight.

Joshua picked up a pine bough that had fallen from a tree and swept the dried leaves from the dirt, and Claire stooped down and raked some away with her hands. Beneath the layer of leaves they could see that it wasn't only dirt any longer. There were tiny white flowers blooming and the shoots of other flowers pushing up, an entire garden about to burst forth.

Claire took a sharp breath in, trying to make sense of it. Her mind leapt from one thing to the next, from believing that it was her mother working her magic, sending a signal from wherever she was, to the realization that it must have been Bruce. He'd planted the flowers without them, without even so much as telling them that he'd done it.

"What happened?" Joshua asked.

"I don't know," said Claire.

"Do you think Bruce did this?"

"I don't know." She looked at him. "Maybe it's Mom. Maybe this is her way of speaking to us." She didn't believe it herself, but she had the compulsion to make him believe, the way she'd had to carry on the myth of Santa Claus a couple of years after she knew the truth.

"Maybe," he said, and she could tell by his voice that he was doing the same thing, knowing the truth but protecting her from it.

"Or maybe Bruce just went ahead without us," Claire blurted.

"Maybe," Joshua whispered.

They looked at each other—they were both crying now—and something came over them simultaneously and they both began to laugh.

"What's so funny?" Claire asked through her tears.

"Nothing!" said Joshua, and then they laughed harder.

"I thought it would feel different," Claire told Joshua when they had stopped laughing. "Being here. I thought I would feel like Mom was here —not just out here, but all around. In the house. On the road." She plunged her hands into the dirt on the edge of the plot, where no flowers grew or were beginning to grow. It was wet and it turned to mud when she brought up two fists of it and then shook it off.

"So what are we gonna do with all those seeds you bought?" he asked.

Claire shrugged.

He still held the pine bough. He tossed it back toward the woods. "I got an idea."

"What?"

He smiled. "Just come on." He left her standing there, starting back on the path without her, Shadow following behind him.

"Come where?" she yelled, without moving. But he didn't answer; she just had to go after him.

As they drove down their road in Joshua's truck and out onto the highway, she remembered she had a surprise too. She hadn't told Joshua what Leonard and Mardell had told her the day before. She turned and looked at him in profile, at his sharp nose that was like hers and at the dark stubble that grew on his chin and across his cheeks.

"What?" he asked, swatting at his face, as if there might be something on it.

"Nothing." She smiled, because she knew it would irk him.

"Don't look at me, then."

She laughed. She felt strangely free, deeply relieved, like it was the last day of school and she would never have to go back.

"And don't laugh at me neither," he said, smiling too.

"So where are we going?" she asked.

"To the river."

She nodded, immediately comprehending his plan, and they didn't say another word to each other as they drove.

The Lookout parking lot was empty. It was Monday, the bar closed. They walked out the little path, to the river. Claire went to the rock and pressed her hand against it, feeling its cool surface, while Joshua spread out the blanket he'd brought from his truck.

"Let's just relax for a while," he said, and sat down on the blanket.

Claire sat next to him and watched the river. The water was high and muddy from all the rain they'd had and the snow that had melted weeks before. The cattails that grew on the other bank were flooded almost to the ends of their soft beige tips. "It's nice to get some sun," she said, and leaned back on her hands, letting the warmth settle over her face. After several minutes, she took her raincoat off and set it beside her. She turned to Joshua. "Len and Mardell want to give you the Lookout. They're going to retire in a year and they just want to give it to you."

"What?" He shielded his eyes with his hand so he could see her better.

"Ruth and Jay don't want it and Len and Mardell saved their money all these years—Len's dad gave him the bar in the first place, so they don't owe anything on it—and they just want to give it to you. They want it to go to someone they know. Someone they trust."

"Holy shit," said Joshua. He sat thinking for several moments. "What about you? Why don't they give it to you?"

She shrugged. "They want you to have it." In truth, they had offered it to her as well—to both of them—but she'd rejected the idea immediately. She couldn't stay in Midden. Their offer had crystallized that fact in her mind. "You and Lisa and Iris can live in the apartment upstairs. Or you could rent it out for money if it's not big enough for you."

"But *you* live there."

"Not for too much longer, Josh." She waved her hand into the new grass that grew at the edge of the blanket and pulled a blade of it from the ground. "I think I'll work through Labor Day while the money's good, but then I have to move on."

"Back to the Cities?"

"I don't know." She shredded the blade of grass into tiny pieces, pondering the question. "Maybe. I could go somewhere else too." She looked up at him and smiled. "Somewhere new to go off and seek my fortune," she said in an intentionally dramatic voice.

"You should," he said, earnestly.

"Yeah," she said, though her stomach flipped with the notion. She flung the strings of grass away from her, but the wind blew them back, scattering them over her and Joshua.

"You're too smart to be staying here, that's for sure. You need to go and be around other smart people."

"I *am* around smart people, Josh. Smart people live in Midden.

319

You're smart," she said, emphatically. When she said it, she realized she'd never told him that. She wondered if anyone ever had.

"You know what I mean."

"No," she protested gently, but she did. She would always be from here, of here, but she could not stay here. She remembered how it felt to walk down the streets of Minneapolis the way she used to, yearning and yearning. For what, she didn't precisely know. Since her mother died that unknowingness had felt to her like a weakness, a hopeless surrender, instead of the glorious question it had been before, back when she was a daughter, a girl. She watched an empty plastic milk jug float past in the river, washed in by the high water, and tried to let the question return.

"Well, Iris is going to miss you. I can tell you that right now."

A tender urge rose in her to take his hand and hold it the way she held it when she went to visit him in jail, but she didn't. It would seem strange now, out here in the real world, where love had the luxury of being diffused and sheltered from itself. They sat together for several minutes in silence. Wispy white clouds appeared above them, blocking the sun for moments at a time.

"So, what do you think of taking over the bar?"

"I think it's interesting."

"I thought so too. It could be a good thing for you and Lisa and Iris."

"It could," he agreed. She could see the thoughts moving across his face as the idea set in. He leaned back on his hands and gazed at the sky and in that gesture Claire could see his excitement and joy, his amazement and relief.

"Would you live upstairs or would you rent it?"

He was silent for several moments and then he turned to her abruptly and said, "I used to live there."

"I know," she replied, not certain of what he was telling her, wanting to let him do it on his own.

"No. I mean, not with you and Mom. I lived there by myself when Mom was sick and for a while afterwards. Nobody knew about it. I sort of broke in."

"Len knew." She watched the surprise ripple over his face. "He told me about it the night before Mom died, when I was looking all over for you. I called Len and he said to go to the apartment and you'd be there, so I did, but you weren't. Your truck wasn't here, so that's when I went out to the lake."

"I always parked my truck in town," he said. "Otherwise Len and Mardell would know I was here. I would park behind the café and walk down."

"Oh," she said, understanding it now. "Of course. How dumb am I?" She laughed, though a bird of pain fluttered into her chest, the entire memory coming to her with a sting. Of course he wouldn't have parked here, she realized now, though it hadn't occurred to her then, in the depths of her grief and fear. If only she had ascended the stairs and knocked, then they would have been there with their mother when she died. They wouldn't have sat for hours on a frozen lake, mired in the ice. They wouldn't have driven the highway to Duluth so fast it made her shake in terror, all to no avail.

"I'm sorry, Claire."

He tried to get her to look at him, but she wouldn't. She stared at her shoes or else she would cry. She'd forgiven him months before, but she couldn't tell him about it yet.

"It seems like we're both doing okay," she said instead.

He nodded. "We're moving on."

Claire remained silent, not wanting to agree or admit that that was what she'd been doing. Moving on, moving away, moving forward and beyond, past her mother. *My mother, my mother, my mother,* she said silently to herself. How much she missed her mother.

"Do you remember how we used to play Blue River Piss Off?" Joshua asked.

"Yeah," she said, a smile spreading across her face.

"We were funny."

"We were."

"I used to still do it. All the way up until—I don't know—not very long ago. I used to skip school and come out here and sit by the river and get stoned and then I'd put stuff in the river and I'd think, *Blue River Piss Off.*"

"It's funny, the way things stay with you." She stared at the water. A jagged branch floated by. She remembered putting the lilac boughs in the river when Bruce and her mother had taken their commitment vows. "So why'd you stop?" she asked Joshua.

He shrugged. "I suppose I grew up." He thought for a while longer and then turned to her. "Iris was born in Blue River. Maybe that was it."

"We don't want Blue River to piss off anymore!" Claire hollered comically to the sky and the trees and the rock and the river itself, as if they would hear and forgive them. And then a hush settled over them all, as if they had heard, had forgiven.

She unzipped the pocket of her coat and took the packets of seeds out and handed one to Joshua. They walked to the river and ripped the packets open and poured the seeds into their palms and then bent down and plunged their hands into the icy water, letting the seeds wash away. Their hands appeared whiter, more fragile than they were, almost glowing beneath the surface of the water as the current moved past them, through them, making rivulets along their fingers.

"Teresa Rae Wood," Claire said softly, slowly, like a secret, like a sacrament, like a prayer.

"Teresa Rae Wood," Joshua said after her.

Those three words were a flame, a torch they would carry forever.

They shook the water from their hands and stood watching the river. Claire was thinking what Joshua was thinking, she knew without having to ask, without even having to so much as look at his face.

They were thinking what they would do now: be incredible. Like most people.